'...through the blood

of our forefathers...'

Æthelstan,

England's first King.

by

G W Lowe

As a boy, I did all but look forward to the lengthy visits the family would often make to my Grandmother's house in Surrey. The 'vacations' in those days had become more of a family ritual, repeated every couple of years or so, whenever my Father had decided to sell up the family business, move lock stock and barrel in search of another venture somewhere across this country, or another.

Of course, until the new business had been located, the family were 'interred' at my Grandmother's house.

In my youngest of views, the only thing that I could concede to being of interest to any rational minded, person when staying in Kingston upon Thames, would have been the town itself. Even at so young an age, Kingston's historic buildings and ancient features drew me close as I pondered and silently questioned the legends, myths and tales that surrounded its every inch. Surprisingly the strangest, yet most magnetic parts of those visits were during the times that I attended the local school, only temporarily of course, but always the same one.

Recently built, it was, and it still is I believe, a typical nineteen sixties school constructed without character or charm and overflowing with blandness, yet for all its design faults, King Aethelstan's Primary school on Villiers Road etched something into my young mind that would haunt me through-out the following years of my life, wherever it was that I would find myself.

Every time I walked through those blue wrought iron gates, either to enter or leave, I would beg myself the same question.

"Who was King Æthelstan?"

...and over the fifty years or so that followed that same question haunted me, until recently...

BETWEEN THESE COVERS IS WRITTEN

A MOST IMPORTANT PART OF ENGLISH HISTORY.

READ IT, LEARN IT, AND REMEMBER IT,

FOR IT IS BOTH THE FACT AND THE TRUTH

WHICH HAS PAVED THE WAY

FOR YOUR TODAY, MAYBE EVEN YOUR TOMORROW.

TEACH YOUR CHILDREN OUR HISTORY

SO, THAT ONE DAY THEY TOO MAY

COPY AND TEACH CHILDREN OF THEIR OWN,

FOR THESE PAGES HAVE BEEN WRITTEN ONLY WITH PRIDE, HONOUR

AND HUMILITY FOR THOSE MANY WHO HAVE SACRIFICED THEIR LIVES

FOR OUR PRESENT WAY OF LIFE FROM ITS VERY EARLIEST START

UP UNTIL THIS VERY DAY,

ALSO, FOR THOSE UNSELFISH MANY

WHO SHALL ALMOST CERTAINLY FOLLOW THEM.

This island Briton is 800 miles in its length

And 200 miles in width.

There are five nations inhabiting her shores,

Engles, Welsh [Britons], Scots, Picts, and Latins.

The first inhabitants were the Britons

who came from Armenia...

And so, began the start of an Isle

Which all races would war over to rule......

from The Anglo-Saxon Chronicles

[Before most men could write....]

INTRODUCTION

I

Within a hill-side plain slightly south of the middle lands, where two rivers flowed towards the east until they eventually joined as one, that is the place where, at first, it seemed to start.

In an ancient homestead known in its earliest days as Tomworðig, within the Mercian province ruled then by those known to their neighbours as the Tomsæte, almost at the very heart of an island once called Britannia.

As the harshest of years gave their way to even harsher warring's and battling's, that settlement became known as Tame's Worth. Yet even though it was merely a hill fort, little less than a Burg, it had become the most northerly ruling seat for the Mercian Realm....

During those years, since the Latin Legions had hurriedly fled that Isle's torment, Tame's Worth had emerged into a 'Common' place where surrounding communities could gather in reasonable safety to peddle their wares, to meet and greet their neighbours over a cup of mead, or to eat and flourish in the summer sun, making it one of the noisiest places within that Realm.

Ritualistically, the start of any morning in the summer of 894 had always begun before the sun had fully spread its warmth across the lands, starting firstly with the chatter of the 'early birds' from the leafy beams of the woodlands, to the fruit orchards which surrounded the barren outskirts of such homesteads that bordered any well protected fort. Habitually, their whistles and chirps would usually be accompanied by the echoed wailings of more than one hungry child desperately screeching their wants towards Mothers who still grappled for the final remnants of another broken night's sleep, disturbing more than just one of the many wattled ærna. Eventually the choir of innocents would rouse everyone within earshot, informing all that another day was breaking......

Often too, as everywhere, came the inevitable barking dog, and then another, registering confirmation that Tamworth had begun to stir begrudgingly into another morning.

It was soon after such a fracass that the clatter of pots and trinkets would be heard echoing across the lower 'ceapstow' accompanied by the scraping of steel upon cobble as the 'dawn riders' came and went through the crowded gennels mixing with the screeching of angry crones as they inconveniently tugged at the arm of a snivelling child, or two, in a frugal search through the squalor of the mead halls and ale houses for the drunkards who dared only to call themselves 'husband' when an empty belly or aching crotch insisted.

Where sweet fruit smoke hung, enduringly tainting the hustling air which rose out from a smithy's hearth to escape through open eaves and breeze away into the walking spaces between the timber framed dwellings that many were forced to call 'ham'.

From an outsider's view Tame's Worth had remained much of a ruin since its sacking by marauding Danes in 874, when, before Ælfred had stepped out of the marshlands and raised his 'fyrds', the heathen invaders had helped themselves to all they required, which would have amounted to everything from weapons to women, from livestock down to the 'bære' that had been stored for the ritual famine of the winter months, all taken by way of payment for their inconveniences.

On that day, the Men of the North had torched what little remained in their wake leaving the smouldering heaps of dismal ashes to the mercy of the night scavengers.

Yet being in part dereliction had more than likely become the reason that Tamworth had been ignored from further visits by her enemies, as well as the fact that Æthelred, Lord of the Mercians and his good Lady Æthelflæd were ruthless to the point when it came to would-be invaders who dared to threaten their worth……..and of course, should she ever have needed, Æthelflæd could always 'call' upon the support of the most powerful and proven individual that had ever walked that Isle, her Father, Ælfred, King of the Wessex.

A little earlier, in the darker months of that year, a great firestone had fallen from the evening's sky, cast down upon those frigid lands far away to the north, screaming its flaming rage from Woden's Halls. Just after Yule it had lit up the distant night.

Some decreed that 'It had been a pious warning against the sinners of those lands.'

Others had whispered in the mead halls that... 'There would soon follow a foul and cruel year of famine and dread', and 'it had been Thunnor's hammer, Mjolnir that had smashed into the northern lands sending a cruel warning to all men....'

Asser had scribbled; 'Such a sign would herald the coming of a King, a great King, even more so than our greatest Ælfred.'

Deep within Tamworth's battered ringwall the heart of Offa's great people had once beat, and despite the rumours of the pessimists, and of course the churchmen, a new heart was threatening to be heard once again...

But that was yet to come...

The hustle and shove of the Ceapmann continued as they hurried deeper into the market's centre with hopes of snatching the best position to set out their wares before the local folk began their new day, exchanging gossip and idle chatter with those who had been missed for some time, adding their banters and boastings with unbelievable and humorous tales that filled the air, making for the start of a normal, yet careful, day.

Welcome to many were the smells.

Of freshly baked breads, offered in all shapes and sizes. Fermenting meads laced modestly with hedgerow spices, imported wines and freshly cooked wild bird stew, thickly skinned cheeses, and mouth-watering pottages, butters and curds, and other delights, all helping to overcome the stench of putridity and horse dung for at least one day each month. And the local folk began to weave themselves in and out of the ramshackle stalls hunting for early morning bargains, grasping at a 'hot bowl' to break the night's fast, or just mingling, for mingling's sake.

As it had always been, the day was keenly watched over by the fattened 'Shire Reeve' who hastily accepted his King's tallies paid by the sale mongers and tenants in lieu for their pitches and places, less of course a 'small' cut for his own trouble.

But the surface of such a peace was a very thin surface.

Those times between wars were still dark and dangerous times, where every cruel day outside the burhs, burgs and stows seemed to begin with a fouler, more suffocating mist than that which had passed over those lands any morning before. Where dampness and chill almost became a custom despite the season and every grey shadow threatened to harbour an outlaw or cut-throat or traitor ever hoping to increase the weight of his purse, or better the steel of his knife, point of his lance or maybe even a sword or a warmer cloak, if the luck of the 'deofol' was about.

Things had become so that war did not always seem the worst of one's fates.

Gestures such as loyalty and trust were only ever made to those closest, almost never to be shared, and then only ever whispered in secret after a second's thought. Words such as pride and passion, honour and chivalry had not yet entered the language then spoken by those Children of Men.

No! There was never anything truly nice about those days. A person merely wandered from 'stead' to 'stead' or croft to 'hus', barely existing, with little hope of finding a full belly at the end of each day, trying without too much effort, in 'missing out' from the dangers that were beginning to become accepted as a normal part of life. Evil had now become an infection that was suffered in silence throughout the daylight hours and trembled over in the false safety and comfort of the night as the blanket of darkness would fall, ending each day, which meant one less to the grave. For others, it may have been the day when the struggle for life in that most miserable of places had thankfully ended and a freed spirit would at last enter the realms of its after- life, to watch over, forever in pity, those who had not yet been so fortunate.

But that is not the part of our past where this story really begins....

589 A.D.

Uriens overruns Din Guarrie and traps Hussa

at the siege of Ynys Metcaut

coveting Rheged's crown….

590 A.D.

Morcant Bwlch has Uriens treacherously murdered,

the coalition of the Britons collapses

and Hussa breaks out of Ynys Metcaut.

The Miathi of Manau rebel and occupy Guidi.

Aeden counterattacks and defeats them

at the battle of the river Teith in Manau….

Caelin's Chronicles

II

This story begins much earlier.

It was the dark time before Dragons. A time so dark that just a mere thought would bring fear and chill into the hearts of men. In fact, the start of this story goes so far back that the 'Men of the Knife', whose descendants would one day walk through Tamworth's lanes thankfully forgetting such times ever existed.

So far back in our history.

To the times before the 'Saxon' and 'Engle' had earned complete control of an island that would suffer more warfare and misery in five hundred years than most lands would witness in their completed history.

Our story goes beyond those distant times when it still brought hurt to remember the years when the 'Foederati' had driven out the last of the Latin Legions from a land that was then cursed as Britannia. Before those years of Penda's alliance with a Welsh King named Cadwalon of Gwynedd, to a time when the most powerful seat was then called Cantawara, and its mighty Chieftain Æthelberht, reigned through fear and might, bringing down horrendous retribution upon any who refused to acknowledge that his one and only supremacy would rule across every hill and valley, from the southern tips of Cent far up to those distant lands north of the Hymbre river.

It wasn't long since Augustine had been sent by the King of an unknown belief, who demanded an unseen God be worshipped by peoples of an unknown place, violently inflicting upon an innocent land the words 'Religion' and 'Christianity'. That is where the true beginnings of this story really start.

During those times before history was barely recorded onto the leafs of calf skin books, sagas were whispered between the flickering flame light of the night fires, by the Elders to the youngest of children, night after night so that they too may remember such stories to be echoed, one day, into the ears of their own offspring, tales of many deeds never to be forgotten.

At the time when our Isle was made up of individual realms which bore such glorious names as Bernicia, Eborac, Elmet and Deira, and were ruled over by forgotten Kings with strange sounding names such as Hussa son of Glappa, Royth ap Rhun, Theodoric Flame-Bringer and Ceretic ap Gwallog, back to those long-lost times that are no longer taught, because folk no longer care….

It was after the winter had broken its hold, in the year of 575, during the warming months when the bard Aneirin sang his laments within the rule of Uriens of the Hen Ogledd.

When the smell of Roman garlic and rosemary still hung foul in the Brythonic air. Before Æthelbehrt's death, and equally before Eadwald of the North and South folk had gained total power of an island he never wanted, a young Engle princess would give her heart to the son of a Brythonic King whose blood line had descended from the very beginnings of the Bryneich, carrying his heritage proudly from the ancestral realms of Morcant Bwlch.

The Engle then was no more than a minority race, an immigrant who had not yet proven his strengths and abilities amongst those people who still held high their ancestral claim upon those northern plains. But as it would soon become a fact through-out eternity, whatever the conflict, love, during any age was always bound to ignore mere trivialities such as politics, tradition, blood-line, or heritage, and the brief but truest of meetings was doomed to failure from the second their eyes met in a misty glade within the lowland leas of God'oddin.

The months drifted by, proving that failure and sorrow would not win its way before their bonding had resulted in the production of an heir, born in a night's secret, deep in that very glade………….

Such were those days, when time was ever too sacred to be wasted and a wrong decision always resulted in death, so to safeguard the life of an innocent baby, the boy, as it was, would soon be discarded by a tearful Mother into the care of the 'estranged' family of a bard who travelled those northern ways by the name of Taliesin, crossing rarely into his southern homelands with his given name of Mervyn.

It was nothing more than a basic requirement that a man, such as the bard, would spend his days on foot, ever embracing the gnarled old black-thorn staff that had, over the years, become more responsible for his balance than his own legs. Scuffling his feet, he would trundle at the head of a rattling old cart, pulled by a disabled old clod pony, and ply his trade from dusky court to the sparsest of outposts visiting the Caledonian Kings, and often those of the Bryneich too, entertaining them with his conjuring's and illusions and sometimes his songs and tales, even poetry, of a kind which told of the romance of forgotten myths. Almost every court was highlighted with his eaves dropped snippets of gossiped secrets overheard from neighbouring Halls, which helped to support a modest living for him and those few who were fortunate enough to follow. Such travels, granted through the grace and favour of the rulers of those ancient kingdoms would also grant the soon to be adopted child a greater education than many as he would quickly become schooled in the variety of beliefs and customs of the day.

...During that most painful of evenings whilst the Lady wept away the night hours with heartfelt guilt for the abandonment of her only child, and fearing for her young son's future, a Bernician raiding party stumbled upon the camp just as her 'weardian' were making ready their return to the southern camps, and in their surprise, were viciously put to the slaughter without mercy nor concern.

Her name had been Arnive and would only be remembered briefly in ancient song, often later to the name Igraine or Ygerna in exaggerated legends, before disappearing into the confines of unwritten history, like countless others of her day.

The child would grow without the love of a Mother, with a half mad bard in her stead, and the last breath that she would cry out across that brutal land would echo her sadness and go unheard by anyone who may have cared.

The boy's Father would never learn of Arnive's peril, and would soon after sink into silent depression believing that his only love now blamed him for the loss of their only son, and had banished his memory from her thoughts for ever. His name would never be associated with offspring of his own, and his fate would be sealed one dismal evening in what he had naively thought to be the safety of his own Father's lands.

Murder, brought upon him by the traitors and spies who despised Uriens almost as much as they detested his son, with his smart new ideas of tolerance towards their new neighbours. Either way, good Bryneich blood would not be polluted with the mongrel blood of an Engle whore.

...For his own safety, during those swaddling years, the boy would be hidden from the gaze of outsiders, smuggled in secret from homestead to homestead as it's 'stoep' Father scrounged out their living. Only to be cared for by a half-blind old hag who held little or no feelings for herself, but freely gave what little she did have to the wants of a growing boy.

When he had lived through sufficient winters to make his own decisions and had grown wise enough to accept their consequences, the boy who had then become a man joined the ranks of the last northern armies that followed King Gwallawc Marchawc Trin, the Battle Horseman of Elmet, as they fought against the new Engle invaders for what was still known then as Bryneich land, and accepted a victory in its capital Din Guarie.

He fought well.

The tactics of battle had come easy, gaining him the respect of his counterparts as well as his seniors. Given his own command had made him the youngest of Bryneich commanders and the reputation that followed showed that he would be second to no one.

But that stage of his life would soon be nearing its end, there were new chapters edging their way to those northern plains of Brython...

What remained of the near annihilated Engle, whose surviving numbers had barely escaped from Din Guarie, had sought refuge in the northern waters upon a deserted isle then known only by the name of Ynys Metcaut. Aided by the relentless weather that kept them safe from the wraths of the mainland, they rested and gathered their strengths in the frosts and snows of the freezing northerly wind, replenishing their losses from a faraway land. Despite all, hope remained in their hearts for they knew then that their own time was just beginning, besides, they now had nowhere else to go.

That young man, known then only by the name of Aedan, played his part in what would soon become known as the last rising of the Brythonic Clans at the Battle of Catraeth. Things did not go their way and in-fighting soon brought about the self-destruction of the 'Gwyr y Gogledd' as jealousy between Gwallawc and his allies exploded into chaos once more. Uriens of Rheged, Aedan's estranged Grandfather, and Riderch Hael of Alt Clut stood shoulder to shoulder against Gwalloc in a small yet fateful civil war.......

The 'Men of the North' rode to their glories no more.

In desperation for a land he had come to love, now deserted by the Kings who had squandered everything, Aedan, alongside Gwallawc's heir Ceretic, attempted to raise what remained of their warriors into a final stand as the Engles lived up to their venomous threats. In seeing the ever-growing weakness of the mainland, they returned from their sanctuary in the breaking weather, striking hard against the Brython's pitiful defence.

But few would listen to Aedan's words. His courageous attempts to rally would earn him small mention in the final chapter of a local tale, which would one day be blown out of all proportion and turned into the greatest legend of all times by those who needed to invent their heroes.

However sincere his intent, the remaining warriors listened no longer to tales and sagas, caring no more for unproven promises. Most had lived the truth of their lives amongst turmoil, treachery and battles lost, they wanted no more of it. Many fled to the far north where things were said to be more 'Brythonic', where folk still honoured the Old Ways. Others sailed south, in small ships to Belerion seeking refuge and new beginnings within the mystical realms of the Kernou.

So, they gave way their lands and conceded their heritage to who so ever laid claim. Throughout the northern plains all had been forsaken, all were now forlorn and those most violent of times slipped rapidly into perdition.

The crumbling realms which had flourished between the two Latin walls began to wither away, and after the death of the Bard, whom he only ever knew as Father, Aeden cast away the sword of a King into a bottomless lake and fled southward with a few modest possessions to what was then the Northumbrian settlement of Mancunium, then on to a homestead which grew in the small shire of the Sealhford, where he would live out the remainder of his years hidden within the shadows of a time that continued to conceive its brutal history.

Fortunately, he had been taught the trade as a farrier during his youngest years and managed to earn sufficient to pay his tallies and fill his stomach, clothe his body and keep a thatch above his head, which leant to a happy and fortunate marriage to the daughter of an Ealdormann sharing his once regal blood with offspring who, after his own death, moved their chattels further south to the lands that were then of the Hwicce, themselves descendent from ancient folk once said in legend to have been graced with the guarding of the Holy Grail whilst it had been hidden within those shores many years earlier.

As the years elapsed Aedan's heirs merged again their blood with those who mattered. Eventually within their veins once more flowed the blood of Kings. Throughout those next years which painfully tore their way through the violence of war, the pity of famine and the harshness of disease, then back to the battles once more, Aedan's legacy eventually mixed with that of Uhtred's Thegn Æthelmund, friend of Offa and Father of Æthelric the last true leader of the Hwicce.

More than four hundred and fifty of the cruellest years after the Latins had fled those unprotected shores, that ancient bloodline, as was the way in such times, was carried by a young maiden adorned with the name of Ecgwynn who soon won the eye of a Saxon nobleman, just as it had been all those years passed in the misty glade of God'oddin.

Eventually, beneath the smile of a King, she had wed that nobleman.

Eadweard Ætheling was the eldest son of the great King Ælfred, ruler of the West Saxon folk. Now that blood of a long forgotten Brythonic Prince was once again as regal as ever and would shortly be pulsating through the veins of a most important body. Soon to be, that blood would become that of a King whose name would be screamed out on the death bed of a Mother, and continue to be screamed through the valleys of a land yet to be named Engle Land, for the countless years that would follow.

'…Then they were weighed down by famine.

They had devoured the greater parts of their horses;

and the rest had perished with hunger.

After, they all went out to the men

that sat on the eastern side of the river

and fought with them,

and the Christians had the victory.

And there, Ordhelm the King's Thegn was slain,

also, many other King's Thegns.

And of the Danes, many also were slain,

their numbers lay uncounted

until their remained no numbers to do the counting…'

The Battle of Buttington 894.

III

894. In this year the Northumbrians and East Engles swear their oaths to King Ælfred, and the Engles give six hostages as their bond. Nevertheless, contrary to their words, the other plunderers go oft with their armies and no more was the truce.

The Anglo-Saxon Chronicle.

It was meant to be.

That on such a morning, just as the mist was smothering the start of a fine summer's day, when the previous night's cooking still smelled of wild bird stew congealing on dampened fires and men folk struggled in pointless agony to rid their heads from the revenge of last night's mead, something different stirred at the echoes still lurking within the shadows of those haunted lands, quivering its threat to the spirits who clutched desperately for the safety of the darkness pulsating through her brown woods, rattling over her greenest plains and quaking over her stony shores......

The exact day would be irrelevant.

All days had been much the same until then, yet the scholars would note that there had been eight hundred and ninety-four dreaded years of turmoil, mayhem, and sorrow since the arrival of 'the one' who had been promised to rid All evil from that cruel world of painful days.

The Lady had been struggling against her wretched agony for what had seemed an eternity.

Nobody had noticed the passing of the day as the chamber continued to shake from her relentless screams of tortuous pain. Nought else could be heard save the echoes of a torrid labour which rattled against the muffled prayers of a half-cut cleric that seeped from the darkest corner of the chamber. Her body had twisted and turned since the earliest of hours as her mind had drifted in and out of consciousness.

Her chest had heaved its deepest craving for fresh breath as the last of her tears had long since dribbled over pallid cheeks.

But now it seemed as if her Gods had found their mercy deeming the torment soon to be at its end.

Erupting from the trembling loins of a would-be Saxon Lady squealed a child into Tamworth's chilling air. Arrogant and positive it bellowed as if it had been the only child to enter that persecuted world.

The Mother's noises followed, drowning away the birth screams of her new born son as another bout of wretched hurt brought further horror and fear into her weakened heart. Her body perspired without compromise as it struggled in torment whilst the flaxen linen beneath gave up any further attempts of soaking away the Lady's secreted agonies.

As a Mother's warmth steamed from an excited child, radiating quickly into the dimness of a busy chamber, the smell of new born flesh fought to overcome the odour of charred fruit wood smouldering on the open fire whilst being fanned by the skirts of the wet nurses scurrying willy-nilly in their attempts to do everything, yet achieving very little.

Anxiously she cried in silence to her Gods for the luxury of a full breath, straining to focus upon her surroundings, glaring deeply into the glowing embers of the central hearth, raising a trembling hand in a feeble effort to fight back its warmth from her over-heated body. Then her stares swept across that bustling place fixing jealously on the silhouettes of two Queens huddled aghast in the room's darkest shadows, their very presence seemingly redundant and out of place…

Why were they both there? The new Mother's thoughts were muddled and confused as those incessant pains surged unyielding throughout her body, but she was now way passed caring. Clustered together in the furthest shadows, themselves too afraid to make a move save their actions cause the dying Lady even more trauma, the two 'Queens' retired deeper into the nothing.

Once of the Hwicce, now within the highest ranks of Mercian nobility, Ecgwynn's beauty had forever been the talk of the courts by all those ladies who mattered. She had been the only one to hold her own against the vivid beauty of Æthelflæd who loved her poor 'sister' dearly. Only married to the Ætheling for the shortest of weeks, being wed on the very eve' that her Eadweard had marched for the 'valleys' of the Welsh, towards yet another fight, they had been joined together under the eyes of their new God, if only to sanctify their expected child's birth, and of course, to guarantee security to a Mother and a wife, and a title to an unborn son should a Father fail to return from his compulsory quest.

... Aghast with a breath that crackled into a whine, before twisting her body taut with a welcome numbness that almost offered sanctuary from the unending pain as it momentarily swept through her tender frame, she felt every strength escaping her fragile limbs, and Ecgwynn knew then that there would be nothing more that she, nor her nurses could do about it. As a desperate resort, they had mixed the 'hælwyrt' with spring water, crushed parsnips in cooled mead and placed their tokens and charms around the birth-mother, but nothing offered any help....

In her frantic attempts to snatch some form of normality she fought back the black mist and fixed her failing vision tightly upon her child, cleansed and wrapped in the arms of a maid. Her thoughts became joined with those of a husband now absent from her side but always present in her memories, how much she missed him now, how much she craved his company, how much she wanted to live, long and old, to watch her new son grow at the side of a doting Father as both would flourish together into the fine men she knew they would become. There were two men now occupying the Lady's final seconds, and she would dearly miss them both.

At the same instant, as those precious memories of a husband began to slip from her thoughts, a heavily draped fabric of an old warn tapestry slipped quietly to one side revealing part of a chamber it had screened, and the innocent looks of an only daughter stared pitifully to witness the final throws of a Mother's pain.

Eadgyth had listened in terror through the awfulness of that day, watching through a faded pleat at the miraculous yet shocking birth of a first brother, amazed in wonder as a new life burst into her world, yet even with no more than six winters to her young life she had accepted that she would never again witness a Mother's comfort or sympathy from such loving arms that now reached out for mercy, 'for pity's sake'.

With an overstated tug by a dutiful maid, the seclusion of the side chamber was returned, and the girl Eadgyth was dismissed back into the safety of her warm cot.

As she feigned her sleep, childish tears streamed down her salting cheeks sponging into the fur lined head rest as the youngster snivelled her sorrow and listened unwillingly to further panic and uproar that echoed never ending through a curtain wall. Small palms shrouded her ears, desperately trying to drown the death cries of her own Mother whilst swearing, even at such a young age, a devout and virtuous oath that she would forever covert the purest innocence's of a child.

She eased closed her eyes squinting back more tears, hammering her thoughts with her only known prayer...

"Fæder ure thou thee eart on heofonum

Si thin nama gehalgod

To becume thin rice......."

"I beg of thee m'lady...." came the whispered plea from a caring maid tearfully mopping a running brow, following her words with a sensitive smile. Her fingers shook as she wiped and patted uselessly with well intentioned comfort. Again, she dabbed at the streams of tears which continued to flood across the sallow cheeks of her dear Lady...... "Ye 'ath a new born bearn, a sunu, a glorious Ætheling to be...." She ended what was until that moment a genuinely comforting speech, with a lie, "Our Lord Eadweard shall return as soon as 'e 'ears that 'e now be a Fæther to such a fine lad."

It had been Ælfred's Law:

A law which applied to all men, noble or ceorl. Duty bound were all to answer the call to 'all arms' from their Ealdormann or Thegn, and join with the King's 'fyrd', except of course for certain 'huscarl' contingents who would remain behind to protect the burgs and their noble occupants, and naturally, to ensure that the harvests were reaped and stored for the 'quiet' winter months.

Aggressively, as the convulsions grew, Ecgwynn pushed her maid free, her eyes opened wide to the point where they may burst, her back arched until it could arch no more then her body slammed back into the sodden linen as she gasped for the shortest of breaths.

Her arms pushed violently upwards, straight, rigid, and strained, and the sadness of a Mother's failing breath loud and positive screamed out a name......

"ÆTHELSTAN!!!!!"

.......and as the wattled walls shook from the echoes of her desperate voice, her dying face changed to a more content expression as she witnessed in her final dreams the fear and worry, mayhem, treason, and glory that was soon to surround her son's destiny.

Then, as her weary spirit approached the gates of her after-life Ecgwynn's earthly presence withered slowly away...

The small private chamber hung in solemn silence as the Mother's final seconds escaped slowly through the dryness of her bluing lips. She had expended every strength in her fight against such cruel labour, but her destiny had been written long before telling all who then cared that she would gladly sacrifice her own life for that of such an important son.

Charred logs broke a second's quiet collapsing in a heap of failing ashes spilling from the fire's grate as the last flames lowered seemingly in respect to the passing of a much-loved Lady, then an uninvited breeze made its way through a half open shutter blowing into the chamber's middle where it also died. The smell of birth mixed with the musk of death intertwined with the fire smoke bringing a brief tear to the eyes of the small gathering standing their guard over the Lady's passing. That new God which had been forced upon them had as little mercy as those of the Old Ways, nothing seemed to have changed for the better in that cruel world of Men.

As Ecgwynn's shrills had pierced the chamber's air with the name of her newly born son, both Ladies had broken simultaneously from their mesmerised states, stepping out from the shadows whimpering with pity and sadness for the loss of a 'daughter', staring down with shock as the maids began to wipe away the visible memories of such a terrible birth, all together whispering a pitiful prayer. Saddened and stunned into silence they clung together in each other's arms as the room scuffed about its terrible duties.

Both were unwilling to believe that such a death could befall their newest of 'daughters'. Everything had been prepared for the birth, just as it should have been, everyone who could had played their part, there was nothing more that should have been done, nobility never had an immunity from death. Shame soon filled them both, then guilt quickly took over, they should have been able to do more.

Such feelings lasted the fewest of seconds.

The humid silence and self-pity quickly broke as a hungry baby screamed its first scream as a motherless son, telling the world with no uncertainty that Æthelstan, son of Eadweard and the grandson of a King had arrived upon those lands. A clasp of thunder hailed in unison far away across the Peake Lands threatening that a storm would soon gather, and the Ancient Ones permitted the beginning of the baby's destiny, whilst a Mother took her rightful place at Frige's side.

After such a finale, there came the slightest movement from the statuesque figure of the silent 'preost' whose stomach had been as upset as his convenience during the Lady's turmoil. He groaned a Latinised blessing, crossed the air, and sank again his pallid face into a robed chest, his part had been played, duty done, and another coin earned.

On the opposite leaf of a heavy door, in the wind flickered light of the hesitant reed torches, a large commotion was quick to pass as a messenger snatched a hasty token of passage, before dragging his noises of desperation and duty along the cobbled way in an excited eagerness to locate his horse.

The trusted rider, Ecgbehrt the second son of Thegn Ecgric, had originated from the small Engle settlement at Beormingas ham, and despite his young age, had recently been selected as Huscarl. In the gloom of that pensive eve he had placed his shield hand upon the tattered calf skin book and sworn an undying allegiance, under the watchful stare of a half-priest, the very instant the cries of the newly born heir had echoed through the wattled corridors of the Great Hall.

Ecgbehrt was more than eager to carry out his first duty for a newly born master.

The lad, with an escort of two well armed 'cnihts' vanished into the appropriate gloom leaving the mellowness of Tamworth's burg with the speed of the wind at their backs, forcing their way west, deep into the ancient valleys of 'Brytenlande', where, after exchanging tired horses and quaffing a 'calic' of something warm at a settlement on route, would finally lead them to a place then known to the Welsh as Tal y Bont.

In that place of war, where other men tried their utmost to emulate hell, and after proving his 'right of passage' to a hundred guards, Ecgbehrt would remove a tarnished spanghelm in respect to his King before revealing both sad, and happy news to the ears of Ælfred the new grandfather.

To his knowing he had never set eyes upon the immediately recognisable figure of his King, so with pride that may have been mistaken for nervousness, in an unbroken voice, he had explained that his King's elder son's heir had entered their world fit and well. Yet such welcome news could only be followed with the saddened words that would tell of the Lady's sacrifice for the life of her only son. Then the King's own heir lowered his head hiding his shock, holding back any grief which may threaten to do battle with his joy, the time had not yet come when it was correct to let free his emotions.

Ecgbehrt pulled to one side his horse as King Anarawd moved first to offer his sympathies as well as his best. The Welsh King was known to all as an over bearing, selfish man who would readily push aside his rightful kin to grant his own achievements. Two days earlier he had brought up his Welsh weapon men to stand alongside those of Mercia and Wessex, against what was then hoped to be the final slaughter of Hastein the Danish Jarl, and yet another group of his marauding Norsemen. Naturally, should they be successful, Anarawd's worth and power would more than double.

Gathered to surround the noble group many Earls and Thegns had come, intent on watching Æthelræd, Ealdorman of Mercia, Lord of Tamworth, pound the enemy with his valiant knights, cruelly punishing their way towards the heart of the Welsh burg, inch by bloody inch. He was himself by far the oldest of Ælfred's Ealdormen, and with age came confidence and an unrivalled experience in warring with the Dane, and on many previous occasions, the Welsh too. It had always been Æthelræd's way to lead the first charge, and it would always be Æthelræd's way to lead the last.

"Doth ye carry more news for thy King?" Ælfred would have asked of his unexpectedly young messenger who would shake the evening dew from blonded locks and nervously mention, whilst over showing his deepest sympathy and betraying his fifteen winters of inexperience, 'that in the last throws before her passing the Lady had screamed out a single name……'

"The name had been Æthelstan, Bregu. Loud and strong my Lady had cried out with her final breath, Æthelstan……"

At that moment, as the Welsh burg erupted into the devil's own fire startling both horse and King alike in the reflective back-ground of the carnage, Ælfred of the Gewissi, who, for many reasons would one day be called 'the Great', turned to his son with much respect for an already missed daughter, and commanded….

"Then be it so. A Noble Stone by name. A Sovereign Rock for the future of these wretched lands. Æthelstan shall be his given name, and may the Gods grant him the

Kingship of a peaceful Land when destiny shall decide that it be his time to rule this place of Hel's own...."

.....And the fires lit up against the darkened skyline as the battle raged in the distance of the night, ignored for the briefest of pauses so that all may pay their respects to the passing of a noble Lady, and a swift calic of mead for the birth of a future King.......Then the ferocity of saving yet another homestead from yet more unwanted invaders would continue to rattle in the foreground as ever rising flames continued to eat their way through a little known settlement where men practiced their rightful gift of slaughtering each other in the most painful and cruellest ways imaginable.

Salutations and sympathies complete, the King of Wessex, followed by his elder son, lead the main body of a powerful Engle-Seaxisc army deep into the heart of Buttington where, alongside their Welsh allies, they inflicted further dread upon another Danish trespasser who was quickly beginning to realise too late that his men, who marched under the banner of the Raven, were no longer a match for that new Saxon army who marched undauntedly beneath the stares of the Golden Wyvern.

That night would not just see the leadership of a small Welsh town reinstated back to its rightful place, that night would also see the beginning of many changes across those cruellest lands that had once been known to the Old Gods as Middangeard.

In his own privacy, as the night drifted towards its close, and the battle sat upon the pinnacle of victory, Eadweard Ætheling heir to the rule of Wessex, shed a single tear for the loss of a perfect wife, then a second was gently guided from a grimy cheek for what he knew would be the most perfect of sons.

At that same time.

Whilst Ecgbehrt had been passing an unwelcome message to his King, the 'birthing' group back in the Great Hall were frantically issuing inherited orders between the walls of the dead Mother's chamber.

Prayers had been said, respects had been paid and tears, many tears, had been spilled as sufficient time had elapsed for the corpse to release its now immortal soul, basically the body had grown cold enough to be certain Ecgwynn was dead.

Firstly, the new born had been separated from its Mother's final caress, reluctantly letting slip her matted locks through crinkled fingers as a wet nurse gathered the child in the softest of wraps, swaddled him tightly to avoid the night's chill and keep the young heir free from such ills that were all too common to follow a birth. Closing her face nearer to the infant she blew the gentleness of warmth into the vaguest wisps of fine blonde hair and began to murmur the nonsensical enticements that only a woman could whisper to a newly born child, and with little encouragement the starving babe began to suckle greedily from a surrogate breast contentedly closing its sightless eyes, tired from his torrid welcome into such a selfish world.

Whilst it had suckled a first meal, a small posy of honeysuckle and blackberry leaf was wafted across the infant pile replacing the day's foul odours with those of nature's own sweetness. She would comfort and protect her ward through that saddest of nights as if he were her own.

Ealhswith and her daughter would oversee the duties of the 'mydwyf' discreetly from the confines of the shadows, watching intently until any 'complications' had set in and then those who were deemed to be 'more learned' and appropriate would step in, as were the ways. The same cautious ceremony was strictly observed after any death.

On that occasion, rigidly supervised by the King's Lady, every remnant from that gory birth was discharged into the flaming tongues of the regenerated hearth fire where they were engulfed without further trace along with the likes of any disease or sickness that may have threatened to lay claim to yet more life. The roar of the flames that bit into the night air was as contemptuous as the impenetrable stench was horrendous; but swift and necessary precautions passed down the lines of time would safeguard all from risk to further contamination that had, on passed occasions, wiped out complete homesteads in the shortest of times.

Eerie and cylindrical had been those ancient chants.

Those chants that had risen softly from the saddened voices of the maids as they washed the naked body free of the blood and grime of child birth, then dried and thoroughly anointed the corpse of their Lady with crystal clean spring water infused with crushed honeysuckle and blackberry leaf. The body was then dressed in a robe of splendour that would befit one who may have herself one day sat as a King's Lady. A posy of seasonally wild flowers and herbs tied with the smallest ringlets of the baby's hair, sat in a wrap made from one of Eadweard's own 'swatlin' and had been tenderly placed within the clenched hands that were folded neatly at the centre of her chest, just below her heart.

Everyone involved took a single pace back and adjusted their own attire as they admired and inspected the final acts of dignity, and a near silent prayer was passed from Æthelflæd's lips to ask for her 'sister's' guidance into the realms of their new God.

As the expected sobbing of an elder daughter was sympathetically, but nevertheless, abruptly dismissed from view, and once the 'Noble' supervisors were equally content that their best efforts had been achieved by administering all possible respects, Ecgwynn's body was wrapped tightly within her resting mat of dried moss and lavender flower with any other linens that had formed her 'death bed'. With the whitest of hand kerchiefs placed neatly over her ashen face and a pair of silver 'penings' placed delicately inside her mouth, to pay the 'boatman', her body was carried, slowly and carefully, into a howling storm that skirted the chapel's yard.

Short footed maidens wrestled against the foulness of the night's worst as their Lady was lowered onto a raft of dried hazel hastily lain above an even hastier dug grave. Despite nature's challenges the corpse was finally covered with a mixture of dried straw and sweetened oil that was all but carried away in the winds.

To the side of a guarding line of shielded Huscarl, vigilant and silent in grubby white cloaks that snapped against the chill and wearing tarnished spanghelms that did all but shine, came the sobbing of even more women folk who had made their own way to gather in the foul weather, to pay their respects, after which in the driving torrents of unseasonably freezing rain, a mortal body was burned to ashes whilst supervised and blessed by the hurried chanting's of a scruffy looking Abbot, who had been roughly and unapologetically dragged from his warmest of cots to attend upon the final rites of an Ætheling's Lady. No further time would be lost, and the Abbot returned swiftly to his own chamber's warmth.

On that saddest of nights, around the shadows of Tamworth's wattled cots, it would be kept as 'secret' by none but a few, that Ecgwynn had been descended from the great houses of the oldest Brythonic clans. The blood that had once flowed through her veins now flowed through the veins of her only son who now carried the inherent line of those who had ruled over their lands, so many lifetimes passed. Tales would be whispered, by that same few, that during her tortuous labour, and on through the snapping flames of the 'wælfyr', fifty or more wanderers had arrived on foot, out of the shadows of the Peake Lands headed by one who, even from a distance appeared so old that he ought not be there.

No person could remember ever seeing such folk and no one had bothered to ask of them, but then no person cared as they had remained amongst themselves on the outskirts of the burg never asking to be permitted an entrance. Yet as the flames rose high and Ecgwynn's body turned to ash the small crowd turned away, back to the hills of the east, and in their wake, could be heard their chanting, almost a song, in words so old that they could never be repeated let alone remembered. The group drifted off into the shadows bringing no further attention to themselves except from the guards who stood in watch along the 'ringwall' and later spoke of a strange odour that had whisked its way through the night with an eerie chill above the winds that had passed out into the direction of the wanderers, followed by a sense of calm settling all, just for the shortest time. Then the strangers disappeared into the silhouettes of the distant hills and their coming had been just as quickly dismissed.

As the winds did all but relax, the mourners slowly seeped from the grave's side in small groups huddled together in protection from the storm's rage until only one figure remained still whispering beneath her breath. Even before a Mother's death, Æthelflæd had been nominated by the King that should the child become motherless, as was sadly often the case, she would become the child's guardian.

Ælfred had known that the strength of his eldest daughter would provide a suitable replacement for any mother.

The good Lady Eostre had not been gracious to Æthelflæd and her much older husband by granting them a male heir, just a daughter of no real consequence, but loved all the same. A girl child, who was right to be born a girl child, who, from the earliest of ages had shown that she would always crave the things that a girl child should crave. More than probable, should she grow, Ælfwynn would more than likely wed an Ealdormann or a middle noble, maybe a Thegn and produce countless children, some of whom may even survive, then pass the remainder of her life unnoticed, as was the way for a girl child at least.

Æthelflæd herself had been born the total opposite of her daughter.

With the will of the strongest of men, a fiery, ferocious, and unyielding will that had deprived her of any maternal instincts which she herself had gladly left to the 'wet' nurses once the inconvenience of labour had passed. Not so for the son of her younger brother. She would most certainly nurture him just as he should be nurtured, in her own shadow, ready for him to inherit all that she as a mere woman could not, maybe even the ruling seat of those most precious lands.

Consequently, upon receipt of her Father's Royal Command, a mere handful of days before the child's birth, Æthelflæd had excitedly selected six of the most trusted 'wyfman' of the best 'earþlinga' from the surrounding settlements. They, who had themselves recently given birth to healthy offspring, sired by the most formidable knights and spearmen, or farmers and smyths who would, without question, delegate the rearing of their own children to another, to fulfil such a privileged post. Their milk would be purest Mercian and their blood lines long and healthy.

As the newly born child had been screeching out its first cries of life into the air that trembled over those unstable lands, across the murky waters to their west, in what was then a Danish Island, those who ruled but did not belong, plotted as they had always plotted.

The conquering masters of that smaller but equally pensive Isle had gathered as they had always gathered, within their fortified settlements along the edges of a black lake known then only as 'Dyfelin'.

Puckered together within the smoky brown fire light of a mead hall that held no real consequence, with a handful of rebellious weapon men from the 'Wealas' who remained angered by the flagrant betrayal of their kinsmen for siding with the Wessex, and any other outcast who wished to add his tones of embittered hatred of those who ruled across the 'brimrad', drank the Irish Dane.

As had always been much of the same on previous nights their plotting and scheming would eventually become louder and more garbled as the mead and ale brought out more aggressive boastings concerning that which they 'could' be doing to their enemies should their Gods grant them the opportunity. The more the cloudy mead was swilled down their necks the more terrible their vocal retribution until no more mead or ale could be swilled and a drunken sleep brought an instantaneous silence into the hall, and a respite to the pinched backsides and bruised breasts of the 'waiting maids'.

Despite their idle threats and drunken banter one thing was certain to all no matter his heritage, Ælfred Æthelwulfsunu had ruled as 'Engla Konungr' for more than twenty years, yet despite his aggressive nature and stoic show of self will, he would soon be nearing his day's end.

But the right time was still not theirs.

The Anglo-Saxon armies were formidable. Ælfred had reorganised them whilst educating his Thegns and Ealdormann in the tactics of guerrilla warfare and more importantly, had re-built and organised a powerful Navy equipped with armed mariners to support his land forces, turning his military might into one that could, and would, respond without notice to the call of the 'All Arms', to march, ride or sail anywhere within those Isles, stand alone in a fight, and above all, win.

A Norse victory at that time would be improbable, maybe two or even three more years of drinking and bragging in the confines of their Hibernian shores inflicting even more misery upon those unfortunate to remain upon that 'Irskr Eyland'.

The sound of Ælfred's war horns would soon be silent. The Saxon fyrd would quickly forget how a real war was fought, Saxon women would grow used to having their men underfoot and idle. Their children were being born into a land where the only mention of war would soon be heard around the hearth fires, taught by elders who could only exaggerate the sagas of the past.

Ælfred's northern enemy had almost been defeated, pushed out from the shores of that once tormented isle leaving the Engle, the Seaxisc, the Geat, and any other outlander who wished for a peaceful life, who would pay his tallies, and honour his King, in a 'quiet' land to call his home.

But the Saxon King's health was waning. Truth be told, he had never really suffered from good health since the day his Mother had pushed him into that world. Now, as an aged man and tiring King he grew worse by the day causing his own kinsmen to show great concern, and an Ætheling to worry that such a task would soon be borne on his unfortunate shoulders.

And Ælfred's enemies, impatiently and frustrated across those 'whale roads', clutching with greedy encouragement every snippet of 'bad' news, almost ready and ever waiting. Their Snekkja long boats with their crews of weapon men urging their leaders to give the order to sail for England, so the blood of the Saxons would run free.

Soon the Seaxisc King would be dead, but they still needed a plan.

So then.

On an ordinary eve' in such uncertain times, born to that ruling House of Wessex, within the enchanted lands of a Mercian Realm came a single innocent child into that cruel world of Men. A child, whose line reached so far back into the histories of those lands that such times had been long forgotten. Now, mixed with the new blood of a Seaxisc Ætheling the baby would grow to become the rightful heir to the ever-growing Realms of Wessex and Mercia……. And much, much more.

I beheld the array from the highland of Adowyn,

and the sacrifice brought down to the omen of fire.

I saw then what was usual,

I beheld the array from the highland of Adowyn,

a continual running towards the town,

and the men of Nwython inflicting sharp wounds;

I saw warriors who made the great breach

approaching with a shout,

and the Head of Dyvnwal Vrych by ravens devoured.

From Y Gododin

by Aneurin

CHAPTER 1

937. King Idwael Foel of Gwynedd, of the House of Aberffraw, distances himself from his English overlord. The Brytons begin to use the term 'Cyrmry' to speak of themselves.

Gone now was the fighting season. In years passed its very meaning had dictated that the driest months, the warmest months, and the longest months were the good months, the very best months for fighting. But since the death of Edward his Father, the fighting season seemed to have no end regardless of the month, so the warring continued. There were no more fighting seasons, every season was now for fighting.

Weary would not have been his word for it. At that moment there was no single word that could have described the extent of his tiredness brought by that hurried march which now seemed his longest, he was exhausted.

From side to side he stared in awe at the vast numbers of men at arms, knights, Thegns and Ealdormann who had gathered to his Order. His special knights, always at his side, and the Thegns, those devoted many who had brought their fyrds to his line, of women as well as men, from many Houses such had been their need, and others not of those isles, all there for that final battle of all battles.

Cold, damp, and dull was that time of year, when the days were at the shortest and the nights the coldest. It was the time of year which the Old Ones had named 'Blodmonað'.

...... 'For then the cattle which were to be slaughtered were consecrated to the Gods and their flesh dried and stored for the empty months'......

Now in that month, Men would do the slaughtering to other Men, how aptly named would be that 'blood month'.

It seemed as if he had been in the saddle for an eternity, searching wide across those northern lands, now at last he had found it. He had found the right place, the best place, the only place. There it would all be decided in a field of nature's quiet, ignorant of any pending conflict.

At a place no longer named Brunanburh, Æthelstan, the first King of all the Englisc sat proudly upon the horse he had long since named Abrecan, staring out far across the flatness of the plains to the east. Until that day such a field bore no significance, but there it was all to be finally decided as to who would rule 'All' those mighty fiefdoms as one mighty Realm, as Engle Land.

Those truly were the worst times of any year for fighting, the days grew the shortest, the nights the coldest, with little cover for hiding an army save a morning's mist or a winter's gale. At least though, if such conditions were so imperfect for his own armies they would be even less so for the armies of his enemies.

The Engelcynn knew their lands well. Those unseen places of strategic importance, the ruts, the crevices, the bogs and the hides, the right places to exploit as the late sun rose, then change to another as it quickly rested. They knew of the places where their enemies would bolt at the height of the battle, places which only seemed appropriate on the surface and would quickly betray their presence, but only to those who knew. That was how they had grown to protect their Lands against any who could only dream of being a part of it.

Edmund Ætheling sat upon saddle close to Æthelstan's left, still nothing more than a boy to many. Only weeks earlier he had seen the passing of his fifteenth summer, even so the King held little concern about the abilities of his younger half-brother, his only heir would soon prove himself a man worthy in title whilst still a boy, just as he himself had done……….

In the year 910, the Welsh bishop Asser, close friend to the late King Ælfred died at Scir burne, and Frithestan became Bishop of Wintanceaster.

During Æthelstan's growing years, those around him who had been part of his upbringing, either as teacher, as friend or merely as his closest guards would see the changing of a boy from noble blood moulded into a strong willed young man who would very quickly learn not to suffer fools, realising from the outset to accept a man for whom he was and for what he stood for rather than the 'House' that he had been born into, or the name of a Father who had conceived his birth.

Daily, as a matter of habit, he was blatantly ignored by those who should have called him 'brother' or 'son'. Very often being left to his own devices he would often witness many things others of his age would miss or ignore for their want of childish things. Those experiences that were equally good or equally bad would be remembered for their own lessons of life.

Unlike others of his age he grew without any individual interests or hobbies that would occupy spare moments, except for one and that would be shared only with his closest friend, Ealdfrith.

Whenever the pair were permitted time from their teachings and other disciplines the boys would slip silently from their quarters, to watch in awe at the training of Ætheflæd's most secret of weapons.

Together, in the shadows of a wattled hut or a ragged thatch, or the overhangs of a weeping tree they would watch and study the evolution of a section of Æthelflæd's military strength. The 'recruits' of that army spent every part of every day in training which was always extended long into the hours of each night causing him and his young counterpart the need to 'escape' their quarters after curfew. When all had thought the boys asleep, both would creep within the night shadows to watch in secret.

Over time, that special army began to express more potential, albeit still in 'secret', than any other within Mercia's ranks, even more so possibly than the infamous Mercian Knights. Those new recruits took no respite, nor asked for any and were becoming a more prominent force within the burg and rumours of its existence had become more than just gossip.

As were the knights and huscarl, Æthelflæd's army of female warriors were paid for their service from the confiscated coffers of previous battles. Each of those selected would learn how to handle every available weapon of the day until they had mastered each one, from the Jutish sling to the smallest 'scramsaex', to throw a javelin with precision then quickly and accurately loose an arrow with speed and silence. They would learn how to kill an enemy swiftly and cleanly with anything at hand in the sharpest, most brutal of ways without compassion, and when they were not training they would freely put themselves through the most vigorous of fitness regimes, toning their bodies until each had grown into a streamlined killing machine.

That infamous group of highly trained females were inducted into their careers with one single intention, to protect Mercia and its ruling House without question or compromise, to the last warrior if necessary, to the end.

Of course, there was just one single trial that remained outstanding, like the young Æthelstan they were yet, untested…

…But that issue was soon to be resolved. That notorious unit of untried warriors would soon make their first mark in one of the land's most decisive and bloodiest battles that would commence their changing forever, and so too the Ætheling, at the Battle of Wodensfield.

During the years of his younger life, which had taken him towards the middle part of his sixteenth year, when a battle had loomed, and the fighting had started, the young Æthelstan had merely been whisked from the ranks to a point of safety where he would become no more than a spectator, whilst Æthelflæd and Æthelræd, along with their experienced Thegns, when the chance arose, instructed, explained, and demonstrated the reasons and intensions behind each tactical manoeuvre. Naturally he had played his part in a hand-full of minor skirmishes, often he had been given little choice whilst hunting down fleeing gangs from defeated aggressors or protecting Mercia's inner borders from looters and land pirates, but all that had been done under the protection of battle hardened veterans with moderate risk, it would not be until the preparations for the great battle of Woden's Fyld that Æthelstan, eldest son of the King of Wessex, would be indentured with his own command, thrown deep into the shackles of a cruel and bloody fight, which according to the chroniclers actually began its intent almost a year earlier.....

Almost from the very start of the previous year the weather had shown little sign of winter's harshness which resulted with the 'fighting season' continuing long after its traditional end, with the slightest of excuses for a 'truce' between enemies during the festivities of Yule and Eostre.

After the Easter month celebrations had hopefully guaranteed whichever Gods had been in favour at the time, another abundant year of ripened crops in their fields and strong young in the bellies of their women, the armies of Wessex and Mercia launched had themselves into a frenzied attack against the 'petty' shire of Lyndsey far to the north.

The Northumberland Danes had inflicted countless raids from that smallest of shires once ruled by the Saxon, against the people of Mercia and the more distant Wessex. Over the years Edward and his sister had tolerated much, attempting to avoid any expensive conflict, but eventually, after more heightened and brutal incursions from across their borders, all patience had run out and the two Houses were left with no other alternative but to act, and would now do so together, with defined strength and precision...

The King had secretly longed for a final conflict against his enemies since the commencement of his reign. He had grown from a child within the darkening clouds of war and they had never subsided, if anything, since the death of his Father, the intensity had increased. Those wars had gone on for far too long, so long that many men had found it difficult to remember when there had been no wars, and all wars were costly in every conceivable way.

Slaughter would not have been a strong enough word for that which was about to be unleashed against the northern Dane as the combined Engle and Saxon armies exploded their lethal intent the very instant they landed upon the northern shores of the Humber river.

The Wessex contingent had been carried north in the bellies of the fighting ships along the rough currents of the 'fish-road', and the Mercians, ever reluctant to travel upon water, swept across country by horse and on foot. Every man, woman and child of Norse origin would be put to the blade of a sword, the point of a spear or blow of a limewood shield, and that part of the Danelaw known to the Saxon as Lyndesege would be subjugated, without mercy....

A harsh and fierce battle brought a much-needed victory to the Mercian and Saxon, but not only through the destruction of the Danish forces and their settlements, good fortune had also left them in receipt of a greater prize withy a final repossession of the Holy relics of Saint Oswald, sanctified patron of all the lands North of the Humber river...

Cut down viciously in the battle of Maserfield in 642 Oswald, son of Æthelfrith, King of Bernicia, founder of a realm which then incorporated all land north of the river Humber after Bernicia's unity with Deira, was also a staunch promoter of the new Christian Religion. Killed in battle by the Mercian Penda and offered as a pagan sacrifice to Woden, his Holy Relics remained hidden from the northern invaders for many years within a battered old casket of flaking gold.

At the command of Edward himself, as a gesture to his Mercian allies, the remains were transported from Bardney where they had lain, by 'fast rider', to be presented to the folk of Gloucester, in an abbey then designated for their safe keeping which would be renamed in respectful homage to their own saint.

...Edward's orders to destroy every Dane in the North had obviously been unsuccessful. No less than twelve months after Oswald's newly found relics had been interred into Gloucester's Minster, in retaliation for the attacks upon their northern homesteads, the Northumberland Vikings assembled a mighty fleet and, supported by their cousins from across the northern waters, called forth every weapon man, and woman within a two-day ride. All now would be under the joint commands of Eowils Ragnarsson and his co-ruler Halfden II of the Danish Eoforwic provinces.

It was no secret to any, that these 'joint' rulers were as incompetent as they were useless in every aspect of leadership. Both had only gained their shared seats of power due to the reaction in the Wessex camp in 902 where, upon the death of Ælfred, Æthelwold of Wessex had contested his cousin Edward's right to inherit the seat of the southern realm, as well as that of Mercia. Outnumbered he had quickly fled by sea to the northern lands conjuring a revolt, after which Edward had seen him slain at the great battle of Holme, along with the rebel King Eohric. Æthelræd of Mercia had taken the greater part of that battle, fighting for the rights of his brother by marriage, putting their enemies to the sword in the most certain of ways. So, the dispute seemed to be resolved, but only just, as despite Æthelræd's intensity the Mercian and Saxon armies had been on the verge of defeat and the northern Danes that survived had never forgotten how close they had come to victory and with Eowils and Halfden united in their inherited seats they hastily replenished their strengths.

What little ability those two 'Kings' now possessed lay only in the vast numbers of mighty spearmen and 'Wicingas' that they had managed to summon when the battle axes were sent out calling their men to 'all arms'. And the response came in the form of three hundred 'Snekkja' long ships, fully manned and armed to the teeth, all itching to meet their enemy in what they now hoped would be their final conflict.

Against the strongest of currents that the River Severn could protest in that year of 910 sailed that fleet of northern invaders deep and swift into Mercia's heartland, and the instant their leather clad heels touched upon the soil of their enemy they began to wreak havoc, decimating every village, homestead and croft that had the misfortune to be in their path, whether or not they had been Saxon, Jute, Engle or even the sparse remnants of the ancient Brython, whatever their religion, or not, they did not show a care.....

Pagans prayed to their idols whilst Christians grovelled to their priests and the fewest of ancient Brythons who had survived the years of invasion and slaughter begged to their Goddess Sabrina of the great waters for her help, but none came, well at least not during those first few days.

With the speed of the sharpest northerly winds the Dane, along with his keenest of allies, and any mercenaries 'inherited' along the way, quickly laid their claim to every item of worth that 'fell' into their hands, and when they could carry no more they buried their booty beneath the ground so that they may return in calmer times to recover it. Once certain that there was no further plunder to hand they turned tail and ran, to make good their escape to the safety of their northern lands slaughtering livestock and burning the crops that stood in their wake, laying waste to everything that could not be carried or buried, just to ensure that those who had managed to escape their wrath would go without.

Yet despite their heavily armed numbers and vengeful strengths the Dane knew well enough from the start that a complete invasion and permanent occupation of the southern lands was out of the question as the combined armies of Wessex and Mercia offered more than an equal match. They were capable only of inflicting immediate slaughter and robbery in a bitter 'hit and run' revenge attack that their enemies would remember for all time.

It would have been a close contest, but if there had been an accolade for the most stupid of the two 'half kings' it would have gone to Eowils.

Eowils had assumed, without any real evidence, that the rumours he had received 'on the hoof' of the Wessex King and his main armies encamped far away in more southern parts had been the truth, permitting his forces a clean sweep of their Mercian targets, followed by a reasonably safe return to their lands.

How he would soon come to regret such idle thoughts.

'The tinder piles were lit across the shires from the summits of every hillock and dune, for as far as anyone could see. So many fires glowed on that first night that only the meanest of shadows were cast along the ridges and runs of the southern lands'.

The beacons had been fired from the highest points of the shires well in advance of the Danish landing. The warning flames had swept along the Malvern Hills, through the middle lands and deep into the wilds of the south the instant the enemy fleet had entered the Severn's estuary. Thanks only to the alertness of the coastal sentinels Edward had received news of the pending invasion with sufficient time to mobilise his southern 'fyrd'.

Edward's urgency would not permit errors.

The armies of Wessex and its southern allies had left Kent's borders instantly and with forced marches and continuous sailing through all weathers they were much closer than the Viking 'half king' had believed. They would waste no time in catching their Mercian cousins, joining the chase to hunt down the intruding raiders.

The Danes, within days of landing upon the shores of the River Severn, had disembarked into a violent rampage deep into Æthelræd's territory where many an innocent had been laid to the fate of the blade. Yet it would not be too long before they had found themselves totally outnumbered and surrounded by thousands of weapon men from Mercia, Wessex and the Jutish shires to the south, and despite their initial attempts to escape back to their waiting fleet at the bridge north of Quatt ford, the Dane would quickly realise that there was no other choice but to meet their hunters in battle and hold out hope that their Gods would be gracious towards them.

This battle would not be spent within a mead tent arguing over terms of surrender or the pledges of 'gelts' in acts of compensation, unlike his counterparts Edward was no fool, after all he was Ælfred's elder son and confident that the ensuing battle would become one which would determine the rule of those Isles for many years yet to follow. There would be no more treaties with the Dane, no more excuses to postpone the inevitable, it was now time for all to face their true destinies.

On those plentiful fields of Middle Engle Lands would be fought the great battle of Wodensfield becoming Æthelstan's baptism into the brutal arena of war.

A.D. 910

In this year

the armies of the Engles and the Dane

fought at Teota's Hahl

and the Engles held the victory.

Then King Eadweard took possession of

Lundenwic and of Oxenaforda,

and so too the lands that owed

obedience thereto......

Anglo Saxon Chronicles,

The Battle of Wodensfield.

CHAPTER 2.

910. Frithstan had taken the Bishopric of Winchester. Asser, his predecessor, had dedicated the final half of his life compiling the chronicles of Ælfred's life, and that too of the dynasty that would follow. His death had come as a double blow with the final ties between the Great King and his descendants being broken from that world, forever.

The Vikings from the north had numbered more than six thousand by the time the final 'karve' had beaten the tides to reach the Mercian shores. It had been almost a full week of arduous sailing up the Severn, tacking and oaring in between impulsively disorganised stopovers for the 'gaining' of supplies, followed by the wilful destruction of the homesteads and hamlets that crossed their paths. From the first spear point that dripped Mercian blood they had been determined to leave nothing of any worth, and nobody capable of reporting the slaughter. Separate raiding parties had affected identical introductions at Netherton's lower farm and Deorhyrst's ramshackle village where, at the former, the small Saxon Chapel was burned to the ground after what little of any value had been confiscated or destroyed. The same too at Saint Mary's Minster where the occupants had fled an evening's mass minutes before the invaders arrival, leaving the Dane able to do completely as he wished. The Northmen boasted little respect towards the Christian religion, the wrath of their own Gods was enough to fear without taking on the new beliefs of an unseen Father of that Hvitakristr.

As the first echoes of foreign obscenities were heard through the crispness of the Mercian air the Norse mariners constructed a defensive perimeter from whatever could be scavenged from the surrounding lands in a bid to protect their fleet from a 'chance' attack. A tactical move by Halfden that was made purely by accident rather than experience and forward thinking. Yet Edward's mariners would make short shrift of any blockade when they arrived upstream, under cover the following night.

Towards the end of their first week of pillaging up river they boasted just a single casualty. One warrior, killed by another of his own over an argument concerning the division of booty from the sacking of the wooden chapel of Saint Peter's at Worfield. A victorious brother had been quite agreeable towards sharing his newly found wealth, but his sibling had held different thoughts insisting that ALL spoils should go his way with him being the eldest as well as the first of the pair to have placed his feet upon that shore, therefore, in his mind he now owned those riches by right. He had also proven himself to be the worst with an axe as he bled out over the mud pools of a Brythonic farm.

Unbelievable to any, who may have watched from the safety of a wooded line or gorse clump as the conquerors had stepped across the bloodied corpse would have been the irrelevance of death shown by the invader.

No confrontation had been offered by the farmer, no armed militia had been ready to provoke a challenge, not even a scuffle as all had speedily fled the scene amongst a hail of abuse and vulgar hand signals at the first sighting of the Danish force. The first Viking death was as necessary as it was glorious.

The Northman's discipline in battle had diminished over the years and they had become lazy and spoiled by the victories of their pasts. Their actions were simply borne out of greed for anything that they may steal or a lust for anyone they may feel to debauch. Their attendances within the ranks once made glorious by their illustrious forefathers were now bought through fear from the rage of the two 'half kings' who repeatedly administered their wrath through a common want for complete power and a total disregard for the opinions of others, including those who filled their ranks. There was little planning and even less organisation within the files of this 'new' Viking army.

No precautions were taken when moving through unknown lands, and very little, if any, research before an attack, they relied solely on their sheer force of numbers and basic brutality to guarantee a victory. To add to those handicaps, most of the warriors were usually intoxicated from a previous night's mead, or at the very least still worse for wear. Surprising facts considering their past successes as an invading force. The truth being told, the 'Men of the North' had grown idle, complacent, and over-confident still relishing in their past, arrogantly believing that they were still formidable warriors in command of their own destiny.

On the other hand, the armies of Mercia and Wessex were as equally well disciplined as they were prepared, moving with precise order, obeying every command within an instant, and without question. Section by section, company by company, army by army they kept their line, held their nerve, and followed their King's Thegns with unquestionable loyalty, without any compromise. Most still remembered their days as youngsters, living constantly in fear of Danish conquerors, witnessing battles, and skirmishes, seeing loved ones slaughtered and homes burned to the ground as they fled, never again would these men submit.

It would have been half way through the hour before the middle of the fourth day of a dry and dusty march when Edward the Elder, King of Wessex and Mercia, and all other Engle and Seaxisc shires, gave his command to stand to a halt.

"Bidsteall" as his right arm reached skywards. Thegns and Earls and Ealdorman all echoed his command as the forward scouts reported 'the enemy, in all their numbers, were finally in sight'...

The march of the Wessex had been long and instant, as were all marches. As much time had been permitted for its preparation as had been allowed for resting along the way, which on both counts was very little, yet that was nothing new, the Saxons, as well as the Engle and Jute, were renowned for their speed when hearing the alarm called. In those days, any weapon man 'worth his salt' was forever in some form of readiness with weapons always to hand. Riders had been sent out within hours of receiving the news and would remain ahead of the main army calling the 'all arms' at every village, croft and homestead along the ride. Disciplined and well equipped the men of the shires, and women also, had been given 'muster points' along the route, so as Edward lead his fyrd north and west, the lines of growing reinforcements joined the swelling ranks, emerging from the hollow-ways, descending from the hilltops, or just waiting where two roads crossed, often to the sad farewells of tearful loved ones.

...The Order to 'settle' had been received with welcome relief with every man and woman swearing that they would not have been able to march or ride another day at such speed. It had been enough to bare when the first day's rations had been delayed and all, but the rear columns and late arrivals had forsaken a descent meal, but after four full days riding, or running against the wind, spluttering dust and 'scitte' from the arses of the horses at the front, it was almost intolerable and did little to encourage any form of appetite.

Edward turned slightly in his 'sadol' towards the knight who had rode at his side since both armies had merged their individual strengths into one magnificent force. The King's health was beginning to betray him more visibly as the battles increased and the years vanished without recall. Whilst his own body felt the stress of the constant riding the fatigue from the responsibilities of being a King flooded through his mind, his once flawless art of being able to hide his aches and pains was also beginning to fail. He stared intensely for a second, as if he needed time to recognise the ironclad figure, covered in dust and grime, with sweat patches through the joints of his thick byrnie dark and filthy. But were all not the same, with their faces masked by the dullest of spanghelms pitted deeply from the dust, knight and weapon man, King and Thegn, all, just the same?

Intently the King ran his eye up and down the form of the mounted figure just as he had done on several occasions through-out their ride, he smiled inwardly, warm and content with what he saw.

How the lad had changed.

How his own guilt now gnarled at him from within for not being part of that change. But many a day could be wasted on regret, he had thought, and quickly dismissed his own pity.

The King spat free a mouthful of dust, cleared his throat of the remainder then spat free once more. His tongue helped to moisten the soreness of his mouth with the aid of a dampened cloth...

"I see thee Æthelstan my son, how proud thy Mother would be to see thee here on such a day, upon horse and at my side…" His voice had croaked free its own dryness almost sounding as it had always sounded, a little older maybe. His gauntleted palm reached across to stroke the mane if his son's horse as it came to halt alongside his own, and the younger turned to face his Father. It was unusual for the King to display such emotion towards an individual, even his own elder son.

Æthelstan's voice croaked and scraped from the same dryness as he too spat out… "I be proud to be here bregu, at the side of the King, my Father."

Edward thought deeply for a second. Words that he would use so often in the past had failed his intensions when speaking personally and had often caused an alternative reaction, this time he was determined that they would be taken in the manner he meant… "Before we venture further my son, ye must be certain of one thing if ye be certain of nought else…"

Edward the Father paused as he dampened again his cracked lips and watched with proud satisfaction as the remaining columns of his armies marched into their pre-ordered positions, coming to a noisy halt alongside his own fighting men, so great their numbers it seemed an age before all were finally still. He watched as they dispersed under further orders, taking up defensive positions against a possible attack with small parties of scouts, scavengers, and spies, splitting from the main body, discreetly disappearing into the tree line.

In the hollows the first of the farrier's fires had already began to smoulder as repairs were made to horses, carts and weapons, every opportunity was quickly taken to maintain the armies. All would soon be as it should.

"…Before we enter this battle with little more than hope as to how we each may fare, know this to be the truth and my most solemn word…"

He sucked again another clear breath allowing himself the time to think again before he spoke.

"...Know that when the duties of a King hath taken the place of those of a Father, most often elsewhere and in the company of others, I have always remained informed of all that thee hath achieved throughout thy growing years, as my son and as Ætheling." The lump that now formed in his throat may not now have been from the dryness of the march. "And know that thee, Æthelstan my first-born son, along with thy dearest of all Mothers..."

As he spoke the King removed his spanghelm and glanced skywards swiftly as if he were seeking Ecgwynn's spiritual permission to continue, maybe there was a tear in the corner of a noble eye as he remembered his first and truest love.

He continued. "...Ye both remain closer to my heart than any other, and though I may not have found the time to show it, thee hath been for always in my thoughts......" a loud intake of breath disguised another clearing of his throat, "....it shall always be my wish, the solemn command of a King, and proudest of Fathers, that when the day comes for my own passing thee and thee alone shall become King, and take forward these precious lands of Mercia."

The Ætheling smiled respectfully, then lowered his head humbly attempting to conceal any embarrassment. Reaching forward he clasped the leather clad hand of his King with fondness as well as a little fear which betrayed an otherwise confident voice, "Fædra, since the youngest of ages I have always held a vision which spreads further than our glorious Mercia, and more also than that of the Wessex. But, 'min bregu', before it be so there be time plenty to learn from thee, the ways to be King, and not always those that be seated in a fighting sadol."

Æthelred's lessons on diplomacy and tact had not been wasted, he too had been the right choice' thought a proud Father as they again exchanged the briefest of glances.

"Now min sunu..." Despite the words his tone reverted to that of a King. "...It be time to find thine own company. Even good men search for their Captain before the battle horns fill the air. So, ride thee proud at the head of thy knights and let all know that thee, Æthelstan, Ætheling, Englecynn, has set his feet upon the field, and remember always that the spirits of thy forefathers shall always ride at thy side. Go with our

God, and with any other God that wishes to look over thee, and offer thee my compliments to Æthelræd and his good Lady, my boldest of sisters."

Again, Edward smiled with a Father's pride as his eldest son and heir pulled back his horse's head and turning at the gallop, his boy had grown into the finest of men, carrying himself tall as an Ætheling should, now the time had come to prove to those who forever watched from the shadows, that he could do the same in battle.

Once again Edward's eyes glanced upwards as he whispered words that were only permitted for the ears of a King, and for those who were no longer of that world...

"May the God's watch over our Lady Æthelflæd for the strength she hath installed in our son......watch over him Ecgwynn my first love, and keep the fields of Glassisvellir warm for when thy husband and son are once more at thy side.... Until such time, watch thee with pride as our dust clouds refuse to settle on our bad-tempered land."

With that, the King of a growing realm that was now more often called Engle Land spurred his horse towards the head of his mighty army, excited to be entering another battle. The thrill of another victory was already beginning to run through his noble veins.

As usual Ecgberht lead the contingent of well armed huscarl closely behind their Lord. Chosen primarily by Æthelred and distantly overseen by his Lady before the commencement of the march, Æthelstan's personal guard was made up from the most trusted 'house-guards' that Tamworth and Gloucester had to offer. Ever vigilant they followed his every step as he returned to head the ranks of his own Order of Mercian Knights supported on foot by a strong-armed force of mainly bare chested, and even some bare footed weapon men who eagerly, if not suspiciously, awaited their 'Captain's' return.

Many within his Company had been raised from the middle shires of central Mercia, the very heart of the Isle, and that alone held great significance as it was from that same heart that was of his own blood. Just as important as their origin every Mercian who rode with his Order was there by his own merit, and always by choice. They were free men, Ceorls, of no wealth or worth just a meagre patch of land to their names, but they were free men nevertheless, riding as knights for one reason and one reason only, because each chose it by his own free will, and unlike the remaining 'fyrd' and 'levy' brought as 'tie' by the Ealdormen and Thegns, the knights received payment for their services. Waged horsemen, not mercenaries, but professional fighters who boasted warfare as their trade, a regular contingent whose one and only purpose was the service of their Mercian commanders, they fought for no other, not even their King.

Their equipment was forged from the best materials available, honed by the finest Smiths in the land, far superior in quality than other weapons and inexhaustible in their supply. One spear or javelin, three battle lances, a sword and a scramsaex ensured that every knight was issued with the same weapons, and the same armour which bore the same insignia and colours. Draped to the right of each horse was a small hand axe, often two, usually used for throwing into an enemy shield wall whilst at the gallop, and to the left of each animal hung the limewood shield which boasted the distinctive Mercian Wyvern emblazoned across the golden cross of Saint Alban all set proudly on a wode blue background.

Then there were the horses.

Descended from the very same animals that had been so greatly prized by the 'foederati' many centuries earlier, the heavy horses were second to no other in their breeding, training, loyalty, and stamina with one horse remaining dedicated to the same rider throughout its life, or that of its master.

The armoured ranks shone bright beneath the golden rays of the midday sun, their excited expressions concealed behind equally gleaming spanghelms, now all were a little more than expectant for the unproven capabilities of their new commander. Riding tall and looking good meant nothing on a field of battle, a noble name and a gifted sword were meaningless if such qualities were unaccompanied by courage, faith, and loyalty towards the knight at your side.

Æthelstan's second, and the one most trusted in his Company was Ealdfrith, a young dark haired Thegn whose own Father had fallen in the great battle of Holme. They had been together during their youngest years, schooling alongside each other, sharing many secrets as they grew into men, bonding a true friendship even before either had learnt the meaning, both were proud to be called friend by the other.

The young Thegn's words echoed tunnel like in the expectant air of a pre-battle din as he passed the message to his Commander. "Our Lord Æthelred bids that we move to the east of his northern position……The spies report that the Dane be strongest at our flanks and now moves their reinforcements towards us."

The Ætheling smiled with concern as the message was completed. He was uncertain and of course nervous, and if honesty had won through, also a little afraid, but who would not have been?

"That may mean fair or foul Ealdfrith……A good commander must plan for everything and expect anything, despite the drivels of the spies."

Like a good student Æthelstan had remembered the times when he had heard of the misgivings and failures regarding second hand information, it was invariably incorrect no matter its subject or source, which in warfare often came inflated and exaggerated to achieve the greatest reward. Æthelred was a good commander, possibly the best in the land, he above anyone would never set his sights firmly on second hand information.

Æthelstan would act as he would have expected his Uncle to act.

"Pass the word to be vigilant. Dispatch the 'weardas', an enemy that be cornered be an enemy with little to lose, and Order that no Knight shall call the charge unless they have heard it from my very lips, and only mine…"

The nod of a helm clad rider was followed by the most serious of expressions as the Ætheling's Thegn turned his horse towards the main line, just as his Lord he too stood in the ranks of war for a first time. As he repeated his memorised instructions the snorting of horse and the chink of armour and weapon steel echoed hauntingly against the rolling hills at their backs. How strange it all seemed to be part of such a mighty gathering, how different that place would soon become.

"....and place watchmen with archers on the highest ground...Our position may hold risk whether we march towards their main body or not."

His master's Orders would be obeyed as the small group of huscarl moved closer eyes wide and forever alert to Ecgberht's silent orders spreading themselves in a protective arc, there would be no assassin's arrow destined for their Lord, not on that day.

Guiding his mount towards the centre of his line Æthelstan gave the order to begin the march towards the north of Æthelred's force, at the same time his blue eyes darted from left to right, then up the rise of the grassy dune ensuring that his command had been obeyed. His horse turned into their front and Æthelstan stared deep into a thousand pairs of eyes, piercing each individual gaze that reflected through the glinting faceguards, penetrating each expression independently as he rode along the heavily armed line, then turned, and rode back.

Most of those who now stood with him were veteran campaigners, battle hardened warriors of whom bore many the scars and signs of still healing wounds from more than one horrendous battle, and He bore none. It would have been impossible not to have heard their earlier whispers before he had been summoned to ride at the side of their King, and now upon his return he could see the visible inclinations betraying their obvious doubts within their poorly disguised expressions. A little closer to their fronts and he slowed, pulling back hard the thick leather tack, bringing the proud white mare he had named Abrecan to a halt.

Motionless and prominent in her attendance the animal stood rigid and still, allowing her steaming breath to rise from overheated lungs, escaping through bellowing nostrils where it condensed into liquid droplets that spilled down onto the crushed green turf at her hooves. The horse's chest again expanded noisily with another breath of grateful air as she stored renewed energy that instinct had promised would soon be very much in need. Unlike her rider, the animal was no novice to open warfare, she had been Æthelflæd's second mount, for her, an unsatisfactory gift from a Cornish King of which she had never found a suitable ride.

The horse had been the Lady's gift to her ward, on the eve of his succession into knighthood.

There to his front stood the lines, three thick in horse borne warriors stretching one hundred riders left and then again right, and to the rear of the horses, pressing their bodies between the animal's flanks, eager to hear a command, came five hundred shield men on foot armed with spear or bow or sling, but always with Daneaxe and linden shields in rounds supporting the mark of the wyvern proudly to the front of every man. Fierce warriors were all, committed to follow behind the knights into an attack, or organise an ambush or form a shield wall or spearhead when taking command in a battle, or providing support from the rear should the battle be turned against them.

All now, whoever they were, looked on awaiting their new leader's speech, for there was always a speech before a commander rode from the fighting ranks to 'support' from a point of safety as 'his' army entered the fight.

Chatter and mumblings within the ranks soon turned to murmurs which turned into whispers which drifted into silence.

"Men of the Shires…."

As the horse steadied herself once again he repeated his introduction to ensure that he held their full and total attention, it also gave him a second chance to assure himself that his words would be spoken only with confidence and dignity, and more importantly with the truest of intent.

"Men of the Shires…" again a nervous pause. Nerves threatened to take hold, for a second he wished he could turn and ride from the line as he overheard the mutters of sarcasm and sniggered expressions of…

'I told ye so….'

And….

'He be just like the rest' from the most hardened of veterans.

His face reddened, palms sweat, and his spine threatened to turn into ice as he tried, unsuccessfully, to push the petty remarks from his mind, forget what he had heard and rise above it all, but for a second he may have failed, until, in the middle of it all the strange sweet smell of honeysuckle and blackberry leaf caught his attention, just for an instant.

Æthelstan stretched his neck, broadened his shoulders, pushed down his stirrups, and belayed his nerves... then in confident voice...

"Ye who hath offered their lives so many times to protect these lands...." and his spear arm drifted left and right as he pointed out across the open plains.

Abrecan remained deathly still, and the mutterings slowed.

"No question doth thee offer when an Order be sent.... No doubt doth thee hold when a battle may turn for the worst...No complaint doth ye make when torn from the arms of thy kin without notice and without reason. How proud I be here, amongst ye all, on this fine day, on this greatest day."

He swallowed the lump that had been forming at the back of his throat and sucked back the tremble that threatened still to accompany his words. Was this truly he, Ætheling and Knight, now at the head of such men, how proud...

And the veterans readied their silence...

"Men of the Shires, I be here at thy side on this day not as Mercia's Ætheling, not as the son of a King just to issue his Order before retiring to safety whilst thou do battle on behalf of another spoiled noble..."

He now had their full attention.

"...Nor shall I be thy Captain, as none need to be told of that which is required upon the field of battle. Yet I be here with thee, as one who holds close much more than a mere position granted by a King's grace and favour... I be here on this day with thee as thy brother, as thy Mercian brother in arms..." a brief pause as he regained his breath, moistened his throat, and tightened a grip around Abrecan's reins.

At last he could make out the fewest of favourable nods, the insults had grown silent. There was even the odd hint of approval.

"So now, as we march forward, content in each other to offer yet further sacrifice should these lands of ours so wish, I ask of thee to remember one thing. I ask that thee remember…" and his voice increased from a loud speech to a roar, louder and more confident than before….

"Men of the West Shires…Ye be the very Heart of Our Land…Ye be Engle Land!!!"

…and the silence was lost as the battle horns sounded above the cheers of the knights who now expressed a vigorous acceptance for their new commander. Spear points were pushed skyward, high above the ranks, blades were held aloft shining bright against the sun's brightest rays, vanished from his ranks was the doubt.

Glancing to his side in relief, his first speech finally over, he would proudly take the point of his Mercians. With Ealdfrith and the other Thegns following close behind they began their ride to the northern flanks and what would soon become another of England's many fields of battle. Æthelstan had earned his chance, at least he spoke a good fight.

The sun passed clean through the middle of the day bright and daring when it was not being candid and shy behind the whisking clouds that were escorted across the Mercian skies by the most delicate of breezes that carried with it the smell of leather and horse sweat mixed with the odour of nervous men choking before the ground dust could attack the back of their throats.

Æthelstan sipped from a 'flasce' spilling a little as Abrecan regained a lost foothold just as the battle ground merged into their path turning out of the valley above the large midland plain, almost precisely central between Woden's fyld and Teota's Halh.

Away in the distance the young family of an 'æcermann' had started to flee as if the devil himself snapped at their heels, in a desperate search for safety, escaping their pitiful lot as the impending battle drew closer to their 'toft'. Last of the families to leave they could be heard in all their panic and chaos struggling to save their most modest of possessions, dragging awkwardly behind them a snivelling young child. A husband, 'hen-pecked' by an angered 'wifman' with a second child at the breast, glanced up embarrassingly at a mounted patrol... 'Should it not also be he now sitting upon a horse's back, shield, and spear at hand, ready to defend the 'hamstede' of his family, to earn the right to walk proudly across such fine lands as a free man, or even to give up his own life for the protection of his children's tomorrows?'

"Efeste hus banda, efeste..."as he received another barrage of abuse from an irate wife, there would not have been a single warrior who would have wished to swap their place with him.

The silence which followed the family's departure resonated across the treeless plain as if all awaited pensively to ensure that all Æcermenn and their 'cynn folc' had left the area. The livestock had been herded away to the seclusion of a hidden glade at the first siting of the beacon line, anything foolishly left behind would be readily confiscated or commandeered as bounty, or slaughtered for food to feed the encamped forces of whichever side arrived first, the ghostly silence prevailed a little longer, eerily pulsating across the open fields, the loudest noise of an anxious nothing...

As the last cries of a hungry child echoed into the distance and the earlier mists that had threatened to engulf the plains evaporated away in their own bid to escape the coming slaughter, the Danish ranks slithered into view. Now they out-stared the Saxon as the Saxon began to out-stare the arriving Scot and signs of relaxed tenseness began to emanate from within the enemy's ranks whilst whispered chatter and nervous fidgeting accompanied a Danish Order to advance more forcefully...

"Framganga...saman" as it was bellowed from the shuffling files.

Previously grounded weapons were retrieved, a last mouthful of drink or 'rip' of half stale bread greedily swallowed and the momentum increased. They surged their masses forward, slowly at first, then more aggressively as the pace increased and confidence grew with the distance between their enemies closing over those once innocent plains. The air between the two sides began to shake with a dreadful fear as ten thousand Danish hearts filled with greed and hatred gathered speed and neared that Isle's only protectors.

No one fortunate enough to survive would remember which had come first, the thud of thousands of footsteps gauging into the dampened ground or the barrage of obscenities and screaming venom that sent shivers down the spines of those who awaited out of sight.

The air above began to squeal as the sky began to fill with clouds of willow that seemed to glide for an eternity almost so thick it sheltered the sun, before finally descending with the deep thud and thump as targets were easily found, and the grasses quickly turned the brightest shade of crimson as the noises exploded the silence with the most hateful surge of suffering ever heard, sending proof to every corner of the land that man was again at war.

"Bordweall!!!" was screamed, the shield walls locked, and the battle had commenced.

Shoulders fused, and feet dug down to embrace the charge. The first three ranks were the sternest, made up from the best of men, armour-clad and ruthless. Spear points were all that passed the limewood barrier, waiting eagerly for the Danish assault, whilst to their rear stood the fyrd, lesser warriors in all but their hearts, common free men who just days since had been tilling their fields far from the cries of battle.

Nerves ripped through him as the unknowns of his first real battle rattled through his stomach and the sensation of adrenalin rode up from his toes and shook his body violently.

Was it fear?

Was it apprehension?

Was it excitement?

And that smell, there on that putrid field of man's disease, the distinctive odour of honeysuckle and crushed blackberry leaf, out there amongst all that misery about to be unleashed upon every man standing.

Æthelstan had no answers and it was not the time for a personal debate. Reassured by the figures of Æthelflæd and her husband to his left, together awaiting their entrance into the fight, breaking through the dust clouds ahead of their armies steady and true, eager for the onslaught. Never in the history of Mercian warfare would there be a more potent partnership between a man and a woman.

In position now.

With his own ranks, their numbers a mere minority within the vastness of the army, his body relaxed, eased itself upright and solid. As his mouth moistened he felt in the right place, he knew that he was born to be in battle, those lands that would one day be entrusted under his rule would be worth the outcome of that day.

To have stood at the lead of any rank, watching the storm of many a thousand enraged warriors rattling their weapons and hurling their curses towards a steady file of staunch weapon men, whilst friends and brothers were torn down at your side by the sting of pointed willow would have been horrendously challenging for anyone. It would have taken the fullest of hearts and the strongest of stomachs to stand their feet firm, yet more likely the truth would have been that, at those precise moments all were too afraid to move an inch, for fear of being struck from above, and found what little safety remained within the numbers of their companions and the protection of the indomitable shield wall.

...And then they hit again.

Hard fast and deadly. Splintering into the first shield wall's defences, made up from the stoutest unwavering West Saxon men. Only the strongest, most daring would ever have been selected, or those who had committed the most grievous crimes against their King or Thegn. With the promise of forgiveness or glory now a distant memory standing firm in their own footprints was their only thought, facing almost certain annihilation as a thousand Viking spearmen hurled their 'shield busters' into the resilient defence forcing lime wood into the ground, now the core of the first Saxon defiance was exposed......

The 'Angon' spears had done their work.

The heavy headed projectiles had struck firm into the wooden shields, their weight dragging the rounds clumsily to the ground. The exposed warriors would have attempted to cut off the shafts, but its 'metal jacket' protected the wooden neck and showed the shield man to his enemy. A hail of battle lances, crossbow bolts or hand axes would then be launched, and the defenders would drop to the ground, mortally wounded and of no further threat. Others who had thought different would have struggled by stamping on the metal necks only to send the shaft's thin metal ferrules painfully through a leather boot slicing into a heel or instep, they were finished just as the others. The Angon was a deadly weapon, and unbeaten.

...A bloody fight would now follow.

As Langsæx and Daneaxe were drawn by the inner ranks, those without grabbed at anything that may kill. Weapons were raised high or horizontal depending on the blade and then hacked down or lunged forward with aggressive precision into the arriving herd of Norse, shattering helm and skull and shield and bone, spurting forth the fountains of blood, bringing on a horrid pain as the Men of Wessex smashed out a fury in their only hope of escape and survival, and an extra piece of a King's 'penig', or a pardon for a now regrettable crime.

As the cavalry maintained their positions awaiting their commands, it became a game of strengths. Pushing, hacking, standing, pushing hacking, standing, the only task of the shield wall was to hold back their enemy for as long their strengths would allow, gain back ground, and fell as many Viking as possible in that first wave of the attack, to kill quickly or perish in the violent storm that neared. But that would only have taken the briefest of seconds until the rear ranks of the advancing Dane had entered the fight, then the shield wall was totally overpowered and lost.

Those on the outer sections of the wall, fortunate enough to have only the fewest of wounds would be able to scurry free their escape, after which the main body of Dane would stamp their way across the dead and dying like a pack of rabid dogs and hurl themselves into the main body of the Wessex fyrd like the berserkers of old, strong, fearless, and irrepressible......

But not before the first lines of their numbers had advanced into a piercing cloud of hardwood quarrels from Saxon close quarter cross bows. So many were their numbers that they were uncountable, and a wall of Norse dead temporarily halted their own advance, until, after a few silent words for the fallen, as their souls were permitted to pass into the Halls of their Gods, they scrambled again over meaningless corpses, deeper into the carnage, spurring on their advance to avenge their fallen brothers.

Just then, as the hoards reformed their strengths...

At that very instant, as the second line of Saxon defences were beginning to accept that they were fatally outnumbered, with their lack of might threatening to fail their King, an unfamiliar sound grew out of the screams that now invisibly shrouded the slaughter.

Almost distant at first.

Then it grew louder and higher in pitch until nothing more could be heard other than that unidentifiable shrill, hailing all those still standing a second's search for its source.

Abruptly and almost out of place it came without warning.

With undaunted expressions of daring and guile, upon the rise of a solitary hyrst, just along the outskirts of man's butchery, as if mystically appearing through the dusty thick stench of death, two thousand in their number, echoing evil and hatred with every movement, they peered down and over the fighting hoards with insolent, contemptible arrogance, and in the same precise second the screeching ceased.

Weapons held high as shield faces were thumped in unison with gleaming blades as a dread like thunder erupted from the top of the once lonely hillock, Æthelflæd's company of female warriors stood bold, disciplined, and defiant as they scowled through the dares of a cautious and confused enemy.

Fearful in looks.

Their leather-clad bodies still and challenging, weapons held aloft and shoulders rigid and proud, with fine lines of ancient Woad enhancing their features. Hearts beat, and nerves rattled with anticipation of the first battle, their skin glistening with droplets of perspiration and oil in the available light. A ghostly vision cut deep down into the painful turmoil below them. Some would say that their presence looked fearful and radiated terror from the summit, others would later say that they looked beautiful, almost enticing, and most definitely captivating.

Set apart from the endless screams of horse and man dying side by side in their own squalor a quietness again loomed over the grassless plains as the smashing of blade upon shield ceased and the field of battle dared to halt its slaughter....

But it would be the shortest of pauses. The Dane took little time in concluding that those who stood along the line of the hyrst were merely a handful of simple, soft, and feeble women, threatening in looks maybe, armed most certainly, but women nevertheless.

'Was the Saxon so lacking in numbers that he had turned out the wifman and sipwif in their stead?' Many laughed at the thought. They would be ignored until the fighting was over, when a true victory could then be enjoyed, and the women taken as a rightful prize after the crushing defeat that they were about to inflict upon the men of that fading Saxon Realm.

Hopeful boastings and other more coarsely descriptions followed the vilest of slurs, crudely and directly to the point, hurled towards the women after which followed a bout of sickening laughter vibrating through the Norse ranks as two spearmen dragged from a pile the youngest of Mercian captives. Hoisted roughly to his feet they took little time in castrating the youngster, purely for the benefit of the 'gallery' above, and as his wriggling body was pushed casually to the side without care he bled to death with the echoing sounds of fear and agony emanating from his dying mouth, then they turned to continue more violent slaughtering.

Ignorance was the only trait that would not be permitted upon a battle-field. As if they felt cheated by the contemptuous behaviour from their male rivals the piercing screams and hollering din recommenced as the fight continued at the foot of the hyrst, more brutal than before, with an added incentive for its completion. That time the female vocals were totally ignored as if their presence was an inconvenient irrelevance.

Still louder.

Their screams increased as they competed for the battle's attention higher and more adamant until it could get no louder, then simultaneously once more the women fell silent with disappointment.

Above the din of battle the female warriors glanced to their left, then to their right angered by the lack of attention from below. Systematically, without a spoken word each withdrew a finely honed 'fransisca' hand axe from the waist, stared down at their proposed targets and raised the weapon high as their bodies leant slightly back.

...The 'fransisca' had been especially designed and developed over many years by the best weapon-smyths, for unleashing into densely populated enemy ranks, ahead of an assault, smashing shields, felling horse, and killing men, causing maximum damage and devastation...

Uncertainty had not been in their thoughts, doubt was never part of their makeup, there was no place for hesitation, so in a single, solitary movement strong and violent each hurled the arch shaped blades out from their files and down into the enemy's mass, and as the heavily balanced sockets sailed towards their targets the 'fransiscan' cloud whistled through the fighting's chill warning of the menacing horror that neared.

Yet still with that stoic ignorance the Dane ignored the warnings and continued their merciless killing, until the threat proved its reality as hundreds of bevelled edges began to bite into their targets emanating cries of shocking fear that filtered from the closest ranks as the axe hammers burst through their shields and began to smash into skull and face and throat and chest.

Halfden's frenzied assault immediately slowed to an enforced halt with writhing bodies by the dozen slumping to the ground, pumping a river of life's blood into the roughened earth along the outer edges of the Viking 'hirth'. Anger, rage, shock, and revenge flooded through the expressions of those who remained, bulging eye sockets, flaring nostrils, gusts of spittle spurting out of speechless mouths as the invaders turned about to stare poisonously up into the eyes of that now dangerous hoard.

Out of the raucous gathering and with a slight tremble of uncertainty Niall, a middle-aged Dane of many campaigns who had boasted some authority within his ranks clambered high upon a pile of mixed corpses steadying his balance before stretching his back. He glanced upwards, shield held high, fearful of another barrage coming his way. Instinctively the limewood 'rond' was pulled tight into his chest, his right arm raised a spear shaft high, his golden locks windswept and his eyes spit fire towards this 'other' enemy....

"Neinn fangi!!!!!!!No Prisoners!!!!!.... Neinn fangi. These be not women for they be Hel's own spawn and we shall not end this day until all be sent back to whence they crawled...."

And the men of the 'Silver Raven', dying brothers at their feet, flew towards the high bank that supported such evil, taunting, and jibing their insults, discharging erratically aimed cross bows which did little more than pierce the bank's incline, their viciousness increased as they climbed. As if Odin, himself were snapping at their heels the Northmen, many from across the Scyttisc waters, clawed their way up the stony face towards these new attackers...

At the first sign of the rush the female defenders stepped back from the hyrst's edge slow and enticing, gathering a breath as they blatantly dared the screaming men to join them, as more Danish quarrels spit harmlessly into the ground inches from the women's feet they kept their enemy's attention from the battle below, which had now increased its threats to all Anglo-Saxon fronts. Hand axes, spears, javelins, even rocks and stones were launched into the climbing rage picking off their flanks just for good measure, ensuring that the Viking's anger would remain at boiling point. Men did not behave rationally when filled with anger, especially if their manly pride was taking a thorough beating.

Further back the women shuffled.

Slyly and without emotion they stared at their encroaching prey struggling with every inch to reach the top of the now crumbling slope, hindered by the mud they strained to find sure footing, to regain a lost balance, or just to grasp a fresh breath before they were pushed further onto the hyrst's top as more of their numbers clambered from behind still screaming renewed insults at those who had dared to inflict such painful deaths upon their fellow countrymen, many of whom lay screaming in unyielding misery, gasping their final breath at the foot of that muddy bank.

Even at such an early point in the fighting the youngsters, many of whom had been forced into their first conflict, previously eager and keen to prove themselves worthy to walk amongst other men, could now be seen wallowing or just sitting amongst the slop of war, bleeding and crying their final noises as young blood and even younger tears spilled out onto the crimson river that now flooded over those northern plains. The final sight that would accompany them into the lands that their spirits would soon inherit would have been the Men of Wessex charging to their rear, hurling axe and spear, lance, and stone into the backs of the climbing Danes....

But the dying went ignored....

Æthelflæd's women, now satisfied that they had permitted their enemy sufficient foot room upon the brow would now deny them the chance to launch a frontal assault. Slowly and at ease they started to coil themselves forward, enveloping the Danish flanks into their fold, teasing and seducing them away from the main body, into their 'wings', cleverly dividing their numbers into smaller, less threatening groups.

These outer sections of women, now confident that any chance of a lunge against them had been contained, reached free the long bows from their backs, easing free the arrows from their quivers. Aiming was not an issue as the numbers still clambering up the incline were so many that their arrows would not miss, their projectiles were dispatched, instantly halting the threat of further reinforcements. There were now sufficient Danes upon the summit, the advantage was firmly in the women's hands.

And below, on the lower plains.

To the droning sounds of the battle horns the thumping feet of the Wessex re-entered the deadly game and engaged once more their enemy.

Many of those 'would-be' conquerors who had managed to remain within the outer ranks had quickly realised that they would not be celebrating the battle's victory in their camps almost before the first horns had broken the day's peace, and had casually started to withdraw from the centre of the fight, until they had caught sight of the 'partner' Kings. Halfden and Eowils were silhouetted against the western horizon within the protection of their mighty entourage, their orders had been precise…

'Hunt down and kill all who attempt to break from the field, of both sides'.

Those who had spotted the skirmishers soon enough reluctantly returned to the fight knowing that death would meet them whatever their direction, no choice had they but to re-join the oncoming carnage and except the fate that their Gods had already destined for them.

Upon the hyrst the Dane, still encouraged by the allure of the women, moved closer, after all they were only women, and some had appeared to suggest that they were worth the risk.

Ever closer they ventured until both parties were almost within touching distance then the women began to move quietly closer, seemingly without any threat even throwing a rare smile towards the men whose expressions now suggested that fighting was the last thing on their minds.

Staring into the eyes of their female adversaries, attitudes relaxed, and guards were dropped, many had lowered their weapons, some letting them slip completely from hand as they became mesmerised and enchanted by the seductive glares. Convinced that they were no longer needed others sheathed their blades or shouldered their bows and let slip their lances before brushing back their unkempt hair, smudging deeper the blackened liner around their eyes, or straightening greasy beards, oblivious and somewhat ignorant to any danger that may or may not unfold.

Or could it have been, that even at that point, they still found no danger in women?

An extremely eerie and haunting alternative had begun across the battlefield.

Whilst the noise from below had increased in momentum with the ever-growing slaughter that was being issued from the hands of the Wessex spearmen the silence atop the rise began, just as it had earlier, before the hand axes had been launched.

The men above were now filling their thoughts with ideas so far from the battle's meaning that many now ignored totally the fight below. It was as if they were all bewitched, and the odd embrace between man and woman had threatened to be more than a mere suggestion.

In the trembling silence that clouded now above the hyrst the breaking sound of horse's hooves treading down the dryness of the outer grasses distracted the women's thoughts. Parting in their centre they turned to be greeted with the satisfied smile of their commander Æthelflæd Ælfreddohtor and her all female escort glistening, golden and gallant. Even amongst the ugliness of a battle's surroundings the beauty of Ælfred's eldest daughter shone free like the brightest of beacons catching the lustful glances of many, whatever their side.

Ice cold was the expression portrayed by the Mercian Lady as she glared pure venom towards the assembled Dane, her own experiences of long ago had bred utter hatred for their race and this intruder had set his foot upon her lands once too often expressing his insatiable craving for that which did not belong to him, how she hated the greediness of the Viking.

Her gaze floated back across her Company, identifying each of her warriors as she knew them, hand picked by her, everyone. Then her feelings sank, and expressions changed to a painful ashen glow as her visual inspection stopped at a clearing across to her left where the body of her only casualty lay crumpled in a pile, killed by a Viking bolt that had ricocheted into deadly splinters off the flatness of a limestone slab, broken and embedded deep in the woman's side. As her heart had beat its last, her death stare had frozen, turning towards her sisters as if she now watched their glories, guarding over them all from the Halls of her Forefathers. The strangest of smiles seemed to approve that which was about to take place.

Æthelflæd turned her attentions to the gathering, silently showing her approval of their actions. She was angered inside at the pointless casualty, a fluke of battle, a curse, a death that had achieved nothing. Then bowing her head to confirm her silent Order she signalled her escort to follow as she disappeared hastily from the hill where a small forest had long since grown. Not once had she acknowledged a single Dane, not even the obvious attendance of Halfden's second, they meant nothing to her.

The women continued to bait their prey…

Every Mercian and Wessex man alike had heard rumours of the Lady's 'different' army, yet none had witnessed its effect in a fight, so it would have been only natural that all who were not readily engaged in the fighting now watched on curiously. At the lead of his own armoured ranks Æthelstan had watched in the relative safety of his allocated position, obediently awaiting a command to enter the conflict, staring out expectantly from the summit, anxiously hoping for the signal, always ready to ride to the aid of a fellow warrior, with or without an order.

…High above the merciless carnage of the lower plains the thicker, more greying clouds had reeled over to conceal the blueness of the sky leaving a suggestion that darkness had started to make its way across the valley, possibly nature's own attempts to offer a curtain, to shadow the innocence of the heavens from that which was about to erupt upon her virgin lands, embarrassed, ashamed, and disgusted by the cruelty and suffering that was all too frequently unleashed by Men.

Brutality as a description, or even a crude explanation for that which was about to follow would have been too kind. Carnage, slaughter, barbarism, butchery, also too soft a word for what was threatening to explode upon the knoll.

……and the women closed in deeper.

The expressions which had, up until then, filled the 'expectant' faces of the Dane changed and their smugness vanished the closer together they were pushed, tighter and tighter, their fate gradually becoming more obvious, then panic and fear began to tremble its curses through the lines of uncertain men.

First to be heard was the stifled whimper of shocking dread as a body part slipped from its torso into the grassy footprints below, then a second, slightly louder but more chilling followed as a shield man looked down to see the nerves of a severed arm wriggling freely and without pain, he cried out louder before the head fell to join the limb, and the eyes closed in saddened anguish as the body's trunk fell across the pile cloaking the crimson mess from view, the nerves twitched a final time ending a fanfare for death which had echoed its way upon that naked hyrst.

That single kill gave way to a concert of evil which engulfed the Mercian plains with its uniquely wretched melody as the superior numbers of women pounced upon their victims with the fury and hatred which to date had never been witnessed, even with man's own gift for carnage...

Intense and specific had been their training which had included detailed instruction of what would befall any of them who may have lost a fight and fall into the hands of their enemy, so all would now readily welcome their own deaths before conceding defeat.

… Without mercy metal cut through cloth then severed flesh before slicing into bone. Stomachs split, spilling out their contents whilst the helpless victims could do no more than stand and watch, entranced by that which now took place against them. Sheer fright washed across the faces of those who themselves had once been feared, for now none could do little more than await their own time to die, horribly. What little defence had been offered by the Dane was rapidly swallowed away as gangs of woad coloured warriors pounced upon their challengers, ceasing quickly any counter attack.

Blood spilled onto the open ground of that solemn hill spraying up into the cold air as if a million crimson gushers had erupted covering everything with the sticky red gore. Men began to scream, to cry like their young sons and weep like their daughters as they realised that resistance was futile. Their executioners had closed themselves so tightly around the Viking formation that retaliation was now impossible, not even to raise a single weapon in defence.

As each Norseman met his death the crushing tactic of their enemy closed around them even tighter, and the killing continued to the sounds of brutality and death which drifted towards the Saxon ranks, themselves engrossed in the slaughtering of those who had remained at the foot of the hyrst. An occasional glance upwards would confirm one unanimous thought amongst the men of the Engle and Saxon, all were truly grateful to whatever God that watched over them, that those women who waged their own war above were part of their ranks and not of those who stood against them.

Hearing screams of horror from the ambush above a handful of Danes punished their way to the foot of the slope readying an attempt to climb the ridge, to rescue their kinsmen. Those who were not cut down by the barrage of lance and axe hurled by the Wessex 'fyrd' were caught in the cloud that flew from the bows of the female archers who rigidly stood guard around the flanks selecting any who may attempt an escape from the summit.

Growing ever louder amongst the unyielding drone of misery could be heard the pitiful cries as hardened warriors now pleading for their lives.

'That was not how it should have been...Their Kings had promised them an easy victory...'

They had been assured that 'the Saxon was now too old, too weak from many years of warring'.

Mercy was begged from their Gods, imploring, without success, for their intervention. Some swore new loyalties to everything and anything they thought may save them from a certain disgusting death. Some, more than just a few, tried a self-conversion to Christianity as they stood amongst the limbs and butchered bodies of those who had once been called brother. But the Father of the White Christ found no pity for them on that day, not even a God could hold back the lust for killing that now possessed such crazed women.

More than five hundred Danes, some had ventured from as far away as Scandinavia, others as close as Northumberland, now alongside those who had once boasted of numerous victories upon those far away Hibernian fields, now lay in the minced vileness that had once been an untouched grassy hill. None would be permitted to survive, not even their mortal characteristics remained, and the cruelty that had been inflicted upon their attackers would later turn the heads of many of the most seasoned veterans who, until such a day, had presumed that they had bore witness to all savagery that could have been inflicted upon another man. The enemy had not just been killed they had been obliterated from the face of those lands to a point that even their own kinsmen, who would eventually summon the courage to search for their dead, would only recognise another by a charm, or a trace of specific clothing, there was nothing evident to have even suggested that what then lay across the hyrst top were ever men.

Once, it had been told in the sagas of battles now so long back in the Old Lands where the Ancient Ones once walked, where a people known as the 'Berserkers' would carry out abominable retribution upon their enemies, so horrid that those sagas were no longer told. Now the sagas would belong to those 'new' lands, where in those idyllic plains of a once virgin valley stood an example of the extreme barbarism that anyone could inflict upon another, and done so by 'mere' women.

...And the pious ones would still speak of their new religion, of a belief that would unite All men in peace, whilst they chanted their Latin verses and moaned their scriptures from the safety and comfort of the ringwall.

Now in silence, trance-like and breathless the women walked from the brow casting back a final look at their 'achievements', their task was complete, and the remainder of their input would be along the outer flanks, separate even from their own men folk.

Their leather clad bodies, tied back hair and wode painted faces were now dripping red with the remnants of their kill. There had been just one fatality and nothing more but the fewest of flesh wounds and scratches, but it had not looked that way.

In the shortest of respites the women were marched from the hyrst by their commanders. All that glistened from their heads down to their feet was the blood of their enemies, as if each had bathed in the gore as they dismembered and disfigured their kill, to serve as a warning to those lucky few, that such a death awaited any enemy who dared to encroach upon the lands of the Mercians. Their actions that day would send out a warning to all, that Æthelflæd's women were far above the merest of challenges. Their enemies would learn well, that should they ever be unleashed again a horrid reckoning would befall any who dared to stand their ground.

Their male counterparts had looked on as the women had marched out to the flanks ready to cut off a line of escape that the invaders may allow themselves. Any who had previously sought to suggest anything like a 'friendly' relationship soon dismissed such ideas, those were not the kind of women they were used to, not the normal 'hore' who ran with the fyrds. They were just as the Dane had screamed out in their final throws before death, they were Hel's own.

These women had fought their first battle and all men would now know of them......but there was still a war to be won.

Æthelstan lowered his head. He had witnessed a battle's aftermath, even though he had never played his part, but even from such a distance he had seen sufficient for that day. Those women who now hurried to the outer flanks were the secret warriors he had watched and admired, honing their talents to become supreme. He had watched, feeling near disappointment and a strange regret that He, and such women marched under the same banner.

Should he have felt disgust?

Would he speak of his concerns to his Lady, his own guardian who had moulded such creatures at her will?

Would he speak to his Father of such things, or even with him as King?

Why? Was this not the beginning of the new ways?

Was not a war, or even the smallest of conflicts and skirmishes there for the winning in whatever ways that may be required to bring the swiftest of victories, at any cost?

Whoever he may decide to speak with would have offered the same answer as another…

'Victory was to be theirs upon the brow at any cost and that would set the outcome upon the field. Their own lands were for protecting even with good Mercian and Saxon lives. Had not the very earth itself turned red through the spilling of so much blood through the countless years of warring?'

Were his thoughts not selfish thoughts, were his doubts those of apprehension, or even fear?

Was it fear that had caused his stomach to churn at the sight of such death, was he, the one who may some day become King, showing the fear of a common coward?

Now as he thought, was it his imagination that sensed a thousand stares from his warriors who sat and stood patiently behind, awaiting his command, whilst doubting his own courage. Did he imagine them nodding their heads in realisation that, despite the finest of speeches earlier they still expected this new leader to 'crack' beneath the stress of his first command.

In the slightest of lulls, amidst the growing carnage, Æthelstan was again taken by the passing of a strange odour, an odour that was clearly out of place amongst such putrid aromas that surrounded him. Sweet and pungent came the distinct smell of crushed honeysuckle and blackberry leaf, filling his nostrils, and easing his senses, then only to be followed by vivid memories of his childhood, of a spiritual Mother and the giant of a man who stood as a Father, not just his Father.

His mind spun in confusion, followed quickly by the warming presence that had begun to settle the shaking of his sword hand, deep down in the distant pits of his memories he saw the visions of his forefathers riding proud into their own battles, guided by the winds of the Gods, victorious and magnificent, without feelings for those who were about to be vanquished.

Æthelstan had decided. His answer had been there all along. There would be no reason to question any person, neither would he question that which was about to take place. He now held all his own answers, they had always been there within since he was a lad, it had just taken the shock of that battle to realise it.

He glanced back behind the entourage that so closely protected their King, back further to the place of safety where the injured lay dying, where the Christian ones portrayed their gleaming silver and golden icons alongside the banners in foreign words, to show all that the Engle and Saxon and Jute that day marched beneath the command of the one true Father of the White Christ. Whatever happened there that day would be justified in their heavens, as 'Their God willed it'…all within their place of safety.

That sight of pious privilege would become the reason that he would never again bring His God upon the field of battle, in warfare there could never be a place for his Christian religion, no place for sympathy or sacred thoughts, in his warfare there would only be the Gods of the past, of the Old Ways.

'That is why they had been there' he had decided 'that is where they would still be needed' and the Father of the White Christ would remain in the homesteads and chapels and Minsters with their pious chanting and praying.

But not upon the fields of battle, there he would be Woden's son.

His teachings and tutoring's jarred him back to the day's reality as that scented breeze caught him once more, and from nowhere came the softest of whispers....

'La, Æthelstan, cild fram se æfonleot, beon thee stillan....'

In a single action, as he sensed a stillness in the fighting, Æthelstan unsheathed the sword bestowed on him by his Grandfather. Raising it skywards, vertical, and still, and to the relief of his own men at arms...

"MERCIANS!!!!!...."

He had reclaimed their attentions.

"Mercians, we shall meet once again at the tables of our Forefathers should we perish upon this plain, on this finest day...."

Watched on now by a noble Father the Ætheling signalled their advance towards the massing ranks of a violent enemy who stamped his enormous numbers beneath the Raven's banner.

And the horns bellowed the approval of Æthelstan's command as rider and horse turned a disciplined trot into an organised gallop, wind in his face, certainty in his heart. Behind him they raced, united and together as one, as had been their teachings, proud and heroic as had been their birth right. At the hooves of their young commander they raced, behind an Ætheling who had sworn an oath to them all. For the first time in their history the Mercian Knights followed a leader who had become their brother...and into the day's glory they flew...

Hooves dug down gouging out the sod deep and certain to launch the following stride, further towards the enemy's ranks that shuffled and stumbled in disarray, still in shock after the rapid 'hammering' of their brothers.

The sun had gladly dismissed itself hiding its gleam behind the darkening clouds that curtained the heavens, what light that remained quickly turned dull and grey contributing to the gloom of their surroundings which had merged into a scene like an afterthought from Hel herself.

…Tabards and jerkins slapped against flesh and hide as banners and flags strained against shafts snapping to the pitch of the horse's hooves, sweat teared down the cheeks of man and horse alike, eyes squinted tight to deny the dust and mouths caked over as saliva congealed upon their tongues as all fought for their share of the foulest air. Their steeds carried them deeper into the open plains, closer to their contact where the Norseman had rallied his ranks, a final stand against the encroaching cavalry.

……and the Danish leaders called out repeatedly for their spearmen to hold the line, 'Halda…. Halda!!!!'

For the shield wall to tighten, 'Rond veggr halda !!!!' To hold their ground and trust in their Gods, and ready themselves for that which would be 'their' fine day.

Æthelstan called out again, and loud…. "MERCIANS". To his right, he cheated a glance towards Ealdfrith where they dared to share a smile of excited apprehension, then to his left at Wulfhere, who shrieked with anticipation, shook his spear in defiance and beamed an uncertain grin to his Lord.

He had ordered the charge.

As the closest commander, it had been his responsibility, and his alone. His spear arm closed in rigid as his body leaned forward across Abrecan's mane, the shield hugging tightly to his left. Booted feet pushed down, his knees threatening to crush the horse's frame as both prepared for the coming impact, and his eyes began to meet those of his targets. His body shook with excitement, fear, and uncertainty as he passed the turning point into his first real battle.

Ealdfrith urged his horse forward, eager to be first into the enemy's shield wall. Again, the two exchanged a glance whilst hands grasped hard and knees squeezed deep and tight into the flanks of their perspiring mounts.

"For Mercia…. For Wessex…. For Engle Land…."

Then, for the first time the chronicles would record that in a strange and unexplained second of silence which engulfed the charge, Æthelstan, King's Thegn and Ætheling to the Mercian Realm then called forth aloud that which would continue to be called out ahead of every Mercian battle throughout the countless ages that would follow....

"GEFYLLAN STEFFNETTAN......Strike Firm, Stand Hard" and the lines heaved above the horns with the copying of their new battle cry.

Within the echoes of such fine words, amongst the sweat and dust and spittle of two hundred mounted men, the riders dispatched a deathly cloud of hand axes, the 'francisca'. Spinning into the pulsating air towards the awaiting columns, flying out from the advancing ranks of vengeful knights who could wait no longer to inflict harm upon their imposing enemy. Turning and cutting through the stale air they screamed ahead until they smashed in contact, stinging with a vicious might that dropped their targets to the ground weakening the shield wall, creating the openings for the horses to pierce the enemy's line before it had the chance to close once more.

...And as the last storm clouds of Jutish arrows and Saxon quarrels ceased as the Knights hit hard against the limewood ring, strong, defiant, and as violent as it was cruel, almost invincible from the first impact. Æthelstan's white charger splintered the shields as she was rightly first to smash her own opening flanked by the ever loyal huscarl, setting the example that all would follow. Loud and painful the Engle, Saxon, and Jute cavalry battered their way through the once indefatigable Viking defence, merciless and without feeling.

Total impact.

The axes had done their worst, then the sheer force and brutality of the muscular animals inflicted further casualties smashing into their defences with unbelievable power and speed, killing out right, or at the very least fatally maiming those who had the misfortune to have stood against the charge, crushing firstly with their powerful bodies enhanced with their own 'breostnett', then trampling down viscously with shoed hooves.

Mercian too, and horse of course were also amongst the first casualties, impaled upon the tallest spearheads, cut down with retaliatory axes or pulled from their mounts as they became encompassed by a sadistic and desperate enemy.

But that was warfare, unacceptable but expected.

Then the blades and points dug in deep, sharply honed for that very task, cutting cleanly through whatever they connected with first, then spun around expertly for a second slice, then a third and more. With the Angon spears from the arriving infantry now launched into the remnants of the Danish shield wall, dragging the defences to the ground, spearmen turned axemen hurling themselves onto the Dane, hacking viciously at their enemy. Battle lances were wrenched from the saddle sheaths and hurled with defiant accuracy into pockets of gathering Danes, first, second and then a third from each rider. Spear points drove their way through human trunks, splitting through back bones and flesh. Blood gushed, frames splintered, and death called eagerly to anyone who permitted his wits to slacken for the briefest second....

.... And on Æthelstan rode with his escort shadowing his every move, he flew through the enemy blockade smashing the shielded resistance to the ground, cutting and thrusting with his gifted sword that whistled the word of truth as it split the air, defending with his dragon shield, wallowing in the glory of his first encounter against the enemies of his Father's lands.

He had been correct before the charge, that was no place for their God, but it was a place for Gods, and under Woden's gaze he continued forward...

Crossing their gazes as the chance permitted, checking the welfare of another the mounted warriors were keen and eager to thump their way through the stout lines of vilified Northmen who remained resilient, far from deterred by the ferocity of the Mercian onslaught.

The Knights rode forward, on into the deluge supported by the spearmen of Wessex who ran to their rear as swift as they were able, their lungs threatening to burst as every heave of air was painfully drawn in to replenish their charging bodies, near exhausted and aching fear and experience forbade them to lower their guard.

The energy boiled though his body the like of which he had never experienced, a newly found strength that seemed to furnish him with unbeatable might. He felt that he was there within that battle by right, by the right of his Forefathers. His Father ruled those lands by the right of Saxon law, by Mercian Law, and by a King's Law, but they were Æthelstan's by right of his bloodline, passed down from a Mother as she first screamed her son into that world. His eyes bulged as a tear formed, at last, on that field of pain he had finally realised his destiny.

To lose momentum, or even glance away from the battle's task would have meant an uncompromising death at the hands of the crazed Northumbrian Dane. Like a machine, He, as did those who stood at his side, cut down any opposition in an instant, hacking at the countless figures that swarmed neverendingly to meet them, to engage in the attack, reaching out with weapon and hand, to drag a knight from the rear of his mount, to crush out his life on the ground below, to destroy that onslaught, to survive that day.

Still there would be no respite from the continuous butchery, the rampant killing nor that merciless violence……

And on he fought.

Through the jumbled ranks of screaming rage, almost unable to identify those of his own. Slicing down from Abrecan's back he rode through each obstacle with ease……until he found himself abruptly at a stop, and face to face with what was most likely the largest Dane on the field, arguably the largest Dane he had ever seen.

Beneath his spanghelm Æthelstan remained still and expressionless, beneath his skin he shook, just a little, but remained stubbornly rigid upon his saddle, whilst the giant, who, even though he was on foot towered down, glaringly defiant, and unmoving.

Both stared at each other, almost at eye level as the horse stumbled nervously, panted for a clean breath, and shook dry her sodden mane, taking her advantage in the unexpected break.

Very tall, stocky, and well fed, even over fed, the giant of a Danish King remained challenging astride a pile of twisted corpses as if he were standing upon a mountain of human flesh, which only added to his threatening stance. Any thoughts of defeat did not form part of his appearance as an arrogant stature expressed the belief that he would truly be the victor that day and that his Gods looked down upon him to ensure it.

The bearded Viking bellowed a moan as his grip tightened around the over large shaft that carried the twin bladed Dane axe to shoulder height allowing it to incline backwards, just a little, for added swing. He grinned a sickening smile whilst spinning the shaft, cockily twisting the blood drenched heads as a daring challenge to the 'young fool' who now sat upon saddle before him. It was obvious by the cut of his purple cloak and the embellishments upon his sword that in front of him now, astride the finest of mounts, was a knight of high nobility and substance. His 'pretty' head would make a fair prize for a victory, indeed.

The half king stood stoically upright and offered the slightest of sympathetic grins towards his young challenger. That mere man who now offered the challenge had probably been spoiled since his unwanted birth on all things that came with a Saxon life, cultivated by the nobles of Winchester and Tamworth for him, King of the Northern Humber lands to defeat and brutalise in the most horrid of ways, there on that great day.

After the deepest lungful, he spoke through a cloud of heated breath in a broken Norse accent, with surprisingly good Saxon.

"Such a pretty boy who dares to confront a King…. There be those in my ranks that would wish for me to keep thee living…" and he laughed too loud as depraved thoughts flickered through his mind.

"I be Halfden, true King of the lands that be to the North, and to the South, of the Hymbre, and I shall relish with the greatest satisfaction as thy Saxon heart trembles its final beat within these hills." The words were followed with a churlish grin displaying a half empty mouth of rotting teeth as it turned into laughter oozing with spittle and slime which instantly congealed where it had drooled. But within Halfden's tone echoed the slightest tremor of doubt.

For a time that seemed an age the Mercian heir remained motionless yet always 'en guard' as his enemy had drabbled on endlessly. Æthelstan had not known that the last Dane to have fallen from his blade was Ingvar, youngest brother to the half king, and that Halfden now sought retribution, but it would be no longer of any consequence, to either men.

Abrecan snorted in contempt as her rider glared at the roughness that purported to be a King.

No grins. No smiles. Just a constant disapproving glare from the Mercian until the Dane had finally quietened. Then Æthelstan spoke calmly and without hesitation.

"I be Æthelstan, Ætheling of the Mercians. Next by blood I be to rule these lands that ye now defiles with thy very presence. Ye be no more than a disgrace to the sagas of thy forefathers and thine own time upon this world shall be remembered only for the waste that it hath brought upon it. I say now that ye shall not succeed" And as he spoke the Mercian brought his left leg across Abrecan's mane slipping easily from the saddle, raising the sword that had been named Caledfwlch by the whispers of a child so long ago, high, above his head with both hands tight as the air about him trembled whilst a mystical tone swept passed the blade as an unseen sun reflected its brightness.

The Dane saw it, the shinning, and heard also the whispers of the breeze about the gleaming blade, and for a second he thought it to be a fearful warning, then he dismissed such stupidity blaming it on the empty mead flask at his side, then spread wide his shoulders defiantly. 'That be a sword for none but a King such as He should wield'.

There would be no further conversation between the two men, it would have served no more purpose than to waste a breath and delay the obvious.

Of course, Æthelstan could have insisted that the half King collect what remained of his rapidly diminishing army, return all that had been stolen and make suitable recompense for that which had been damaged or destroyed. But such a demand would have been naïve and foolish, so their breaths were saved.

The clouds had thickened in the skies above and there was the suggestion of a storm brewing across the distant hills, but that was always so in those parts. In the din, the battle's noise had grown louder in desperation for an end before nightfall, vibrating across the melee as man's weaknesses set in. Horses struggled in their attempts to find sure footing amongst the corpse strewn ground, the smell of blood, and vomit, and other human waste had long since sickened the stomachs of the hardiest fighters.

Shinning and daring he stepped one stride out from that vision of torment, immediately following with two further paces that accompanied a swagger of natural born confidence. His eyes pierced through the niches of his spanghelm cutting deep into the figure of that foolish Northern King….'Who would not pass'….

In retaliation.

The invading giant launched his awkward mass into what had been intended as an explosive statement, hurling his body aggressively into what resulted in no more than an idle leap across the cleavered body of his favourite Jarl who had once been named 'Oddr' and had proudly sacrificed his own life for that of his King's.

In an uncontrollable mead fed rage Halfden Half King slipped clumsily through a blood pool that had clotted at the dead Jarl's side, cheeks reddened even more as he struggled to regain good ground, an incapacity for proving his own words had always been a handicap and once more the Norse King secretly cursed his own ineptness.

Ignored were the bolts and reused arrows that pierced the ground at their feet penetrating grass and corpse alike. Dismissed were the screams and groans, the cries, and the whines from the surrounding savagery. Æthelstan could find no time for further trivialities, under any other condition he may have felt the slightest of sympathies for his challenger's awkwardness, but such a place refused to welcome such feelings of pity or remorse and that so named King at his front was a fool, and would be treated as such.

Gone were any nerves of a fighting novice, only confidence and certainty of a battle-hardened warrior showed in his step as he parried to his left then took a controlled lunge forward as if showing the Dane how a challenge should be executed. With a quick breath he glanced to check his rear, then smashed down hard with the golden blade slicing cleanly the willow shaft of the giant's axe, as well as the right wrist that held it, severing a hand by all but one remaining sinew, dispatching splinters of bone and willow and clumps of flesh into the air around them.

The redness seeped slowly for a second then gushed freely as the Viking cursed loudly in his natural tongue failing to disguise his screams of painful surprise. Even so, despite the trauma, Halfden reached down with his only hand finding the splintered shaft, retrieving the damaged axe which was brought immediately to the ready.

Both men stood their ground rigid and certain, glaring poisonously at the other whilst every chance to regain a breath was taken.

The Dane stared away with disbelief, his severed limb dribbling through a hastily made bandage into the same pool as his dead Jarl.

There was no warning, no sign of the half king's intensions as he screamed out once more, louder through his own agony as the broken nerves contracted in the open air, stinging, pulsating, beyond bearable. Defiance and retribution were his only thoughts as he lunged himself forward unbalanced and single handed, swinging the shattered Daneaxe that shamefully dripped with his own blood, his only aim now was to kill the young Ætheling.

Again, Halfden slipped. Once, twice, and then again before finally steadying his pose, ready in hope at least to pronounce his kill. As if it had all been rehearsed a thousand times he took deep a fresh breath, cushioned his injured hand, and flared his reddening cheeks with enraged defiance. A jumble of words splintered from his lips, but they went unheard adding to his anger as he rechecked his guard.

Agility and physical fitness had always been a strong point within Æthelstan's character, instilled by his aunt from his earliest years. The young Thegn stood firm, silently accepting the challenge that now stood before him, there was no other choice, he had met the challenge, one of them had to die.

His eyes cut deep into the stares of his opponent. He streamlined his body and lifted again the blade, as high to his right that he could stretch, inflated his lungs to their fullest extent and moistened the dryness of his parched lips, then stared deeper.

Now for the first time Æthelstan felt the strength of the blade within his grasp, the power that came with it as a thousand visions of unknown conflicts flew through his mind and the whispers from the blade echoed…

…and a shiver surged through his body bringing ease and confidence into an already stalwart mind. He could almost feel the thoughts of his opponent radiating from the Dane's anger, 'how dare he stand there in contest'.

The wounded King's expressions had betrayed him, pain had started to overtake cause, anger over rationality, and doubt over certainty.

Now was the time. Head upright, shoulders broad, one step…stop, second step… twist, and with every ounce of strength within his young body he brought down the sword for a second time in a crushing blow that clean cut through Danish 'skrud' deep into the thick flesh of a Nordic back. With a single pressurised swipe, the blade sliced through the invertebrates of the spine instantly taking away control of his legs, slipping him pathetically onto his knees.

There, in that mess of war he half sat, half knelt confused and in shock, yet still daring his superior, impudent to the end, but ashamed also that the fear which now shook through his crippled body caused his only hand to fail any attempt to remove the battle's grime from a dying brow...

A war left no time for ceremony or audacious speeches, and even less, no Kingly respect, and certainly no place for mercy, as neither had been earned. The battle was far from over, still a war was there to be won and could still be done so by either side as a thousand spear shafts snapped whilst the sword blades clashed into the engulfing hoards that were highlighted by a dying sun.

...Without further thought Æthelstan's blade swiftly and silently sliced down and across removing the Dane's head from what were arguably once noble shoulders, without grace the single action ended with a gusher of blood from a now open neck as the torso crumpled into man's own sludge and fell into a never-ending 'sleep of the sword'.

"Here passes half a King named 'Half a Dane', the other half being that of a fool……may his forefathers take pity upon his tormented spirit as he passes through Hel's gates."

As a final courtesy, he stared down into death's gaze there motionless at his feet. There was no emotion, no remorse and certainly no care for his first significant kill, neither was there any elation for ending the life of his first enemy King. All that he had held for the man was sheer and embittered contempt for one who had deservedly met his rightful fate after ordering so many foolishly to their pointless deaths, and still, so many yet to die, and for what reason? For the greed and wanting of another man's worth in a realm that would never belong to 'his house'. Edward's elder son again found the saddle, settled himself once more as he cleaned the blade of Danish life upon a cloth pressed tightly beneath his seat before turning again towards the centre of the enclosing fight.

Relieved, Ealdfrith had at last found the side of his 'hæsere' thankfully still in one piece. Stumbling closer he stared down at the bloodied corpse that lay in pieces between the fetlocks of his mount, the response was silent.

The young Thegn had searched the field frantically for his Lord battling his way through those who dared to offer a challenge, ever since they had shattered the Danish line, splintering their attack into smaller more manageable groups. Ealdfrith placed a free hand upon Æthelstan's shoulder and the pair exchanged a respectful nod, the Ætheling was safe and what was more, he had taken the life of an invading King, despite all, it was becoming a good day to be Mercian.

"Bregu...." a breath. "Our King sends word that our armies are to leave this field for this battle be all but won...." another breath. "He Orders thee form the knights in a line to his right."

"Does he not wish to end this fight here, and now, return them all to Woden's fyld back and through Hel's gates, now with their fool of a lonely King?"

The Thegn looked deep into his master's eyes, they were cold and even more cruel than before, but that was but one of the many silent injuries of a war.

"This fight be far from its end Bregu" as Ealdfrith motioned across to the east with a badly scratched spear arm, over to the outer plain on the edge of the clearing below a slight ridge, on the outskirts of the place long after to be known as something other than Teotta's Hahl.

Æthelstan lost his breath. Almost choking he sucked deep another with amazement and shock, or was it in awe of the numbers that had now assembled along the base of the Brunesweald, heaving beneath the banners of the Black Raven, fluttering in a final hint of sun burst. There, within striking distance, in densely packed groups and rows and gangs and clans stood thousands, maybe as many as five thousand, even more, Norse, Dane, Scot, mercenaries from anywhere, and possibly everywhere. There was a second army, ready and waiting to receive their Order, an army of men whose strengths had made the previous fight irrelevant. Eowils may have been a stupid King, but he had just proved how cunning and sly a stupid King could be, Halfden and his spearmen had merely been the decoy, the temptation, the starter, and the sacrifice.

He had all but won his first battle, now Æthelstan would be contesting his first war, and at the enemy's head sat their King with all his decadent glory and arrogance, possibly the most ruthless man alive.

"Now that bregu, be an army to beat," and both men shared a nervous smile as the remnants of 'their' fight now scurried through the carnage to join their one King.

Finally, Æthelstan exhaled a clear breath, his chest relaxed, and his stare had thawed, but only slightly....

"Sound the horns.... Form the lines.... Our King and Our Lands call to us yet again...." He sheathed his sword, settled the shield on his left and withdrew the last remaining battle lance from the saddle sheath. Ealdfrith was right, that would most certainly be an army to beat, that would most certainly be an army to destroy, for if they did not then the Engle and Saxon tongue would no longer be spoken across their lands and the Golden Wyvern of Wessex would no longer fly across the plains of 'Engle land'.

If, at that precise moment, as they rode from that field, the future King of an embattled realm had found the time to cast a glance down to the 'grizzled' stare on the corpse that now lay crumpled and broken between Abrecan's hooves, he may have recognised the face as that of the æcermann seen fleeing the field with his family before the battle's start. His grubby hand still gripped tightly around the broken half of a lance's shaft, yet despite the torn looks of a painful death that strained across his once placid features there was a strange veil of comfort about him, a glint of self-worth and pride that he had found the courage to leave his family safe and return again to the fields he had once ploughed, to join his fellow man in combat, stand his ground in defence of His Lands, for the futures' of a nagging 'wif' and their 'cyldru'.

As they rode from a field of dead, and half dead, to the echoes of the forlorn, they who were still able to stand on either side of the shields hobbled back to their ranks battered and bloodied yet relieved not to be amongst those who were now forsaken to the feastings of the night carrion. The flocks of crows and rooks and ravens that had earlier threatened their presence now began to hover in earnest around the outskirts of the carnage, assembling correctly in their aptly named 'murders' slyly awaiting man's retreat from the day, and the dogs, also in their wild packs, hurried from the shadows, as did the two-legged foragers who had callously awaited that time with bursting excitement.

How their numbers had depleted.

The lines had grown noticeably shorter and their colours gleamed no longer. Not a man who sat, or stood before him did so without an injury, but they were alive at least. He cursed himself, more than once, for not recognising those who were missing, finally relaxing in the knowledge that their spirits would still be amongst them. How costly this war against the greed of man?

At the head of his reformed ranks the depleted force joined the surprisingly vibrant face of the main Wessex army. An exhausted Æthelstan permitted himself a glance along the shallow incline to his east and found the relieved expressions and acknowledgements of his Father, and King. Edward betrayed a thankful nod of relief, but it went ignored by his son and the Father in him knew then that his boy had changed, as did every Father's boy after their first taste of a battle's scar. His welcome humour would, from then on, be no more than a distant memory, the dark stares would be more common, and the periods of silence would lengthen, whilst tolerance would become a rarity that would be gratefully appreciated by those few he may eventually allow to be close. There would follow less compassion in his moods, on and off the field, words of pity and mercy would slowly fade into the unused vaults of his vocal memory. That was how it always was in the Land of Men, but maybe not for his son, maybe his time would be different.

As a noble son reached his strategic position, a rider swiftly left the Royal Column above, passing spirally down the grassy dune until he had caught the lead, just as an ordered manoeuvre had brought their ranks into the files of their allocated place. The standard that a squire then viciously thumped hard into the grassy turf bore the sign of a double headed wyvern in a field of green and would tell 'ALL' that 'There' camped Æthelstan, Thegn of Mercia, with his victorious knights.

Embroiled in a constant cloud of that hateful dust the messenger struggled his horse to a halt, coughed, spluttered, cleared his vision through his helmet with a right hand, dusted out a knotted beard and nodded a token of respect as he exhaled another tired gasp.

The day had been unacceptably long. He had ridden countless messages to every part of that field heralding his Master's Orders to the ears of the 'fighting' commanders. His position was the most hazardous, riding through enemy lines unescorted so as not to boast attention, chancing his luck on many account only to be berated by his superiors as he dispatched his usually unwelcome news, to commit themselves further or push their battered warriors deeper into the fold. Then back he would fly, cheating death once more, to the side of his King who would again dismiss him ungraciously to the rear until another task would allow him to repeat once more his near impossible quest. How he wished many times to have been chosen as an ordinary knight, a spearman, or even a shield man, but again, as always, whilst he glanced across the carnage of a battle he would pray for his wishes to remain private.

"Æthelstan..." a pause to recover lost breath, "Bregu, our King requests thee join him upon the hyrst." Horse and rider panted loudly, almost more than the spoken words, and continued to do so as they turned, ready for their return.

To join his King would have meant leaving his knights, and that would never happen, Æthelred and his Lady would never have considered it, not at such a stage in the fighting, and neither would he...

"Tell my Father..." he coughed at his deliberate error, "...Tell our King that I shall remain with my knights, for this be where I shall serve him best."

Eager to leave the front line, the King's herald bowed his head and without further to do jarred his mount into an instant gallop, back to the safety of the summit.

A sense of acceptance could be felt radiating from the ranks behind, from those who had overheard the 'tactical' response to their King's request. It had always followed since the first conflicts, many Kings ago, when victory over a battle, or even a war had threatened to become less certain, the Earls, Thegns and Ealdormen would retire to the safety of the King's Line to await the outcome from a 'better' distance, whilst their knights and weapon men continued under relayed Orders risking almost certain death and probable defeat. Often, they feasted and wagered the outcome over a calic of mead, as they had watched their own men fall to the onslaught of a better prepared enemy.

It had always been the way, until that day.

The King had offered the safety of refuge, to 'view' the oncoming fight beneath the safety of the Royal banner, but Æthelstan had declined. He would be the one who would again lead his knights into the enemy shield wall, that was his place, his right, and his destiny, and the King would be proud of his eldest son when the messenger had relayed his son's answer.

And after all that, despite the previous need for haste and fine speeches, to move their lines and change their tactics, there would be no further fighting on that day.

The evening had arrived at its fullest bringing a dusky gloom across those saddened lands, reducing visibility at the closest of ranges. What little sign of the sun that now remained was escaping into the darkness of the far west as the chill that followed escorted an impenetrable mist deep into the valleys, warring for that day would soon ease, rests could be taken and where possible the wounded would be cleared from the suffering heaps below. Man's hurtful intent upon each other could gladly await the sunrise of a second day.

The King's 'Arthegn' had been the first to spot the enemy's intensions running excitedly in front of the royal horse pointing and shouting....

"Min Cyning, min Cyning!!!!"

Away across the plain flustered Eowil's banner, barely visible in the murk of the eve. Even more haunting in the misery of the descending night were the horns, eerily sounding their King's calls upon his warriors, to retire from the field and return to the camps. To continue further would have been futile, almost suicidal for either side, it had reached that point in a day when the shadows were indistinguishable from their masters.

'These men came from three tribes of

Germania, from the Old Saxons,

from the Engles and from the Jutes.

The commanders were two brothers

Hengest and Horsa who were the sons of Wihtgils,

Wihtgils was Witta's offspring

Witta was Wecta's.

Wecta was the first child of Woden,

From that so followed the Noble families

of the Anglo Saxons.'

From Bede's Ecclesiastical History.

CHAPTER 3

The Wessex King had copied.

Much to the relief of those within the ranks of his combined army, Edward had ordered the lowering of the guþfanan permitting the retirement of his armies into their night camps. For most, such camps remained in the field where they had fought, with the night sky as a canopy, still in their fighting positions, still amongst their dead, still, and ever ready. The Dane could never be trusted, even under a night's truce.

Within minutes' supplies were being scavenged and camp fires hurriedly kindled, bursting into the reddest of flame, while soups and stews were slopped from basin to bowl and stale bread was unceremoniously ripped into rationed portions... 'One piece per man, and two for the shield wall, they shall be certain to need all their strength on the morrow' had been the repeated command from the King.

Yet no battle fully ceased in lieu of the darkness, it never had.

There would be the 'arrows', there was always the arrows. Randomly the aimed projectiles pierced through the night, loosed by archers on all sides, pointed out into the dark when the sounds of the enemy had echoed from the silence, or the roar of an over stoked fire had highlighted an interest. Rarely did they ever prove fatal, their main intension had been to unnerve the enemy, especially should an arrow unluckily find a target, keeping them from sleep and rest so that fatigue would set in upon the morning's field.

There was usually more risk to the archers. Foolishly believing that the dark offered an impenetrable shield they would move out from their camp's protection for a closer aim, sometimes running into their own sentries who would mistake them for an enemy raiding party, or they would fall into one of the many drunken gangs over loaded on battlefield mead, drowning their sorrows over the death of a friend or to forget their own failings in the heat of the fight. Not to mention that the quiet would often be broken by the infamous gangs of Hibernian Danes, whose bellies slopped full of sour mead and back bones burst with a drunkard's courage, hell bent on seeking their revenge over the day, or merely staggering back to where they thought to sleep off the night, often stumbling upon the sentinels of a better prepared army.

Edward was not a foolish King on any count. He had descended from good stock and had been taught well by his Father who would possibly be remembered as the greatest of all Kings. He knew too well that many of his own numbers would swallow a calic or two in respect of a fallen friend or brother or father, or just to ease some physical or mental pain, and rightfully they would be entitled to do so providing such indulgencies remained modestly controlled, without affecting their actions that would certainly still be required.

Apart from such on goings, which only gave way to a much-needed sleep, there would also be the runaways. Those who had witnessed more than they had expected on their first day and now wished to witness no more. Both sides would be plagued with desertions as was any large army called to arms without notice, with little bounty or reward in the offering and even less to be rifled from the dead, now that all trinkets of any worth had been forbidden from the field. It would often be, what had seemed the correct course on the day would swiftly turn into a 'fool's errand' once good men had begun to fall.

Many would slip away under the cover of a clouded moon intending a return to the Shires, or the fleet, unless of course they were captured by the sentinels, then their fate would certainly be decided behind the limewood rounds of the morrow's shield wall.

A night between battles is often a lonely place, especially for a King.

As Edward had listened deep into the darkness, surrounded by heavily armed house-guards, as well as a few thousand knights, he sipped slowly on a calic of imported wine that had been gently warmed over the first fires before being laced with a touch of imported spice.

The haunting sounds that had survived the day's violence chilled his spine. It was something that he, nor any reasonable man would never grow accustomed to. The screams of the dying, as their bodies bled out whilst the carrion refused to wait for death's final scent, which, more often than not came accompanied with the sobs of those who had followed the 'fyrds' and searched in desperation for their kinfolk, tentatively fumbling about the half naked corpses, in the dimmest of a torches light, for the slightest sign that would prove the identity of a husband or father, or brother, even a wife....Which was only too often followed by the sudden screech of horror as proof was gruesomely found.

In the opposite vane, with a strange note of welcome for battlefield humour, the King, as did many others, listened out to the countless obscenities and curses that were yelled and screamed across the blackness, from all sides. It went from common name calling and insults to criticisms of another's actions upon the field, changing to doubts about one's parentage, then crude suggestions of what may be done to another's wife or lover should he ever gain the chance. Even similarities to various animals, goading's on the inadequacies of a leader or a King, all were thrown into the darkness, and for the shortest of time the night almost seemed pleasant, in an unusual way.

Finally, there came the worst screams of all, sharply dismissing such humour as agonising yells and torturous roars told all that the carrion had found a feast, curdling tempers, spreading reality back to all corners of the darkened plain. Then, as a wolf called out to a jagged moon there fell an instant silence as all camps knew that those who remained upon the crimson field would soon be walking the path of another life.

The highest ring of hastily scavenged thorn hedge entwined with brambles and saplings and pinned down tightly with sharpened stakes had been constructed into a large circular wall to offer the best protection for a secure 'nihtwic'. Situated far enough from the wooded lands the 'nihtweard' would see well in advance the silhouettes of any would-be raiders, and if their eyes had failed in the darkest of night then their ears and noses would pick out the signs, betrayed by the night's breeze, should the 'ræcc' hounds not smell them first.

There were only two points of entry, or exit from the thorny burg. A main entrance pointing west, used by the large bodies of infantry and cavalry alike who were vetted and searched by the most observant of guards.

The second faced south. Much smaller and far less obvious, mainly for use in emergencies such as a surprise attack, or for their own clandestine activities. Both accesses were equally guarded by vigilant spearmen, charged by the most trusted of Thegns.

At the centre of the camp were the horses, tethered, groomed, and fed by the squires whose only duty was the welfare and safety of the animals, grooming a horse in virtual darkness had become second nature to them over the years.

The few fires that were permitted were also strategically placed and glowed dimly behind cloth screens as the rushed preparations for an evening meal were ordered to the muffled reply of a cook's insults who longed tirelessly for the curfew that would soon follow. Hot food and a little sleep, an excellent way to prepare for the following day's war.

In the shadows of the dead, as Mercian Knights assembled on the edge of the day's fight, the oldest surviving veteran ignored the pitch of the night-arrows as he stole half a pace forward allowing a second's silence for the thoughts of the day's experiences. Sigric had played a part in every fight since his fourteenth summer, from Ethandun to Holme, now, thirty years of warring showed heavily in his eyes as he eventually removed his spanghelm took in a breath before the deepest of sighs had permitted a solitary tear. Then he called out, loud for all to hear, respect and pride thundering from his tone...

"T'is told, in the Halls of the 'Ærfædra', of that which hath been granted to us through their blood, must be safely guarded through the blood of those who now be their sons..." a permitted pause to regain control of his speech.

"So, then may the innocent voices of our children's children still speak forth the names of our fallen, with the pride that we do upon this very eve."

And the knights repeated...

'That which hath been granted to us, through the blood of our forefathers...must be safeguarded, through the blood of their sons...'

And then, the names of each of those who had fallen were called out by he, or she who had been the closest.

Every knight present repeated those ancient words then followed with the strictest silence, a time to remember those who were now at their side only in spirit...

The grave be terrible for any knight

when the corpse quickly begins to cool,

and is lain in the bosom of the dark earth.

Prosperity declines, happiness passes away

and covenants are broken

as the wrath of the new men

rattles the dawn.

A Rune Poem.

CHAPTER 4

910. This year the Engles and the Danes fought at Tootenhall; and the Engles had the victory. The same year Æthelflæd built the fortress at Bramsbury.

If you have never woken to a battle-field's morning and witnessed its uniquely haunting atmosphere, then those who have may say that you are surely fortunate, for it is an experience that can never be sought in one's imagination, and only realised with the slightest hint of accuracy in the report of another....

After the sudden reprieve from a night's sleep induced torments are finally over and relief fills the body as it emerges that you are still sadly amongst the living, you desperately struggle to beat away the sleep, forcing yourself reluctantly back into the land of cruel reality, and as the aches, pains, strains and stings from the previous day's fight for life herald forth a new day, the first thing that hits you is the stench of yesterday's death alongside the fading embers of the funeral pyres and scorched dressings from the makeshift 'læcehus' that attempt to rid the world of bloodied bandages and severed body parts which dry the nostrils to a point where your first action of the morning is to choke violently and snort back the first breath of a new day.

Then comes a spitefully harsh realism.... Yesterday has not yet been finished.

Following that memorable feat of mental effort and abrupt realisation of those dreadful facts comes the strained creaking of the body as it forces itself to sit, untangling the knotted muscles of earlier exertions where sinews and cartilage were stretched beyond conception in a successful attempt to survive the agonies thrust upon it the previous day.

Once you have regained the energy and summoned the will to accept a morning's contest and you finally rise to your feet, the full challenge is cast.

Opening dried eyes, wiping away sorely the night's crust from their stinging lashes and piercing a gaze through the loosened tent flap your vision will focus onto its first target which would usually be the streams and drafts of charcoal coloured pyre smoke bellowing 'too and fro' across a tortured landscape. Then, as the breeze splits the dark clouds in half, your vision is dragged into the open plain where another day's desire from Hel shall soon be unleashed.

Then come the noises.

Nothing at first. A sheer silence as the mind still craves for what little remains of a sleep driven refuge, where silent dreams fight for their right to be believed and the numbness of denial still challenges the nerves of acceptance. Then the sharp realities of that life quickly echo through the spiritual seclusion and you painfully accept that another night's torment is truly over.

As you dare to rise, struggle for that first awkward pace towards the canopy's porch, you decline the temptation to 'down' another calic as the screams from the wounded and dying still beat out against your senses whilst even now they attempt to claim their mercy, or at the very least, a dignified release from their lingering and unimaginable persecution. It was one thing to die instantly within the fight, but to do so after a night of torturous agony to the sympathies and pities of others, is inconceivable.

Evident are the broken minds of those who have wandered the camp aimlessly throughout the night, tears still streaming down cheeks of grime, jerkins barely hanging with the saturated and congealed blood of others as they wrestle with their own guilt over the cruel and barbarous acts and unbelievable sights they had witnessed, neigh, that they had been part of, in that other world of yesterday.

Far across the forlorn openness into the enemy camp similar sounds can be heard emitting through the dimness of its hollow echo. When a man, or woman is suffering through the final seconds of a violent life there is nothing to separate them from their enemies who struggle to survive the same fate, only the accents of the dying are different.

Such a solemn, almost holy start to the day is quickly substituted by the chilling sounds of scratches and scrapes and grinds as weapon men and serf alike sharpen and prepare their blades and points and shafts for another day's killing. Diligently the 'arthegn' attend to the reparation of a knight's mail and the strapping of leather onto the already sore backs of dun ponies, then you discover the fear of, yet another day reflected in the pitiful eyes of those animals who, unlike their masters, were not there by choice. Its not just Man who is tormented by the memories of yesterday's fight.

As an aged 'erne' hurries between tents slopping his master's 'morgen drenc' of sweet honey mixed with almost warm goat's milk, another busies himself with the contents of the 'night bowls' and Æthelstan watches, watches as his knights, now awakening from their rest, begin to drag their own aching bodies through the same ritual that he had just suffered.

Hardened veterans, survivors of countless battles be they so stern, yet their faces portray the guilt of the brutal slaughter inflicted upon their fellow man. Added together with uncertain and vacant expressions they silently ask of themselves what a new day may bring, who else would they secretly be weeping for at the close of another day's torment, or who maybe, would remain to weep for them?......They would not have been knights if they had not felt such a way.

With the stifled nod of a struggled greeting man passes another with a stifled 'Morgen' as a face is recognised......and the day now begins in full.

Silently, more on instinct than habit, each man, no matter his status will visit the communal 'gangtun' at least once, to relieve himself of the last evening's meal, if you are caught short in the field there is only one alternative and the discomfort from that is more than unwanted. Belly gases are thankfully permitted to escape, without apology, from both orifices as the innards awaken after the mind, then in turn they all wash free the night with tepid stream water in surprisingly clean basins, then without privacy nor comfort dry themselves upon the body 'lina' held out by obedient ernes, or even scylcen. After maybe, some will take a second calic of sweet milk for sustenance before cramming flatbread and head cheese into now empty bellies, which is always followed by a final 'stretch' that takes them back to their 'ganggetelden' where recovered weapons and cleanly oiled breostnett are taken as the day's dress code and what remains from a thousand Mercian Knights, assemble, alert and ready, at the side of an equally 'dressed' horse, awaiting Order from an honoured leader, that the time had once again come to resume their barbaric butchery that only another night's welcome darkness could offer the slightest relief.

For those who still believed, the Holy Men who ritually trailed behind every Christian army had set up their 'gebedstow' where, for the cost of a silver coin they would offer a prayer, which would be spoken by the 'gebedmann' whilst the 'believers' were in battle, as a possible plea for a soul's salvation should they be amongst that day's fallen, or absolution for their actions against another should they survive….and for those who did not care there would always be the justification of their own council.

He spat twice. Both times solidly into the dew soaked turf, each time almost clearing the congealed filth from the back of the sorest throat. Finishing the final dregs of milk from its calic he stared into the awakening eyes of the knights, shaking free from aching fingers spilled droplets of the liquid that had broken his fast. Before he spoke he returned the empty drinking vessel and remnants of a crust to an older, but efficient erne whom he had always named Bod, mainly because he could be trusted with the carrying of an ærende, Æthelstan accepted the cleaned purple cloak in fair exchange.

Ealdfrith had found his master's side, a little late as always and through his stuttering apologies he clumsily assisted in the cloak's fitting.

Æthelstan spoke to no-one, yet addressed everyone.

"What I would not now give for the comfort of a single day, with nought more to do than rest and game play…"

Sighs, grunts, and groans of agreement came from the assembling riders amidst the 'slurps' and 'scoffs' of unfinished 'undernmete'….

… "And with a little deer hunting, just to ease the boredom?" laughter proved their agreement.

"Like us all Bregu, thee should not know how to deal with such comforts" again a humorous addition brought a chink of laughter that rippled through the ranks then petered into another silence suggesting that the realities of that day were returning.

"Thee be right Wulfhere, but it would be very welcome to try."

The slightest trace of emotion crept into Æthelstan's tone as he began to address his ranks more formally.

"Men of the West…." He paused to swallow. "Knights of the 'middel scir'… we have no true plan for this day's fight, for our King insists of us that there be nought but one true task, with nought but one result…" another pause, then his voice grew louder "One result only… To destroy, without pity these Orcs from the north… to rid our lands of such 'hrot' who dare to impose their company upon us without invite… and to do so as speedy and as certain as we may… Complete this day without mercy or compassion, as a warning to others who may still believe that this realm of Mercia be theirs for an easy taking."

He had long since named his horse Abrecan not only because of the animal's cloudlike mane which continuously wavered in the slightest of breezes, but also for her thunderous hooves which had clattered above all others upon Tamworth's stony cobbles. The animal stirred and jumped nervously as the knights took to their own mounts assembled in front of the long line of night tents that were already being dismantled by those who would, or could not fight.

…As Abrecan turned regally to show the ranks her rider's back Æthelstan stared out across the open plain. The mists of the morning had been slow to clear eventually showing once more the 'litter' of the previous fight. How strange it all seemed, so quiet and inviting it appeared despite the putrid looking remnants of yesterday's fallen. Was his vision a warning, or a welcome?

His concentration broke.

In the distant vestiges of that morning's haze that still fought its own battle against the coming of a new day, the bellowing of a horn broke the silence with three short but deliberate bursts which were quickly followed by a fourth and a fifth that echoed for longer. Then the notes were repeated with the accompaniment of many more horns in the distance. It seemed that they would scream forever telling all that the King had set his feet upon the battle's field and his banner, the Golden Wyvern set on a deep red background waved vigorously proud in the morning breeze to offer proof that Edward was still King of the Engle's Land and that the folk of Wessex stood proudly at the side of their Mercian ally.

A separate horn, loud and long was then followed by many more across the English ranks, almost becoming melodic as they greeted their King and told All to prepare for the battle that would now most definitely not be ignored. In the briefest seconds of their notes the horns had brought the morning to all, alert, eager, excited, blood pumping and veins swelling as knights and weapon men, archers, and spearmen, along with the serfs and their 'levies' expressed an urgency to rekindle the fight, and their intent readily transmitted through the assembled armies.

.... And the realisation that there was now an enemy present interrupted the assembly as louder horns, bigger horns, but not melodic horns tore into the sky telling their God's that the Men of the Raven had also arrived, themselves ready for the challenge, and the drone was followed by thousands of spear shafts, sword pommels and axe heads smashing down hard onto rounded shields that brought the noise of thunder crashing down onto Dane and Saxon alike. Neither Man, nor God, in Heaven or Valhalla would oversleep that morning.

Ignoring the horns and chants and crashes of their adversaries Æthelstan, as did all commanders and captains, watched expectantly as Royal signallers hastened to the lead of their King carrying armfuls of multi coloured banners which would be used to indicate in turn royal commands as the battle commenced and gathered in pace, therefore Edward would hopefully remain in control of his armies.

'Enough was the wait.'

'Now was the time.'

'Just get the start underway', a thousand minds wished of their King, and they would do the rest. Æthelstan had waited all his life for what he now saw.

The double headed wyvern of his own colours, his own 'gupfana' presented now by the King, and endorsed by his guardians, held high by a 'beacen mann', and a second, that of Mercia's own Golden Saltire on a wode blue field flying high together in a glorious brilliance spreading pride and honour across the ranks of excited warriors.

Anticipation streamed through the Ætheling's body, now finally he would accompany Æthelflæd and her husband, into battle. Together they would ride like the wind, through the shield walls of the Dane, into the ranks of their allies who now rushed to assemble their disorientated numbers across the crimson tinged field and beyond.

Not for the first time, he glanced across the large numbers of Anglo-Saxon fighters intermingled with Jutes and Britons, together with those from the shires of the East Saxons, the Middle Saxons and those of the Saxon south. Across further he stared to where his aunt would be waiting, far from his sight, and sensed that she would also be staring towards his direction, where he now sat exchanging thoughtful wishes of good fortune and pride and duty and passion, and into the Halls of the Old Gods he prayed with each thought for hope of that day's glory….

Then they flew…

The instant the 'gupfana' was sighted upon the King's rise, waving their King's Order, almost one thousand Mercian Knights, with the spirits of their forefathers behind their young Thegn, beat the wind in their race for the field. To his far right came a thousand more, led by the fiery Æthelflæd and on her own right, her husband, Æthelred loud and excited as he brought up a third more. With wind swept hair and cloaks flapping in their wake, what a sight they would have been as they spurred the horses for greater speed, He would not be second into that slaughter, not on that great day.

Bolts and arrows were first to seek targets, launched loose in sporadic clouds of steel and pointed willow, showering down upon the lifted shields of Mercian Knights, and ignored, as the first casualties fell, stumbling over horse, veering left or right, toppling back across their mounts, and the horses, speared and spiked just as their riders, without quarter…their fate was inevitable, there would be sufficient time for mourning in another life.

Close enough, and the hand axes were dispatched in retaliation for the second time in that fight, piercing the clouds ahead as they twisted and glided through the course air, until they stopped, embedding into their targets, bringing disarray amongst the front lines, opening weakened points for the approaching horses to take their advantage. Both Dane and Scot expressed their fear equally as the impact from the approaching riders became inevitable, the panic brought an added incentive into the charge.

Æthelstan's knights had won the race. They pierced the shield wall first with a crashing collision that drowned out all other sounds, splintering lime wood and willow, hazel and yew, only then to be followed by the chink and sting of metal upon metal from battle lances thrust forward, bursting through the backs of writhing weapon men, forcing shredded pieces of lung and heart and any other human offal into the faces of the second rank who had themselves began to hack and batter and pull at every mounted figure that dared to enter their protected wall, desperately dragging down any knight from his saddle where only the most horrendous deaths would be suffered upon the battle's floor.

Then came further dread as bare-chested spearmen caught up with their cavalry leaping like hares into the Viking clump, bringing down a mighty rage, where louder screams issued every obscenity as men cursed a final breath within the mix of a fighting's clamour.

Now the fight was truly on, there would be no end to it until one side had been annihilated.

To his left, through the squint of an eye, Æthelstan noticed the silvery greyness of a knight as his horse stumbled across the growing barricade of corpses. An arrow had found its way beneath a shield and into the thigh of the rider puncturing the artery in a flow of red. On through the leg it had passed into the side of the horse piercing the animal's lung. It was the expression upon the horse's face that had highlighted the action as it accepted in all reality that it was done for as both horse and rider's fate shared the same blow. To add to the scene, intermingled between the panicked hooves of the falling steed screamed a bare-chested Scot, spear point splitting his ribs and opening his bleeding heart for all the world to witness. Blades fell to the ground, shields slipped from a grip and the knight's lances dropped onto the dead, no longer did either have the need for such things as they died out in the fight's beginning.

Above the metallic din of chaos came the added noise of wailing and screeching that would have sent shivers of terror down the spines of any should they have taken the time to listen, but remaining alive was now the only importance of the day through the killing of the man at your front. The noises that echoed were those of Æthelflæd's women as they neared the battle's core, quickly recognised as they closed their distance towards the fight. They charged upon horse, but they were not the riders.

Just as it were told to the children about the night fires of Bryton, in the sagas of the great Boudicca and her vengeful assaults upon the Latin invaders, Æthelflæd's warriors clung to the straps and tethers of the rear columns of Æthelred's own Mercian cavalry, as if their lives depended upon it, from an extra stirrup lashed to the saddle they crouched, keeping their feet from fouling the ground as the horse and its rider delivered their deadly bundles into the Danish lines. With screams of rage they all but flew from their male couriers pouncing like agile cats onto the invaders, hacking and cutting their enemy to pieces....

But that time, unlike the previous day, they also suffered casualties.

The Dane would no longer regard them as women, not that they held any respect for women in the first place, especially Mercian women. They had all been warned, every one of them, before the start of that day's fight, of those women who fought at the side of the Mercian Lady who were unlike any other. 'They were all to be dispatched into the jaws of Garm', the blood-stained guardian of Helheim's gate, without further thought. As the Dane, had cornered a female, just as they had leapt from the horse's side, or found their balance or took a guard, little quarter was offered and even less pity. No mercy would be granted, to male nor female, whatever their ranking, and a killing as quick as it was certain was suffered by whoever had been the weakest, no more than would be expected by any on that day.

The battle had now approached the point where each man, or woman realised that they were only there for themselves and the warrior at their side. There was no opportunity to glance around, to search out a friend, or a brother, in doing so one's own death would most certainly be guaranteed. There could be no other outcome than victory and the only way to ensure a victory was to remain alive. Of course, the only way to remain alive was to kill, and continue to kill until there was nothing left standing to be killed.

Then, at the height of battle, as Æthelstan struggled to turn his horse east against the mass that had gathered about his position, he was suddenly aware that he had become the enemy's main target. Since the killing of the 'half-king' his own death would bring a great prize around Eowil's victory fires, an even greater prize for the one who could slay Edward's son and claim a captured sword as a gift to the one new King. It seemed as if all Danish eyes were upon him, as if there were no other upon that field but He, and his Huscarl were paying dearly for the protection of their Lord.

Hacking their way free from the curdling hoards that endlessly pushed towards them, his 'weardian' ushered him onto a small rise that seemed easier to defend with their now depleted numbers. It was safe enough, almost, to take a breath, gain an overview of the fighting, and plan his next move, just as a good pupil had been taught, by an even better tutor…

…and immediately she found his side.

Æthelflæd, who would have ridden through half a battle to be with him remembered the previous night's words of her King, in the most discreet of whispers….

"On this night sister, I have come to realise that it shall be my eldest son who shall be the future of our Lands. Our own Father knowing it to be so told of it to many, and I, above all others failed to see it...until now. So, my Lady it shall remain with us, with all of us, to ensure his safety on the morrow, and on every morrow until it be his time."

She had agreed then without argument, there was little point, Edward's words had been those of a caring Father more than those of a King, and she had always known there was more about Æthelstan than others had realised. Her brother's eldest son was more capable than many in surviving a fight, but a helping hand would never go amiss. Besides, she had also spotted the safety of the position for her short respite.

Still the screams and shrieks from the female warriors cut through the battle's deathly pitch....

"Brodorsunu..." interrupting her greeting as she cut through the torso of an attacking Scot chancing his luck as he leapt upon the rear of her mount, and failing as her blade run him through from front to back.

"My Lady" was followed with a struggled smile.

The quickest of welcomes were exchanged as both commanders were reinforced by the remnants of their Huscarl over dressed in armour and waving frantically with Dane axe and flail, stabbing with spear and sword, lashing out at anything that dare offer a threat towards their charges. Spearmen locked shields tightly as lances were pushed forward automatically falling in to an instant guard atop the battlefield's rise, and for the first time Æthelflæd's banner flew alongside that of her ward, Æthelstan lost a breath as he stared proudly, almost for too long.

The Lady brought back his attentions as she jarred at his 'armoured' ribs painfully with the pommel of her sword, "Do not give these vermin the slightest of advantage...." as she lashed down twice to her right.

The Huscarl closed in, tighter.

Now, the Golden Wyvern could be seen flying clearly on three of the four major points of the fighting. Edward was playing a shrewd and dangerous game with his ally's superior strength, allowing the Mercians and Jutes to engage their forces in total, fully enticing the enemy into the fight, then once both armies were committed he would circle with his Wessex men to the rear and to the sides of the fighting, and in 'the boar's head' formation slowly march into the perimeter picking off the enemy as they met, piercing their lines and ever cautious to avoid their allies, although some 'friendly' kills were inevitable, even acceptable.

As the King's army had advanced a small section of spearmen would linger at the rear, lie in wait at the farthest side of the fight, to cut down the Dane as he would predictably attempt his escape from the field.

The 'newcomers' were easily made out. Entering from the west, they cut their way through the smallest of outer skirmishes and into the fight came the small group of Wessex mariners. Wearing cloth skull caps, three quarter length smocks tied loosely at the waist and open toed sandals they were more readily noticed in how their blades sat. Long blades, sheathed across the shoulder, strapped to their backs for easy access aboard ship. They carried the javelin too, long, and almost weightless, swift to fly across the waves from boat to boat. Across the land from Bridgnorth they had come showing no signs of injury which readily told of their success, now there would be no escape for the Dane, not by seas at least. Now their fight was on land and they engaged with ruthless determination, eager to join their fellow warriors...

...In the melee that now pulsated between him and his King, mixed in between the colours of Wessex could be seen other assembled allies also fighting for survival. The new children of Hengist were the Cantii, valiantly cruel warriors who knew no fear and would grant, nor accept any quarter, loyal to their Wessex King, but always putting first their own lands. Welsh, from the western valleys and Saxons from the lands of the Engles had rallied to Edward's call, as well as more than one thousand mercenaries from 'wherever' following the enticements of another Noble's purse. All, little matter their reason, had offered their pledges at his side, and had flocked to the aid of Mercia.

"Our King has sealed the exit of the Danes with his 'Brimwudu'" reported Æthelflæd as she guessed the same conclusion and directed His attentions with her 'slaughter dewed' blade, across the misery towards the battle's edge.

It had not been the mariners who had caught her attention. She had become aware of small Norse bands who, ever since that first charge, had realised defeat was looming and were attempting, without success to escape to the 'awaiting' fleet unaware that Edward's navy had made such an attempt fruitless. The King's skirmishers were picking them off in small groups, ambushing their withdrawal along the battle's fringe, permitting none to leave, denying any of a future return.

Æthelstan nodded in angered agreement, "....and He used 'My Mercians' to do it."

"They still be 'MY' Mercians nephew..." she corrected sternly, loosing the humour amidst the surrounding horrors. "...Thee only hath but the loan of them..."

She caught a breath and continued... "Thy Father knowingly used those better to achieve it, inflicting as much hurt upon our enemy, granting us first blood, proving the better with least loss to our numbers. Thy Father acts as a King, as thee shall one-day copy in his stead...and hath he now almost brought us the victory?"

His silent reply was a simple nod before his blade swiped down through the skull of an aged Dane who had bloodied his way through the dwindling Huscarl line. His attacker's glare turned from a violent hatred to one of complete surprise as Æthelstan's right boot cleared the confines of a stirrup and kicked away the dying body which rebounded from the arse end of a Huscarl's mount into the forefront of his own. Abrecan stood her ground, reared half a stand, raised her front fetlocks then dismissed the corpse from view.

"A battlefield be no place for one of such an age" his comment ended any further discussions over the King's tactics.

Politics to one side, he had permitted his guard to falter, the battle was no place for such discussions and without further warning, Æthelstan screamed out with a fearful scream of surprised terror as he struggled to believe what he now saw. His outburst had been so loud that he threatened to drown out the noises around. There, in its centre Æthelred, his uncle, could be seen half slumped across his horse's back, clinging to the animal for his very life. The Mercian Lord held tight a gauntleted hand pressing hard onto a gaping wound across the top half of his chest where he had instinctively removed the stinging head of a Viking's hand axe, allowing it to drop onto the ravaged ground beneath him, but not before killing the axe's bearer with the same blade, following it with the pommel of his own sword which had smashed through the helmless skull and left his attacker dying in the bloody ground where he would be finished off by the hooves of the Ealdormann's angered mount.

Æthelred's hand still managed to grip tight his sword despite the obvious pain that now wreaked its way through his upper body, the pommel still dripped with the congealing remnants of the Dane's head as his fingers struggled, in near panic, to stem the flow of his own leakage glistening dark as it pumped out over tarnished steel and down the left side of his horse's tabard. He glanced out towards Æthelstan, his expression showing the seriousness of the wound as the numbness of the blow began to wear away and sheer pain started to strike its way through every nerve. Æthelstan needed to reach his uncle's side without delay.

Abrecan flew into the gallop pushing her way through the remaining Huscarl, parting her way through the Danish onslaught with growing authority and Æthelflæd shouted an ignored warning.

'Could she not see that it was her own Lord in the gravest of danger?'

He hacked, chopped, cut, and rammed his way through the enemy's flanks dispatching the blade of his Grandfather's sword in every direction to clear his path where, the urgency of his errand would show the intent of his aid. He refused to look back in answer to her calls, this was not the time to offer his enemy his 'blind' side, nevertheless he hoped, no, he knew that Æthelflæd's presence would be as close as that of his Huscarl...

The battle had come to its peak.

The full numbers of both sides were now in the fight, even the reserves had been committed, any thoughts of leaving that arena would only result in certain death, to anyone, on any side.

The noise, the smell, the sights, even the putrefying taste of the fight itself had reached its limit. The scene was like a vision from the infernal pits of the underworld. Every man, woman, even children had been thrown in to make up the numbers that now tore, ripped, stabbed, and sliced through the first body within reach, often failing to recognise an ally, or even a neighbour, often there had not been time to look, sometimes there had not been time to care. All on Hel's field now fought as rabid dogs, like men possessed, like the berserkers of old, to kill dead the man in front, or to the side, or to the rear, and to stay firm upon both feet, and miss the blade of the next attack.

To stay alive.

No man at such a time ever thought of the loyalties to a King, or a Land or even to the brother to his left or right, all a person thought of at such a time was his own selfish need to survive.

...A flurry of enemy bolts flew to their left offering no immediate danger, nevertheless the intent was there as Danish archers recognised their valued target and hastily reloaded their hard-wood quarrels into the tautness of leather draw-strings. Æthelflæd scrutinised the group as they moved further right to correct their distance and improve their aim, she hurriedly bawled an Order to her bowmen, they would now deal with the problem.

With the greatest difficulty, and at more than one instance near to failure, Æthelstan eventually broke through the oncoming 'Scyttisc' advances at last able to sight his mount alongside that of his uncle, with barely enough time to save him from completing his fall to the ground, averting further injury.

"Stillan thee Bregu, stillan" he managed a whisper, so violent had been his charge, so defiant had been his adversaries, that in the shortest space of time he had expelled what little energy he had remaining, smashing, and lunging at anything that had dared to stand in his way.

Dehydration and near exhaustion, added to the painful strains and bruising's that covered his body, flooded through his limbs, yet there was no time for rest. Drifting from semi consciousness a Viking bolt whisked beneath his helm, passing by his left cheek, leaving behind a stinging mark that seeped into his partial stubble, standing out vividly against his blondness. His head clouded with that which might have been while his body still lacked the energy to break free of its trancelike state, he knew once again he offered an open target to any... Then, amidst the odours of the battle's dead he caught again the welcome scent of fresh honeysuckle and crushed blackberry leaf from nowhere in that world. Instantly his thoughts were shaken back to the quest at hand.

With the Huscarl protection finally in place, and a dozen Thegns bringing their aid to his side Æthelstan was finally able to sheath his own dripping blade. With both arms now free he lifted his injured Lord back upon saddle and, despite the unsteadiness of their excited animals, managed to keep Æthelred erect, but not without a struggle to keep himself upright.

With half a hand Æthelstan pulled to a sit his uncle's lifeless torso roughly shaking the collar of his jerkin, painfully dragging his senses into reality, "Strength Bregu, keep thy strength."

The sharpest single worded command was interrupted by a single wisp as the air was split by a score of Mercian arrows, and the growing threat against them was reduced within an instant. What few remained of the Ealdormann's battered but still mounted Huscarl had gathered around the pair relieving the young Thegn of their master's weight, with a newly found energy Æthelstan instinctively unsheathed his sword raising the blade skyward, his voice carried loud to any who were close enough to hear his words...

"To the 'fyrdwic'..." he bellowed aggressively "to the fyrdwic." A 'servant at arms' nodded in compliance as he escorted away his wounded commander. The remnants of the tattered guard followed alertly, all protected by the spearmen of many loyal Thegns.

Æthelred's fight was now over for that day, maybe for every day.

"It shall not be an easy wound My Lady" as she rode alongside.

"There be no such thing" came her answer, "Our Lord Æthelred never did observe the easiest of ways, for anything." The smile which followed betrayed the doubtful hope in her words.

Still the battle continued...

It was as if the enemy was refusing to die, no matter how many fell their numbers never seemed to decrease the continued push into their own ranks. There were now no reserve forces on either side, no secreted companies concealed behind a hyrst or within a glade awaiting the final minutes to step out and inflict the ultimate onslaught and change the tide of the battle, even so their enemies would just not die.

Amid the swarming rings of the Northman's shields, the specifically embroidered dress of the Hibernian and the chequered costumes of the mercenaries, precisely central to the fight, could be seen ragged banners, still held high by heavily outnumbered Kentish men now frantically protecting themselves against the vast numbers sent to destroy them. The enemy completely overwhelmed them.

A group of dark skinned warriors, who had originated from a land many weeks away to the south but now fought beneath the Raven's banner, ferociously tore into the men of Kent as they had tried to regroup, to make more difficult their 'easy' slaughter. Without an ally close enough to offer aid their efforts were about to be sacrificed for better things...

...Until Jutish battle horns tore out their warnings through the denseness of the slaughter, then vigorously answered by a distant tune, immediately followed by the curdling screams of two hundred spearmen from the old realms that were once those of the 'Suthseaxisc'.

The descendants of Ælle, whose line went back five centuries, were led by a red haired one-eyed Thegn who had always claimed, around the hearth fires, to have been a bastard from the very loins of the infamous Ragnar Lothbrok. He encouraged his followers with enthusiasm and rugged audacity as he battered and blundered his way through the Danish ranks, on into those of the 'dark skins' then further until he had reached the depleted numbers of his fellow countrymen.

Too close for the arrows and javelins the fighting was now down to the short lances and the blades of all shapes used to slice their way through a hastily erected shield wall towards the men of Kent. With brutal desperation, they forced open a corridor into the centre of the fight and a place alongside their beleaguered companions, only then to find that they too were now embroiled in the same trap.

Shoulder to shoulder they fought.

Side by side and back against back, cousin reached cousin and neighbour collapsed alongside neighbour. Their banners were swallowed in the turmoil mercilessly unleashed by those who fought beneath the Raven's stare which had now 'swamped' its way through the weakened defences, overrunning the battle's heart.

Wessex bowmen let loose their projectiles, reclaiming others from corpse and ground as their own quivers had emptied, all attempts to assist were hopeless. Spearmen attempted to open another corridor with their typical 'vee' shaped shield wall to spearhead their attack into a new flank, but they too were beaten back without success, too great a risk at such a stage would be their commitment into that futile engagement that had been strangely engineered by the remaining half- king. For once in his reign Eowils had made a commander's decision and at the wrong time for the English it seemed to be working, taking hold the advantage and turning it against his enemy.

All attempts of a rescue or at least reinforcement had failed, no further efforts would be chanced, and the Kentish men would fall alongside the Saxons of the South, and a sea of Viking men at arms would flood across their battered corpses drowning any further attempts of liberation.

'There lie the men of the south, and may the old God Seaxneat now welcome their spirits to settle forever in the Halls of their Forefathers.'

As his neck twisted and stretched to the left and then to the right, massaging the muscles along his spine, caressing the bruises and eventually finding relief from a battering with a Danish shield edge, Æthelstan's glances located a hillock and as he focussed the sight that confronted him sickened his stomach.

A dozen or so Preosts, clerics or similarly intentioned individuals who had hailed from the local parishes of the surrounding homesteads, all assembled in a neat Order 'ghosting' the shape of the cross repetitiously in the ungodly air of the battle, blessing those who marched forward to their deaths, condemning to Hel those who opposed them. There was no place in his battles for such men, such pious hypocrisy, such blasphemy, and he turned from their sight in disgust.

Away from such pretence he watched on, cursing as good men fell to the massacre, desperate to do anything to turn the tide, and it was then, at that time, when he had allowed his attentions to once more drop from the battle, that Æthelstan felt the dullest of blows to the rear of his right shoulder precisely at the point of his earlier injury, painful enough to bring out the sharpest scream as the impact stole his breath, strong enough as it pushed his body hard against the horse's neck startling the animal to surge forward into a short gallop.

He had let his guard slip again. Permitted his enemy the advantage. Just for the slight of a second, but that was all it had taken. He moaned again trying to check the extent of his injury and taking a fresh breath in relief, it could have been worse.

Fortune in that case most definitely favoured the brave, on that occasion at least, Abrecan's shortest gallop had certainly saved the life of a future King.

He managed a turn despite his new pain, pushing himself upright, clenching tighter the hilt of his sword, coming face to face with his attacker.

The fatted bulk of the last enemy King had picked out Æthelstan amidst the battle, seized the opportunity and rode in from behind, launching his attack. Eowils had excitedly lashed out against his opponent in the heat of a second, but it was hurried and unthought and for the Mercian's good fortune that his attacker was as useless as his dead counter-part misjudging his lunge, over-balancing in his own saddle only to catch the Ætheling with the flatness of the blade, doing nothing more than painfully winding him. Abrecan's sense to gallop forward had lost the Northumbrian any significant advantage, denying him the time to correct his aim, twist his blade, and repeat the assault.

Close by and ever vigilant had been the Lady Æthelflæd. She had witnessed the wasted assault whilst dispatching another aggressor into the next world with spear and blade. Instinctively she came to his aid, dug hard her heels, hastily urging her mount forward into a reflexed attack from the left and in the same action had punched fiercely through the Dane's 'herklæði' with the sharpest of spear points, driving deep the metal into his lower back through whatever organs it met and out through the quivering mass of bulked fat that had made up that 'kingly' stomach.

Without hesitation, in an act to make certain, and with the force of any man, she smashed her painted shield into the Danish side freeing the spear's point from the wound's vacuum hailing a noisy 'gushhhhh' as it left the gaping hole, without delay she repeated the act driving the spear once more into the lower stomach twisting the shaft twice before pulling it free. Two wounds, both equally fatal, the first had been for her husband, the second, 'just in case'.

Bulging eyes of an oversized King widened to bursting as he struggled to remain conscious. Despite the pain, he leered at Æthelflæd's 'soft complexion', almost salivating over her beauty, was his destiny that day also to be cursed by the want of a woman?

Fear and shock streamed across his sallow cheeks as a gusher of arterial blood escaped from his trembling lips, spilling down his unkempt beard, over a winded chest staining the Raven's Head emblazoned upon his front.

Eowils looked about in disbelief. He had thought it certain that following Halfden's death and that too of his cousin Scurfa on the previous day, and five Jarls also, including Ingwaer a second brother earlier that day, his own survival had been more than guaranteed, if only by sheer chance. 'How could two shared Kings, three brothers and so many Jarls be slain in the same fight?', Where were their Gods? ...

Weakening rapidly his body sloped clumsily to the right becoming more unbalanced, finally slipping gracelessly from the saddle, smashing his withering form pathetically onto the ground splashing mud, blood, and grime onto his distorted expression. The horse stamped hard upon the turf in welcome relief from such a bulk and the last northern King to set his unwanted feet upon Woden's Field attempted to struggle impossibly to his knees.

As the life eased away Eowils stared upwards almost childlike into the eyes of the female knight, she, more so than her Lord had long since been the scourge of his miserable existence, all the way through to its now bitterly undignified ending.

The Mercian Lady tore her gaze defiantly from her victim and stared deep into the eyes of her much thought after protégé visually checking him for any injury, her flick of a smile told of her lack of sentiment, her words held back any emotion...

"One injury in this family be sufficient for this day."

Both Aunt and nephew turned their backs on the writhing body as it drew a final breath, attempting a feeble cry for mercy, but the haemorrhaging that continued to erupt 'gargled' away any further efforts and the King fell side wards, half rolled twice before falling rigidly still and dying in the bloodied plains of the Mercian Lands which he had mistakenly thought should be his with the easiest of taking.

As Eowils life had expired in his own pity, during the afternoon of the fifth day since Lammas, on a sunny August month, so too did the final threads of his dynasty and the reign of the 'twin kings' from the lands north of the Humber river which had started first in the year that had followed Alfred's death, by the killing of Aethelwold of Wessex, finally ending eight expensive years of continued warring, and with their deaths had vanished another threat to the future prosperity of Engle's Land.

As the dead King's body had continued to cool in the fading sunshine of a dismal afternoon the mixed armies of Scot, Hibernian Dane and Northumbrian Viking had started to fall in greater numbers. Their advantage had been lost through the tenacity of the English fighting man and the stalwart tactics of their leaders.

The mercenaries had been the first to suffer the quickest of endings, surrendering their ground the instant the incessant battering's of the native forces had weakened their last lines of defence. Shield walls had been splintered into a non-existence, the first sign of defeat. The Saxon had not invested too much in the way of mounted weapon men, but what few there were had merged with the Knights of Mercia and rampaged their strengths through the lines of disarray, efficiently dispersing their enemy into smaller, less volatile groups, allowing the infantry from the Shires easy targets to dispel with blade and bolt, arrow and spear point, club and fist, whatever, anything which held the ability to kill.....and kill they continued to do until the numbers that survived were not worth the count.

It would have been more than difficult to show anything which may have been remotely mistaken for sympathy towards of any kind after taking part in the aggressive destruction of an enemy over a two-day battle where more than eight thousand men, and many women had sacrificed their lives to wage a fight for or against the whim of an idiotic pair of 'would-be' Kings.

Yet, as the Lady Æthelflæd had knelt at the side of the body that almost resembled her husband, she offered as much concern that her breaking heart could summon. As he lay in increasing discomfort and obvious torment upon the floor of a hastily re-erected night tent her eyes fixed magnetically onto his naked chest, at the extensive 'hack' that was splitting his shoulder away from the rest of his body. His breostnett could not be completely removed for fear of causing further damage, even though its presence added further complications to the horrific wound. Blood oozed unendingly through a neatly folded but grubby sheet, that had been desperately 'stuffed' into the pulsating 'gape', easing out through its weave onto the grassy floor turning the clean green into a bloody mess of crimson froth. Vibrantly into the battle's air his screams were instantly absorbed into the cries of hundreds more that lay about injured, wounded, and dying, and those who were so near to their end that they had been set aside, to suffer their final minutes in that world, alone.

The Preosts, cleric and other ranks of Holy men moved from litter to stretcher passing the last rites to those who wished to listen as they were relieved of a purse or trinket, for the good of those 'less' fortunate. How could anyone be less fortunate than those who writhed at their feet, in Hel's torment of unstoppable agony until a greater power than they had permitted an end to such misery, and the corpse then lay still at their feet, and the cleric moved on to the next.

The injured now covered the largest area within that thorny fence, the sounds of the 'after-war' continued to increase as hundreds more were carried or dragged in to receive what little aid was on offer.

As had been expected, Edward had exercised his right as Victor and ordered the raising of the 'sigethuf' before the battle had fully ceased, to show all that the day's glory lay with the armies of the Anglo-Saxons and their allies, but to any other who had just ventured upon that field, victory would have been the furthest thought from their mind.

The fighting was not completely over.

The Danish fleet had been burnt to ashes cutting off any escape to their homelands meaning the skirmishes would continue for several days as pockets of resistance held out in the lowlands, the peak lands, and the glades and on into the surrounding shires. Desperate men fleeing for their lives, scrapping for every step to survive a few seconds more. The worst part of any battle was hunting down such desperate men, like wounded boar there could be only one outcome for them.

As the threats fell away from the decimated field the last of the arrows did the same and the King rode his tired mount into the centre of the camp shaking a saddened head as his eyes met those of the injured. Wounded men of Wessex were still being brought together, as were Æthelflæd's warrior women, and allies from the furthest shires who had flocked to His 'call'.

"So many" he had thought, "but then, there was always so many".

And then came the duty that only a King could carry out and still hope in the keeping of good conscience.

Leofric, a Shire Reeve from Oxenford ran wearily to the side of his King's horse removing his spanghelm and lowering his head in respect. His spearpoint dripping as the coolest of air blew welcomingly through his matted locks sending a brief chill down his spine, it was then that he realised, as the eve's cool caught his brow, that the battle, no, that the war was over. He stretched his neck and caught the eyes of his King...

"Bregu, the enemy that remain standing?"

Edward's eyes closed as his head dropped for an instant, the reply was silent but expected.

"And their wounded?"

The eyes shut momentarily once more, the Order was given.

The Reeve sighed and slumped his shoulders, this was the part of a battle that no single person would relish. He turned from his Lord and stared out to where a collection of tinder and bracken had already been started and with little remorse he moved his left hand to steady his sheathed sword and broke into a trot to relay the command....

There was no room in the 'laecehus' for what remained of the hundreds of enemy wounded, it did not work that way. Those of the injured who were not put to their deaths immediately on the outskirts of the makeshift burg were left to bleed out in horrid suffering as the scavengers and crones sliced their way through the pitiful numbers robbing the dead of anything valuable, from either side.

Remaining mercenaries who had managed to evade the blade now begged to be freed claiming they would 'turn' their loyalties against the Dane, for the cost of a King's shilling. They received no shilling, just the point of a spear or edge of a blade, an arrow was too costly to dispatch. The kind of man who would turn sides against a previous employer would, on any future occasion, do the same just as quickly should the need arise.

Danes, who claimed to be of privileged blood, or at the very least, of some noble value had also asked for mercy, and on many previous occasions had been granted the 'privilege of ransom', but there would be no such privileges that day.

Edward's words were final. "No Dane, or other who has set his foot upon these lands with hostile intent shall be permitted to leave that field." Too well had he, and before him his Father, learned to their detriment that there was always the risk that a freed prisoner would return another day with a mightier army. His men came first, neither the lives of good Anglo-Saxons nor their allies would be jeopardised by paying aid to an enemy.

Total annihilation was the deterrent that would be sent from Woden's Field along with the solemn promise that the same reward awaited any other Jarl, Hibernian King or Pictish chieftain who thought to chance his own destiny.

"What sort of dream be that?" Odin spoke,

"In which just before the day broke

I thought I cleared the Val hall

for the coming of slain men?

I awakened the Einherjar

bade the Valkyries to rise,

to strew the benches and scour the mead calics.

Wine to carry as for a King's coming

here to me I expect Heroes coming from the Lands

of Men, certain great ones, so glad is my heart…"

By Gunnhild, on the death bed of her husband, Eric Bloodaxe.

CHAPTER 5

At the closing of the battle's second day at a place later named 'Teotta Halh,' the sun had started to fade as if lowering her radiant head in respect for those who had fallen. The first of the funeral pyres had initiated their glow and as more bracken and twigs and tinder were packed tightly beneath even more corpses King Edward stepped reluctantly into the centre of what would soon become, a burning ring.

Already the hint of darkness had spread the glow everywhere, sending the shadows of those who had gathered deep towards the horizon, as the fires grew more intense they took away the day's own light. Fidgeting ceased, whispers quietened, all were still as those who could turned to face their King.

For the time being, the thought of victory and any celebrations that would come with it were disregarded as the King raised his head and lowered his eyes. In a second movement, he lifted high his sword upwards and straight, towards the Halls of the Slain, then loud, and clear, and briefly he started to speak...

"That which hath been granted to us, through the blood of our forefathers, must truly be safeguarded through the blood of their sons."

...Then, as the wind began to sweep away the souls of the glorious fallen, skywards towards another life, his head dropped upon his chest in a moment of saddened respect. Anyone close may have caught sight of a tear trembling its way down a noble cheek, so many dead would bring many tears over the days that would follow. They would now 'all' be greeted by the 'spirits of the waiting,' who would guide them into the Golden Fields of their afterlife, to rest deservedly in eternal peace...

After a respectful pause paid by those fortunate enough to do so, Æthelflæd humbly took the place of her King...

Much sterner than her brother she could hold back any sign of a tear, she had more practice, yet she felt his sadness as she caught a breath and stared deeply across the fields of dead…

"So… may the voices of our children's children still speak of their names with pride…." then she too lowered her head joining her brother in silent prayer, as did those who now stood around the perimeter also in a silence that seemed to drift on forever as each of the dead were remembered in what would not be their final prayer.

As the short rituals neared completion, the Preosts were permitted to enter the field to bless those whom 'they' thought of as deserving and curse those they thought were not, even they would find difficulty in justifying their religion.

Away from the heat of the biting flames, the stench of burning flesh, and the wailing of saddened kinfolk, the knights of Mercia had assembled with their leaders and sauntered their way to the bases of the camp fires where bowls and pales of the hottest water had been laid out, alongside bowls and pales of the coldest. Now would begin the Mercian's customary ritual which had proceeded every battle since the days when fighting had become Man's habit.

The knights gathered without Order, to cleanse the battle's filth from their shields, to repair and ready their weapons. It was a task that would never be left to the serfs or ernes, but a task for each individual, where, during that ritualistic act a solemn and strict silence would be observed as each man remembered every possible second of the fight, committing their exploits to memory, reliving in their thoughts the slaughtering, the beating, the winning and the losing so as to improve upon their own abilities, for the next time, because of course there would be a next time, there 'always' would be a next time.

As they cleaned and honed their weapons until they were as excellent as they could be, although ignored by many, a priest or cleric would wander amongst them whispering and blessing in poorly spoken Latin, and forgiving in the name of their unseen God, whilst in the minds of each knight the names of the absent would be silently recalled, never to be forgotten.

When that process had been completed and weapons readied they would turn to their horses, and begin to attend to their needs with balms and salves for cuts and wounds, whispering gentle words of gratitude for the animal's strength and loyalty during the fight, and the bond between horse and knight would be cemented even deeper…

Legends of the Mercian Knights were famous throughout their lands, also the lands of their enemies. No man, or woman would ever remain behind after a battle, whatever the outcome. The spirits of their dead would be released in an energy of pyres for the riders and their mounts, for no warrior would ever contemplate leaving his trusted animal. It was driven into their souls, that should a rider fall his trusted mount would continue within the glorious ranks, seeking a fate of equal glory. Then legend said, that in a final breath, a golden tear could be seen trickling from a tired eye as its soul met again with that of its knight, to ride then together through eternity, in the golden fields of Glassisvellir…Later into that sorrowful eve, before the darkness had chanced to cover the scars of war, more than five hundred horses had shed their final tears, in those peaceful fields that would always remain with the old Gods.

…And as the night had completely won its own battle, after the beacons had started to burn down, providing just enough light still to remind all of their meaning, Æthelstan sat at the base of his night tent, a calic of spiced goat's milk in one hand, the bloodied helm of Halfden in the other…

Both had been presented to him by his Father who had expressed his relief for his son's safety…

…Edward had passed a noble, yet nevertheless grubby thumb meaningfully across his son's blooded cheek and smiled, "Marked in battle, by the battle…." He looked deeper into the cold eyes and forced a smile "…it be a good scar, and a true scar. Each morning when thou wake ye shall be reminded of this battle at Woden's Fyld and of all that hath been done here, and know ye that in thy heart the taking of an enemy life…" Edward swallowed in correction, "…Nay, the taking of any life be the easiest of things to do, yet the hardiest of things to forget."

He smiled again towards his son continuing to express the pride he held.

"The helms of two Kings and many Jarls shall grant us peace from the north, and it be only right that we should both share the prize, even though we may not yet share their lands..." It was then that the King had passed the dented helm to his son. "...A token. To remember thy first victory, and the killing of thy first King. Ye must never forget that such a fate may await any man whoever he be, even thee my son, even thee."

Æthelstan's cheeks reddened slightly and a cold shiver travelled down his spine as he remembered his own lapse, 'Æthelflæd' he thought thankfully.

"One day Your Grace..." Æthelstan choked and corrected himself "Father..."

He would always be his Father before his King and Edward interrupted "...Maybe those lands to the north should remain severed, in exile, until a younger man may stand in my stead. From this day onwards, in the shadow if thy dearest Mother, I shall declare to all that ye be known no longer as a King's Thegn, nor as a King's son, but as Ætheling, Ætheling of these lands that ye love so much and still name Mercia...With it ye shall serve alongside my own sister, as always, until her Lord shall recover or pass from these lands, as be his destiny."

"Bregu..." A pause as Æthelstan cleared his own emotions. A status within the House of Mercia. It had been everything he had ever wanted, it would be his most precious. "...and as for those northern lands. They may await the actions of another day for there be no hurry this day for further slaughter, in any place."

The King nodded in silent agreement, one battle at a time...and had not that battle been his most important to win, maybe even since that great battle at Holme, or possibly even those battles won by his own Father.

Æthelstan watched with sympathy and feeling as the tired shadow of his King struggled to his tired feet and limped across the clearing before vanishing behind the dusty canopies of the Royal tent, then he glanced deeper into the hectic atmosphere of the camp, on such a night when celebrations and feastings would have been raucously welcomed by other armies, the mood throughout that field was one of sorrow and fear, pain, and guilt...

The sentinels had been doubled, even quadrupled in some places, for many a time had passed when there had been, on the first night after a battle's winning, groups of a defeated enemy who had managed to evade death, cornered in a foreign field, robbed of their booty, thieved of their pride, in a final bid for their freedom, or just in revenge for the deaths of their brothers they had attacked the victor's camp whilst they feasted over the spoils, quickly killing many, even a King. A war that had been won through such a battle may never truly be over for many days, sometimes longer.

...Dying, and those who still queued to join them cluttered every vacant corner of the once crisp grassland. Corpses were still being placed upon freshly stocked pyres, and would continue to be long into the night. The flames would again begin their dance deep into the darkening gloom forming strange looking silhouettes that many had sworn were the spirits of the fallen searching their way free from that land of mortality to the valleys of their forefathers where they hoped for eternal peace. Others, who believed differently had said that the shadows belonged to the tortured souls of those who did not wish to leave the Land of Men and were searching desperately for one final chance to remain, before being carried off into the cold blackness, never to be seen again.

Ealdfrith was his chosen second and closest friend.

They had known each other forever meaning such trivial things such as rank, and title had rarely mattered, to either of them, yet respect had always been shown. Æthelstan had been disturbed from the deepest of daydreams as Ealdfrith had dropped to his side, painfully crushing an arm as he did so. In the combat's frenzy, his hose had been torn so badly they were now beyond the talents of the most gifted of seamstresses, his jerkin had also been ripped but that would repair, and he had lost his spanghelm, yet that was less of a worry there were so many helms that now lay spare he could choose a different one for each day.

Æthelstan shuffled into a more comfortable position freeing his newly crushed arm and glancing down at a poorly tied, blood stained, and filthy cloth wrapped loosely around Ealdfrith's forearm. Desperately he failed to conceal a grin which only resulted in a bout of laughter at the other's obvious misfortune...

Æthelstan laughed "I see at least one Orc bested thee my friend?"

"Nay Bregu. T'was no more than a mere accident, a slip, no more..." toying needlessly with the make-shift bandage "...besides, the maids at court shall find it a 'lucky' wound, and I see someone had dared to spoil thy looks."

Æthelstan grinned sallowly and wiped the drizzling blood from his cheek "It seems we both have suffered the same misfortune"

Their sorrow and fatigue gave way momentarily to a sniggering bout of laughter, soft enough to maintain respect for a passing litter, but their solemn expressions quickly returned as guilt for such humour was realised simultaneously with a thousand visions of the battle awaking their bitterest memories...

"Shall not these files of our dead ever cease" Ealdfrith sighed, "T'is truth that this be our first real fight, yet surely so many good men have never fallen in one battle?"

"By the grace of some God Ealdfrith, we have survived such rage. A rage which the Ealdor Fyerdmann whisper to be the fiercest since those fought even in Ælfred's day."

Ealdfrith pulled tighter his bandage to stem a modest seepage as Æthelstan shook his head in dis-belief at his companion's overreaction to such a minor 'graze'.

Bandage adjusted Ealdfrith continued, "Surely all battles must seem fierce and damaging, but it not be until such a fight such as this that it be proven how deadly man's anger may be. I be no 'wise man' Bregu, yet even I concede that there will ne'er be an end to such fighting...."

"The only end shall be with the final battle which may be so fierce that none shall walk free, not even those to do the counting of the dead." Æthelstan sat forward shocked by his own response. He slipped the dead King's helm into a tattered leather satchel and pushed it guiltily beneath the tent's wall, out of his sight, it meant nothing more to him than a trophy.

"Then Bregu, for what purpose do we then serve, to be born just to wage a war upon our neighbours?"

"Then maybe the teachings of the White Christ and his one God, this, this Father of everything, be nought other than an invented tale. Maybe it be that the Lands of Woden All Father be the only true way, the right way, and we be here for no more than their pleasure, as they watch us do battle and die amongst ourselves whilst they feast and drink and wager the outcome in the golden lands of our forefathers."

Struggling with tired and aching limbs, as did all, Ealdfrith rose unsteadily to his feet and stared down once again as his Lord, still insisting on cradling his wound, and he winced more than once as he peeled back the cloth to look once again at the 'scratch'.

Æthelstan shook his head "It be a greater man than I to answer such questions, but we must remain thankful to whoever watches over us, that we have been spared on this sad day."

As Ealdfrith stretched out his good hand to aid his friend to his feet, both looked out across the glowing plains, sharing the same thoughts and feelings as they studied what was now no more than a ruined and pitiful field lighted only by the unending pyres that burned and crackled their golden embers high into the night's shadows. They strolled aimlessly towards the cooking tent shaking their heads at the barrage of unanswered questions that flooded their minds. One thought that they would forever hold in common, along with every man and woman still capable of thinking, 'that there was more fighting yet to come, much more fighting, before the time would eventually fall for their own pyres to light up an evening's sky'.

For the best part of the remaining night, until it was too dark to see the next footstep, the chroniclers would record that Æthelstan had made his way through the carcasses and remnants of the battle alone, murmuring quietly to himself in the insufficient moonlight that had tried its very best to hide from the grim sights below. Serfs and huscarl went to him with torch and drink but were keenly dismissed and ordered to leave him in his own company.

Some 'scribes', who had made it their task to document the events wrote that 'He had wandered freely, alone in that field of the slaughterer's fight, talking with none but himself for many hours....' Others added '.... Or maybe He spoke to the spirits of the fallen, thanking them for their selfless sacrifice, assuring them that their deaths would not pass in vain, promising that their kinfolk would be cared for now that they were alone.' It was an act that many a commander had carried out after such a battle, and an action that many more would continue to do after the countless battles that were yet to follow.

One chronicler, a Breton Abbot who had been visiting a nearby Minster, travelling by the name of Erwan, wrote that 'He had witnessed the heir to the Saxon throne praying for the souls of their dead. Insuring them that if their new God truly did not exist, then their spirits would be gratefully accepted in the Halls of their Forefathers and that they should keep ready his place in the lines of those who were never to be forgotten...'

There had been a second priest by the name of Godwyn, from the Minster of Medulf, who had made it his personal quest to record as much of Æthelstan's life as he were able and had created the historical diary since the earliest years. Godwyn had detailed the important, as well as the trivial at the secret bequest of King Edward who was himself at that time Ætheling to those Lands then ruled over by Ælfred. He wrote in the Latin words, in a heavy calf skin book embossed with the finest of gold lettering, 'That the new Ætheling, Æthelstan, was speaking to the spirit of Ælfred, whose heavenly presence constantly watched over his Grandson and had been congratulating him on the success of his first battle, promising again his word to always watch over his son's heir in the many battles that were yet to follow.' It would not have been the first account of such a conversation with the dead King, neither would it be the last.

Half way through the following morning, the victorious, yet heavily depleted armies of the Engle, Saxon, Jute, Lombards, Frisians and many other ancient groups who served the Wessex King assembled beneath their appropriate banners within their specific 'Houses' before the start of the long march back to their 'homely shires'.

The Royal contingent, which consisted of anyone above the title of Ceorl, had collected themselves at the centre of the formation....

The air that day was as much as any other except that it carried a much sweeter smell than previous morning owing partly to their victory, and an easterly breeze that not only kept the climate a little cooler but also swept higher the smoke streams from the remaining fires that would burn into a second week before they were fully extinguished, the last of the corpses turning finally into ashes.

The stench of burning flesh was a stench that was known to all men, suffocating and horrid it stuck for days in the back of a throat, almost tasting like a roasted chicken, only more sickly and sweeter, the easterly breeze was welcome.

Thickly greying clouds swung in across the eastern ridge covering that tarnished plain with a semi shade that threatened at any time to erupt into a torrential storm urging all for the need to hasten, take their leave forever from that saddened place always to be named Woden's fyld. The coming downpours would be nature's own means of washing away the signs of Man's inborn cruelty that had stained away the greenery and defiled the beauty of yet another season, men stoked higher the pyres hoping to out do the rains.

...It had remained the duty of Edward, as King of the Anglo-Saxon people and Head of the House of Wessex to motion his horse a few steps forward out of line, so that he sat alone, easily recognisable from the most distant ranks. The banner of the Golden Wyvern flapped aggressively overhead, as did the 'gupfanas' of other Houses, but more prominently that day, snapping higher in the breeze than any other, was the 'sigethuf', the victory banner that was carried in the trail of the King by the proudest of Thegns.

To Edward's rear sat Æthelflæd showing her continued support for her brother despite the absence of Æthelred who would now be writhing in his own agonies as his wounds tore deeper, ingesting their infections as they ate hungrily into the flesh of his deteriorating body. With God's grace, he would now be in the hands of Tamworth's physicians.

Edward's first attentions had been drawn to the vast numbers of men, and women, even children, that still formed the fyrd. It had not been until then that he had realised how large a force he had originally assembled, and how vast were the numbers of injured and dead now missing from his ranks...

"As ye march back to thy Shires," he had opened, "where ye shall replace the tools of war for the tools of the mills and the fields and the smithy's fires, remember those who will not return with thee in body.... But shall always be with thee in spirit."

He spurred his mount and distanced himself from the Noble's line, glaring deeper at the remaining numbers of his 'fyrd'. Gone was the brightness of their armour, grey and torn was the once crisp colours of their clothing, missing were the cheerful expressions that, only two days previous had beamed within his mighty ranks. The King steadied again his horse as he fixed his eyes upon the blood-stained blaze of the Mercian banner that still flew defiantly in the chilling breeze.

"Min Eorlwerod!!! Westseaxe...Myrce, Geatas, Brytas and all thee who rode to join this fight from far away shires and realms that lie proudly and remain safely between the shores of this most noble of isles...

...Even though it be that we shall forever pray that such warring upon our lands be no more, and that our enemies, with God's kind grace, shall hopefully accept that Englisc ac Seaxisc land be no longer theirs for the taking, we must all realise the truth of the times in which we now live, in which we have always lived... That no sooner do we return to our 'cynnfolc' and the fylds and burgs of our shires it shall come to us yet again, the call to take up the arms of war and stand again together against another attempt to steal away from us our rightful lands...

...Our borders may soon change...The great burg at Lundenwic and Oxenaford shall now fall beneath the banners of Wessex, granted to the House of Wessex by my own sister's husband, as a better way to offer folk protection and safety should we again be called away to battle once again in their names..."

The stern expression that had spread across the face of his elder sister did not say that such a 'gift' had been offered freely, there was always payment to be made when assistance and ally be called upon by another 'House', even if such a 'House' be that of a brother who became a King over her because the new God insisted that she should be born a woman. Her 'gift' was expected payment, the result of a full night's bartering, finally granted in her husband's absence, on behalf of the Mercian people, in 'part' payment for their assured victory. She also knew that through the days to follow, more 'gifts' would be required, that was the way...would she not have insisted upon the same if she had sat in the place of her brother?

"...Yet borders within our realms be nought but a matter of treaty and organisation, to install and keep our laws because all of us here who dwell within such borders, noble and freeman alike are as one whether we be Wessex, Mercian, Jute, Bryton or Weales, we all be of one kind...we all now be Angelcynn..."

The closing speech of the Wessex King was greeted with a rapturous bout of cheering and screams of agreement, except of course from groups of Welshmen, and some Brytons who would always remain their own men regardless of whose army they gave service to.

Æthelstan was more cynical...

From within the centre of nobles he had whispered to Wulfhere and Ealdfrith too loudly. "They cheer not for the meaning of such words but for a hurried end to such a speech, so that they may be on their way sooner, back to the arms of a loving 'wif' and 'lytling', at such a moment they would cheer anyone."

His Father had heard. Half the fyrd had heard, but for once Edward had excused the criticism as an immature comment that he would soon learn to disguise and keep for the privacy of his own chambers. His son had fought well, made proud his family line, and their Forefathers would now know for certain that there was an Ætheling most worthy to succeed when Edward's own time arrived. Æthelstan could be permitted at least one indiscretion. Nevertheless, he had caught his Father's disappointment as he completed his 'whisper' and realising his outspokenness had fallen silent, almost ashamed. His complexion had blushed as it had never blushed before and only returned to its post battle paleness after a nod of forgiveness had been received. The 'boy' had only made the smallest of errors and it was in his nature to learn swiftly, could he not be seen regretting those words as soon as they had been spoken, despite those around him openly showing their agreement.

At last the fighting was over.

Victory was theirs and those who could were returning home. The battle had not been a war, but it had been the end to one that had been going on one way or the other for a little over eight years. It had been a battle of all battles and it had been brutal enough to be remembered. The fighting on the plains of Woden's Field and Tettenhall had kept over nine thousand men and women from ever returning to their shires. Highlighting against the glow of the pyres were the naked corpses of fifteen thousand Norse and Scots who had sailed and marched from every direction, now left for nothing more than the pleasures of the carrion that shadowed the withdrawal of that still mighty army.

At the bridge north of Quatt Malvern the bodies of more than two hundred mariners had been left to float their way down the river's current no more than food for the pike and leeches as their charcoaled ships lay as nothing other than burned out hulks smouldering in a morning's sun.

As they rode, all nobles within the company of nobles, along the outskirts of that northern plain, Æthelstan pulled Abrecan to an immediate halt. Those around him instinctively copying his unexpected actions, including the King.

All eyes fixed intently on the younger, surprised, and waiting his explanation.

There was anger in Æthelstan's face, but no rage, pity in his eyes but no sadness, excitement in his manner, but no delight. Eyes pierced deeply into his company, his behaviour was solemn, almost trance-like...

"To this very day our heritage hath been wild and brutal. Since our Forefathers trod their first steps onto the stony shores the time of the Saxon, Jute and Engle hath been both victorious and cruel."

He turned his face to the skies as if he sought inspiration to continue. His pause was almost long enough for those around him to show concern, when he did finally continue it was as if his words were being spoken to others elsewhere.

"Yet all those battles and fighting and cruelty and sorrow that hath brought us to this still uncertain time be nothing as to that which lies ahead in the years that will come. A cruel war be winding its way towards us."

Coincidentally, as his tone began to match his disturbing speech the greyest of skies loomed over-head causing an eerie chill to fill the air, a shiver to run down spines and nervousness to jump the horses...

"Soon, in these coming years our lands shall bare witness to a fight that shall be unlike any yet set against us..."

Even his horse brayed concern.

"This war shall tear every man from his woman, father from his son and Saxon from Dane. Such times shall be more than cruel, bringing with them pain and sacrifice worse than any of the sagas told around our hearth fires. It shall become more vicious than the coldest of winters and more violent than the worst of any Norse attacks."

He finally took a deep breath, almost choking on its dryness as he visually inspected those close as if he had forgotten where he had been and who he had been with, even his Father.

The 'spell' returned and the raised pitch of his voice startled some.

"But should we stand firm... stand together as one, then a victory over such terror shall be ours and we shall be the ones permitted to rejoice in a new and golden age... An age that shall become known to all as the time of the Engelcynn."

A well-disciplined silence remained within the confused assembly after such a prophetic speech. Some had thought the terrors of the battle had sent him a little mad as indeed it had to many others. But his Father had recognised the expressions beamed across the face of his eldest son and for a second felt envious as he had only witnessed such a thing on the face of his own Father, during similar speeches. Edward wished for a second that he had been more like Ælfred, more like Æthelstan, but jealousy soon turned to pride and realising the meaning of his son's words urged his horse to his side touching gently a shoulder, bringing his boy back to reality...

"To some thee speaks the strangest of words my son, yet my only fear be that thee are correct. Yet I feel such days shall be for the conscience of another King, maybe one such as thee...."

Then the King himself began to feel prophetic...

"T'is truth, that the taller a man stands in the paths of his enemies the more his enemies shall gather in their attempts to knock him down, maybe they will continue to gather and fall until there would be none remaining to stand against that man. Then, by such a result there would be none left for the tallest man to rule over."

"Then Your Grace, if such be our destiny then all warring would be for nought."

"Maybe thee be right. But maybe, if two or more Kings agree to stand together, and as tall as the other then maybe man shall wish no more to gather against them... Still such a day hath yet to come." Then Edward closed again the distance between them until the sides of their mounts rubbed away the day's dust from the dry hide. He reached across and whispered private words into the ear of his son...

"For such a war that ye speaks shall be for the fighting of a King such as thee shall one day become. I see it in thine eyes as did my own Father, thee shall be a true and great King...a glorious King, maybe more so than any before."

Amidst their tired smiles, a father and his son, a King, and his heir, moved to the head of their column, together, united leaders of a mighty dynasty, and continued in their return, to the welcome that would await them within Tamworth's gates.

Æthelflæd had watched intently from behind, as the bond between father and son had grown into something it had never yet been and a flood of jealousy surged through her body. Deep down she knew that there was little reason to fear, Æthelstan would always be hers, her brother would soon be on the move, back to his new wife and sons, just as soon as he had been fed and rested at her expense and, of course took collection of the agreed charters... Guilt dismissed all other feelings, did she not have more worrying concerns churning in the pits of her stomach, was not the life of her Lord and husband hanging dangerously in the balance?...

"The King came into the Hall,

Amongst his Knights all.

Forth he called Æthelbus his steward,

and to him spoke thus,

'Steward, take thou here my foundling

for to teach of thy mystery,

Of wood and river, and tug o' the harp

with his nails so sharp;

And teach him all that thou

listest that thou ever knowest;

Before me to carve,

and devise his fellows with us, other service.

Horn child, thou wouldst understand,

teach him of harp and song."

Romance of Horn Child.

CHAPTER 6.

910. Ragnall I Ivarrson, grandson of Ivar the Boneless seizes the throne of Dublin after years of roaming the western seas.

911. Hrolfr Ragnvaldsson, otherwise known as Rollo besieges Paris and is awarded the lands to be known as Normandy by Charles the Simple of France.

Whilst sadness, grief, and exhaustion, and maybe a little guilt had replaced the joyous feelings of victory and relief for their own survival, the various armies of the Anglo-Saxons marched solemnly from the ruined beauty of yet another once virgin plain. In every direction, they rode, on horse and in cart. They marched, or limped on foot, arm in arm, towards every Shire within the land, and the warmest of welcomes that would hopefully await within their homesteads, farms, and burhs. No man had been permitted his leave until the last of the funeral pyres had been set, and all watched with continued sorrow as the ashes of their fallen had smouldered away with the western breeze.

Those who would remain, within the heat of the 'adleg' would be the 'bæl weardian' to watch over the pyres until they had finished their burn, ensuring that the scavengers, who would always be watching from a place out of sight, remained in the distance until nothing more remained for them to thieve.

At that very same time, the hectic 'cycenen' of Tamworth were becoming dark and smoky, noisy, and alive with renewed commotion as 'cocas' and 'flaescmangereas' and 'baecereas' and their countless helpers busied themselves with the food preparations to celebrate the return of their ruling families, Thegns and victorious armies. The kitchens of every home, regardless of size, became a hive of activity to prepare the finest of meals and with it came the hope that their efforts would not be in vain. Ravenous appetites would be unending as they arrived from their campaign where everything, if anything, had been scrounged or scavenged or stolen from the land and its folk. But the food of the æcermann, eaten on the march, was no substitute for the delicacies that could be prepared in a Mercian kitchen.

An anxious cook tripped over a nervous baker who in turn stumbled over a scrounging dog who bit a slovenly serf who spilled a calic of cream over the 'water-boy' who was chastised by the same cook who had started the 'tumble', and all eventually settled back into the chaotic regime as excited preparations continued to pulsate through the cooking houses, and the constant delivery of yet more rations and supplies were hastily accepted, then sorted into their appropriate piles. The freshest and sweetest were set aside for the 'top' table, the lesser for the 'side-boards' and the lowest of all would be sent to the square where wives and mothers and daughters busied themselves with the same preparations of hope.

Æthelred, Ealdormann of Mercia had left the battle site the second a victory had been assured, and not a second earlier. His stubborn refusal to leave before the declaration had done nothing more than worsen his already critical wounds. But he was his King's man, he always had been and had vowed all those years ago, to the Father of his brother by marriage, that 'he would ne'er leave his King amid any war, whatever be the reason.' He had always been true to his word.

The physicians and apothecaries at the time had insisted that the basic services available in the field 'læcehus' did not offer suitable treatments to deal with such severe wounds. The truth be known, all had accepted the obvious and neither wanted the responsibility for allowing their Lord to die under their hands, his wounds were passed their treatments and would never heal. All were adamant in advising his return to Tamworth, without delay.

Many of the Huscarl who had survived the battle had suffered some sort of injury and despite most being weary, beyond the point of exhaustion, had marched through the night safeguarding their Lord under the dullest torch light, narrowly missing the dangers that would always be present in any post battle darkness. Through into the following morning, slowly and with the utmost care for Æthelred's welfare, without the smallest excuse for a stop over, excepting for a single occasion to change the left Shire of the main wagon. The proud animal had been taken lame in the fighting and within the first hour of night had been released from its suffering on the grassy bank of the hollow way.

The lack of grandeur portrayed by the carriage and escort would have told any of the urgency in their mission, if anyone had been near enough to see, but the sound of war and mention of 'levy' and 'fyrd' kept any who lacked the stomach to 'assemble' far away from view, even the 'wolf's heads', those outlawed and banished as 'utlaga' were themselves well away in the south, far away and out of sight from the Jarls and Reeves. The shield wall would have been the only place for them had they been caught.

Two messengers had ridden ahead on the fastest available mounts, riding as if 'Hel' herself gave chase, to warn the burg and ready those required for the arrival of their wounded Lord. The first, and older of the pair had fallen from horse before he had completed half of the journey, dead before hitting the ground from a bolt head of a Norse cross bow discharged in the penultimate seconds of the fighting. It had been lodged below his left armpit troubling him little after the shaft had been snapped away in a 'too late' defensive shield swipe, only to work itself deeper into his body as he urged more speed from his mount. The point had sliced an artery as the evening sun sank away and life left his mortal remains in the dust of the Mercian road, his eyes closed shut for the final time.

There had been little notice to prepare as was often the case, yet as the rickety old cart rattled its way through the fortified gates a cluster of serfs and other would-be carers descended upon the wounded Ealdormann as if their lives depended upon it.

Everyone wanted to take charge, but nobody wished the responsibility of their Lord's welfare yet after the exertions and struggles of being transferred from cart to litter and the upheaval of being man handled through doors and passageways, Æthelred's broken body was made as comfortable as possible in a 'ward' just off the Great Hall, facing west so he may watch the setting of the evening sun.

Taken aback by the putrid stench of already rotting flesh and congealed blood the 'læceas' inspected, examined, and pondered uselessly over the fatal wounds. They argued with their open leech books and slopping potions like children, as to the 'obvious' course of treatment each had differently recommended, but with no certainty for cure or commitment. The truth was evident to the most stupid present, none who considered themselves to be doctors had any hope in healing their Lord, and even less guarantee of his survival.

The Danish axe blade had smashed down through the 'healsbeorg' and 'byrnie' sliced on through the flaxen 'hemejje' into the flesh and bone, dissecting part of the rib cage and splintering the shoulder blade, all in that one single, but fatal sweep. The infections that swelled within the putrefying muscles and organs had been caused through filthy slivers of mail and jerking forced into the body as the blade sliced open the body, enhanced by the congealing marrow that spilled from the various fractures, until that itself had formed an infectious pulp.

Despite that which the chroniclers may have recorded, mainly to suit those who paid highly in one way or more for their 'scribblings', Ealdorman Æthelred was not a religious man, irrelevant to any beliefs of that 'New' faith continuously sounded by the family in which he had married into. He was a realist, always had been since the first time he had been forced to think for himself, at the age of six when he slew his first Dane with the split end of a shaft from a dead man's lance, and he would always remain a realist. If he could not see it, nor hear it or even taste it, then it never existed in the first place and could not bring to him any help, and in the same way do him any harm.

Still, Æthelred was not expected to survive a week.

Æthelflæd had wept at his side since the echoes of the army's return had spilled in through the open shutters, as wives had found their husbands and sisters their brothers and the screams of horror and fear pierced the sounds of joy as other wives did not find their husbands nor sisters their brothers, she had wept since then, and every day since.

And he had let her weep as she did not do so that often, and in the strangest of ways her tears had been a comfort to him to see her private show of weakness and sympathy. Æthelred was many years her senior, but that had made little difference to their relationship which had been born from the intelligent planning of a King long since dead. She herself had seen enough wounds to know that those that tortured her husband's will would be his final undoing. Growing weaker over the years his health had begun to yield to the afflictions of many unknown illnesses, also naturally there were the wounds of battle, many of them, some of which had never totally healed. Her husband's body no longer held the strength to win another fight.

And it did not.

But he did last through the festival of Yule, into the following year, passed the time when Baldur's Bane had finished its sprouting from the bark of the 'Æppel beam', but only just.

Æthelred Langlocc, Lord of Mercia passed into his after-life during the week that followed the festivities that would normally have welcomed the New Year. In a drunken stupor from a continuously full calic of the finest wines, in the arms of his Lady and a saddened Æthelstan soberly at his side, the only son he had ever wished to be his own.

The apothecaries had poorly disguised the foul smell that continuously swept free through Æthelred's ever-bloodied wraps. The salves and scents from herbs and potions were sufficient only to offer the slightest of distractions, so the dying man's final speech was witnessed by the fewest, and went almost unheard.

"Æthelstan..." He had strained to croak the name with everything that was left in him the pain in his eyes telling of the torment that resonated through his crippled body.

"Æthelstan..." after another half-breath, and the saddened Thegn leant across the body of his dying Uncle, ignoring the stench.

His free hand trembled raising from the flaxen sheet.

"If I had been blessed...with a son such as thee... then no more pride...could be shown than that.... which I now show...."

Tears were exchanged and quickly hidden away and the weeping of Æthelflæd accompanied them both as they delicately embraced each other.

Æthelred's voice was becoming shallower, harder to hear, but it still was not in him to concede, not yet.

"Thee hath a great destiny...to fulfil my boy, and at the side of My Lady thee shall start."

Again, he struggled for breath, what little he had managed to inhale would not be sufficient to keep him alive for much longer. His voice had grown coarse and dry and a crimson stream of saliva and puss bubbled in and out over his lips as he strained to be heard.

"All of them know so...that within thy veins..." and his eyes began to bulge from their sockets. "Within thy veins, thee carries a blood line so ancient within these shores that there be no scribblings of its record..." a desperate cough brought a splattering of thick blood from his throat and he coughed again to avoid choking. "Thine own Mother..." he continued. "...descended from the lines of the ancient ones...who first began these lands...passed down to thee the noble blood that flowed mightily and victorious through those forgotten times."

Almost unconscious, vision almost gone, and the want for everlasting relief taking its hold he spoke his last.

"Thee carries within thee...the blood of the Brython...as well as that of the Engle and Saxon too...and with it...the strains and gifts...of the ancient ones from the north...Do not waste these gifted things..."

The dying man battled against his fading strengths yet still managed to prod a shaking fist into Æthelstan's chest pushing towards his heart "...And when the time comes, and all seems lost, such gifts shall come to thee, so...use them wisely without selfish..."

Æthelstan did everything possible to restrain his sadness in the presence of one so close, and so nearly dead. His sadness choked back any thought of words, all that could be managed was a nod in agreement even though he had not understood fully the meaning of his uncle's words. Fingers that had dug deep into the younger man's forearm as the words of a dying man had been whispered, began to ease their grip, and so too did the life of Æthelred who, in all but title was the last 'King' of the Mercian Realm.

Mercia's Ætheling stood awkwardly forcing a glance skywards…

"La!!!…Here passes Æthelred Langhær, Ealdormann of Mercia, the only son of Ceolwulf. May his spirit watch over us for eternity as he stands forever as a Dragon of OUR Engle Land…"

And those same words were echoed once again, towards the end of the first month which had commenced the year that had been numbered 911 in the old calendar, when the body of Lord Æthelred was entombed at Saint Oswald's priory in Gloucester, the construction of which had been paid for by Æthelred himself.

He was greatly missed as a husband as well as a learned uncle, but during those final years, due to his age and intensified illness, he had started to falter making it necessary for Æthelflæd to increase her rule above his. It had been his wish to 'step back' as if knowing his own end was close, and as his strengths faded those of his Lady had increased.

Æthelred Longhair had died knowing that in his mortal absence his lands were safely in the best hands.

Æthelstan had been hard hit by the loss of his uncle's company and guidance. He had wandered aimlessly about the bur without purpose and without point. He would sit beneath the rays of a dying sun each eve, searching for a point to all that had happened, and he dreamed…

...Dreamed back to his childhood when the days were easy, full of adventure and purpose, when duty did not govern the day and the only responsibility to a child was that of being...

"So, having spoke, the King of Gods arose

and mounted his horse Sleiþner, whom he rode.

And from the hall of Heaven, he rode away,

to Lidskiaff, and sate upon his throne,

The Mount, from where his eyes surveys the world.

And far from Heaven he turned his shining orbs

To look upon Midgard, and the earth, and men."

Balder Dead. [Matthew Arnold]

CHAPTER 7

A.D. 903. This year died Alderman Ethelwulf, the brother of Elhswitha mother of King Edward; and Virgilius abbot of the Scots; and Grimbald the mass-priest; on the eighth day of July. This same year was consecrated the new Minster at Winchester on St. Judoc's advent.

The young boy's eyes gazed rigid into the expressions of the man who now towered high above him. His young back pressed hard against the wattled wall of the single-story building, his neck cranked to its fullest as he continued his stare, defiant and cockily into the dark eyes of an aged huscarl. Æthelstan inched closer towards the half open door, there was a dare in the child's eyes that made his actions seem ever the more innocent, albeit unauthorised, even for him.

Another wider side step to his right and he found the opening, skipped another pace, and gingerly began to pull behind him both large oak doors that lead him into the Great Hall's gloomy entrance. The guard smiled betraying his jealousy for the boy's childhood, Æthelstan shrugged both shoulders uncaringly turning his back on the servant with the wryest of grins.

As he had disappeared from the cycene, finally escaping the risk of being 'caught', he dragged free from beneath his jerkin the largest leg of spit roasted chicken that had been to hand. With a greedy rumble in his belly and the slobber of incurable hunger drooling from his chin he ripped his teeth ravenously through the crispness and chewed, triumphantly savouring the flavour of his greatest prize. A greasy smile of victorious satisfaction dripped from left to right covering his grimy face as he imagined his contraband had been intended for an important Ealdormann, or Thegn.

Once again, he shrugged his shoulders with even less care as he stepped out into the courtyard and whispered...

"It be mine now" another smirk followed as he scoffed the remainder, his Lady's roasted chicken tasted far better than head cheese, 'King's meat' or not.

Summoned to Tamworth's Halls, often in much haste and without given notice, Æthelstan was aware, even at his young age, to the purpose of the 'war gemot' even if he was still ignorant as to its full intent. Even so, as a youngster, such things were easily shrugged away as meaningless and unimportant, maybe another of those uprisings somewhere, or just a Danish fleet spotted by the fishers crossing the Hibernian waters...

Only recently Æthelred had returned at the head of the fyrd, back from thrashing, once again into submission, the unruly armies of the Eastern Engles at a place named Holme. That time there had been the added prize of killing a King and four Jarls. The boy had been presented with a heavily jewelled seax, 'Taken from the dead King' his uncle had boasted. Yet despite such great excitement it had meant nothing more than a mere gift...

That was all a battle had meant to a child of those dark days, bringing further inconvenience upon his day which was often accompanied with more exaggerated tales from the elder 'fyrdrinc'.

Mesmerised, just as young boys of such an age would always be, he had watched with innocent awe as the pristine ranks had assembled outside the fortress 'tun' their colours flashing in the breeze, banners snapping on their shafts, weapons chinking as they glowed in an early morning sunlight. Always he would watch as they made away to yet another fight, proud and excited for its coming, keen to do well in the service of their Lord. Yet he had quickly learned, from an early age, that when they returned, always much lesser in numbers, as victors, or sometimes not, they would look quite the opposite to how they had left, and not just in their dress, but in their manner also...

The shine had not only vanished from their appearance and their blades, their excitement and energy had remained upon the battlefield, the clean edges of their colours so ragged and torn. More than anything else it was their facial expressions that had been the most noticeable, blank, and distant they stared seeing nothing, and some would never change.

But now there were more urgent priorities within a boy's day as he hastily made his way through the 'secret' exit in the outer ringwall which he had discovered by 'accident' the previous summer.

It had never been 'missing' of course. Constructed deliberately just in case of a siege, for escape, inflicting a night attack or just replenishing the burg, such openings had been placed at strategic positions many years earlier, but not in the mind of a child.

His own 'covert' escape would lead him away from the confines of Mercia's northern seat and with the ringing of feastings, loyal chants and war songs disappearing in the background he crossed the open stretch of always clear ground, on through the shoulder high gorse and into the dark forest where he would once again bathe in the safety of its mystical dimness.

'Strange place for a young lad to seek sanctuary from his elders' some may have thought, if they had actually known, just like all boys of that age he had sought a seclusion from the pit falls and bindings of reality.

Without a care in the world, or regard for his own safety, Æthelstan skipped merrily along the hollow way that would lead him deeper into the forest's heart and further away from the protective shelter of the hill fort and the staring eyes of Ecgbehrt his loyal huscarl.

Strolling carefree he would pass the time identifying the trees and bushes as he skirted passed, firstly in their West Saxon names, then with their Mercian alternatives, and finally in Latin just as he had been taught in his lessons...

"Se Æsc and acbeam, bremelberie, morbeam and netel."

Squinting through childish eyes, transfixed by the rarest shards of sunlight that broke their way through the strangles of the leafy canopy and blinded him for a half second, then refocused allowing him to continue his way reciting a poem, or calling to a frightened deer before launching a victorious attack upon an imaginary enemy, thrusting into an invented battle, flaying and slaughtering his opponents with the finest of willow blades, before relaxing back into reality exhausted and out of breath as he watched again the glories of nature's gifts.

Not so far above, swimming in the woodland's everchanging crown, proud parental birds taught their young to flee their nest and make ready their own shelters for the onset of the cold months that would soon be threatening to turn all within the Brunesweald into white skeletal beings until the goddess Eostre would reawaken with the new Summer's sun and win yet another battle of the seasons, breaking through with her warming charm for the start of a new summer of plenty. Æthelstan was content.

Just the fewest of paces had been skipped along natures secret lane before he stopped.

Still, he froze in his tracks with a sudden jerk coming to a halt, almost falling as his feet stuck in their steps. Catching his balance, he focussed his vision. A sudden distraction had released him suddenly from his thoughts of make-believe, something unusual had caught his stare.

Lying upon the leafy crust was the strangest of objects. He glanced around sharply for signs of others, maybe within the knee-high shrubs or gangly trees, awaiting an innocent to come upon their trap, but nothing seemed out of place. He stared at the thing, suspiciously twisting his head in confusion and curiosity.

Gingerly the boy leant forward cranking his knees, slightly lowering his body, yet all the time looking about him for signs of danger from outlaws or 'wolf-heads', cut throats, or worse, Elves, just as he had been 'taught' by the old maids, but there was nothing.

Slowly, with the greatest of care he reached out hesitant and afraid but eventually, after his third attempt he found the courage to touch it, lightly at first, and then a grab…

"Mmmmmm…" as he cautiously inspected his find. To his amazement, the thing was rather pretty. A ringed cluster of acorns bound with a soft branch of hazel and expertly formed by a sprig of neatly stripped lime wood, of which the bark had been used to bind each piece tightly together.

Certain now of his safety the youngster let free an overheld breath quickly replacing it with a refreshing pant as he straightened his knees easing himself upright, all the time staring deeply at his precious find with growing confusion.

He held it up into the speckled sun-light, then back down against the shadows, he had never seen anything like it, certainly he had not expected to find so enchanting a piece discarded along a barely known woodland path.

Inquisitively.

Recording to memory every section of the trinket, closer, at the circle of dried acorns bound between fresh-wood, he puzzled for the reason as to its making, or even its being, even at such an age he knew that Ac, hæsel, and linden wood were never found in the same parts of the forest. They had been brought there. Why?

'What kind of woman…' as it could only have been a woman, '…would make such an object so delicately, so precisely and so deliberately only to discard it upon a woodland path?'

The find was too intense for a child to comprehend, and even more confusing was that a person would make such a thing only to leave it behind on that leafy path just for him to find, in that place where it was forbidden for any folk to venture alone, for 'elder' reasons that he could not be bothered with, let alone understand. Was such a thing just a Lady's unwanted trinket, or an enchanted gift from one child of the 'tun' to another……or was it evil in disguise?

As the boy's heart began to quicken with renewed fear his imagination began to break from reality, his body dripped freely with sweat as panic welled up from the pits of his young stomach. His fingers trembled, knees rattled, and at that very point, he dropped the devilish object as if it had come alive, bore a curse which had painfully bitten into his flesh. He took a pace back, away from the evil and drew in a deep breath...

...Then, just as the strange object had settled once more upon the crispness at his feet, the breeze blew the leafy canopy, the bushes rattled and dead leaves swirled around the trinket, fear flooded through his every sense as his imagination once again broke free, Æthelstan's hands clasped together hugging his chest, his left leg dragged backwards to distance his body from the chance of an evil magic, or a Wiccan's curse and again, in his self-inflicted commotion he scared himself witless, worked himself into a deep frenzy, lost his breath to blind fear and turned on his heels to flee...

Then unlike the conjuring's of a child's imagination came real panic.

Truly now he could not breath.

His body began to shake with fright, terror filled his every thought as he found himself trapped in a canopy of darkness that shrouded his whole being. Suddenly he was unable to move, held still as something wrapped around his upper body tightly, but not painfully tight, just enough to ensure against escape. He attempted to scream out, raise an alarm, but found himself dumbstruck and dazed, barely able to gasp at each precious breath through his strangely scented darkness.

Sweat soaked from every pore, his mouth went strangely dry, and his joints began to shake uncontrollably. Was it fear or had he been cursed by one of the cruel elves?

Those Elves he had been warned about, threatened upon him by the wet nurses and maids save he chanced to venture from his wards, the very reason the forests were out of bounds.

Terror struck deeper, maybe he had disturbed the Wiccan who were rumoured to inhabit the forests during the 'mystical' times of a year.

Was it one of those times in which he had perilously found himself spellbound and caught?

Still entrapped within the darkness he attempted to wrestle free an arm to reach for his waist where he would find the bone-handled 'scramsæx', slip it quickly from its scabbard and lash out relentlessly in his defence, set himself free and escape, back to Ecgberht and the safety of the huscarl...

There would be no need for a weapon, no need to fight back...

Slowly the pressure of his restraints eased, but not completely. He sensed the presence of someone else, close enough to him for the warmth of a gentle breath pushing through the shroud, and the scented air that filled his own breath calming him as his restraints relaxed completely. He knew that odour and his fear began to fade. Gradually the darkness which had blinded his senses turned back into the dim light of the forest...

Nervously, and extremely slow his mind swirled from his capture, his eyes opened fully and focused as his remaining bonds caressed his shape gently ensuring he did not panic and lose his balance. They 'washed' through his unkempt hair, onto his shoulders, down the length of his arms and entwined with his hands offering comfort and warmth, and all the time he breathed that fragrant odour.

As his thoughts began to gather he quickly realised that the darkness had been no more than the soft woollen cloak of a radiant young Lady and his bonds had been her slender arms that had done no more than catch hold of him, instinctively fearful that he may stumble and injure himself. Now kneeling, that same Lady gazed into his eyes and smiled with affection as she spoke in an accented voice that sounded as soft as the shimmer of the rarest of cloths...

"...La, Æthelstan, cild fram se æfenleoht, beon thee stillan...Be thee not afraid, for no harm shall come to thee here, not for a child of the even' light, not in these most special of places."

The boy looked about him, it did not seem that special.

She stared fondly at her 'prize' as a flock of pouting doves landed upon a flowering beam watching the youngster's highlighting cheeks as he stood foolishly silent, stuck for a reply. Another smile as her eyes swept passed him slowly, down to the pathway until they located the object he had nervously dropped.

Her stare returned as she smiled once again at the clumsy childishness that all boys of his age portray when in the presence of a beautiful Lady. She saw the boy for what he truly was, nothing more than an innocent child.

He was staring now.

Entranced, almost mesmerised by her looks which on any other occasion would probably be thought of as rude, he found it impossible to turn his attentions away from her radiance as she knelt in front of him engulfed in that enchanting odour.

Who was this Lady so far from safety, and alone?

And for a second he thought he may have answered his own question, did he know her, or was it just his imagination?

Her smile would have betrayed her thoughts, but not to a boy so young as he.

"I be not afraid my Lady." He stuttered insistently, attempting to dispel the very thought. "T'is nought but surprise in finding someone other than myself so far from the burg. I thought, until this day, that no one else would dare to venture so deep into the Brunesweald."

Again, she smiled at his boyish excuse whilst her softly manicured finger tips swept away the blonde fringe that had dropped across his right eye, now he could see more clearly, and his cheeks turned crimson once again.

"Of course, ye be not afraid, not thee...min deorlic Æthelstan."

And the young lad swooned as the gentle words had left her lips.

"I see thee hath stumbled upon my looking glass...?"

Æthelstan looked at her as if she were mad. 'What looking glass?' and he reached out to recover the object...

"There be no looking glass my Lady, just a jumble of..." yet as his fingers made contact a chill swept along his spine as he spun the piece between his fingers. Then, and only then, as the invisible sunlight caught the glistening mirror the boy fumbled, almost allowing it to slip away again.

Not for the first time he felt distressed, mesmerised, and confused at what he now held...

It was truly a mirror, just as the Lady had insisted.

No more was it the 'twistings' and 'turnings' of woodland make-believe but an actual looking glass now held tightly within his grasp. Trapped within a cluster of shining, golden acorns and entwined with loops, knots, leaves and buds of gold and silver around a shining mirror.

Closely inspecting its every part, he could see, plainly around the handle etched in sweeping forms, the strangest of letterings the meanings of which were unknown to him, 'probably unknown to many' he had thought deeply staring at the ancient forms.

"But...but...?" stammering, nervously rubbing the side of his head as if he were trying to free an explanation from the depths of his mind. Attempting to prove its reality, he tapped, twice, on the shiny front as it returned his own reflection, confirming for certain that he was in no dream.

Spinning the thing three or four times in a still shaky grip, again to convince himself of its reality, he remained certain that it was now not as real as when he had first found it.

'Elfish magic', he was now starting to believe.

Another smile from the Lady…

"Many things are never as they may first appear my young Thegn…" as she carefully slipped the mirror from the boy's nervous grip, then nodded fondly as she nestled it safely within folded arms.

The boy's head threatened to lower, almost guiltily as his eyes stared into hers. Who was this Lady, where had she come from?

'She could have been from somewhere far away' for now he was certain that this Lady did not hail from Tamworth, neither was she Mercian, nor would she have been part of his Aunt's visiting dignitaries for she would have had huscarl of her own, most certainly a 'maeg' or huscarl at arms in attendance.

He thought deeper.

'Such a Lady was fine and noble enough to have been almost anyone, from anywhere….'

"Respectfully my Lady, I must ask, have we met somewhere before. How doth ye know of me?"

Another angelic smile. He had brought delight to his new 'friend'. She turned with her reply, allowing the breeze to catch her own blonded locks showing its well-kept glimmer as it nestled back upon her shoulders.

"Why, Æthelstan, my young Ætheling of a realm yet to be named…"

She returned to her kneeling position.

"...In the lands of an unyielding summer where I shall dwell forever, all wait for nothing more than thee and thy 'ealdorlege', etched so long in the fires of man's destiny, a destiny that ye hath been born to follow since thy truest of hearts beat between the shores of this land. When thee took thy first mortal breath thy Mother sighed at the sight of such a perfect son." Her words were followed by a silent tear that flowed gently down her softest of cheeks, and again there came that odour. She lowered her eyes, saddened with her own words.

Confused would have been acceptable but how he now felt was unexplainable. He had understood her spoken words, but as far as their meaning, that was something entirely different, and he told her so.

Then added nervously...

"...and I be Æthelstan of Mercia.... Elder son of Edward, Cyning of the Westseaxe, ward of the good Lady Æthelflæd who rules with her Lord these fine lands. And, my Lady, there be no such place that thee speaks of, not within any day's ride."

"...And in better hands thee could never be. For ye hath the bestest of teachers to guide thee through the beginnings of what shall soon become such an important and demanding life."

There seemed to be the slightest hurt, maybe even a hint of jealousy lost in her tone, but nothing that would catch the attention of a boy.

She could see he had lost track of the conversation once more.

"Ahhhh, Æthelstan, Ætheling of Mercia, and some day also of the Westseaxe. One day, King to be of the great land of men. Thy destiny was etched amongst the tablets of the old Gods and housed in the great vaults of a distant land long before thine own father had set his eyes upon the lands which now be his. There, in that Land no longer dreamed of by men, such words have been guarded in a place where nought can ever change once it hath been written. I told thee, ye hath the greatest 'ealdorlege'.

"How thee speaks my Lady, why, some who know more about such things may think thy words to be blasphemous."

Her turn had come again, and she turned smiling with true humility and politeness, her cheeks reddened in the dim light, and at that point Æthelstan grew ever certain that he knew of her...

She stepped forward leaning towards his cheek in the same movement to whisper, again that calming odour filled his senses.

"It be called blasphemous only by those who know less than they who know the truth, or be too afraid to concede that what they do know be more than that now taught by these new 'Cristenmann'." Angered by the thought of such hypocritical teachings she raised her body and stood, ran her hands again across his scruffy hair and held out a hand as a gesture for him to follow, it was time to ignore such a subject.

He looked unsure at her invitation...

"Thee hath my word young Lord, that when in my company, ye shall always be safe..."

"But there be little time left my Lady. I shall be missed, and I shall be summoned. Why, my Lady Æthelflæd may even order out the knights..."

She understood his childish nervousness.

"If thee dare to follow, and permit me to tell of the answers to thy questions, if only for the shortest of visits, I shall promise that thee shall ne'er be missed by 'those' who only care...not even for an Elf's whisker..."

There it was again, the mention of Elves.

Everyone knew that elves were to be found no more in that Land, at least not since his grandfather, who had been the only King of men who bore no fear of them. The elves and their kin had all left those parts long ago, in golden ships with silver sail, bound for a far-off land that would stay forever green, before man's new age had begun, or had they?

Such fearful stories swirled through his imagination sending a chill the length of his back bone. The sweat increased between his palm and the hilt of his scramseax as he thought of his coming actions, doubting himself, unsure whether to follow.

But the longer he remained fixed to her radiance the more he became convinced that her words were spoken only with kindness. There was a comfort within the brightness of her eyes that was intensely reassuring, she could never speak a lie.

Overcome with certainty, yet cautious nevertheless, Æthelstan stretched out a hand until it became entwined within her fingers, and as they touched he became even more relaxed. It was then that he had realised, unlike many other ladies, she wore no jewellery, something that was not usual for a person who held such obvious importance. There were no amulets, no rings, nothing, save the smallest lock of the finest hair held in a modest clasp which hung from a basic leather lace around her slender neck.

The ease that continued to fill his body as they began to walk, alarmed him at first, until the warmth of her company swept through him, then he felt certain that he would come to no harm. He was now convinced that at sometime, within his shortest winters he had known of that Lady, but where?

The incandescent aura around her figure glowed as she glided effortlessly over the leafy path of the hollow way and on further into the eerie dimness of the Brunesweald, but even such gloom seemed to radiate a safe, encouraging brightness that he had never felt before, and that odour, never had it faded since they first met.

Æthelstan had never ventured so deep into the forests, nor had he known of any other who had, it was always strictly forbidden, a rigid law insisted upon without compromise. A cynical smirk crept across his face as he realised the possible implications of his disobedience, only though if his secret were betrayed.

At a gentle, unhurried pace they strolled as he stared intently at everything.

As a hare played with it's young, allowing newly born kittens to clamber upon a mother's back and tumble awkwardly scratching a mouthful of stolen fur in the excitement, birds flew from branch to branch, types of which he could not remember seeing before, cart wheeling in mid-flight as they chirped and whistled in their own type of pleasure that strangely added its own melody to the shadowing glades where a young fawn, resting at peace whilst it soaked greedily the sporadic warmth of the sun, then sneezed as a mayfly flattered its beauty along the tip of its nose. The young deer stared back at the boy undisturbed as he hastened his step to keep with the lady, who still glided her path freely into the upper woodland.

At one point, it appeared as if they had walked for miles further and further into the forest's heart, only to discover that in the next glade it seemed as if they had yet to leave the path on which they had first met. Even so, however far, or short they had come he could not remember when he had realised that things were very different to those elsewhere in the woods.

It was unexplainable, but he felt the strangest of feelings, unlike any he had ever sensed whilst previously exploring the leafy outskirts of the forest. But then he had always been amongst others of his own age, sharing their confidences and courage whilst gaming and skylarking with nothing more than the cares and concerns of a child, any danger then would have been shared and quickly dispelled by those who had 'known better' or were too afraid to show weakness. Of course, on such occasions, somewhere close by, there would always be the ever loyal Ecgberht of whom he had known 'forever'. He had always been close, always in attendance 'since the moment of his birth', and always so poorly hidden, barely ever out of sight, instructed by his guardians to keep a watchful eye upon her ward, also the other children, fearful she always remained that 'wolf heads', those out of law, or pirates, or worse, 'Wicingas', would relish a captive of such standing. What a bounty they would have commanded if they had held the life of an Ætheling in their hands.

None of the wildlife they passed, sometimes close enough to touch, showed the slightest signs of fear or alarm towards them. That was the obvious difference within that place, all signs of danger had disappeared, the threat of fear had long since passed, or more so, there had probably never been such threats. Within that part of the forest the same gentle warmth flowed, there was a governed cordiality everywhere with the softest glow of resting light, not too intense just very tranquil and serene.

Engulfed in the magic of his surroundings, for what had seemed like forever, Æthelstan hadn't noticed the weathered old cottage that all but miraculously appeared directly in their path, not until he had first smelled the fire that plumed its smoke upwards, escaping through the charred thatch of the open eaves, accompanied by the noise of a poorly fitted shutter creaking in the slightest draft as it tapped gently against a crooked opening. It seemed obvious then that not only nature had found refuge within those enchanted lands.

Again, an air of caution snatched his attention as he remembered the tales that had been hammered into his young imagination by the unkempt and toothless old crones with creased up faces and double noses, who scrubbed and slopped their way around the cooking fires of the Great Hall, chewing their tongues and scratching parts of their bodies that should never be scratched, especially in a kitchen.

"...Be ye aware young Bregu..." would be the crawl, "A'fore the dægcandel begins to set, of the Wælcyrie and the Nihtgeng that wisp their evil selves free from the deepest of shadows hidden within the Brunesweald..."

Followed within seconds by a curdling chuckle would come...

"...Care ye agin the Ælfwine, that hide and wait for ye young'ens to fall asleep after thy playing, and scurry 'em off to a land not known and far away, ne'er to be seen agin..." and their croaked out tales would always be followed by those dry, wretched cackles that passed for laughter as the boy and his companions ran off to hide from their sight, whilst a huscarl who had 'watched-on' grinned half-heartedly at the boys' expressions as he greedily stole a toasting 'crumpete' from the fire's grate.

Back within reality where the hairs on the nape of his neck stood up rigid and fear began to engulf him as the rotting old door of the 'cot' started to strain open from within...

The stretching of aged leather hinges, groaning as they burdened the weight of the ancient door and the rattle of a loose section of oak as it 'scuffed' against the 'thresh' unnerved the boy. Quickly he sought her protection shuffling his feet discreetly until he came close enough to hide within her warming aura. He may have thought to himself until that point as brave, but after all, one as young as he could only be 'so' brave.

Content that she should be of comfort the Lady smiled allowing an arm to fall lightly upon a young shoulder, gently reassuring the lad of her presence, and his head tilted backwards offering a stare, she returned the look and read the deepest concerns within that innocent of expressions. Young eyes fixed into hers and again he thought he had known her, but still not remembering from where.

The creaking door drained back into the silent shadows of the old hut until it reached its limit, leaving in its place the withered form of an old man dressed in a single grey robe that draped loosely upon his over relaxed shoulders ending where his feet would otherwise have been. A baggy hood that had once guarded against many a winter's cold had slipped onto a bent over neck, it appeared to the boy to have lain their forever. Yet despite the age of the once heavy cloth with its patched repairs and fraying hems the old man looked pristine with his greying locks and sturdy shoulders that still hung as if they had borne more than just the worries of the world. Two very dark, piercing but kindly eyes sank deep into his wrinkles puckering like field farrows across reddened cheeks. His right hand held down the door's latch whilst his left found the door's frame, steadying his ancient form, allowing him to take one short pace bringing him almost outside the dilapidated structure. He stared directly into the boy's gaze with the suggestion of a smile attempting to break through an even greyer set.

Æthelstan felt the tell-tale signs of cold fear that threatened to sweep over his body forcing the slightest tremble into his hands and his knees did all but buckle as the stares of the old man penetrated his young mind. He was now more than just afraid and despite his attempts to hide it he knew he would not be able to keep his feelings secret for much longer.

Regardless of the brewing tenseness between the youngest and the most ancient, the birds continued to sing their calls, undisturbed and free they sensed no danger, yet the boy's young wits still guarded against complacency.

A firmer smile tentatively crept from behind the creases of the old man's face as he saw through the boy's false expressions, the smile soon grew into laughter as the youngster's nervousness won through.

"So!!!" The old man eventually spoke with a coarse, dry voice which suggested his weariness in such effort. "So, here must be the 'cnihtcild'. The youngling that holds tight the destinies that shall soon fall upon the Children of Men?"

The boy shuffled deeper into the Lady's dress, he hadn't any idea as to the meaning within the old man's words, he grew more afraid.

She lowered her head respectfully and answered…

"T'is He, Alfæder."

And the old man laughed again, that time settled and a little louder…

And the boy feared …

"Be ye not afraid eorðcynn, there be nothing to harm one such as thee, not here in such a place."

But the elder's attempts of reassurance did nothing to quell the boy's fears, if anything the situation worsened as his clammy palm grew ever tighter around the bone handled knife still nestled within his waist belt.

The old man spotted the uneasiness and his smile widened further sending the boy's knees to shake even more.

His first instinct urged him to break free of the Lady's embrace, to turn and run far from that strangest place, but he kept control, stood his ground, and remained still as her left arm increased its pressure. Fearful that he may 'cut and run' she pulled him closer resting both hands gently, but securely upon both shoulders, her palms slipped down onto his jerkin and maternally patted his chest beating time with his racing heart.

Yet Æthelstan still felt unsafe, ever more afraid. He had no inclination as to where in the woods he was. He did not know the old man, and only dared a thought that he knew this Lady.

"There be no reason to fear my boy" came her whisper as she lowered her face alongside his left cheek. It was clear, her own ease told that she knew this old man. "In these lands, there be no more than warmth and good things for one such as thee."

"Then these lands be much different from those outside the Brunesweald my Lady…" he hesitated a nervous pause before he turned to face the old man. With a found confidence, he continued, "…And who be this elder man who speaks as if he doth know me, why hath thee brought me to such a place?"

"Why, Æthelstan, if ye are to ask for so many answers should thee not first make thyself known to an Elder of the Brunesweald, and hope that he may return the same?"

The Lady exchanged a wry grin with the old man as the boy glared in silence whilst thoughts of anger and caution filled his mind, however, such suspicions finally gave way to those of common sense. He smiled in agreement shuffling his body forward, barely half a pace, then a complete step as he left the security of her shadows.

Reluctantly she allowed her hands to role from his shoulders.

"My Lord!!!" Polite, yet very cautious. "I be Æthelstan, elder son of Edward, our King and ward to the Lady Æthelflæd, Ælfred's dohtir…" His bold introduction eventually ended with a respectful and calculated nod, yet still holding his stare against the old man's gaze, he began to realise, in the mind of a child, that the Lady's safety may rest also within his young hands. "…But I believe thee know this already."

For a short while there remained a silence seemingly to be shared only between the old man and the youngster, as if that point of the meeting did not include the Lady.

Still no response.

Not a single word came from the cottage, and the two, one extremely short in years, the other, whose years covered so long a time that even he had forgotten their beginning, stared deep into one another's glare, as if both were reading the other's thoughts, or maybe each were daring the other to be first in ending that strictest silence.

Finally, as if it had been quiet forever, the old man conceded. His words were now soft and without threat, with delicate pronunciation, in an accent that clearly did not belong to those parts.

"I know who thee be Æthelstan ring-giver to the bold, how proud thy Mother should be of thee."

The boy strained to understand.

"My Mother be dead my Lord!!!"

Æthelstan's sharpness caught the elder off guard. The boy's cold response was not expected, he had not anticipated such a reply from one so young, not from anyone.

"...and I have been taught that it be courteous to return an introduction after one hath been offered."

A spluttered laugh came without the slightest hint of apology.

"Of course, ye be correct...why should thee not..." the old man grumbled as he cleared his throat, "I be just an old man who takes delight in meeting one whose hands and mind shall make the future times of which I, and others, have long awaited."

A sigh trembled passed his aged lips as he remembered just how long he had waited.

"Just an old man" he continued "whose final days seek the comfort of the smallest of life's trivial offerings." Then his aged form struggled in a turn and began to float back awkwardly within the dimness of the cottage reclaiming his assistance from a gnarled old wooden staff that had supported itself behind the door's jamb.

"Wait!!!" shouted the boy whose tone had now lost any respect. He repeated his words twice more and just as loud, the final time more assertively.

"Wait, I command thee!!!"

The old man stopped in his own shadow, let free another sigh from his ancient lips, shook his greying locks and turned on his heels with the speed and agility of one half his age. In the same movement, his body had arched angrily, allowing the wooden staff to fall noisily upon the sour thresh, bouncing twice before it rolled to a rest.

Both hands pressed hard against the entrance frame, as his eyes now pierced coldly. His cheeks became pale, the creases in his olden neck stood out like the ancient hedgerows of the Wessex farm lands.

"Yeeee!!!!" He dragged in another breath. "Yeeeee!!!! Command of meeee?" And the yell drowned out nature's all from the surrounding glade sending the wild things that remained to seek sanctuary of their own behind anything large enough to offer the meanest protection from such a rage never seen in those parts.

The old man's words had cut through the air like the most violent 'maelstrom', even so, despite the obvious threat towards him, the boy remained calm.

The response continued with the same level of anger, yet quieter, but not too quiet...

"Command be a bold word for one so young Æthelstan peace bringer to all."

More words that he failed understand.

He had never witnessed such temper or rage, even at his most mischievous, yet he still retained a confident manner, nervously brushed down his ruffled cloak, and ceased his quivering.

"I apologise my Lord...but I must know who thee be... for how may I address one of whom I have had the honour of meeting."

Again, the boy's reply caught the old man off guard. His anger slowly eased, replaced by the sharpest second of silence which was broken once more by the instant howling of unstoppable laughter. Louder and louder the old man laughed until his bones began to shake. Both hands slipped from their baggy sleeves and clung to his waist as he attempted to steady himself, in fact at one point, he was laughing so much that the Lady thought he may laugh himself into the grave...and he kept on laughing, until, without the slightest of reasons, his laughter began to grow softer, and as it grew softer, his appearance began to change.

Inexplicably his expressions began to alter, just a little at first, barely noticeable, but then a definite change became more obvious. Gone were the wrinkles and skin spots of old age, the greyness of many haggard years, the lines of time, all just seemed to vanish, and in their place a smoothly tanned skin, glistening and younger beneath a polished spanghelm that now sat immaculately upon his golden hair, and around his body the ancient, tattered robes had been replaced by pristine hose and jerkin over lain with glistening mail that had found the shining of a sun that had long since set... The mightiest of swords hung from a thick leather belt in its own sheath of encrusted gold.

After a thousand sighs and gasps the boy eventually found his breath...then a form of words seemed to follow...

"...What...tri...trickery be...be in this?"

The lad then lurched backwards, into the protection of the Lady's soft hands. In his excitement, he had almost drawn his knife...But only almost.

She towered over, finding his eyes once more, and again her look began to calm his quaking spirit. Her softest whispers eased his panic as he breathed the sweetest smell of honeysuckle and crushed blackberry leaf, feeling certain once more that he knew her voice.

"It be no trickery my son...I promised that no harm should befall ye here in this land, and it be the truth."

Æthelstan stared back, their eyes bonding as if they had always known each other, but still he struggled to remember where, or even her name.

"I shall now take my leave…" His frustrated confusion told in his voice, embarrassment, and anger too, that still his questions remained unanswered, he felt foolish that he had not the years to command respect from others.

"The time to leave be not yet" she answered, "there be more things still to learn, things that thee must know a'fore thy return to thy guardian."

"I cannot wait my Lady…"

Suddenly, without any warning there came an almighty smash of oak against daub as the elder slammed the door against the inner wall with the strength that almost shook the ancient building.

"Yeee. Ye shall leave my lands when I permit thee to leave my lands…" replied the golden warrior. His words may not have been louder than those spoken by the Lady, but the tone was more convincing.

"…Harken ye to my words boy, if only for an instant!!!"

He continued more rationally. "No mortal child hath ever been granted such privilege that be offered to thee upon this day."

Now, Æthelstan was totally confused, even curious.

"Then my Lord…" he still shook nervously, and his fingers still trembled. "Have thee at least the good manners to tell me of thy name, and why thee be here, then perhaps I shall remain, willingly."

A pause passed between all three before the Lady re-entered the conversation.

"The boy be correct, my Lord…Cease thy toying, for he be still no more than a child despite his name…Tell him…Tell him for he be young and truly knows nothing of thee." Her words had been precise, and strict, spoke with a maternal tone, protective and stern, how could He not…

Conceding with a nod, the older man, who had miraculously become much younger, straightened his body until he stood tall and erect for the first time in their meeting, proud and dignified with an air of respectful command about his noble presence, glistening bright into the forest's light. To the boy, he seemed a giant.

Staring deep into his eyes, serious and direct, he grabbed fully the lad's attention, she was right, the time for playful games had now passed.

"Why, Æthelstan, boy who be yet to walk as a man, doth ye not know of me from the 'ealdspell' told as ye sat around the hearth fires, or doth ye now believe in All that those 'Christians' whine from their calfskin books, dreamed up in their wattled cages?"

"I do not understand my Lord, and I apologise, but I do not know thee." He felt a stupid awkwardness inside, as if he should have known and even understood everything, he cast back another glance seeking her reassurance...

A smile of approval came from both. Now the man spoke again but his tone offered only comfort and understanding, for the first time he almost seemed friendly...

"...I, young Æthelstan, be the One thy forefathers knew as All Father...I be the one who begat these lands, who brought forth the first of thy line in a far away place many winters passed. I be he who guarded thy kinsmen through the ages, now only boasted of to children who sit around the hearth fires, or mead soaked men who secretly want for more than the nothing they now possess. I be the one who protected thy Fathers, and their Fathers also, through such times that have since brought us all to this place, together, to these lands..."

Confusion still highlighted the boy's expressions as the giant's voice deepened, echoing high into the forest's canopy.

"I be He who commands the thunder..." and he lifted both hands, palms upwards, and directly it thundered high above the trees, shaking the earth from its evening sleep, but it did not rain.

Then...

"...The one who welcomes the rain..." and as he raised his bearded face it rained, and continued to rain until he lowered his sodden beard, and the rain ceased, but not before all three were drenched, almost to the skin. Yet even the wetness seemed mystical, warm, and silken, as it disappeared from every surface leaving all clean, dry, and fresh.

Thunor's mighty clash disappeared as it echoed into the distance and Eostre's tears eased slowly away until they too had vanished, leaving all that remained pure and at peace.

Then he continued...

"...I be he who permits all things to happen the way they be meant to happen upon this Land of Men...For I be Woden, Woden All Father, creator of All...and the sagas that ye were told in thy forgotten days be true."

Woden stood proud and erect as his spoken words had unleashed their closely guarded secret that had been withheld from the ears of such mortals for many lifetimes, since man had long since forgotten to believe in them...The boy remained dumbfounded as if he were trying to rouse himself from the strangest of dreams.

They shared another of those vibrant silences, granting the time, at the very least, to register all that he been told. Surely that which he now witnessed could never be the truth, even in the mind of a child. If that were so, then it would mean that everything he had been taught during his short life, about the world and its beginnings, would have been lies and those who had taught him such things would have been liars.

Her interruption came as a surprise.

"Nese!!!" insisted the Lady reading his tortured appearance, "No!!! thee hath just been taught the new ways, the ways that be now in the world of Men...That doth not mean that the old ways never existed, and that such old ways do not still exist, now and forever. There be more than one truth to a tale and there be room in the minds and hearts of Men for more than one belief, if they so permit it...and more so, should they so wish it."

"Then my Lady... who art thee? What be thy name?... Which saga be thee from, for I be sure that I know of thee, and that we have met, some place other than here."

Sadness now filled her eyes. A tremor flitted across her lower lip.

It wasn't difficult for the boy to notice the single tear that slipped down the dusky pinkness of her primrose coloured cheeks.

The one who had long ago been called the All Father now broke the short silence and answered with humility and sincerity.

"Why, Æthelstan sunu...doth ye not know of her name?"

He paused to find a more comfortable kneeling position set back but in front of the boy, and that same odour of honeysuckle and blackberry leaf shimmered passed once more, already he felt his own tear escaping...

"Doth ye not know the name of She, she who be from thine own saga, from the saga of Æthelstan...?"

And another tear joined the first on the boy's reddening cheek. He shook his head not wanting to believe the words he thought he would soon hear.

"...She who was first to scream thy name into the fires of Men. She, who loved thee more in the final seconds of her mortal life than any other Mother could ever love her son...Doth thee not know the name of thine own Mother... for She be Ecgwynn?"

Æthelstan was stunned.

At the mere thought that 'this giant should dare to speak of such a thing'.

He was afraid, again.

Afraid that his young mind would not cope with such horrid untruths.

And he was very angry.

Angry that he lacked the years and authority to cast out a punishment against those who thought and spoke such blasphemous and hurtful things, of course he had not known who 'She' was, how could he know who she was, he had been but seconds into that world before his mother had been torn from him.

His Mother?

Ecgwynn?

Again, as he wiped the tears from the edge of a cheek with a grimy cuff, Æthelstan felt that he should now flee from the Brunesweald and its curses forever, escape their presence and hurry himself back to the Burg, where he would scream to all of the terrible game that had been played on him, if at all anyone there would believe such a tale.

But move he could not...

His feet seemed as if they were fused to the ground, maybe through fear and panic...or maybe there was another reason fro keeping him there...

No matter how much he tried he could not move from his invisible bonds, however hard he willed, because for the strangest of reasons, deep inside he knew that Woden had spoken the truth. No matter how absurd it seemed, it was the truth.

He had known that Lady who smiled upon him. Somehow, in some strange and mystical way, maybe through the Old Ways, she was truly there at his side, his Mother.

The struggle was over. Gone were those invisible bonds. He could lift his feet, free those imaginary ties, rid his mind of the disbelief that had fought against all things real, and rest his mind on what he now knew to be the truth.

Standing alone, no more than a boy he relished the dreams of a child which had now become reality. As if he had been stuck in the essence of the moment, without consciously knowing, he ran into the clutches of the Lady Ecgwynn, into the embrace of She who was his true Mother, into the arms of She who should be seated at the side of his Father, and together they wept for a time that could have been eternity…

Yet it was just the briefest of seconds, as they held each other's emotional embrace…but to the boy it seemed as if those shortest seconds had been forever, and his true life had been there with her in that glade, all else that he could remember about his younger years appeared now to be the fantasy.

…And a Mother wiped away the tears of a beloved son as she smiled her warmth into his reflection and her newly found child copied as he wiped away the tears of a Mother's newly found joy.

Within the innocent harmony of nature's wilderness, watched over and protected by the All Father, who discreetly permitted their privacy, they remained in a silent hold as each had so much to tell, however little had been needed to be said.

A child's mind became entangled in a thousand or more questions, yet out of them stood only one that should be asked, in the simplest of manners.

"Modor…?" the plain sound of that word as it escaped from his lips sent a shiver through her body.

"Modor, what shall now become of Ælfflæd my Father's Lady?"

How much had he despised that woman's presence? She had never the right to sit at his Father's side. How much he would now relish her departure from court. Would he now, at last, see the back of her?

Ecgwynn looked down at her son and shook her head in confusion. For a moment she had felt nothing but pity for the bewilderment that clung to her son's face. Was he still too young to understand?

Could anyone be too young to understand?

"When we return to Tames Worth…" he continued, "and my Father sees that thee, my true Modor be not dead, what shall then become of this Lady Ælfflæd?"

Laughter rang through the lips of the All Father, discreetly occupied in the distance, who, on seeing the ire within Ecgwynn's eyes immediately followed his rudeness with an apologetic cough as the boy's childish anger bore into his face, seeking explanation for this new found 'humour'.

The Father of All Fathers returned from the shadows of the glade and knelt, placing the heaviest of hands upon the smallest of shoulders. His palm pressed down supportively and squeezed reassuringly whilst his eyes stared deep into the troubled glare of a youngster who could then only dream of the adventures that would soon befall him as a man.

"Young Æthelstan..." Woden, the creator of all that man had possessed and everything else that he did not, swallowed uneasily, then filled his lungs with the deepest of breaths. He was far from comfortable when discussing such things with a child of man, or any child if it came to that.

"...Ætheling to the destiny of man...Ye be permitted here, on a day such as this to receive a gift that hath rarely been granted to a mortal born out of Middangeard. Since those dark days before Asgard none but a few hath been granted such a gift, for here, in these Lands that belong only to 'those never to be forgotten' ye may sit alongside thy Modor for as long as thee wishes, and within that wish, time itself shall remain still... But when thee returns through the forest of Dearaldia, back to the Land of Men, thee shall forget that such a day hath existed for it shall only be remembered in thy dreams, hidden away, until such a time comes for the need to remember, for at such a time ye shall know all that be needed to know."

Confused? More so than ever before.

"No, my Lord... Such a thing cannot be. For if it be so, then what should be the reason for summoning me to such a place that rightfully belongs in the dreams of a boy?"

Woden's face reddened as he strained to choose between rage and laughter... 'such a question, could he not just accept things for what they were?'

"Noble son…" laughter had won the argument, but only in short, respectful bursts. "…Of course, thee be here… for if ye were not, then all ye need to do is wake…" His mighty hands swept across his front pointing out into the woods. "…All that thee doth see be real for if thee be dreaming let it all vanish, let it all go within the shake of Fenrir's tail" and his hands came together offering his challenge to the boy.

Æthelstan squinted, concentrated, and wished hard, but when his eyes opened he was still there, in the wooded glade, with his Mother at his side, and the giant of a golden warrior at his front. He lowered his head and finally succumbed to the fact that all about him was real, at least for that time. He had no other answer, for there was no other explanation.

"…Boy…" The All Father's voice had now lowered sympathetically. He also wished for that meeting to end so he may return to the mead halls and drink and laugh with those of his own kind. But there, in that place lay his duty to those whom he had created, and to the lands of which he had made.

"…As thee grows into a man, thee shall need the aid of many to complete thy destiny, for it shall be shared by more than just thee. Be certain, there will come tests of many kinds that will threaten thy path, for these darkening days that befall upon men shall be the darkest, and most evil yet to descend upon their lands. If ye are to succeed much of that aid shall come from those around thee, allies and friend folk who shall share in the same goals as thee, also from others who just wish to serve because they know nought else, but other support, which may not be found upon the land of men may only come after thee hath taken the years to understand the true meaning of thy ealdorlege."

Young eyes again burned hard into his words, he had never heard such a speech and had never felt so confused.

"Then my Lord, apart from these precious hours with my Modor, what shall be the purpose of such a journey?"

Another smile returned to his lips, 'only one such as this child could ask a question of a scholar with such innocence then return to the simplest words of a child…Whose idea had it been, so long passed, to create these children of men' and he laughed once more, but that time only to himself.

"Such a gift young Æthelstan, may be the gift in knowing that which thee must never know…"

A pause, even one so great sometimes had to choose his words.

"Know that thy Modor be here in these valleys of Glassisvellir, and that I too be here watching down upon thee, alongside those who have been before thee, for it be not the words of the 'plain robed preosts' who speak of nought but the White Christ, that ye may lean upon in troubled times, as troubled they shall truly become."

His young mind may not have understood all that had been told, yet he was certain that he would always remember his words and one day everything may well become clear.

As he tried yet again to understand the All Father's words his mind drifted between dream and reality, such a day had been too much for one so young. Deeper, his mind sank into a realm of comfort and peace and as his eyes closed, Ecgwynn stroked the softness of a son's cheek whilst she sang the words of an ancient lullaby. For the shortest of times he would at least know his Mother, albeit in the land of dreams.

Æthelstan floated deeper, contented, relaxed, and comforted, in a way that can only happen when a mother shares her love with a precious son. A golden tear slipped down her silken cheeks, onto his forehead, soaking its way into his young skin carrying with it the memories and knowledge of his Mother into the heart and mind of her son, with the scent of crushed blackberry and honeysuckle to the echoed words of the All Father…

Woden rose to his feet and took a pace closer to the pair…

"…Slæp þu Ætheling cild…and when thee awakes know only that the eyes of thy forefathers be always upon thee, and within them the guidance of the Old Ways, for should ye fail in thy destiny's tasks, then so too shall fail the future of Men."

It was too rough, too hard…almost unbearably painful.

The way the boy was dragged from his 'afternoon nap'…half sitting, uncomfortably crouching against an elder trunk, wasted chicken on the sod at his side, and a golden tear stain still resting on a grubby cheek…

Æthelstan opened his eyes twisting with hurt from the second 'slap', he cried "Modor" loudly and escaped from his dreams.

He could not remember the subject, but he could still the strangeness of the dream itself, as he continuously swept his brow from a fallen fringe that became dislodged once again on receipt of a third 'crack' to the back of his already smarting neck. He now woke fully and caught the passing of the sweetest smell of crushed blackberry leaf and honeysuckle clinging onto the last wisp of an afternoon's breeze.

The only thing he remained positive about was that the odour most certainly did not come from his aggressor.

"Modor?" Ground a voice. "I'll give thee weep for thy Modor…and ye shall soon be wishin' she be 'ere to save ye…I be in right bother now ye nawiht…Ætheling or not ye won't ever disobey those what 'ath Order over ye agin…"

Such angered rants had come from an irate Huscarl as he 'man-handled' the boy towards the small gate that would lead them back into the protection of the burg. Rough was the hold about his neck that his feet barely scraped the ground as the guard pulled again at the lad's jerkin, scratching the youngster's scruff painfully more than once. The Huscarl had been searching high and low for the boy since the middle of the day and always with the curses of an incensed 'Servant at Arms' at his rear.

"Run off like that would ye…and where there be noble guests and all…ye be lucky that Our Lady 'ad not called for ye…got me in bother thou 'as, ne'er the less…"

As they made their way into the safety of the fortified walls the guard kicked open vigorously the smallest of doors to allow them entry, slamming it shut just as harshly with the back heel of his opposite boot, and they passed through the crooked jamb.

A puzzled spearman slipped an ill-fitting peg to secure the entrance holding a cynical smile across dry lips, watching the boy wriggle pointlessly as his eyes scanned the buildings and gennels for the slightest sign of Ecgberht, his trusted friend, but he was nowhere to be seen, then so came an explanation for such treatment. Ecgberht would never have permitted such punishment to be brought upon him, at least not by the lowest of Huscarl, and he knew that.

"Ne'er agin boy...ne'er agin shall ye make such a fool of me...not if ye ever wishes to be King" and with the inside of his palm the guard added two more unwarranted slaps to the tally, hard and loud to the side of an already reddened neck, just because, at that point in the huscarl's life, he could.

Æthelstan shook off any trace of his dreams, he was now most certainly back within the Land of Men.

Still smarting from his earlier pasting, Æthelstan was left alone that night, in the single chamber with a young hound pup contentedly curled in front of a glowing fire, a single candle, and a mind full of dreams as his companions. He would never speak about the incident with anyone, but even at his age he accepted that the bullying guard would need little help in being a fool.

The following morning the burh was snatched from a night's peace by a barrage of horrific screams. Two butter maids, on their way to the earliest of starts, had found the huscarl still at his 'night post', rigid and very dead to that world. There had been no sign of infiltrators or thieves across the ringwall, nothing more than the normal occurrences of a normal night. No physician could explain why the guard had died, and none could make any sense as to the large red mark etched across his forehead...Unnoticed too went the clumped sprig of honeysuckle leaf and blackberry squashed in the dust at the dead man's feet. All that could be determined when observing the petrified expression on the dead man's face was that he had been frightened out of his wits...and died in a silent frenzy of terror.

...Then so was Helgi Hundingsbane

Behind the Einherjar

Like the bright growing Ash

beside the thorn bush,

And the young stag, drenched in dew

who surpasses all other animals'

and whose horn glows

bright against the sky itself...

From the Poetic Edda

CHAPTER 8.

918. For seven years plus, Æthelflæd had ruled as Lady of the Mercians, in the wake of her husband. She built fortresses and pushed her way into the territory of the Danes. Leicester submitted to her without a fight...

It was not just the incessant confusion brought through his dreams that made 918 a terrible year. It would probably prove to be the worst year of Aethelstan's life, always to be remembered by him and his King for the most unwelcome of reasons.

To begin with it had started with one of the coldest winters that anyone could wish to recollect. Even the toothless old Thegn Bedwig who had originated from the middle shires and was thought to be the oldest living Mercian, could not remember a winter ever being as cold, although, at his age, remembering anything more than a few days old would have been an achievement. He did little more now than just sip at his mead, suck on the softest bones from a wild bird stew or coney broth and tell tales and stories to those young enough to believe them. Despite the infirmity of his age he always supported a 'childlike' smile as his stories grew more exaggerated each time they were repeated.

At the start of that year Guthram II, who had ruled over the lands on the eastern bulge of the isle, had been killed by Edward and his army at the battle of Tempsford following his over-zealous attempts at the destruction of Bedford. He had died along with his Jarls Toglos and Manna and hundreds of their followers who had truly believed that they held the rights to another man's land. By default, and persuasion by numbers, Guthram's lands were 'encouraged' under the rule of the King of Wessex without any further outbreaks of revolt.

At the same time, similar uprisings were occurring across the Isle...

Around the western shores a large fleet numbering as many as forty fully manned Snekkjan sailed into the mouth of the Severn. At their head stood two insanely greedy Jarls from Breton named Ohter and Rhoald who wasted little time in dispatching their heavily armed warriors upon a quest of savage plunder on every town along the northern coast of Wales.

After filling the bellies of their ships to the point where they could not be filled further for the fear of foundering, they entered a port then named Ircingaford where they took the resident Bishop, Camlac hostage. The Breton Jarls imprisoned the bishop and his clerics, aboard the largest of the warships and proceeded to taunt the 'locals' with their prize. After weeks of negotiations King Edward finally agreed to pay a ransom of forty pounds of silver for the Bishops safe release.

Almost as predicted, after the receipt of the ransom the invaders set sail once more, but instead of returning to the Breton coast they entered Archenfield and held its whole population captive bidding for more of the King's silver.

Still caught up in his troubles in the eastern shires Edward ordered the dispatch of the East Saxon fyrds from Hertfordshire and a Mercian contingent from Gloucestershire who joined forces along the Wye river at a place named Hereford. Now under the command of a Wessex Thegn the combined army of Mercians and Saxons crossed the Wye and marched upon the invaders. Firstly, a naval force from the southern shires besieged the invasion fleet with all but a few of the invaders ships burnt beyond use. Then the newly formed land army surrounded the Dane on all flanks until they were starved out. Fleeing for their lives the Anglo-Saxons ran them into the ground killing many at a place named from that day as 'Kill Dane Field'.

It had all been a truly national effort where the southern forces had taken up arms in defence of others, an action which had been encouraged more often since the days when Alfred had taken his rule upon the Winchester seat. Those very actions had displayed a new unity across the shires, one which had gone unnoticed by their enemies. The time along the Welsh coast had finished with the annihilation of the invasion force and the return of the 'booty' to its rightful owners, less a small percentage for 'expenses', and a little more to balance the Wessex coffers. The fyrd had also commandeered the remaining enemy ships which were converted for use within the efficiently reorganised Anglo-Saxon navy.

If the troubles of the west, added to those in the east and south were insufficient enough, then those erupting in the north would not pass unnoticed. By that time of the year, Ealdred, the new heir of Bamburh had convinced King Constantine of the Scots to 'rightfully' reclaim back the lands of Bernicia and thereto persuaded the Scot to engage his 'enemy' at the battle of Corbridge, which ended with the deaths of many good men from both sides, and lacking in victory to either.

At the same time, Æthelflæd, with her tactful way had managed to 'peacefully' convince the burh of Leicester to re-join her Realm and after, had slyly begun to 'stir up' rumours of discontent and talk of rebellion in the outer 'tons' around York, leaving an intendedly uneasy peace in the northern air.

On a brighter side, two Welsh Kings, Idwal Foel of Gwynedd, and Hywel Dda of Dyfed, along with a suspicious looking Prince named Clydog of Deheubarth swore their allegiances to Edward and the West Saxon Houses.

All such on goings and the country itself still froze in the full span of a winter which lasted long after the seasons 'usual' end.

Finally, to the greater relief of the population there began a most welcoming thaw urging Æthelflæd to finally declare that the 'fighting season' had at last arrived. Yet as the days lengthened and the 'Shires of the Four Winds' burned with retribution in the shorter night skies, the middle lands were now ready to have their 'say'.

Already prepared for many weeks, and heavily armed, she mustered and marched her Mercian army across the hills of the old Pecsæten to Deorby where after the most hellish of onslaughts upon the river homestead and the loss of four of her most trusted Thegns, she would violently evict the Danish garrison, along with their families, dogs, and anything else that proved to be tainted by the touch of the Norsemen...

...Such greed that was endowed by the Danes had urged their raiding parties to encroach upon Æthelflæd's lands once too often, taking for themselves that which they had wrongfully deemed to have belonged to them. Her tolerance had worn thin since Tettenhall and after continuous receipts of increasingly serious threats to remove the Mercian Lady, she had ordered her retaliation to coincide with the thaw. She now aired an intended viciousness that would decimate her Danish enemies beyond recovery.

As battles went the attack on Derby was as fierce and as cruel as any other, with its outcome greatly hindered by the deepest of thawing snows and still partly frozen waters of the river Derwent.

Their attack had been launched well into the traditional fighting season when the climate would have normally been more hospitable towards the dying, but mother nature never did consider mankind's position when changing her moods. Besides, if the Lady of the Mercians had waited any longer, the waters would have thawed fully making it easier for the Danes to receive much needed supplies and reinforcements from their Hibernian allies...

Over the volatile years of occupation these 'colonising' invaders had built their stockades upon the crumbling ruins left by the Legions of Roman intruders discarded by those 'innocents' who had foraged for house stone and stock walling between invasions. Despite its deterioration, it had been the best tactical position for thwarting an attack, or even to suffer the recriminations of a long siege upon their new riverside village.

Entering any town during the heat of battle would always be the worst type of fight, but in the deepness of winter's harshest retreat it made things harder and deadlier, many lives were quickly sacrificed. Sadly, one of those lives was that of Æthelflæd's most senior Thegns. Æthelfrith was the most devoted of all those not of her blood, yet had sworn an undying allegiance to his Lady as their Lord Æthelred had expired his final breath.

The Anglo-Saxon had always preferred the open plains to wage his, or her wars. A horse could charge, and turn with ease, a spear could be thrown accurately to its fullest and there was space enough to divide an enemy, contain him in small groups and pick off his numbers with minimal risk. But in a village or homestead a shield wall was useless, there were too many restrictions and the fighting always took longer, costing more and there would always be the unnecessary casualties...

No reasonable man relished the slaughter of children, for any reason. Their frozen corpses lay innocently bloodied along every path of the 'vil', some accidentally speared or cut, others used by their own kind as living shields to deter their 'morally correct' attackers. But their survival was not on that day's agenda, and the children wept their last as any thought of mercy was dismissed.

After five days of brutal hostilities, with many accounts of callous hand to hand engagements, on a slightly warmer Sunday morning, the battle was finally won. The few survivors who had managed their escape had done so towards the lands north of the Humber river where hope of sanctuary lay with their Yorvik cousins and the cost of that campaign would be counted as the last prisoner was dispatched from that mortal world.

It would later be deemed that the capture of the Danish trove at Derby had been worthy, but not all, as it would have only been a matter of a few short weeks after her victory that Æthelflæd passed away from fatal wounds received in the final minutes of the battle.

The Lady Æthelflæd died on June 12th in her beloved stronghold at Tamworth, just nine days before Litha. After a funeral procession, which followed the length of her realm, her body was tendered by noble and servant alike being laid to rest alongside her husband in the Minster of Saint Oswald's at Gloucester. None present that day would realise that many years later she would become known as the most formidable female warrior since Boudicca set her revenge.

Æthelstan mourned the passing of his beloved aunt greatly missing her support and companionship through his remaining years. Her death had not come as any great surprise, in fact he had conceded in a small speech on the eve of her death, that it would be the only way her life could end, 'with the dignity of a notable victory behind her, the cementation of her lands, and coffers overflowing. This Lady had not been placed upon the earth to rot into old age.' A fitting end to a woman who had ruled as a queen in all but title.

The loss would convince him that no other female could ever hold the same value than that of his dearest aunt, and therefore, in the years that followed, he would never take a wife, as any suitor offered would never stand in comparison to Æthelflæd, or was that a mere excuse?

What had haunted him consistently over the following months was the flashes back to those final seconds of the battle when he had been at her side. Together they had ridden into the final throws of the conflict jousting for the lead position, an end to the fighting in sight and the sense of an important victory within their grasp when all seemed to turn as the Danish 'short bolt' shattered its hardwood quarrel into her side, missing him only by the length of his horse. Eventually he would come to terms with his 'guilt' as he committed to memory Æthelflæd's surprisingly impious words whispered only to him during the misty throws of her demise...

"When Woden rings his bell, the way of the old ruler shall be gracefully conceded to the path of a new, and if the old ruler be so fortunate, she shall join with the Einherjar at Woden's glorious side..."

...And, as graceful as she had been in life, despite the severity and extent of her fatal wounds Æthelflæd would not cry out a single tear during the weeks that would lead to her tragic end.

'She died, at Tamworth, twelve days before midsummer, the eighth year of her having rule and right over the Mercians...'

Edward, followed by the most modest of escorts, had ridden for Tamworth's gates the instant the news of his sister's death had reached his encampment along the Great River Ouse, interrupting his supervision of two fortified burgs at Bucca's meadow where there had been too many years of 'too'ing' and 'fro'ing' from the eastern Danes.

Respite from continuous fighting there and at Stamford was more than welcome to the King, even more so to his armies, even so, the last thing he had expected to undertake was another journey north to witness the burning of the pyres that had been offered by the 'loyal folk' in celebration of Æthelflæd's great life.

The pious chroniclers wrote that…

'The realms of her rule were littered with the beacons from every forest for ten nights and more, to let all know, that Æthelflæd their Lady no longer rode upon her lands.' They were said, 'To have been the greatest display of loyal offering since the deaths of Offa and Penda.'

The Christian service that gave up her soul to their new God was also spoken with extracts from the old ways passing through most of the first night. It was followed by two or three days of mourning and remembrances which were then celebrated by the drinking and feasting and paying of generous compliments from every shire, realm, and land, along with further mourning which refused to stop until the end of the second week. By that time her body was well entombed in Gloucester's Minster within the walls of the eastern porch.

Æthelstan had grieved with his Father and on the final evening, as they had stood side by side staring out towards the western sun, sadness filled them both but for entirely different reasons. He had waited long enough, ensuring all around were silent, a stern look about him guaranteed that it would remain that way…

"…Nu geleoran Æthelflæd, Ælfreddohtir…Myrcna hlæfdige…" a tear was dismissed as he repeated his words "Now depart Æthelflæd, Ælfred's daughter…Lady of the Mercians…"

"…and the most valiant leader that our Isles shall ever see." Edward had added.

Over the first few days that followed her burial, almost before her spirit had barely entered her afterlife, some had said, a significant argument threatened to considerably taint Æthelflæd's memory, over who held the right to rule the lands within the borders of that middle realm.

It had been instigated by Ælfwynn, Æthelflæd's only heir, and directed towards the King of Wessex himself. The argument put forward declared that only she could inherit the right to rule over Mercia, in the stead of her Mother. The declaration itself would not have seemed as bad but for the way it had been presented...

Her single demand had been expressed to the King by way of a messenger, not in person, as would have been the respectful route. Sent from Ælfwynn's own hand to the quarters of the King who was housed no more than a few paces from her own. It seemed as if the 'Lady' deemed herself too important to carry the message herself.

Despite his anger, that single action had left Edward granting her the benefit of any doubt by declaring that 'his niece's attitude was nothing more than an emotional triviality based on the loss of her Mother and deep concern for her own future'.

At first light, Edward marched hastily from the Mercian town returning, in a foul mood, to his semi constructed burgs. He had stated his intensions regarding Mercia's future on more than one occasion and saw little need to repeat himself any further.

Yet, no sooner had he reached Bedan Ford, Offa's final resting place, did a messenger from Tamworth laden him with another declaration regarding the intensions of the 'new' Mercian Lady.

The rider was sharply dismissed, narrowly missing the brunt of Edward's rage and the documents were dispatched into the flames 'where they belonged'. Over the weeks that followed continuous messages were delivered into Bedford's fort, receiving little attention only from the bishops, who at that time were acting as Edward's clerks. The contents were 'discussed' with the King, but no answer given, and more than one messenger arrived back in Tamworth with little more than an empty satchel.

Then the messages became insulting, even to the point that threats towards the King himself were suggested. Now it became clear to the King that his niece was suffering from a great deal more than grief for her parental losses.

He did not wish to fight his niece verbally or otherwise, neither did he care to enter a war against Mercia, for more than one reason, especially that of not knowing which side his own son would stand. Neither did Edward wish to chastise Ælfwynn in public, or any other way if it came to that, but as the messages became more frequent and were now to a point of being offensive, he realised that the disagreement would not just 'flitter' away, nothing less than his own attendance would be required within Tamworth's walls.

Æthelflæd's daughter was not going to accept a few hastily scribbled charters carried to her by a lowly herald or two.

By the time he had made his second visit in as many months, Edward was far from being upset, any sympathies he may have previously held towards his niece were now rapidly diminishing.

Æthelstan, who had tactfully kept out of any arguing, greeted his Father at the wall's southern gate offering the most cautious of pleasantries before riding the remaining distance in silence. Even though they had spent little time in each other's company his son knew Edward's habits well enough and saw no requirements to add his comments to the petty squabble which was now in grave danger of becoming more than just a greedy declaration from a spoilt cousin who had normally gained her way by stamping her feet and shedding a few tears. Such actions would not win her that argument.

Unfortunately for Ælfwynn, she had not inherited the strength of mind, or body, from either parent, neither had she learned the tactfulness that had normally granted her Father the 'upper hand' in his negotiations, even when he had argued with the highest levels of any council. She had been brought up by wet nurses and hand maids who had pandered her every whim and too late into her Uncle's second 'visit' did she realise she had over stepped her 'petty' position of nobility, taking things much too far.

She was only a woman, and when it had suited she was just another worthless woman.

Edward granted her no warning, no offer of compromise and no concessions towards the future of his spoiled niece. Even Æthelstan remained silent within his Father's shadow knowing that then was not the correct time to speak out. Much to the outrage of many of the local folk, Thegns and eardlinga alike, the King of Wessex claimed direct control of the Mercian Kingdom and sensing the certain probability of an uprising from those whose interests lay firmly within those middle lands, appointed his eldest son as his representative.

Æthelstan had lived in Mercia for most of his life and was well known and extremely well liked by those who mattered. He had gained much respect as a capable warrior and tactful commander, which meant that he would be instantly accepted as their Lord, albeit governed by the 'strings' of Wessex. Æthelstan would remain seated between his beloved Tamworth and Gloucester as his Father's heir.

In the King's own eyes his decision had been the correct one. He was Edward, Elder son of Alfred, and had witnessed his own Father's declarations many years earlier when he had bequeathed in charter that Æthelstan should become 'ward' of Mercia, and in time, when the position should allow, he would inherit the kingdoms of the west.

Yet despite the 'half welcomes' of the Mercian folk towards their 'true' King, which was also echoed by many Welsh nobles, the common right to rule should have settled with the 'heiress', as wished for, allegedly, by her own Mother. But the King's challenge was the most powerful and in those times, it was power and spearmen that counted, in short, the King had added Mercia and its shires to that of his Wessex authority.

To avoid further upset, and any misplaced empathy that was certain to be shown by the hard line Mercians, Ælfwynn was taken into the King's 'protective custody' and escorted directly to Winchester under a Wessex guard in the first weeks of a cold December, in that sorrowful year of 918.

As was appropriate for a meddling Lady of the times, Ælfwynn was placed within the security of the nunnery at Wilton, 'for her own care', under the direct watch of the Abbess, herself coincidentally Edward's daughter Eadflæd and Æthelstan's half-sister. There, in the pious shadows of a cold and sparsely rationed convent she remained a recluse with only her new God as companion, ignored and in total silence for the next thirty or more years until her reticent and unnoticed departure from a tormented world in another cruel winter of 950. Within her final days, her only wish to see the sun set was granted, it was to be the first time she had seen the sun since she had been 'escorted' from Tamworth.

Thee Prince...Thee be called Æthelstan,

a Noble Stone.

Take this as a happy omen for thy life,

thee shall be a Royal Rock fighting with a

mighty strength against fearsome demons.

But take thee the Holy path of learning too,

and should peace come, pray that thee may

seek it and that God may grant the promise

of thy noble name.

Anon.

CHAPTER 9

Almost six years to the day since Æthelflæd's death, on the 17th day of the Anglo-Saxon month of Ærlitha 924 in the old calendar, two full weeks before the anniversary of Offa's death, the rule of King Edward came to its end, during his fiftieth midsummer, by the aid of a deep wound received whilst quelling further unrest between Mercia and their Welsh neighbours.

His more than painful demise had come, ironically in a shire he had founded less than four weeks earlier, named Legeceasterscir. In the homestead of Fearndune, on the dusty floor of the Chapel of Saint Peter, so close to the river Dee that the King would have heard the water's currents as his blood drained freely from the gaping hole that had fatally ripped open his stomach.

Æthelstan had been saddled alongside his Father, taking stock of the battle's progress, when a Welsh spearman, half naked and blazing with anger, had broken their erratic defences before fatally piercing his lance through the King's tarnished mail. The immediate expression upon his Father's face was one of disgust and shame as he readily accepted his own fault in the battle, then his gaze changed oddly to calm and humility as he dropped his sword and fell from horse.

During those final minutes of King Edward's life, He had taken immediate control of the fighting, and in turn, Mercia. His first command came by calling an immediate halt to a battle he had deemed unnecessary and without purpose, and was himself relieved when the Welsh, led by Elen Ferch Llywarch, daughter of the late King of Dyfed and wife of Hywel Dda King of Deheubarth, accepted the truce by retiring back into their valleys with a Saxon King's death to their credit, and an extensive band of Mercians discontent with the Wessex rule, within their numbers.

His second command, made only as a precaution, was to dismiss the ranks of the Wessex guard so cherished by his Father, and call his own knights to his side.

No outbursts of sadness had been expressed for a passing Father, Æthelstan had merely stood and turned to the west. There was a kind of sorrow in his tone, but there were no son's tears as he spoke into the wind...

"Now then God of these lands, who so e'er thee be. Take into thine arms the spirit of my Father, Eadweard, Elder son of Ælfred, both great kings of the Wessex folk. May he rest in the lands of our forefathers as he hath earned more than his right to walk always alongside the truest of men."

One single day was set aside for the mourning which was observed in the nearest burg, then named Legacæstir, and was followed by a regal procession under a close guard as it escorted the body of the departed King from the plains of Chester's shire to his own new Minster in the Wessex ruling seat of Winchester, where alongside other family members, which included Alfred, Edward was ceremoniously entombed...

In his wake, Æthelstan's Father had left a legacy of children to the future of the growing world. They would include four Kings, two Queens, an Empress, a Duchess and even a Saint, sadly it would bring anything but stability to a continent that was becoming more than full of greedy nobles, and even greedier religions.

...As it had always seemed in such days after the death of a king, Æthelstan inherited a slight obstruction against his 'rightful' inheritance with regards to the seat of Wessex.

Ælfweard had always been a hateful and much disliked half-brother, nevertheless he was also the King's eldest son through his second marriage to the Lady Ælfflæd. He had truly believed that the rule of Wessex should have been his through right of birth and had always gossiped that Æthelstan held no entitlement as his Mother, Ecgwynn had only married Edward a few weeks prior to his birth, therefore, consummation could only have taken place outside the bounds of matrimony, or so he had often bantered.

With that in mind, and upon receiving confirmation of Edward's death from the previously dismissed Wessex guards, Ælfweard instantly put into place the ceremonies which would guide his ascension onto the Wessex seat, and in turn Mercia along with the remaining lands that were then ruled by the Anglo-Saxon.

The good folk of Wessex and Mercia, which included freemen of all ranks and titles, were becoming tired of the constant battling across their 'friendly' borders and would have wished a halt to anymore infighting. Overall, they would have been more than satisfied to have left both brothers dividing the rule and governing each province separately, as had been the way many years earlier.

But that disagreement was only set to continue for sixteen days after the death of their Father, as Ælfweard more than conveniently died. Immediately after, Æthelstan had ordered the body escorted to Winchester where he was buried without ceremony alongside Edward's still fresh tomb.

Suspicions from all levels, some more than mere whispers, hinted that Ælfweard's death was anything other than natural, or even accidental. Rumours were quickly scorched by the countless supporters who rallied to Æthelstan's side including the support and open backing that he gratefully received from the church. The assistance was sufficient to invalidate all accusations, and it had been more than helpful that his cousin held the position of Canterbury's Arch Bishop and dutifully guided the 'see' in the direction of their 'rightful' leader.

Even so, as should have been expected, and local gossip being what it was, and a good story was always worth an extra calic of mead, which also aided the intensity of the rumours as they continued to circulate, especially across Wessex.

Within hours of his Father's death, the new King in waiting had done no more than had been deemed correct by immediately dispatching his messengers to all corners of the land to inform all that their King, had fallen in battle whilst protecting his lands and that He, their new King would soon be taking a new seat of power. No sooner than the messengers had taken flight so too did a second band of black cloaked riders secretly head south, stopping for nothing more than to water their horses.

Those times were no different to any other, so rumour and dark tales were quick to follow the riders' trail through the woods and shires and forests of both realms, finally reporting them coming to a halt in the gloom of night along the outskirts of Oxenaforda.

Allegedly the black riders were met by a spindly figured, torch bearing cleric who guided them secretly through the shadows of the burg. It was there that the rumours had ended, as there would be no further sightings of the dark riders. All traces of their arrival had vanished, and no credible account could be given as to the reason that within a few days Ælfweard had been mysteriously taken ill from an unknown allergy and soon after had painfully died, installing further suggestions of misdeeds ranging from witchcraft, elves, and more so, Mercian assassins.

Again, such tales were dismissed as ridiculous and treasonous.

So, the gossip had faded away into the shadows of the shires like the wraiths who had instigated them, and Æthelstan stood rightfully as his Father's elder son and heir, to both Houses.

Regardless of the facts, the West Saxons seemed to be without a King as Æthelstan, who had unanimously been hailed as King of the Mercians, delayed his ascendance for almost a year before accepting the 'complete' coronation. His plans not to hurry into the 'grabbing' of another King's seat were tactfully as well as politically planned to settle any further suspicions the 'land folk' may have held over his half-brother's untimely departure. It also removed a tool from the hands of his neighbouring enemies who had extended their efforts in stirring up further trouble within the borderlands.

His delay would also permit the planning of his ascent so that it would be entirely different to others of the past, a marker for the chroniclers that his rule would also be unlike any other.

And it was.

Æthelstan was anointed as rightful ruler over All Lands Anglo-Saxons on 4th September 925, in the same place that had blessed his Father's rule twenty-five years earlier, in the richly adorned timber and stone chapel at Cyningstan on the banks of the great river Temes.

The ceremony of Edward's heir, between the walls of an old Saxon chapel within the settlement of an even older Brythonic King, was far from the lavish ceremony that would have normally been expected. The rule of Wessex, and by that the whole of Anglo-Saxon Engle Land was received as he knelt alongside the King's Stone that had been placed at the forefront of the Chapel's alter, of which had been built with funds provided by his late Father.

There was no person still living at that time, whose memory stretched back far enough to tell how that stone had come to be in such a place, as far as anyone knew, it had always been there. The stone was a mystically carved section of sandstone unlike any stone obtained from the surrounding areas. Ancient sagas of the Old Ones had told that the stone was transported across the Isles when a new King, or Chieftain was about to be declared as head of his 'clan'. Ancient legends, so old they were barely remembered, told how the stone had been brought across the great waters from far and distant lands, by those who had first settled those lands long before records were kept in anything other than a memory. The stone had been fought over for centuries, by the Cantiaci, Regenses and Atrebates, and many others whose clans had long since vanished from the hills and valleys of that turbulent Isle. But it was still said, that whichever group held its possession, the stone would hold close the destinies of all folk within the Brythonic south.

'He, [Æthelstan]

With Sihtric having died

in such strangest of circumstance,

armed his fyrds of Englisc

for battle

through-out the Isles of Bryton.

{Carte, dirige gressus...]

[Letter, direct thy steps...]

CHAPTER 10

Æthelstan;

924-925 King of Mercia.

925-927 King of Mercia, Wessex, and All Lands of the Anglo-Saxons.

927-939 King of the English.

From the very commencement of his rule Æthelstan 'hammered' the Danes showing little mercy and even less compromise. Whether they were Vikings from the Northern Fjords, or from the vast lands north of the Humber River, or Irish Dane from across the Hibernian Brimlad, He cared not and set to slaughter any who would dare to threaten his rule and the safety of the folk who now lived out their days within the new Engle Lands.

During those earliest years the new King's military priority was to forge a permanent alliance between the lands of the Anglo-Saxon and wage a merciless campaign against the Danish inhabitants of the northern shires. He rode at the head of his armies like a man possessed, smashing his enemies out of 'tun' and 'stead in his fervent obsession to unite All the Engle Lands under one common banner, and one single belief, that of the new Christians.

Whilst at court Æthelstan dismissed the fantasies of a youngster and the old ways becoming a religiously devoted and committed Christian, passionate to the point in spreading the words of the Holy Gospels, endowing upon his Cirican and Minsters the greatest iconic gifts of the day. Also to the good, he ordered the translation of the Latin Bible into a common Anglo-Saxon language, to offer his people their chance to read and understand the 'new words' for themselves.

Yet upon the field of battle his attitude was quite the opposite.

Naturally, rapidly becoming part of the 'etiquettes of the day,' clerics and priests from every religious minster followed his campaigns as God's representatives for the 'fyrds' and 'herga' gathered from every shire, in support of their King and defence of their 'faith'. As they marched across hillock and dune their crosses of gold and silver reflected the sun's rays upon the ranks, then as they moved into their fighting positions, echoed chants and blessings escorted the warriors towards the front lines and the wrath of their heathenish enemy. Whether it had been superstitious nonsense, or a deep-rooted tradition inherent from his forefathers, or the teachings of Æthelflæd and the old guards, Æthelstan warred in the names of the old Gods. He battled beneath the eyes of Tiw the war God, under the protection of Woden the All Father, and in the name of Saxnot, Woden's brother and their 'first father' who walked the golden stoned floors of the Wæl hæl.

Once his own borders had become secure Tamworth became his great project raising its status again to Royal capital of the Kingdom of Mercia becoming one of the most important towns in the land, all quietly to honour his still missed guardian Æthelflæd. It also made great tactical sense as Tamworth was sited virtually in the centre of the group of nations that were widely becoming known as Engle Lands.

He 'colonised' what was once just a locally important stronghold, turning it into a well fortified and prosperous urban development, which held all the important industries of the day, including a Royal Mint for the fabrication of his own coinage. The lands under Æthelstan continued to be prosperous, maybe more so than they had been during the rule of his Father and Grandfather.

The King's unrelenting pressure and distinct refusal to concede a decision, or even compromise against his chosen beliefs and ambitions inflicted mighty losses upon the ranks of his hostile neighbours, none more so than the infamously despised Northumbrian Dane's lead by Sihtric Caech.

Four years earlier, in 917, when his Father still held the throne, Sihtric 'One-eye', along with other kinsmen from the House of Imair, which included Ragnall and Gothfrith, had sailed their united fleets onto Hibernian shores dispatching their

Vikings into a heinous battle against the ancient clans lead by Niall Glundab mac Aodha of the Cenel nEogain, High King of Ireland and grandson of Cinaed mac Ailpin King of the Picts and first King of the Hibernian Scot.

Between the three of them they managed a complete disaster.

Ragnall took the 'longphort' of Waterford slaughtering any who stood against him, and even those who did not, and remained upon the island for a short while before becoming unsettled and bored, when he sailed across the waters to the valleys along the river Clyde venturing south to York, insisting he sat as their King.

His insistence lasted less than a year before being struck down by an unknown and incurable illness which made way conveniently for Sihtric.

Following his overwhelming defeat over Niall Glundab and the armies of the Irish at Islandbridge a few months earlier, Sihtric had taken the rule of Dublin as his right, but after hearing of his cousin's sudden death left Ireland for 'better' places, gaining command of All the lands within Danish Northumberland. From there after he took the title of 'King of the Dark Foreigners and Fair Foreigners.' Five years of devastation on both sides of the Mercian border would follow as Sihtric made his intensions clear by using the Mersey River as his favoured crossing point, trying his utmost to rout the English King.

As a mighty commander in all forms of military campaigns Æthelstan also excelled as politician, always encouraged in his youth to believe that words could often be a better way to negotiate rather than a sword. He 'summoned' Sihtric to a 'feasting' conference at Tamworth where much was discussed, including peace across their borders, and as always, the topic of the day was Christianity.

Before the meeting's completion Æthelstan had the Dane converting to the new religion 'on the spot', swearing his allegiance to the English King. In turn, Æthelstan 'gave' Sihtric the hand of his sister Eadgyth, as a settlement of marriage, therefore cementing both families in the unison of blood.

Eadgyth would be his 'eyes' in the Danish camp and as it would soon prove, would be his only loyal servant in the Northumberland courts.

To the astonishment of everyone, except of course the King, rumours began to flood across the waters of the Humber and Mersey, reaching ale houses and mead halls, and inevitably the ears of every ferend and ceapman who instantly set about reporting vividly 'Eadgyth's reluctance to commit herself to the new marriage' once the couple were in the confines of the marital home.

Eadgyth and Æthelstan had been close as children, sharing everything that siblings should share so he, and only he, knew she had obsessively convinced herself from the time she had bore witness to her brother's terrible birth, that such 'wifely' ways would never be for her. There would be no children, no attempts of having children, no matrimonial duties of any kind, and that had been her will, always. Knowing that, it had come as no shock to her King that before the marriage could celebrate its first year a more than frustrated Sihtric had renounced his newfound religion along with his 'Saxon' wife, whom he had banished from the bedchamber to her own quarters far out of his sight. That would suit Eadgyth, for despite her self-imposed celibacy she also found the Dane repulsive in all ways, especially the habitual way he had of staring incessantly at her through his permanently squinting eyes, whilst drooling like a rabid animal from his bottom lip.

A few months later Sihtric was found dead in extremely suspicious circumstances, and that time there were no rumours of 'dark riders'.

Æthelstan, as if he had known that such a time was nearing, instantly gathered his ever-ready army, and marched to the side of his bereaved sister, now alone in a land of unruly Danes and in her 'sorrow' found the excuse he had needed, or possibly manipulated.

As Æthelstan had marched his army north reports were received that Sihtric's kin Guthfrith had sailed from his continued dominance of the Ciannachta at Annagassan and Dublin, to inherit his cousin's worth, but had returned his fleet to the Hibernian shores once the English King's intensions, and military strengths, had been confirmed.

Northumberland was now under English rule by right of his sister's marriage and, as she was merely a timid woman, her 'inheritance' would befall upon him and therefore Northumbria would automatically become part of Engle Land.

There had been no warring, not even the smallest of scuffles as a 'united' submission of all peoples was volunteered, it was as if they relished the coming of a normality that they had never experienced under Sihtric's rule, or the rule of any Dane.

More rumours had spilled from the shadowy corners of York and on through Deira, suggesting that Eadgyth had been 'deposited' in the Danish courts by the English King by way of an 'engineered' marriage, and once the relationship had been 'set aside' the embittered wife merely sat back and waited until the time proved right and had cunningly slipped a 'potion' into Sihtric's night drink bringing about his agonising death. But such accusations could not ever be proven. Whatever the truth, Æthelstan's dream of ruling a United Isle was becoming reality, the Engle Lands were now the largest they had been since the rule of his Grandfather.

Eadgyth's hopes were now fulfilled. Her duty to her brother and her people had been accomplished and in return she was permitted to enlist within the small nunnery at Polesworth, where she gladly lived and prayed out the remainder of her days in the service of her God, whom she had solely believed, forever in the debt of her King.

Things did not always go his way...

Almost immediately after Northumberland's reclamation, the Scots, led by Constantine and supported by Sihtric's ever returning heirs, then gathered with a large group of extremely unhappy Danes who had themselves once dominated the plains north of the Humber. Combining their forces, as well as their hatred for all things English, they rekindled their acts of cross border fighting against their 'new' neighbours.

The petty conflicts posed no great threats, becoming more of an inconvenience than anything else, but they still brought an unwanted expense, as well as an uncertainty towards the people, outraging Æthelstan and his Thegns, whose attentions and finances could have been spent better elsewhere, with more productive outcomes.

So, it would be arranged through embassies, equerries, and messengers of all kinds, over many months, that on the twelfth day of July 927, Æthelstan would convene a gathering at a small, insignificant place then named Eamotum.

The first treaty between the lands north and south of the Latin wall, pledging the Anglo-Saxon English and the Scots of Alba not to lend their support to any unchristian Kingdoms, which meant that Constantine could not openly side with the Dane, or any other Viking, who still at that time laid claim to parts of the north, as well as much of Ireland. Those who eventually swore their oaths, signed their names, or made their marks upon Æthelstan's treaty were King Ouuen of Strathclyde, Constantine mac Aeda of the Scots, Hywel Dda of Deheubarth and Ealdred Eadulfsson a noble from Bebbanburg, once named Din Guardi the ancient capital of the Bryneich folk.

Ealdred's mark upon the treaty was significant only to Æthelstan because of the historic connection Bebbanburg held in the north.

The 'Gathering of Kings' had been held on the shores of the river Eamont along the most southerly extremities of Ouuen's lands. The plains and woodlands were sparse, the closest shores were unsuitable for the birthing of a fleet, so the area was as safe a meeting place as any other.

The tents were raised on each side of the 'pen rhyd', an ancient crossing place, where Æthelstan had ordered the construction of a small wooden bridge in advance of the gathering, to link both sides of the river, as a sign to show those arriving that the treaty was there for the benefit of all, who were free to come and go, unhindered across all lands.

The signing was carried out with little ceremony within the confines of a small 'henge' of stone erected thousands of years earlier by those who first walked the lands, when there was little need of a treaty to walk peacefully alongside their neighbours. Æthelstan insisted no weapons would be carried within the 'circle' of stone, and to show his credibility a 'table of shields' was erected in a circle without a noted place for a leader, sufficient for seating all, plus one, and unlike the traditions of passed gatherings there would be no mead, no ale and no wine served, no refreshment at all, save a single flasc of fresh spring water, there for all to share, as equals.

"For who be set this empty place…" Hywel Dda had asked, certain there would be no latecomers.

Æthelstan had expected such a question, there was always someone ready to ask the obvious… "A seat such as this shall always be set and ever empty, to represent all who have given their lives in the fighting now passed, for those who have done battle in our names, and the names of those who ruled before us. T'is there, so that His spirit may sit at our table, and hear all that we agree upon, so that He may return to the lands of the unforgotten and say to all, 'That we be united now, as one. No more shall we waste the lives of good men.'

"Then who be He, this one messenger, who sits at thy table?" asked Constantine.

"He be no one" replied Æthelstan, "yet he be everyone."

His companions had felt stupid, they should all have known the answer.

From that minute on there had been an eerie silence as each noble made his mark upon a document that would be forgotten in time as the first treaty between the lands of the Scot and the English. The process was completed as each man turned to his neighbour and clasped their hand, satisfied with himself, they could now relax for the first time in the company of their 'enemies'.

On its completion, after the expected small talk that always followed such gatherings the King of the 'new realm' of Engle Land presented each with a gift that had been forged by the Smyth's of Tamworth… Each received a golden ring of the highest quality, which, on the outside seemed nothing more than a modest yellow band, but on the inside, inscribed in perfect Anglo-Saxon, was Æthelstan's name along with that of the receiver, and between each name was the single word…'Frið'…peace.

Æthelstan knew too well that it would be far easier to etch a word on a golden band than to uphold its meaning.

From that day on, the meeting was named as 'the treaty of the five rings', and the ancient henge of stone was named locally as 'Æthelstan's Table'.

A Hall stands there, fair, under the ash called

Yggdrasill, by the well, and out of that comes

three maids who are called thus;

Wyrd [fate], Verdandi [present], Skuld [future].

These maids determine the length of men's lives;

we call them Norns; but there be many Norns;

those who come to each child that is born,

these are the race of the Gods.

But the second are the Elf-folk…

…Most sundered in birth I say the Norns are;

They claim no common kin:

Some be of Aesir-kin, some are of Elf-kind,

Some are of Dvalinn's daughters

CHAPTER 11

928. This year William took to Normandy, and held it fifteen years.

There was always a certain amount of boredom with that time of year despite the 'petty' matters of the gemot, Æthelstan had often called it 'idel menn monað' as all men seemed to him lazy during that time of year. February, or Solmonað, was also the quietest of months, bitterly cold, sickeningly damp, and frustratingly tedious, with no crops to be sown and even less to be harvested, the moon still drew in the shadows of the night giving way to the day's light even later, yet that had not deterred him from taking an evening's walk, alone.

On a dry chilled evening, as the freshness of winter tide let all know that the mighty Tiw's only hand remained strong enough to hold back Eostre's warmth, Æthelstan stepped out from the comforts of his Great Hall where those who kept his favour drank the last of the season's mead whilst feasting on salted pig and overstored vegetables. He walked casually passed the night guards who were as vigilant as ever, despite the cold, passing others who braved the freeze, bantering their way from the fire of one ale house to the warming flames of another, all within the safety of the burg.

'Was that the reason for such fighting, such warring, such wounding, such slaughtering, for the safety of the 'true' folk, whose only requirement was to innocently pass their days in the service of their 'masters' without the slightest consideration to robbing a neighbour's possessions, stealing his land, or even taking his life for the sake of greed and wanting?'

His thoughts were deep and many.

Unintentionally or not, he would never recollect his reasons for leaving the defences of the ringwall through the same 'secret' exit he had used so many years before, but that was just a distant memory.

How things had changed since those early days, not always for the better. Often, he had longed for the return to those innocent, childish times when he knew just enough to pass through a day, and little enough that the days never seemed to have an end.

Nowadays Æthelstan had to bend and twist his body almost in half to avoid painfully hitting his head on the stone lintel that had barely scraped the curls of a boy, all those years ago. Had it been that long?

Once free from the fortified restrictions he stretched back his body, upright and relieved, long, and high, towards the night sky that was then bright and clear despite its blackness, hence the crispness of the ground underfoot. How the night stars had seemed so much larger than on any other night, providing their heavenly beacons as he aimlessly strolled across the open grounds, nearing the distant line of mystical trees that had always remained 'the forbidden Brunesweald'. Now the heat of his breath, condensing in the cold almost blocked his vision with its intensity, it was an extremely cold night.

He could think of no specific reason for his venture on such a night, leaving behind a fire's warmth for the bitterness of a winter's chill, and more so, how had he so quickly reached the Brunesweald, and further, but truly at that moment he did not care and kept on walking.

That night was not his first visit amongst the shadows of the forest, there had been many occasions in his youth, whilst at play with those of his own age, and later as a man, just to escape life's pressures and monotonies, but that night the Brunesweald seemed different, very different…

Ambling his way further into the charcoal night, as the naked limbs of winter's trees excluded most of the heaven's light, huddled against the chill in the thick wolf's fur that covered his purple cloak, he ventured deeper into the leafless surrounds, and the forest appeared to change around him...

Not just in the way forests change, thicker, then thinner, bushier then thornier, but brighter and greener.

It also seemed much warmer. So much warmer that Æthelstan opened, then shouldered the heavy fur that had protected his body from the harshness of the winter's eve.

The light also seemed to increase, more so than would have been expected from the half moon which had danced its way between the modest wisps of night cloud, it was almost light enough for the sun to rise yet he knew that to be impossible and his own curiosity, as ever, bade him advance closer into the strange brightness.

During those early years, when he had entered the forest, whatever had been his age at the time, any caution or suspicion had been quickly dismissed as the trees seemed to grant him nature's own security, and that time would have been no different, in the mind of a child.

Alas, the man that had since grown from the boy had gained mistrust and scepticism at the slightest of changes. Instinct forced his right hand tightly about the grip of his sword, guided his eyes as they scanned sharply, and his ears pricked as they listened. His senses set themselves deep into the woodlands, preparing for anything that may suddenly rise out from the secrecy of nature's 'innocent' shadows.

'...And what in the Lord's name was that?'

Ahead, surrounded by the brightest circle, within those ever-mystical woodlands had been laid a table, a table draped with a fine cloth, embroidered with signs and letters of which he had never seen. In its centre had been placed a single calic, moulded in the brightest of gold and encrusted with the largest of gemstones shining enticingly against the brightness. What had begun as an innocent stroll was now seeming more of a dream as all signs of reality seemed to be exchanged for those of the unreal, had he really ventured out into the night, or had he fallen deeply into another strange sleep within the comforts of his quarters?

Wherever he was, and why ever he was there, the warmth of the light and the opportunity for quenching his thirst was almost too tempting. He stopped alongside the table staring down at the calic and its inviting mixture, but that was where his wits had rescued him.

Regardless of his thirst nothing could, or would persuade him to drink the contents, whatever it contained. He was ever uncertain of the reality to that which he now stared down upon, nor anything else around him for that matter, more certainly he realised that nothing about him seemed at all safe.

Æthelstan stood alone, in the spell of the Brunesweald, vulnerable and unprotected.

Away to his left, just as he had first set foot from the shadows, there had been a rustle from within the walls of evergreen, an animal of the night he had thought, yet the noise had continued as he had approached the table, still nothing more than a rustling breeze he had hoped, and a slight glance in its direction offered no better answer, then the rustling had stopped.

The brightness seemed to have peaked spreading outwards from where he stood, illuminating the woodland carpet deeper into the distance, highlighting the greenness of the trees, bringing out the wild things as they gained sufficient courage to investigate his arrival, suspicious of his coming, angered that their world had been invaded.

And the chatters and cheeps of fur and feather filled the air as nature debated his presence…

"But!!!" he realised amongst the commotion, "It should still be the night." There had not been time enough since leaving the burg for the sun to rise and the wilderness around him to waken. Even if it had, it was not yet the season for such things…and the warmth?

The chattering of the birds eased a little, but silence had not replaced their song…

The strangest sounds could be heard, a kind of melody, the rustling within the gorse had restarted, and still there was the rush of the gentlest breeze, but without the disturbance, and the 'hush' grew louder as it carried the ghostly chants towards him, louder, until his own thoughts were taken by the hypnotic sounds that carried upon the ever- warming draft. The stillness around him woke his senses and half a drawn sword threatened to cut the air as his feet began to slide cautiously back into his earlier tracks. In a silent bid to forge an escape he scoured the evergreen for any target that may launch an attack, until the breeze became more insistent and filled his breath with the calming odour of fresh honeysuckle and blackberry leaf, and his feet stopped still, the sword returned to its rest and Æthelstan stood statue like and confused yet at ease, nervous yet comforted, more so he started to feel any danger that may have threatened swiftly disappear. Defences relaxed, fears calmed, he knew then that he belonged within those wooded lands.

And the chanting's 'hush' quietened slowly until it was almost exchanged with the melody of a harp, the trickle of clear water, and the softness of...

...A scented breath which spoke softly against his innocent cheek...

"La, Æthelstan, cild fram se æfenleoht, beon thee stillan..." and a tear began its escape followed by a second as a hand that was not his wiped dry his cheek as the face of a Mother appeared in front of a son, and another tear escaped, but that time it was not his.

Words pierced her smile, whispered in the softest of tones, almost an echo...

"Once my son, in this same place stood as a child, here, alongside his Mother."

She wiped away another tear as her son was permitted to remember those times long ago, he returned her smile.

"Now here before me stands my son, in the form of a man he be...A hero of battles...A noble of truth. Here at my side stands my son, the Man who shall become a glorious King within the lands of men."

"Modor." The voice of the man had long since replaced the tones of a boy.

"Sunnu, my son" and they embraced as if they had never been apart, but were immediately disturbed as the gorse began to rustle once more, that time louder, more definite as Æthelstan reached for his sword...

"Gestyllan Æthelstan... Be thee calm. Here there be no danger, not for one such as thee."

He knew that. Something from the past had told him from his memories.

Then the bulk of another, from the dreams of yesterday, stepped forward from the treeline, rattling again the gorse as he filled the whole glade with his presence. He was remembered as a giant, and still he remained a giant. His armour-clad form glistened in the golden rays of a false sun, just as it had done long since, and his thickened beard flared rigidly from a reddened face sending the illusion that flames burst free from his nostrils as he thumped his heavily booted steps towards the pair.

A true silence now smothered mother and son, permitting the giant time to assure himself that he now stood in front of the man he had expected. The years had done little to preserve his memory, his own excuse anyway.

"Ahhhh... Æthelstan, Cyning of Mann." A sigh joined the words as he confirmed Æthelstan's identity, "Soon, thee shall become more than a King. A King of all men who tread between the shores of middengærd. Destiny still speaks of the great things yet to come to the shores of this realm of man. 'Hleothop still chants his decree, now even louder as the days gather towards thy time...Middengærd'... he calls loud in the Halls of the Gods, 'the Lands between heaven and hell, where true men walk tall. The lands of the Engle and Seaxisc.'"

At first Æthelstan stuttered trying to accept that which he had always thought a dream, a myth from the memories of the elders, or a saga from the hearth fires of a child, again he remembered that time long ago when he had sat with his Mother, in that same forest of peace and tranquillity.

"Woden."

His temporary stammer had gone as he declared his recognition with a returned confidence...

"Eallfæder t'is thee" and his head dropped respectfully as his Mother fondly took his hands.

Arms flew out from the Godly bulk, joyful laughter, as much in relief as in delight, burst up from the All Father's heavily quivering stomach dragging the young King into his hold, squeezing tighter and tighter as if the very life would burst from his body. It was then that Æthelstan remembered the truth about that most special of places, for gone at last were the feelings of a dream.

"Æthelstan Trueheart soon to be All King to the worthy" he humoured his proud response, now it was his turn to lower a respectful gaze. "Thee hath yet to be known as Rewarder of Heroes, Slayer of Greed and Champion of Peace. Thee now stands here, at my front, as the man spoken of in the Halls of thy Fathers, for many ages passed."

Embarrassed, humbled? At the very least he was confused that one so great as Woden should bestow such words upon him, still unproven in the eyes of many. He felt uneasy and out of place...

"Father. I be nothing of those things of which thee speaks. I be no more than a simple man who through right of birth be honoured as King. Nothing more than a lowly man, who believes in truth, who hopes for peace and plenty for the good folk, and defeat to the breeders of greed and hurt who for too long have been drawn towards our shores."

Woden laughed a little too loud and corrected himself instantly with a deep... "Hmmmmm..." followed by an enforced cough before saying... "That my son be why thee be many of those things now, and shall be all those things, and more, in the times that are about to unfold." A pause saw him turn away. He walked the few paces toward the solitary table and turned to them once more, this time holding the single calic in his right hand, then raised it high enough for both to see...

"Why did thee not drink from Woden's cup young King? Especially when thee held such a thirst."

Æthelstan looked directly into the eyes of the All Father…

"I do not care for wines and meads of man, nor the ales of mishaps and false courage…"

He looked towards his Mother, then back towards the table staring incessantly at the jewelled cup "I have seen enough of its effect upon others. A little may be accepted as a cure for illness maybe, but only when it be prepared with spring's water from the 'firgernstream', or goat's milk and spices from our own feld."

"And thee tell that my words of compliment do not apply to thee…Why, t'is the very reason thee are, and why thee shall always be…"

Æthelstan still failed to understand and said so.

"Blunt as an old seax, just as thee were as a child" he laughed "Why, doth thee never frequent the mead halls, or suppen ale with thy knights?"

"Nese!!! I see little reason in the drinking of one's fill, ne'er remembering why thee did so, or what thee did whilst drunken. T'is not wise to place the trust of a man into the hands of a mead soaked erne when such drink can turn a mind and corrupt it to say and do such things that would not be said and done without it."

Woden had to agree, he knew well enough that past times had proved the King's words right.

Ecgwynn took again her son's hand in silent agreement, in her time within the Lands of Men she had witnessed everything her son now spoke of, and much more. Bad decisions were often made with a belly full of mead.

Woden's voice had now lowered into a calmer, more serious note. "There be other temptations that may divert thee to be a lesser man…"

Now the meeting had reached the point that it was intended to reach.

"All those years passed, when thee were nought but a child, and we sat here as one, together here in this same place, my words spoke to thee of cruel days, evil days that would soon be upon us, Man and God alike, and of the sacrifices needed to bring victory across thy lands."

He remembered, not until that minute, those dreamlike times now real in his memory, just as any other memory.

"Then, Æthelstan, should thee still wish to fulfil thy destiny and the wishes of thy Forefather's, just as it were written long ago, with the chance to bring thy lands all the good things that thee do wish for, there be yet another sacrifice that thee must make. An oath must be taken, that ye must swear to uphold its every word so long as thee shall remain within the Lands of Men…"

Again, confused, concerned…

"And I told thee that there be much to learn through the years, with more gifts for ye to collect as thee grew."

He remembered that also.

"What be such an oath of such sacrifice, to be greater than my oath already given, to do All for the folk of my land?"

"There be more than just folk of thy lands within thy destiny, Æthelstan Truehelm, much more than thee could ever imagine."

Woden's right arm lifted in their direction and beckoned them to follow, across the glade to a cluster of small rocks, where he sat upon the tallest then sighed with exhaustion as an arm rested upon his thigh. Mother and son sat at either side staring left and right, inquisitively waiting for him to continue.

And continue he did with a tone of voice as serious as his expression, but not until he had completed the deepest of thoughts.

"Thy bloodline Æthelstan, was passed unto thee in the womb of thy Mother..." he motioned towards Ecgwynn as if there were still a need to confirm her as his true Mother. "A bloodline which hath flowed with honour through the bodies of the many who have walked upon these lands since times so long passed that even I struggle to remember them... Before the times when they who only spoke the Latin dared to set sail upon the mighty 'whale-road' and threatened to take all things within these shores for them and no other. Before the times when far off lands were hurriedly left in search for a promise of plenty, and thy forefathers first came upon these shores. So much of their blood, and that too of others, hath been spilled into these lands that the soil now begins to turn its own colour." The All Father reached down to his boot, tore a fistful of earth between his fingers and allowed it to sieve back onto the land. "Yet despite the fightings and battlings brought about by the enemies of those who shall never be forgotten, there hath been little to halt such slaughter. Slowly, from those past times thy 'blodfolc' have grown fewer until now, when such blood flows only through no other body but thine within this realm, or any other within the land of men."

Æthelstan shook his head removed his bright helm for the first time and piled the thick over fur at his feet... "But Eadgyth...Is not my own sister also of the same blood of our Mother?"

Ecgwynn's eyes closed as they lowered towards the ground and her cheeks reddened bringing an awkward silence to the glade.

Regardless of his adamantly enforced tone, Woden's voice was a welcome disturbance to the uncomfortable quiet "Thee, and thee alone be the last of thy bloodline, and there be need for no more to be said." He shook his head, there would be no further explanation in his answer, it would remain another of the strange mysteries that he would need to accept.

Woden continued, "The era has long since passed when those who also came from thy blood did leave the ways of men forever, and now, allow such men who remain in thy stead to fall and rise by their own fault, or gain, as it may be. There shall soon be no place upon these shores for one such as thee. The Men who follow Ælfred's line shall be no more."

He eased his bulk backwards finding a little more comfort upon the rock, let out a sigh and replaced the breath slowly before beginning a story that had never been shared before, with any earthborn man...

"In the world of mortal man, the God's have always been honoured. Though known across many lands by many different names, they have always stood to represent the same. For many ages, Man hath fought against the will of the Gods for supremacy over the lands, some may say rightfully so, but there hath ne'er been a time when either was victorious over the other, and despite the greatest powers of the Gods, man's own heart hath proven strongest, but never powerful enough to conquer fully. Many lives have been taken in the cruellest of ways, for the rage of man be unending. Yet now the chances of us all are drifting away. There is coming a new age to the Land of Men. An age where all shall kneel in the name of the White Christ, or another of his kind. There be no place now for the spirits of thy forefathers who walk proudly in the Halls of Fallen."

Sadness high-lighted Woden's own silence as if he had only now accepted an imminent defeat, and with such a defeat would come his own redundancy as the All Father of everything that, up until such a time, had been granted to Man.

"Thy bloodline..." he continued his whisper "...be the last of the old ways that were set upon this land for what was then thought to be 'for the good of man', at a time when a mortal needed protecting from no one else but others of his own kind. Even though such a need may remain it now befalls upon thee to leave them in peace, and that peace can only come when thee reaches the end of thy destiny."

The more he tried the harder it grew to understand. The more his mind repeated Woden's words the more complicated things seemed.

"Then what shall become of the Old Ways, the ways of my Fathers?"

Woden's tone bore sympathy. "They shall be left in the tales and sagas yet to be told around the hearth fires of future years. To be remembered in myth and in legend forever, and no more."

"Then what of mine own Ætheling, how would he fare?"

Ecgwynn moved closer in the pause, to offer the comfort she knew her son may soon need.

"There shall be no such heir my son..." a short wait for a response that did not come, and she continued, "Thee must be the last of our blood, and that be how these lands must remain, long after we be forgotten, in the times not yet dreamed. When all earthly traces of our presence are removed no mention of us shall be permitted. Soon we shall exist only within the dreams of man, as a testimony to that which he could never possess, to that which he shall always wish, but ne'er truly want..."

"And what be that Modor?"

"It be that which thee shall search for, and receive at the end of thy days. That which shall vanish with thy memory never again to return to the World of Men, for it be nothing more than Peace my son. Peace among men..."

How right she sounded. The lessons he had been taught, about the histories of his 'fellow man' and the sights he had witnessed during his own short life, he could not argue with his Mother's words. Man, did not want for peace, all man wanted for himself was More.

"...There be no place now in Middengærd for the mystical ones. The times of New Men are about to begin."

Æthelstan shook his head, waving his blonde locks from left to right in frustration...

"Confusion and chaos now fills my head, and all else with it be..."

"Indeed," broke Woden "there be nought else but confusion. Harken my words Æthelstan Ælfscreon. Thy destiny must be fulfilled in the short times that follow. It shall rest upon thine own shoulders to search for the true peace that shall spread through the lands. A peace that shall do battle against the greed of man through the countless ages, until Man has found in himself a stronger belief. Thee Æthelstan, last King of the Ælfen ways, shall win thy battles true, but to do so thee must first swear an oath, an oath never asked before of a Man by a God, an oath, here and now within the ears of thine own Modor, and I…"

"Oath, what oath?" he slammed and shuffled his feet in frustration, a little childlike, he had never appreciated being forced to agree the unknown.

All eyes met, fixing upon the figure of the All Father, eagerly awaiting his response.

"This be a most important and sacred oath and one that thee must agree to uphold, if only for the future of man. Whatever thee shall do upon these lands, be it now, or in years yet to come, thee must ensure that ye shall ne'er leave an heir of thy blood, to follow in thy stead. Thy bloodline must end with thee, as I say once more, it shall soon be the time of Man."

So deep in concentration were his thoughts, almost loud enough to be heard.

"Hath thee e'er lain with a woman?"

Cough, splutter, heavily reddening cheeks, and a feeling of angry intrusion welled from the King's stomach, no one would ever ask such a personal question, and never at the side of his own Mother.

"Thou ask that of me, here, within earshot of my Mother? Thee be the All Father, forever knowing of all, so why be the need of such a question?"

If the situation had not been so serious, Woden would probably have smiled at the response, but he was as equally embarrassed at the asking as was shown in the tone of his reply…

"There be things that even a God shall not be privy to. If all had been known to the Gods my son, about the ways and wants of all things, then we would not be here at such a time."

A further pause, but no reply…

"Then, my answer be told with thy silence…'nateshwon', by no means."

Æthelstan's deeply reddened cheeks highlighted against his blonde complexion whilst his head lowered in an expression of failure and shame, "No Lady hath yet taken my eye, t'is as I spoke 'afore, I do not frequent the mead halls, nor other such places, for any kind of false pleasure."

"…And thee must ne'er do, throughout the years that follow."

Embarrassment still told in the King's eyes, even so, he managed half a glance towards his Mother. Then eye to eye.

"Celibacy, thee both ask of me an oath of celibacy?"

There was no shame betrayed in the All Father's response. "We do not ask for it… For the future of 'mancynn' we insist upon it."

Silence.

A long silence that seemed as if it would never end again filled the glade, not even the creatures in the wild dared to break the quiet. Whether it was the shame within the question, or the embarrassment in owing an answer, the silence seemed to go on forever.

Finally, he shook his head, rose slowly to his feet, walked three or four paces, then turned back to confront the still reticent pair. "No wife, no heir, no son?"

"No kitchen 'mægden', no lass from the vil, nor even the dohtor of a Thegn even" added Woden, "nothing that may risk the true fulfilment of thy destiny."

She watched as his face dropped in sorrow, not for the denial of future pleasure but for the sacrifice from every King's duty to leave behind an heir, to follow in his path, to continue the line of his forefathers into the future years, and in such an heir a Man's memory would be kept alive, his own story of life.

Ecgwynn sensed his feelings. "T'is the way that it must be, thee must leave no heir to thy bloodline, to our bloodline…" she pulled him a little closer tugging at his cloak. "And in return…,"

"What Modor?" His tone dropped for a moment to that of a spoiled child, scolded by a parent. "What be it that I shall receive for such an oath, what can be such greatness in place of honour, apart from the shame of childlessness, and the subject of gossip behind hastily drawn draperies. For that, what great thing shall I receive in return?"

The threat of yet another silence was quickly dismissed as Woden interrupted.

"Honour may come in many ways…The honour of a man may be nought but his own pride, yet the honour of a King be that which he leaves in his stead…" Woden now stood. "Thee shall receive what e'er be needed to achieve unending victories in the battles and wars against thine enemies. Victories shall bring treaties that shall then bring peace between all thy neighbours, a peace within these lands such as ne'er been known, and a place in the chronicles that shall read as the most glorious of all Kings to rule these lands, the first of many Kings for a united Engleland."

The proposition did all but delight him. "And my Ætheling, who shall…?"

"…Thee shall choose thine own heir, the way that it hath always been. He shall be who so 'er thee wishes, for one of thine own choosing shall have the right to follow."

"…Then my lands shall remain at peace, for ever more?"

Woden groaned slightly before a smile of confused awkwardness drifted across his lips, "Would thee believe my words if I answered Yeah…knowing the greed of those about thee as ye do?"

"So then, what be it that changes with such an oath?"

"Ahhh…" another expected question, and he returned to his 'seat' upon the widest rock. The weight of the world that had been set upon his shoulders for evermore was now easing, his own time was coming to its long awaited close and he would welcome its arrival with delight, forever had been such a very long time.

Yet, until such a day came, there was still much remaining...

"...The White Christ hath already begun to change many things about this world. Those who speak of his ways have set their path within the hearts and minds of man, and so too shall man follow with those same beliefs, and the beliefs of many others like Him that wish to destroy the Halls of thy Forefathers with their pious speaking through dreary chanting. But men alone shall always remain in search for things greater, even beyond that of the White Christ and his familiars. Thunor, Tiw, Eostre and Saxnot, even Loki, Hel and Balder, all those within my world be tired. They have struggled everlasting for the good of 'mancynn' and have little stomach left for the hypocrisy of such 'Christian' ways... The first change for man, Æthelstan, shall be the ways of the Christian."

Another quick thought, then without searching out further argument Æthelstan accepted that all that remained was to ask the obvious.

"Then what shall happen here, upon these lands, should I refuse, should I leave an heir of my blood, what then shall happen to the destinies within this Land of Men?"

Woden bellowed loud enough, almost beating the wind...

"Ye must not refuse. Ye cannot refuse. Ye shall not refuse..."

And Woden stared into the King's eyes. He had feared that question's asking, but Æthelstan would not have been the man they had hoped for if he had not asked it, but that did not mean the All Father could take such a question lightly. He rose again to his feet and closed the distance between them. Taking the deepest of breath, he placed both hands firmly upon Æthelstan's shoulders, then...

...Gradually the silence became the past as cold winds brought free their howlings from the evergreen and the chants and earlier melodies echoed within the breeze. The voices of the frosty chill increased until nothing else within the glade could be heard, and hear they did....

'It sates itself upon the lifeblood of fated men,

paints red the powers' home with crimson gore.

Black becomes the sun's beams

in the summers that follow.

Weathers all treacherous....

Do ye still seek to know...?'

And Ecgwynn took to her feet, crossed through the dust clouds, and found the safety of her son, then the frosts fell deeper as the winds continued their eerie knell...

'Brothers shall fight and kill each other.

Sisters' children shall defile their kinship.

It shall be harsh in the world of Man...

Whoredom rife...

an axe age, a sword age, shields are riven...

A wind age, a wolf age

before the world goes headlong,

no man shall have mercy upon another.'

Woden raised his hands free from the King's shoulders, lifted his arms high in silent command, shouted high and loud...

"Be not yet the Norns' time" and the winds fell with a hiss of discontent. The wild things called, and the brightness returned to the glade, Æthelstan feared, Ecgwynn trembled...

"The west wind speaks through the voices of the 'spæwife'... They speak of Ragnarok!!!... Thee knows the sagas of the Norse told when a child, to scare thee into thy cots at night, to make certain that thee should not leave them until the sun itself bade thee. The sagas of Ragnarok, the final battle for Asgard against her enemies, the end days that the Christians call Armageddon, the last of All that we know, all we have ever known. Oblivion, upon these very lands, upon all lands...Ragnarok shall come."

A true fear swelled up inside his stomach unlike any fear he had ever felt, a chilled sweat ran down his spine, his belly threatened to empty, he choked as his fingers began to tremble, in his mind the clouds turned grey the winds screamed and the cruellest of weather blasted every front, he tried to visualise what he had been told, how the end of their world would seem...

...As evil swept through the Lands of the Engle and Saxon, creatures never seen in the Land of Men strode free from forest and wood and broke out alive from the skin of the earth surging a path across the Realms of Engleland, and into the lands of their neighbours, leaving the putrid stench of death behind them, defiling the women, feasting on children and tearing his warriors limb from limb as they tried in vane to stop their onslaught, until nothing else remained of Man or his makings within that, or any other place. The end would follow as raging infernos blew melting rocks from the heights of the world sending out their rivers of molten fire which would mingle and congeal in the flooding streams of mankind's blood before there came upon that world...nothing. Nature herself would then rise, call forth her children from their longest sleep to stand against the terror, fight for a return to normality of what was once her lands, only to be ripped in half by horror's own beasts, devoured in a feasting frenzy, digested in the myths of history, gone for all times.

There was no time for choice, there was no choice, no time for further questions, no further questions were needed, all arguments had been made.

"The choice be made...The oath be given. I shall uphold the words of my destiny...So here, upon this very day, to the ears of my Lord and my Mother I vow an oath and a promise that no son of my blood, of our blood, shall remain upon these lands when my own time comes…But with all this I have sworn, permit me one, final question."

There would always be one final question. Woden agreed with an expectant frown drooping over his eyes. Glancing towards Ecgwynn for a final time he agreed that Æthelstan may ask…

A full breath exhaled into the now warming air of the glade, "If it be that I am the last in the line of the Old Ones, the last line of Ælfenfolc, then, when my time comes, and I pass from this world, where shall my spirit settle, in the Halls of my Forefathers, or within this place, this 'paradise' that be told of by the Christian ones?"

There was no way that even Woden, a God of All Gods, creator of all things now and all things passed, could answer such a question, it could never have been answered by anyone.

"The answer which thee seeks lies where it hath always lain for every man, through every time…Thy destiny's end can only be shown in the final seconds of a life, when one's own deeds upon the mortal world be taken to account. Then, and only then may thy 'ealdorlege' be taken, and not just by any God, but by the 'Norns'."

Her Motherly instincts told Ecgwynn that the answer was insufficient for her son, and his expression confirmed her feelings, so she explained…

"Thee must live the remaining years of thy life in truth to thyself, and in return thee shall be true to the lands and its folk. If that be, then so shall it be that the judgement on that final day be taken fairly for the way thee hath spent each day of thy life, and it be unlike a son of mine to accept anything less."

Æthelstan nodded, her words were acceptable. Naturally she was right, she was his Mother, was not every Mother?

He turned without speaking a word, walked half the distance towards the edge of the glade and stopped without cause or intention, staring into the gorse bush that had first conceded its secret presence…Again the yellow berries had been covered in a thin white blanket which like before had been ignored.

There he was, swearing an oath of celibacy, promising to leave behind him no heir to uphold any legacy that he may strive to leave, and yet he had been King for the shortest of times and had barely forged the lands, as one. He turned sharply on the balls of his feet with another question almost upon his lips.

Where had they gone?

Alone, he stood in the clearing, freezing cold against winter's chill and wet from winter's curse. All that remained inside the gloom was his fur over cloak, neatly folded within the small circle of stones, where he had left it. Now they too were covered by the same white blanket...Had he been dreaming again?

The cold had found its way into his boots. A freezing cold that bit hard into his flesh making its way deeper into his body, and the rain that had accompanied it started to turn more from a frigid wetness to the light dusty flakes of whiteness that fluttered down erratically in the hollow breeze, that picked up its force just as he had reclaimed the fur, and as he struggled for its warmth against the ever biting winds, Æthelstan, King to the Mercian and Saxon realms turned and hurried from the Brunesweald, stopping only once, for the slightest second, when he could have sworn, that a cloud of honeysuckle and blackberry leaf had swept its fragrance through the wind. He smiled, knowingly content with his night's walk as he made for the safety of Tamworth's ringwall with an excited confusion and the knife sharp cold as his only companions.

How soon hath Time, the subtle thief of youth

stolen on his wing, my three and twentieth year.

My hasting days fly on with full career,

but my late spring, no bud nor blossom shew'th.

Perhaps my semblance might deceive the truth,

That I to manhood am arrived so near,

And inward ripeness doth much less appear.

That some more timely happy spirits endu'th

Yet be it less, or more, or soon or slow,

It shall be still in strictest measure even

To that same lot however mean, or high,

Toward which time leads me, and the will of Heaven;

All is, if I have the grace to use it so,

As ever in my Taskmaster's eye.

John Milton.

CHAPTER 12.

He had admitted to himself, but only in the briefest second, that 'he had expected the storm to have been much worse,' and the instant his eyes glared up to the charcoal skies he cursed aloud for his optimistic thoughts.

Within no time at all he was saturated from head to toe, despite the heavy cloak, soaked through to his skin. A freezing stream poured over his tarnishing helm, cascaded across his unkempt face, and soaked every part until every inch of him became waterlogged to its limit, and it did not stop there, there was worse yet to come…

He should have listened to the advice offered by his Ealdormann at Oxford. For once in his stubborn life he could have listened and humbly accept in the vain in which it had been offered. "Bregu, delay, just until the morn'" Thurold's invitation to spend the night in his company, under the roof of a friend, remaining dry, well fed, and warm, able to continue his journey on the morrow. It had been dismissed, kindly, but dismissed all the same. Even Ealdfrith and Ecgberht who knew him better than most had both lost their arguments against his stubbornness…The King had won his right to continue his quest…and continue he did…alone.

…His horse Abrecan was aptly named. Standing herself against Thunor's rages, contemptibly ignoring the brightness of Loki's fire, unlike most other horses of her standard, but there were signs now that even she may betray her stoic character.

There had been nothing like it in years, and there he was alone, trapped in God's own fury, at the side of a Brunesweald hollow way, sheltered beneath a leafless willow without a single Huscarl at his side, far from any 'friendly' burg where he could expect the warmth of a loyal Thegn's fire and a hot meal from his kitchens.

A hot meal?

The King was hungry as well as soaked, and although he would not admit it, he was also lost. Not that any other could have found their way out of such a storm, but lost he was nevertheless. The skies were too black to read the stars and the night too dark to recognise the land's signs. Being in a strange place had never previously caused him any concern, and neither would he have worried much over an empty belly or wet back as there were always those whose 'pangs' would last longer than his own. But alone, with the storms turning worse by the second and the blackness of the night now only illuminated by the white bolts of forked lightning, Æthelstan had good reason to worry about more urgencies than an empty belly.

Little more than a trudge. Battered by the winds and hindered with a foot's depth of sodden mud his goings were slow. Despite the usual concerns for Abrecan's stamina he knew, for both their sakes, that he must remain mounted. Her own instincts against Nature's unheeding wrath were greater than his, to dismount now and proceed on foot would bring peril upon them both.

…And the rain teemed harder as the thunder shattered above the hustling clouds, he had to find shelter however modest, nothing could last out the night in such ferocity.

Suddenly from nowhere his face was slapped smartly by what leaves remained upon the straining branches of a struggling tree, dragged back and forth by the demonstrable winds. Branches, thicker than a spears shaft were sharply wrenched from their trunks and hurled into the mighty storm, only adding to the danger. That night was truly horrible, and the noise…

Visibility was virtually nothing, and the wind's rush took away any hope of coordinating a route, so it was little wonder that the King had not heard the excited screams until he had found himself between the horses of both knights…

All were as bemused and surprised as each other. Other riders out on such a night was anything but expected, both parties had believed, up until then, that they were the only fools within the Brunesweald.

Each rider struggled to snatch a breath from the howling wind, attempting to be the first to speak…

"Where be thee bound for?" asked the King, his left hand instinctively pulling the cloak's hood across the lower half of his face, the helm's eye guards should do the rest, ensuring his identity remained a secret until he grew certain of his own safety.

"We make for Aglæca's 'stead at Swin Dun, and the house of our Thegn…" gasped a rider as he spat free a gob full of rain. "Our quest this Hel's own night be of escort to our Lord's 'dohtor' Ymma, from her praying's at Wintanceaster's Minster." As he spoke between the gusts the huscarl motioned back into the shadows at their rear. It was only then that Æthelstan had noticed the covered cart highlighted only in the brightness of a thunder flash. The way in which the vehicle was thrown about in the gusts and hammered upon by the relentless rains brought thanks that he was travelling upon a horse's back, in the open.

Caution, and the lack of his own huscarl warned him still to hold secret his identity.

"May I ride with thee?"

There would be no question against the request. Their Lord would be furious if his huscarl had agreed to anything other. No decent man in those lands would refuse another the shelter of his 'ham', and the benefits of another sword increased their strength, even in such weather gangs out of common law, and even land pirates could bring an attack.

Being part of the escort, or just in the company of others had not made the storm's force any easier to bare but it had offered reassurance, and the possibility of warm food next to a roaring fire, making every step worthwhile. Apart from the storm he would be grateful to rid himself from the cart and its occupant, as every lump and bump, sweep of wind, and sheet of hail that hit the cloth canopy was highlighted by the screams and roars of the female occupant who was most certainly proving her ability as a contender against the storm's noise.

'Probably a spoilt crone…' he had thought, 'overweight and foul to the eye, whose own Father had failed long ago in his attempts to get rid.' With a smile at such a thought he lowered his head failing to miss a cloud of leaves which slapped against his drenched cloak, stinging into his sodden face, sticking like an outer skin, until the storm sent another shiver which snatched them away into the cart's canopy bringing forth another scream that threatened to drown the gale's whine.

The struggle through the merciless weather seemed as if it could continue forever, damned by the Gods of the 'hidden world,' to travel endlessly through the continuous deluge of that merciless squall, into oblivion without purpose or meaning, yet, just when any hope of respite seemed no more than a hopeless dream, a welcome light pierced its way through the dark fury, shining ever brighter as they passed through modest fortifications to enter the smallest of courtyards. Almost immediately the outer walls, though slight, had reduced the torrent of the winds bringing an almost silence. The riders dismounted, relieved they had reached the safety of their destination.

The first impression that would have beset any newcomer entering that 'Hus' would have been how modestly it had been furnished, openly lacking in the touch of a Lady, without the necessities of a large family, only the barest of essentials.

'But it was extremely warm, almost hot, compared to the outside' Æthelstan had thought as the party was ushered urgently into the main hall by the first rider, who seemed to be the most senior Huscarl, wasting little time in presenting the newcomer, as the 'lone rider', to a tall, thickly bearded figure who continued to sup slowly the warm contents of a calic in the glow of a most welcoming fire highlighted only by the thunderous outrage that was continuing to hammer beyond the walls.

"…and they bring with them a stranger my Lord…" were the late words stupidly repeated by a hunchbacked 'thrall' who had hurriedly slithered his entrance whilst conjuring with a tray of barely warm refreshments and dry towels. The hurried welcome, along with a keenness to provide the expected told Æthelstan 'he had entered a noble house, a Saxon house.'

His cloaked figure stepped forward into the light, his hooded garb fused against his iced skin betraying only a damp, pallid silhouette. He followed with a second pace towards the fire's warmth, closer to the side of his 'host' and cleared the storm's filth from his throat.

"Thee hath my sincere thanks for the good manner of thy Huscarl and their unexpected rescue…" a right hand reached from below the wetness removing a dripping gauntlet, exposing a perfectly jewelled ring.

"It be no more than right…" came the reply as the Thegn's eyes cemented on nothing more than the ringed finger, "…and what be thy…"

Æthelstan interrupted the Thegn's response as he more than awkwardly pealed back the wet hood and removed a dripping helm that had helped to conceal his identity…the whole room fell silent, a few shuffles as those within sank to their knees respectfully in shock at the sight of their King.

"Bregu, min Cyning…" nervously taken aback, "if we had but known…"

"How could thee have known anything on such a night…If I had known myself I would have kept the night at Oxnaford…" then the company sighed a laugh in light agreement with their King's reply.

The older man returned upright, then lowered his head respectfully…

"Ic am Aglæca Bregu, Thegn of Swin Dun, by thy Father's good grace and favour. And it be our honour for Oxenaford's loss."

Æthelstan watched with concern as the old Thegn looked about the room nervously. The expression told of shame and embarrassment that the lack of comforts within his own house would be insufficient to afford their King. He placed a still cold hand upon Aglæca's shoulder. "There be no need for formality my Lord Thegn, not on this night. I be here only by the grace of our God and the goodness of thy Huscarl…I ask of thee all…be at thy ease."

"Bregu…" relieved, he lowered again a grateful head before turning towards an opening door where a tapestry curtain had been pushed to the side allowing the room's warmth to escape, and the unkempt figure of his only daughter entered.

Again, nervously embarrassed in the presence of his King, that time for the dishevelled appearance of his only heir.

"My…my wind-swept daughter Ymma."

Æthelstan was rarely stuck for words. He had earned a reputation for knowing the right things to say, and when to say them, but on that occasion a speedy response would have been inappropriate and most certainly fumbled. Within the hollow way, with no more than the rage of Hel's own storm in his mind, he had imagined the girl to have been a woman, much older, not as pleasing upon the eye and large, much larger than the trim figure who now stood in front of him. He did not know why but he was pleased with his mistake and smiled at his stupidity, then continued the smile in a show of good manners.

"My Lady" he greeted and lowered his own head in respect.

Keeping the upper half of her body totally erect the girl slowly bent her knees, her eyes following those of her King.

"My King…" she sighed, "and I remained within the dry, out of the storm's worst whilst thou rode in its fury."

"T'is how it should be" Æthelstan smiled, "T'was I who took the easiest part my Lady" his head lowered respectfully. "No true man would have left a Lady to the mercy of such a storm" he bowed his head, took her right hand in his own and squeezed slightly, etiquette of a noble when meeting an unwed Lady. But he would not kiss her hand, that would have been too forward and far from a noble requirement.

Sensing the uneasiness Aglæca's fatherly instincts cut in as he distracted the clumsy silence that had emerged between the King and his only daughter. It would be more than wrong for him to assume anything more than a courteous welcome and a slight sense of overwhelming on his daughter's part, after all, how often does a young woman get to meet their King, and in the privacy of her own home? The top half of his body disappeared through the still open door and called to an invisible serf for food and drink, "...and more dry towels."

Usually, during those years, a Thegn with an unmarried daughter who had long since 'come of age' would be elated at the thought of an unscheduled visit by their King, or any other noble more prominent than the Father. In any circumstance, the thought of romance, or at least a short flirtation would have occupied his thoughts, but with this King, whose reputation was nationwide, who did not partake in casual 'liaisons' or affairs and had put his private life on hold for the good of his lands, nothing should be assumed.

Æthelstan was morally observant, his interests did not incline towards women, the taking of a 'bryd' did not at that time form part of his agenda, so Aglæca's conversation eluded towards anything other than a 'managed' relationship, or any other association between his only daughter and the most powerful King those lands had ever seen.

He had by no means been prying for information, just the making of interested conversation from a loyal Thegn when he had enquired about the 'gathering' at Eamont Bridge, and the treaty with the Scot, and when he had asked about the campaigns in York it had been with the same intent and interest as his queries regarding earlier subjects.

The old Thegn's excuses had been natural, touching, even expected, if not a little embarrassing. Aglæca, as an able-bodied Thegn had been too old, and even too infirm to take part in such operations. He had tapped his 'wretched' leg too many times to be just a subtle hint, as he explained, clearing his throat with an overexaggerated cough to gain a little more sympathy...

"...But many of my æcermann, eardlinga, and own Huscarl had been sent to join thy fyrd...I for one served proudly alongside thine own Father at Holme, and 'afore that with thy ealdefæder Ælfred, in many battles," he added his declarations, hastily accompanied by the genuine shadows of happy, as well as saddened memories reflecting in his aged complexion, then he tapped again his leg, suggesting a battle's wound.

The King nodded as if he had already been aware of the Thegn's passed loyalty, which of course he had not, but it pleased his host to think that the King had remembered his own modest contribution to his fyrd.

...And Ymma, seated to the left of the King, also appreciated the unselfish gesture. Her Father was old, older than many Fathers, his real times were of Ælfred's times, but it was only his body that had accepted it, his mind was still that of a young warrior, the fact that he could no longer play his part in the fightings' had brought him a dreadful guilt over the years, especially when travellers had brought news of his King's victories.

But Ymma was at least content that her Father, if only in the shortest term, had found himself another purpose, after all, entertaining his King on the night of the harshest storm in living memory was no small accomplishment, and would certainly be something to boast about in the neighbouring courts. However, some of the furthest of his neighbours may not have taken the gesture in the same way, Æthelstan for many, was still an unwanted and unentitled King.

Aglæca had married late, after the 'duties' of a younger man had been completed. Wed to the daughter of a Kentish Thegn more noble than himself, he had done his utmost to keep 'his Lady' as she had been accustomed. Sadly, during the 'joys' of childbirth she had passed away leaving him to mourn his loss over many years as he allowed the 'wet nurses' and maids to bring up the child...Ymma sighed too loudly, her dear Father had not lived the happiest of lives.

The hurriedly prepared meal was accepted as if it were a feast, and to all intents and purposes, it was. Although modest, and put together by half sleeping cooks, who had quite possibly cursed the air blue during its preparation, it was surprisingly delicious as well as hot and fulfilling. The Swine's Hill kitchens would not have needed to be fully stocked all year round, noble visitors were uncommon, especially during such a season, the old Thegn would not have been sought after by other nobles, not at his age. Even so, every delicacy that had been available had been prepared with intricate care and brought out as an offering to their King as such a visit would probably never have occurred save for the weather, but it would now be at the centre of everyone's conversation, and more visitors were certain to follow. Æthelstan had admitted secretly, in a whisper to the daughter of his host, that the spiced milk was probably better than that from his own kitchens, and the company as good as any other.

Finally, dry, relaxed, and fully at ease he soaked up greedily the heat from the ever-roaring fire and attempted to smooth away the creases from his now dry jerkin. His cloak had been removed by the 'inthinen' who would wash, press, and dry the garment through the night, making it pristine and ready for the following morning.

The storm outside was still as obvious, penetrating the chamber through the thinnest cracks of the shuttered windows, blowing about tapestries and upsetting the regimental forms of the hearth fire's flames, interrupting conversations as a wind howled and the skies threatened again to crash upon the earth. Nothing could have travelled on such a night, there would be no early respite from its ferocity, but it was now far from the minds of those within the warmth, and too much spiced drink and a full stomach brought about the excuse to crave his host's forgiveness and be shown to a room for the night. He would have been thankful to have remained in the settle, next to the open fire, but the Thegn had insisted earlier, that the King should make use of his own quarters for the night, or longer should he require. A refusal would have offended, even from a King.

That eve, in the warmth of an oversized bed, and despite his exhaustion, the King could not sleep. Maybe it had been the varied spices mixed in his drinks that had caused his head to swim from topic to topic. From the memories of his coronation, to those of his Grandfather, to the thoughts of all who were no longer at his side, whose companionship and advice he had often missed, then back again to that night. Then away to his dreams as he played as a child within the outskirts of the Brunesweald, and the strangest of experiences as he had ventured deeper into those same woods...

...And as he drifted, in and out of his slumber, sometimes grateful for the release of his thoughts he had broken his only oath to the All Father...

The daughter of his host had been quiet under foot as she had slipped her brightness through the room's draperies hanging heavy across the entrance, and even heavier across the bed's framework. Tender and caring as she caressed tenderly the perspiration from his forehead, and far from shy as she comforted her King through the torrents of the night...

...And when morning came, Æthelstan rose drearily from his bed, alone with only the vaguest suggestions of the previous night pecking at his early morning thoughts. Yet as his mind swam fully into the realities of the day He remembered clearly what had occurred. She who had entered his bedroom and warmed away more than just his outer chill would now need to be his only secret. It needed to be more than a secret, and he prayed to who so ever could hear his thoughts that She would keep that secret with him, but he would never forget.

The storm had vanished as the morning sun had burst through the hurling skies, he may have rose in another land, how different it all seemed and once dressed, washed, and refreshed from the contents of a serf's tray he guardedly made his way to the main hall and the day's greetings from his host, who instantly added his excuses for the 'rude' absence of his daughter, with the vagueness of a caring Father.

A raised hand proved that the King was not offended, but he was secretly disappointed.

"Of course, t'is nought but expected...Such a storm would have kept the 'deofol' from his rest."

A smile in reply. "Yet Bregu, I hope thee slept well?"

He lied and agreed that he had as he pondered the most private of thoughts over his night's companion. Such vivid feelings that swept through his mind and body, surely, they were no dreams, it truly did happen…And again the King prayed that his secret would be kept, and that his host would always remain ignorant of their indulgences…

However, for everything other than his daughter, Aglæca was owed some reward for his hospitality and loyalty, merely through the noble courtesies of rank, whether it was expected or not.

With great difficulty, the Thegn finished a mouthful of flatbread whilst he watched his King pace the stone floor, transfixed in the deepest of thoughts, expressionless except for the times when he stared at the wall hung pictures, one being that of a passed over wife, before moving to the half open window shutter, helping himself freely to more spiced goat's milk, freshly 'jugged' on the cup board.

Aglæca swallowed gently the contents of his own calic which helped to dismiss the bread lodged in his gullet, gulping visibly in relief.

Æthelstan turned confidently and faced the older man, his right hand resting habitually upon the handle of his saex, his left still clutched the half empty calic. He stared appreciatively into the elderly eyes of his Thegn…

"For a King to speak of gratitude to a Thegn, or Ealdormann, may have been sufficient reward to one such as Aglæca, but a loyal gesture to one in difficulty or danger be the greatest of deeds offered to a man whether he be King or not, and when such gestures be freely and honestly given, they must deserve reward…"

Surprise was nothing more than a hint that flashed momentarily across the face of the old Saxon, yet, even in its shortest of glimpses the look of expectant hope almost betrayed him, and Æthelstan saw it, hesitated slightly then dismissed it as a sign of modest embarrassment, and if it were not so, then it be the look of any man loyal to his King…

"Thurbold of the Suþseaxe fell in his last meeting with the Dane, and until this time I have not seen fit to pass on title…" He glanced over his host once again, his age and health may have been against him, but what he would lack in those attributes he would make up with experience, loyalty and good intension which had struck as obvious since their first meeting. "I wish for thee, Aglæca of Swin Dun, to accept the position of Scir Gerefa, and with it the King's favours that accompany such title...As Shire Reeve thee shall answer to Ælfric, King's Reeve for the Westseaxe."

Enforced speechlessness? It would not have been proper to have shown his immediate delight, it had to seem unexpected whether it was, or not. So, after an exaggerated fumble of half muttered words he managed to respond with genuinely shocked excitement...

"Min bregu. To grant aid to a traveller, whether he be King or otherwise, be the duty of every Saxon and should be done so without expectance of reward. However, it would be a life's honour to accept my King's favour."

Æthelstan smiled in acknowledged satisfaction, he was pleased at his own choice. "There shall be a charter drawn, as soon as I reach Winchester, to show of my choice..."

"...And thy daughter..." he feigned an absence of memory for the sake of modesty and politeness, but he was a poor actor.

"Ymma" Aglæca assisted.

"Yeah, thy daughter Ymma...With thy consent, Ymma shall join my court in Gleaweceaster, as maid in waiting to the Ladies of the court." The old man remained silent. "I trust that such a position be acceptable to ye both?"

It was more than acceptable to the old Thegn, and more so than expected. Shire Reeve was a position that only the most trusted few had been granted, under any King, and would see him now ascend the ranks of respectability higher than any of his 'younger' neighbours, providing he remained a King's mann. With a position at court for his only daughter it could mean she may be secure in the years that followed, and whatever the King's purpose may have been he was certain for her future. It would see her settled, maybe even married, into a life that would guarantee her future, and if the God's allowed it, should he live long enough, provide for his own comforts when the years began to take their toll.

Such trivialities were over, a charter would be scribbled in the weeks ahead recording officially the King's wishes, now Æthelstan stepped forward as his immaculately pressed cloak was politely returned with a smile and a curtsy from the inthinen, and another compliment followed to the maid who had diligently prepared the King's most precious garment, and a silver halfpenny was exchanged in appreciation bringing the slightest squeal of happiness as the girl skipped from the chamber. What a story she could now tell.

A second smile from the newly appointed Shire Reeve was followed by a respectfully short bow...'Things could not have passed better' he had thought, 'he would never again curse the rantings of Thunor's temper.'

The small assembly watched as the King rode from the courtyard accompanied by four house guards insisted upon from a distance by Ymma who had been heard to mutter, 'Our King be brave and mighty, and the storm of the night may be passed, but there be many out of our laws that may cut a Royal throat in the hollow ways of the shire...'

She had waited, nervously peeking through the half-pulled drapes of her own bed chamber, watching her King as he rode beyond the outer wall, praying that he would turn back and pay her one final complimentary glance, and maybe a smile to accompany it, but there was nothing, not even as his silhouette disappeared into a much calmer morning.

Upset, sad, tearful, and ashamed of her feelings for someone she had known for so little time, until she turned to her maid who had been watching her uneasiness.

"T'is for thee my Lady" she uttered, almost giggled. "Left for thee by our King it be" as she handed her mistress the finest of kerchiefs and whisked herself away giggling loudly amid her duties.

Ymma inquisitively opened the folds of the fine cloth and stared into its secret. Immediately gone were the tears of sadness and in their place, smiles of joy and happy thoughts as her fingers rubbed delicately across the top of the embossed golden wyverns that matched the clasp of the King's most precious cloak.

A grinning wolf, a grunting boar, a raucous cow,

a rootless tree, a breaking wave, a boiling pot,

A flying arrow, an ebbing tide,

a coiled adder, the ice at night,

A bride's bed talk, a broadsword,

a bear's play, a Prince's children,

A witch's welcome, the wit of a slave,

a sick calf, a corpse still fresh,

A brother's killer encountered upon the highway

nor a house half burned,

a racing stallion which hath wrenched a leg

Are never safe; let no man ever trust them.

Havamal

CHAPTER 13

The storms had eased dramatically since Æthelstan's night at Swin Dun, most had already forgotten. That season had thankfully passed for another year, but his memories of that 'special' night would include much more than just foul weather.

For the first few weeks since leaving the burg his mind had been filled with her vision, he had found it difficult to concentrate on the tedious problems of his court, such trivialities as petty law breakers and family squabbles had bored him extensively, yet eventually that passed, and his attitude returned to the positive. Those about his court had assumed their King had been ill, a fever from the effects of the great storm and had excused his state, all were relieved that whatever it had been had now passed.

Aglæca had instantly settled into his new role. He had good teachers who took a respectful consideration for his age, he was quickly showing that his years of experience gave him the upper hand over his contemporaries. Reports that reached the King proved that he had made a wise choice and things would pass with little upset.

Ymma, on the other hand caused him greater concern. Yes, she had settled easily into her new Gloucestershire chambers and had immediately taken upon her duties without argument or worry, but there was an air about her that had given Thegn Eanberht cause for concern, it would be for him alone to inform his King...

After a two-hour ride, continuously at the gallop, he had slipped painfully from his mount finding instant respite from a battle wound that had never correctly healed, he found his King without delay...

"Bregu, the Lady in question..." one of multiple pauses in the man's short speech "...the Lady Ymma, it be reported, be with child" and when his King showed little surprise Eanberht instantly realised the delicacy of the 'situation' and took it upon himself to keep any 'secret' that there may, or may not have been.

"I shall leave it to thee to ensure, that the daughter of our newest of Reeves has all that she may require. Maybe, for the ease of thy household, she could be moved to a private chamber...until the birth of the child." His orders had slipped off his tongue as if they had been rehearsed, almost as if the news had been expected.

The Thegn agreed assuring his King complete loyalty.

"Should a child be born Eanberht..." Æthelstan thought quickly, this part had not been rehearsed "...it may be that we find a homestead, or even a burg where the grandchild of our loyal reeve may grow."

Again, the Thegn agreed.

"I also know my friend, that should a time arise, when the new born should require a guardian, this, this new Lady may also be permitted to call upon thee."

"Bregu, the arrangements shall be made, and confidences kept should it be so required."

Strangely Æthelstan was more at ease knowing his secret had been shared with a loyal friend and that safeguards would now be made, such news would fill his thoughts for many weeks, until....

The Royal Burg at Winchester had been the ruling seat of the West Saxons since it had replaced Dorchester after the then Wessex King Cædwalla defeated his Jutish rival Atwald of the Wihtwara as he purged the Isle of all its inhabitants in 686.

Two hundred years later, King Ælfred had been responsible for the added strengths which now protected the boundaries to the fortified burg, and had spent many of his final weeks personally designing a complexed street plan which would survive over many centuries. But other than Edward, who used the burg as his main seat of power only when dealing with matters pertaining to the south and the building of a minster, nothing much had been done with it since. Apart from a few royal funerals, the odd uprising and invasion, and one or two noble marriages, Winchester had seen little entertainment and even less 'investment'.

Æthelstan had visited the burg on many occasions as a child, at the wishes of a devoted grandfather who had 'seen' great things in the boy's eyes from his earliest years. But now as King he openly preferred Tamworth as his main seat. He relished every one of his days spent there which lately had become fewer, more were his visits to the oldest Mercian seat of Gloucester.

Winchester had never offered Æthelstan the feeling of ease and welcome, even as King absolute he could sense the disrespectful stares and crude suggestions from the local folc as he rode through the heavily guarded gates and on into the bustling market square. That far south the days were much warmer, but the reception he received in Winchester was the coldest within his lands.

Without her master's command Abrecan had eased to a halt as the party rode to the lane's end, the entourage that followed copied. The horse's ears twitched erratically, her eyes flicked from point to point and her head shook in disgust, it was not her place of choosing either.

'At last' he had thought with welcome relief as the rear guard of his cavalcade approached the grounds of the Old Minster. Finally, a 'friendly face' as the beam across Byrnstan's toothless mouth made up for the lack of welcoming expressions upon the many faces that had slowly meandered to gather along his trail.

His only ally within the burg, Byrnstan was Bishop of Winchester since he had replaced Frithstan back in '31 when the latter had resigned his 'see' due to increased ill health, and an ever more increasing dislike towards his new King.

Old Frithstan had shown his true colours when he had openly refused to attend Æthelstan's ascent to King, silently taking the side of the 'new' King's recently deceased brother Ælfweard, and openly declaring his intent by his adamant refusal to hold mass in Winchester's Minster to celebrate.

Rumour of his actions had swept the shires of the south and once the formalities of the new King's appointment had been completed and the 'necessaries' had passed, Frithstan had been seriously, and without question, put in his rightful place during a hurried visit from Æthelhelm of Canterbury, himself openly adoring his new King, and cousin...

Frithstan the renegade had died in his sleep just a few months before Æthelstan's visit, and another rumour monger and religious adversary had been removed from the equation. Was it God's will, or something to do with another small band of 'Dark Riders' fleeing from the burg as night fell in Frithstan's bedchamber for the last time?

'Regarding the health of Bishops' Æthelstan had conjured mindfully as he slipped himself gently from Abrecan's saddle, 'Byrnstan did not look as well as expected' and the looks upon the faces of Wulfhere and Ealdfrith read the same...

...Nevertheless, the haggard Bishop was more than pleased to greet his King...

"Wilcume min Beaggiefa, Wilcume to Wintanceaster" and the Bishop fell enthusiastically to a knee grasping the King's right hand pulling it close "T'is good thee be here Bregu, safe and well" and he respectfully placed his lips onto the Royal seal that sat tightly around the King's middle finger.

It was the 'safe and well' part that jarred a thought in Æthelstan's mind, as if Byrnstan had expected different.

"Ic þancie þe Byrnstan, god wine...As I know that thy welcome here may be certain and true of heart" he replied. "Yet the same may not be said of thy preostscir" and a grin of expected disappointment flicked across the Bishop's face, which also reflected in the expression of the King.

Byrnstan rose to his feet with the difficulty of old age and arthritis in the left knee brought on by a lifetime of paying his penance upon the freezing stone floors of many religious houses across the shires. The embarrassment upon his face reddened deeper as he glanced around at his own parishioners.

'This was their King, here, now, before them' he felt as if he should be openly beating the whole of his congregation with a shredded birch, but he quietened his inner temper and turned to bid his Master entry into the Old Minster of Wessex...Yes, there had been rumours of rebellion and assassination from the outlands, but he would have thought something dire if there had not been, but surely someone else would have been overwhelmed to see their King.

Notwithstanding the obvious signs of hostilities towards his presence, which grew more apparent in the faces and actions of the folk who continued to gather along the hollow ways, Æthelstan stood down his extra body of Huscarl which had gathered from the column's rear. He had insisted, before accepting his Bishop's offer of much needed refreshments, that he would first visit the tomb of his Father to pay his due respects in the short form of a prayer, adding also a blessing for his long-passed Mother whom he was certain would now be at his Father's side. Then, after a token had been laid upon the late King's 'stone' he walked slowly across to that of his Grandfather where he spent more than an hour paying his respects and whispering his secrets, which some had thought at the time to be a little out of place, considering the increasingly heated noise coming from the outer assembly.

But when it came to anything regarding Ælfred, Æthelstan did as he wished.

There came no surprise to any who trailed behind that the King had omitted to place an offering upon the tomb of his half-brother Ælfweard, not even a whispered prayer or glance in its direction, no recognition of any kind.

Formalities complete and a small purse of silver was respectfully placed upon a platter left specifically for such a purpose before walking casually through the corridors of the Minster with little concern for the continued bellowing from the crowds beyond. He passed through the Læcehus, where the festering wounds and empty stomachs of the latest passing pilgrims were attended to by the clerics, as always, for the smallest of monetary donations or a few hours' work in the fields. The King placed a second purse in a large receptacle at the feet of the Holy Virgin's statue on the western wall before passing into a smaller, more private graveyard, to pay his respects to Swithun, its only occupant...and the crowd's frustrations could be heard all the louder over the stone walls, the unfriendly words and chanting could now be made out more clearly, and signs of the odd scuffle with the Huscarl became evident. Obviously, without sight of 'their' King, the people had grown a little bolder and increased their challenges against his absence.

...Æthelstan knelt on the smallest patch of turf alongside a modest tomb and prayed as if he were surrounded in total silence.

Swithun had lived a full and pious life becoming the legendary Bishop who had been responsible for the healing of so many sick and infirm. He had dedicated his life to their serving, never once refusing to aid the needy, whatever their condition, or station in life. The west wall of the nave was adorned completely with countless canes, crutches of all shapes and sizes and other strange implements once used by the crippled, now discarded as redundant by those who had been cured by their saviour. No longer needed, they had been permanently fixed to the stonework as a memorial to prove the extent of the Bishop's gift, and there they would stay in homage to a great and kindly man whose memory may one day be rewarded with a sainthood.

It was after he had paid the proper respects to the occupants of the Minster and returned outside, that the attack had occurred...

Whilst the King had been carrying out yet another of the Royal duties that had been compulsorily passed down through the line of Kings', handing out the 'penig' to Winchester's poor and needy who had assembled 'forever' in the Minster's only square, a large section of the crowd, including the earlier hecklers, surged forward too fast and too loud, and defiantly too close for the liking of the Huscarl. Swords were drawn, spears were raised and two Thegns stood at the side of their King, ready.

Byrnstan had been deeply engrossed, at the rear of the party, chanting his Latin from Mathew's gospel...

"He will reply...'I tell ye the truth, whatever thee did not do for one of the least of these, thee did not do for '..." Then the hustles and screams from the crowd had brought a swift end to his ritual prayer...

Unusually, Æthelstan had not heard the roar of verbal obscenities being hurled in his direction, maybe he had just grown to ignore them. Knees bent, and eyes lowered to help a small child who had been forcibly pushed to the ground by the volatile crowd. The youngster was more than likely too hungry and exhausted to keep any sort of balance against the 'rush,' after standing with a Father since the morning's earliest hours, in their desperate hope that they would be one of those fortunate enough to receive the 'ælmesse'...A Father did not have to 'like' his King to accept his silver.

It was solely due to an action, so natural, that the King's kindness had saved his own life...

He was pressing a newly minted coin into the grubby palms of the hungry and sick, as had always been normal on the first day of any visit, when he had spotted the child whimpering and crumpled in a bedraggled pile at his feet, and in imminent danger of being stamped upon by the greedy and irate crowd. Wretched, filthy, and crying, the King had stared down at the child for a second, almost beneath his own feet. His own instincts had caused him to crouch down and assist the helpless waif, if he could, after all, 'It was not the fault of the lytling that his belly was empty.'

It was at that precise moment, as he had bent towards the child, that the 'seax' had passed where Æthelstan's head had been mere seconds earlier. The knife had sliced its way through the air, unseen and unheard by any until its flight had finished with a dull thump. A second later a scream of absolute horror followed as a shocked ealdwif collapsed to the ground, the knife blade housed deeply at the base of her left breast. It had been launched from the strongest of arms, sending the blade deep and fatal to its hilt.

The handle of the knife could only have left its assailant's hand for the shortest of time before six or more Huscarl had pounced upon the heavily cloaked figure of a would-be killer displaying anything but ease and compassion towards him.

"Bregu, we must get thee inside" from an attentive Huscarl "there may be others..."

But Æthelstan had seemed to care more for the injured woman than he did for his own welfare, insisting immediately that she be carefully carried away to the læcehus, where she would be cared for by the 'sycan'...

Despite the hurry and eagerness displayed by a caring few, by the time the woman had reached the first available space, and a priestly nurse had been found to attend upon her, she had bled out, dying within the walls of the Old Minster. She was granted the last rites, covered fully in a ragged cloth before her family were called to reclaim the body, her name would never be known to anyone other than those who would grieve her loss.

The commotion about the square was at its peak when the King had turned from watching the woman's body disappearing into the Minster, back to facing the unruly crowd. Those who had witnessed the 'near miss' were dumb struck, astounded and in shock that He had been so fortunate as to survive what would have otherwise been a successful assassination.

'Devine intervention' someone had whispered.

"The Will of God' from a shaking milking maid.

'Our Lord's sign of a true King' came another voice, louder.

'Bad timing' well there always would be those who could never be appeased.

Despite the hassle, the King appeared, on the surface, to ignore every comment, and many others vehemently emitted in his direction. Whether he had heard them or not, his concentrations and thoughts were turned to the seriousness of the situation...

His mind raced as he walked reservedly towards the arrested assailant who, by now had been completely overpowered, beaten harshly before being dragged viciously to his knees, to answer to 'his' King...

But not before another beating had been administered in the most delicate of regions.

"This be the one my Lord..." reported the closest Huscarl as he keenly pushed his blade, threatening to slice open the throat of the failed assassin. "I saw the knife leave 'is filthy 'ands." The Mercian's tone was proud, his accent rough, accompanied with an additional air of success and fulfilment. At that instant he had possibly felt like the most important man in the kingdom having almost definitely saved the life of his King...Well, that would be his version in the ale houses for many years to come.

Æthelstan lifted a hand, a silent command for the wilful battering to cease, at least in view of the 'common' folk. As he stepped towards the prisoner something caused him to stop himself, an expression of absolute shock and dismay replacing his visual anger, as a grey hood had been snatched free from concealing the captive's face. The King's fingers started to tremble in confusion and worry, as he recognised the man now being held for an almost murderous attempt upon his life.

Apart from the filthy grey cloak, which had obviously been a disguise to assist his concealment within the crowd, he was well attired in the garb, almost of a noble, because he was almost a noble. Until the end of the previous year the man held there, in front of him as an assassin had been a member of the 'Witan', one of the trusted 'few' depended upon by the King.

Notwithstanding the viciousness of the overpowering arrest the assassin still managed to hold his posture with a sense of arrogance, almost contempt towards those who now retained him, especially so against the man who now stood before him.

"...Ælfred?" questioned the King his head still spinning in a mix of confusion and anger. "Why thee Ælfred, why thee...Have I not returned thy loyalties...hath thee not received sufficient favour...what be the name of He who offers more for thy service and sets his claim upon thy loyalty?"

The prisoner raised his head until the Huscarl's blade dictated further movement, wincing as he tried to ease the pressure that continued to force the point harder against his throat. His face held the expression of a man who had just failed to murder his King and now accepted readily all its consequences.

"Yea, t'is I, Ælfred" he snarled with increased scorn "I, Ælfred, named so after thine own Ealdefæder," came the answer cockily, "and there be no He to sway my loyalties, as I have no loyalties to thee or any other."

No terms of respect had been offered with his reply, the once 'loyal' man now clearly held no liking for his King. But that had only brought Æthelstan greater confusion. It had been less than a year since He, King of the Engle lands, had signed a Royal Charter granting the lands around Stanham, just south of Winchester, to the man who now knelt before him in human shackles.

Then out of the crowd pushed Byrnstan...

"I know of him...I know of him" still out of breath. "I know this man."

He had pushed himself excitedly to the forefront, snatching his 'trapped' habit behind him, almost collapsing into his King's arms as the garment pulled free. Concerned he checked his King's welfare, then looked skywards crossing his own torso to give thanks as he caught his breath before continuing...

The King's eyes also swept skywards, but his were in disbelief 'Was all folk in that place an idiot?'

"...I know of him Bregu" the Bishop added whilst still grasping for more breath, the shock of the attempt upon his King's life was too much, and there, in his 'Preostscir' of all places.

"He be known as Ælfred..." a little more relaxed "and a Thegn, by thine own favour...he be Thegn, Thegn of Stan Hamm...a...a quiet man on all accounts." The doubt in the old Bishop's tone told the King that the attempt on his life would have been sincere and intended, albeit poorly planned.

'A quiet man, who had brought with him little or no notice. The way of a spy, or an infiltrator.' Alfred, until recent months one of the King's own military aids, had obviously harboured a serious grievance. Yet he would not have acted alone, that man would never have owned the initiative to take on such a task as that, at least not alone. He would soon learn the truth of it all.

"A quiet man, says ye?" snarled the King "Of course ye know of him" he jibbed, "we All know of him." As he mocked his Bishop, Æthelstan gestured to his guard, then the culprit was dragged roughly from the small square with over enthusiastic force. Not another word was uttered from the prisoner's lips, but as he attempted to rescue what little skin that remained on his knee caps a blow from a second Huscarl knocked Alfred unconscious...

"The crypts" informed Byrnstan knowing exactly what would soon follow, "Thee may use the crypts. T'is a silent place, and private." The lead Huscarl nodded his response to the Bishop who had again started to recover from yet another case of embarrassment.

Heavily armed Mercian knights, who had always escorted their King, wasted little time in reacting against the threat upon their Lord. Before the knife had embedded into the chest of an old woman, they had urged their horses forward, forming a mounted ring of protection around the immediate area with spear and shield at the ready. If there had been any more than a single killer within the crowd their show of force would have deterred any further attempts upon the life of their King.

Regardless of all that had occurred, and against the advice of his Thegns, Æthelstan remained insistent that the alms giving would be completed, although there was much more haste than had originally been planned, and the knights continued to 'encourage' the crowds to disperse 'to whence they belonged' allowing the square to settle back into its empty quietness.

None but the small boy remained, glancing up innocently at the man he thought may be of some importance, but was too young know why. The King leaned forward, bent lower and lifted the youngster, cradling him within his arms, lifting him high so that both their faces came level...

"Above all here, would thee show respect to thy King, would thee?"

The frightened boy nodded a grubby face, unsure of what he was agreeing to and Æthelstan lowered the lad back to the ground ruffling his greasy locks in reassurance, staring into his dark, young eyes. A silver coin was pressed gently into the boy's sticky palm, as he continued to speak the King scanned the courtyard intently, back, and forth, left, and right, until he found the skulking shape of a Father who quivered ashamedly behind the wattled corner of a building.

"I speak my words to a man who should ne'er be a Father" his eyes portrayed the scorn he held for the failings of a selfish man. "This 'ere be they son?"

The man slipped free of the shadow and nodded the poorest attempt at respect.

Æthelstan beckoned the man closer, he reluctantly obeyed.

"What shame hath ye, that a Father would use a son for gain?" The King's glare told the boy's father of his anger. "Thee are to care, in a right and proper manner for thy son for it was not he who asked to be brought into this world."

He thought deeper for quite a time, he would not leave things as they were, there was a shortness of trust in the man's eyes.

"Thee are to report here, by my command, on the first day of each month, or closest to, a front of my Bishop, with thy son, to show how he fares. In return, the bishop shall give thee two penigs, one for thee and the second for thy son. However, should ye fail to do so, or should I hear of any undue harm that may befall the boy, then I shall know where thee may be found, and who it be that shall take the blame."

"Yea bregu, my King" lied the man.

"If thee doth not comply, I Æthelstan, guardian of all folk good, shall return to this burg…and a mighty hurt shall befall upon ye."

The King's tone proved his words were no threat, and the Father agreed once again, that time with more conviction.

"What be thy name lytling?" as his eyes returned to the boy.

Nervously and after a short stammer "Cuthred, my Lord, son of Nerian" and the boy's grin brought a hint of delight into one of the King's poorest days.

"Then be gone with ye boy...and remember this day as the day that a King wished that he too were again lytling."

As he watched the boy's shadow disappear from the yard he knew that day may have been his worst.

Æthelstan could have questioned the folk of Winchester in person. Each one if he had wished. Held a court, or a council, gathered the Witan or a more local Moot, all who had probably been hovering somewhere safely within the shadows, aimlessly watching what had occurred. He could have asked them all individually or as a group, why it was that such people held so obvious their intent against his rule, pleaded with them for their understanding. He may have offered them inducements with the lowering of taxes, reduced the levy upon the Shire to bring them onside, or even scribbled out another charter granting more to a Shire that already boasted of more than most, but that would have been the sign of a weak and desperate King who could not control his people. Those people were Engle, Saxon or Jute, and part of his kingdom as one, and they 'would' come around. 'Besides' he agreed with himself 'why should the folk of other Shires pay more taxes than those who seemed so adamantly against him and his policies?"

He would be their King, and more so, they would be his loyal folk.

The chamber had been especially prepared for the King's visit two days before his arrival, to ensure all had been prepared in the best possible manner and that nothing had been forgotten. That visit, which had been intended as a celebration of his rule, with the signing of more charters granting further power to the Minster, had been a visit any one would be quick to forget, and the signs on that first night proved that things would not get any better.

Besides a few stout candles that littered the flat surfaces of the chamber 'bords,' the hearth fire had offered most light, as well as a welcome warmth. It had been whilst sharing a modest supper, with his closest Thegns, of freshly skilleted flat bread and cold meats, that the Mercian interrogator had offered his account.

The fact that Alfred had not been eager to share his explanations for such treasonous acts, offer not even the slightest indications as to why he had attempted to take the King's life, had come as little surprise to any within the small group. What had concerned Æthelstan most of all was the discovery of a small tattered document that the 'accused' had kept, secreted away in the inner side of his left boot.

For an assailant to carry proof of his crime upon his person whilst committing the offence was not only incredibly foolish but also unbelievably open. Either that, or it showed a huge amount of over confidence. Had it been Alfred's intention to lay blame in the direction of another, or was the assassin merely naïve, easily led, or just plain stupid?

Ælfric was the King's High Reeve and had been so since Kingston. Chosen for his devout honesty as well as his undeterminable loyalty he was also well known to many for never being swayed in a decision, just like his King. Since his promotion, he had often given advice to the Witan regarding all types of matters and requirements. He had coughed and spluttered on half a mouthful of warm mead as he had read the note's contents silently, but saying all through silent expression.

Then a stoutly man, Deormud, whose sole responsibilities lay with ensuring the King's properties were always well provided for regarding food and drink, and all other 'important' requirements, had almost dropped the document into the fire's raging flames as it had ben passed across for his comments. Again, his contributions were silent but visually his thoughts had been those of the others within the group.

The well written message had been scribbled in Saxon, and in a 'good' hand, which had told more than a thing or two. The note had not only informed the assassin of the route that would be taken by the King and his 'weard' on their march to Winchester, but had also provided the date of their journey, as well as the estimated time of their arrival, it also included the precise number of knights and spearmen that would make up the guard. Stupidly such a precise and incriminating letter had been the author's betrayal as it could have only been written by a handful of people who had been privy to such detailed information, and a well educated one also.

His appetite had died, his stomach threatened to violently reject what little food he had already eaten. He sipped lightly on his 'very' weakened wine to settle his gut and stared deep into the luminous flames of the hearth fire...

'It was enough to send a man to the mead halls' he had thought. 'Not only had a Thegn of chartered lands openly plotted against him, and one who, until recently had held a high-ranking position within the Witan. The writing was easily recognisable, the way certain letters had curled, only one other, to his knowledge would openly write in such a manner, the assassination had been instigated by Edwin, his half-brother.

Everything seemed to fit into place as he recalled his last visit to Amesbury, for Yule, where his beneficiary had been granted to one hundred and twenty of the burg's most needy. It was there, within the ancient Halls, that his half-brother Edwin had joined his entourage, or at least his presence was vaguely recollected around the feasting tables...

Things had always been estranged between them, as it was with most of his Father's 'other' children, except of course with Edmund, who had always been a loyal brother, even if a little young. Edwin had always been the most distant, instigated without any doubt by the Mother, the 'other' King's Lady, Ælflæd.

...It was during that same gathering that the now assassin Alfred, then a full Thegn, had requested his King's permission to be released from his Royal tie, as a sickly wife who had not long given birth to their second child, was then in need of his presence. Before that week of festivities had ended both Edwin and Alfred had left Amesbury, nothing more had been heard from either of them until that day in Winchester.

The King leant sharply across the 'food bord' hand outstretched, snatching free the note from Deormud's hand, almost dragging him into their suppers remnants so fierce was the action. Æthelstan re-read the writings twice over before rising from the table, pausing for a moment half standing, then shaking his head in confusion and frustration more than once as he stepped away from the still seated group, then with the rarest displays of anger paced through the shadows of the fire's flames pushing down hard on the seax within his embroidered belt.

The contents of the note had personally wounded him, dug deep like the sharpest knife, more so maybe than if the assassin's blade had found its correct target, a half-brother, a son of his own Father, was it hatred or greed?

'Had he not made ample provision for All of his family, whether half-bloods or other, granting them much more than just a King's favour, ensuring that they all, apart from his Father's 'other' wives, would always be catered for.'

Since becoming King, he had showed no malice against them, except for Ælfweard of course, and the only provision he had placed upon them was that they should respect his position and show loyalty towards him. Had he not forgiven them for the way they had treated him as a youngster? His hurt was for much more than just an attempt on his life, it was an insult, an insult towards him and all that he stood to achieve.

There would be no further need to interrogate the prisoner, no cause for further investigation as to the identity of the 'spy within their camp'. His half-brother Edwin had foolishly and arrogantly signed his name at the end of the note, adding his personal seal, and on the rear of the note had been scribbled a pledge, a written promise signed and again sealed by Edwin, granting great riches and a powerful position to Alfred, Thegn of Worthy Mortimer, should he succeed with the assassination of the 'false' King, which would then pave the way for his own rightful ascent to the seat of Wessex.

Without warning Æthelstan's attention was dragged out from his deepest thoughts. As if to provide further evidence of the treasonous guilt, and conclude the impending fate of the prisoner and his absent 'master', Byrnstan's senior cleric, Elwin, entered hurriedly, a little crude in his manner, just as those types often were. He did offer the slightest hint of respect, almost lowering his head...

"Yea?" Byrnstan was again embarrassed "thee better have good reason for such interruption."

There was no apology. There never was from 'those' who had given their lives to the Minsters and Priories, they were openly the strangest of all, in every way.

The celebrant's head moved from left to right in order of noble priority, clasping both hands tight into his chest as he spoke…

"Bregu…bisceop…leofan" King…Bishop…Sirs "the prisoner hath offered confession, unto my ears alone. He names the Earl Edwin…" Elwin the cleric paused, expecting a verbal barrage from his King, none came, so he continued "…the Earl Edwin as his only Lord…" his eyes reached into those of the Kings "and true instigator of this…this darkest of crimes."

There was no shock, no argument, no outrage, Æthelstan had always known that Edwin held no goodness towards him, as brother or as King…

"…Did he ask for mercy?"

"Na Lord" he may have lied "He did not crave for mercy" His reply was high-lighted by the now agonising screams and cries that seemed to echo up from beyond the stone steps that lead up from the crypt, vibrating through the whole Minster, it confirmed, if confirmation had been needed, how the confession had been obtained.

One final curdling scream rattled the building and all within before there came a strangely 'tranquil' silence… the unnamed cleric glanced back through the corridors displaying a sickly grin about his gape.

Æthelstan browsed at his council as each in turn had lowered their heads in quiet agreement with whatever their King would declare. There was little option remaining, apart from the obvious, there could never be any other option, the law was absolute, to all.

"Once the Huscarl be certain that the traitor is dead, his body shall be taken far from this Minster, where it shall be dragged behind horse through the lands of Stan Hamm as they ride for all to see…The Reeves shall tell of this great treason and misdeed brought about by their only Thegn against their land and their King. There he shall be buried in unholy ground, at Bæddi's Weald, without marker or note and let the elves of the Brunesweald feast upon his spirit."

Ælfheah, one of two mass priests in the King's company, raised a closed hand to his mouth and coughed intentionally until he had caught his King's attention...

"...And his worth, Bregu?"

"...And his worth?" questioned the King, "Of course, there be always someone's worth when it comes to the church."

He paused as his sarcasm was dismissed for anger.

"His worth shall be forfeit to the King...Na, that shall be too obvious. A new charter shall be scribed this very night..." and Ælfheah reached down for his satchel readying himself to comply to his King's wishes.

"...The charter shall grant the rights of the Lands in and around this place named Stan Hamm, be taken into the folds of the Minster, and its loyal house, until the day comes that a lad now known to Byrnstan by the name of Cuthred son of Nerian, reaches his fifteenth summer and shall take by title that which be defaulted by Ælfred..."

What happened then was the part of his duties he disliked most of all...

"...All cynfolc that remain within Ælfred's halls shall be taken into servitude, for a minimum of two years, within this burg that bares witness to the shame of their Thegn. Mann cynn shall loose their right as 'Freomann' and spend the remainder of their days in servitude to this Minster, as followers of Swithun, and mædencild shall be sent to the kitchens until such time they become of age."

Byrnstan smiled at his King's 'generosity', then grovelled and bowed over zealously in a single movement before 'signing' the cross in another over indulgent gesture of appreciation, things had not turned out too bad for him, considering how the day had started.

The shallow cleric also bowed and left in a more respectful manner than he had entered.

Edwin had been the younger brother of Ælfweard, and his own feelings of contempt towards his half-brother's rule were well known throughout the 'moots' of Wessex and had been openly supported by Ælflæd, Edwin's mother and Edward's second wife, herself now confined to a nunnery. 'But even so...' Æthelstan had thought 'assassination, surely not?'

As his companions flustered about he stared through the open shutter, out into the courtyard beyond and thought deeper. None knew of any words of consolation, if the culprit had been any other than a member of his family, however distant the relationship, they may have offered some discreet advice, but it was best, they had all agreed, to allow their King his own decisions, after all he would do as he wished on any account.

Æthelstan turned and glared into the illuminated faces of his silent advisors as they fumbled discreetly, sitting in the strictest of quiet around the spitting fire, cautious not to disturb his thoughts yet eager to share his answers, keen to comply with his wishes. 'The most telling trait of the bestest of advisors' Æthelstan had always insisted, 'is their good sight in knowing when not to advise.'

Longer and deeper he thought. Without the slightest hint of disturbance, not even the servant-at-arms had dared to take his leave, until he was sure that his King's Order had been completed.

At one point within the vibrant silence there occurred another of those strange occasions when Æthelstan could be heard muttering to himself. Such incidents were becoming more usual as the stress of his reign began to tell. He would often speak in whispers, and as on previous occasions, it seemed as if he were holding a private meeting with an unseen presence, similarly he did so without care or concern for the thoughts of those present...

He continued his Order, as if there had been no pause...

"...and as for Edwin..."

Every ear locked tightly onto the voice of their King, Byrnstan mouthed a curse whilst Ælfheah signed the cross.

"Have my Father's son detained without matter or cause and escorted here to this very Minster. Should he offer argument, or resist he is to be placed under arrest and dragged to this Minster…"

He then turned to address Wulfric as he often did in such times.

"…Thee shall lead the Huscarl. To ensure that the journey be safe." His words were followed by a calic, which he had long since emptied, dispatched across the chamber into a long since faded tapestry. The calic landed upon the stone floor spinning noisily until it scrapped to a stop, it had been the first physical show of his anger.

"There shall be no reason to cause delay in his leaving," he insisted "nor concern for his own arrangements. If he be naked when thee finds him, then he be naked when he arrives here."

"Certainly Lord, as thee wishes" then Wulfric left the chamber without delay, followed by the servant-at-arms, who, once out of the King's sight could be heard bellowing his own orders for an armed assembly as he marched behind Wulfric into the darkness of the small courtyard.

Less than a week had passed since Wulfric's hurried departure from Winchester and little had occurred to occupy their thoughts, not even a hunt had been arranged, it would not have been appropriate, no one was in a mood for entertainments.

The King had prayed with his Bishop, for hours at a time, and when he had finished praying he had spent the remainder of the days and nights walking the grounds of the Minster, often alone, and regularly talking to himself. The growing habit had become more noticeable during times of frustration and concern, but as far as Æthelstan had been concerned he seemed to get his answers much quicker when consulting his invisible advisors.

Nervously for all within the Minster the time eventually passed seeing Wulfric's return, and with greater numbers of spearmen and knights than had followed him north.

Whilst Wulfric had been leaving through the main gates of Winchester on his quest to detain Edwin, riders had been dispatched through the side gates of the western wall, in secret, hurrying for Mercia, where a full body of heavily equipped knights had made ready and rode south to join the ranks of the returning escort. Should the situation have grown volatile, and Edwin had been granted the sympathies of the more prominent Wessex Thegns the Mercian Knights would have formed the guard that Æthelstan would have trusted, to beat back any size of rebellion against his rule.

Edwin was not granted the time to consult with his advisors, in fact, it had been arranged so that all who were thought to be sympathetic to his views, excepting of a single Bishop, were denied access, there would be no opportunity to conjure excuses for his treasonous acts, there had been sufficient time wasted on that subject, more urgent matters were brewing across his lands.

Some may have expected a 'turn out' of local folk, showing their support to the one next in line to the seat of Wessex, to offer Edwin a glimmer of hope against that which was about to be cast upon him, but since the violent display of a King's retribution, when Alfred's battered and bloodied corpse had been dragged through the fields of Stan Hamm, and left to rot for two days in the local woodlands before a party had been dispatched to bury what little remained of the carcass, there was little likely-hood of anyone being that eager. Besides, since Æthelstan's 'miraculous' escape from near certain death and his compassion shown to a young boy, the folk of Winchester had begun to change their opinion towards their King.

Edwin, once escorted into the Minster's main Hall minus any courtesy's that would have normally been afforded to one of his ranking, stood in silence as Wulfric, the arresting Thegn, read out the charges...

Æthelstan had sat to the right, as the injured party as had Byrnstan, raggedly dressed as usual, who would offer proof of the assassin's confession, under the eyes of God.

Ælfric, as High Reeve, sat in the centre of the gathering and would take charge of the proceedings until such time a verdict had been reached, then, as injured party, the King would award the punishment. To Ælfric's right stood Ælfheah overlooking proceedings from a religious point, as a gesture that their God would condone any decisions of the court.

Wulfric spoke nervously, he had never been in that position before, and hoped he would never be again...

"Thee, Edwin son of Edward, until this day Earl and half-brother to Æthelstan, King of all Anglo-Saxon..." he paused until the 'husting' showed their King due recognition. "Be charged that ye did conspire and plot with others to murder thy King, by means of assassination at the hands of one named Ælfred, in this very Minster..." Wulfric stepped forward half in Ælfric's eyeline, the other in Edwin's sight...

"...I offer as evidence the confession of Alfred given on that same day to the ears of Elwin, cleric of this Minster" and his left hand pointed across to the scruffy figure who immediately rose, eager to grab his few minutes of fame.

But that was instantly denied as Edwin himself stepped forward, pushing away his guards...

Once he had seen the looks of anger upon the face of his King, Edwin had decided to appeal his case for mercy. The proof against him was undeniable, there was nothing he could have said in his own defence.

He swore that his loyalty was incomparable to that of any other within the King's council and that he had actively gained support for his half-brother's policies. Not once had he asked after Alfred, which told the court that there had been spies amongst them who had sent news to Edwin before his arrest, maybe even along his journey to Winchester.

The accused's own Bishop Wynsige of Dorchester, had been permitted to accompany his patron, vigorously attempting to provide an over-exaggerated reference to Edwin's good character, passionately claiming that his benefactor had been acting in haste and with poor judgement, plotting with others under duress and misguided loyalties... then he had been cut short in mid statement by Brynstan who adamantly stated...

"The King himself shall already know of any words credible that may be afforded to his own Father's son, so there be no requirements for outside assistance." With those bluntest of words ringing in his ears the visiting Bishop had no other choice but to remain silent for fear of claiming the King uncouth, incompetent, and poorly informed, and without feeling...

There came a quiet lull in the verbal interrogations, where those who had already spoke patiently waited for the continuance of others, and those who had not yet said anything deemed to be of the slightest relevance, had decided that they should remain unheard for fear of misleading their sympathies.

Wulfric walked casually towards the accused who now stood in the central shadows of the Minster, unchained, and ruffled with nowhere to run. From his waist band, the King's Thegn withdrew a folded parchment, grubby and creased but ever so important. He held the note high, in line with Edwin's face, separating their stares as it was slowly and carefully unfolded.

The young Earl's expression turned into a pallid gaunt as he recognised the written proof of his own hand. How stupid had been Alfred, how stupid had He been to choose someone more stupid than himself...It was all that would be needed to prove his guilt, further words in his defence would be conceded as useless...Yet he still had more to say, much more...

"Our same Father..." he repeated his claim "...Our same Father had sworn throughout his reign that the rule of Wessex would settle with my brother Ælfweard, and follow on to his own Ætheling upon his death."

Æthelstan was almost impressed. Despite the pressure upon him, and the now certain conviction, Edwin, who had never been known for his composure had found a new lease, perhaps another tact that would sway the King's mind and offer some hope of survival. Remembering his place, and feeling the stares watching on he quickly crossed his body in pious respect for their Father's spirit, then silently prayed to himself that Edward would now be watching over him.

He had tried on every occasion to move away from his position of arrest, pace across the stone floor of the Quire, attempt to give his voice an added air of importance, and impress his confidence as he spoke out in his own defence against the courts near certain decision, but he was dragged back and for a final time, forced down into a high-backed settle by two Huscarl, he would not be permitted to move again.

But even that did not stop Edwin from attempting to make his point, after all, he knew now that he had very little left to lose.

"...Our Father had left thee Mercia, and Mercia alone" he swallowed allowing time for his courage to increase "Surely that should have been enough?"

So far Æthelstan had remained silent. As was his way he had watched and studied the expressions of those gathered to his left, the nobles and so-called advisors who formed the Witan. He listened intently to his own Thegns whom he trusted as much as a King may trust anyone, and at the centre were the Holy men, bishops, clerics, and priests who guzzled on imported wine, nibbled on local cheese, and said all they had to say, so long as it benefited them.

He had allowed the prisoner to rant freely, putting his own predicament deeper into trouble as he spoke out in treasonous retort, but now the time had come to declare his own view.

Æthelstan shuffled a little in his fur-lined settle all eyes sweeping from the accused coming to rest upon their King. Regardless of their representation all within the court knew that Edwin's end was nearing, they remained silent for fear of incriminating themselves. He stared deep into the coldness of his half-brother's expression searching for any trace of humanity but there was little sign of regret, of guilt, he was now a man, and accountable.

"Thee Edwin, third son of Edward...who cares only to name me as brother when conditions suit..."

He still refused to name Edwin 'his' brother and had done so since his sibling's birth, as he had with all his half-brothers, since the open rejection of his Father's second wife.

The King stood, gone now was any polite need to remain seated...

"Thee, and those of my Father's 'other' families look down upon me as last in line for any considerations, forever keeping me to the rear of decisions, pushed out of mine own Father's light, and for why? For greed, and title, and ultimate power, to create riches and worth for thy self, and thy hack of a Mother. Even the ealdor clerics recall, that here in this place, in this very hall, the great King Alfred declared me whence still a child, to all, as future King of all lands Anglo-Saxon, and thee hath nerve to deny it."

He stepped back pausing briefly, ridding his mind of passed upsets and quarrels, it would not do for a King to show others that his decisions were made through anger and retribution...

Calmed again in his usual composed style he paced slowly back and forth, in full view of the Witan, in full view of Edwin...

"Ye, asks of me if Mercia would not have been enough for a King such as I, to grant unto me sufficient worth...?"

Edwin remained silent, he had not the upbringing that would have taught him how to 'hold his own' in a verbal conflict, he had always relied upon a Mother.

"...Did thee ne'er learn, from the man who was a Father to us both, that a King may not be King for his own worth, nor to bring unto him vast riches and power... A King may be King solely as example to those within his lands, for the security and care and worth of the land and its folk."

His strides widened, then shortened as he came within inches of the accused, his face reddened as his voice threatened to betray his inner anger...

"Cyning sculan rice, for þin landleode...eac næfre for gegan." Louder and more positive he repeated his words so that they filled the Minster. So, that all should hear as he glared defiantly at the gathering, as if he spoke a lesson for all Kings that would one-day follow.

"...A King must rule his lands, for the folk of that land... and never, never just for himself."

The assembly remained silent, deep in thought. They were fine words, honourable words, new words. Gone with this King was the self-greed of the past and the lust to always have more. It had started with his Grandfather and then Edward, the land would always come first, and hopefully so would the people.

Echoes of a single cough, the rustle of a cloak, the scraping of a Huscarl's spear shaft across the cold stone floor and the closing of a Holy Book, but otherwise, silence...

...Until Edwin himself boldly restarted the conversation...

"Æthelstan, Bregu Cyning...Be it known upon this second day of Winterfylleth, in this year of our Lord 933, that whatever judgement be taken upon me, and all that be mine, be done so in contempt of the wishes of our late King, who was Father to us both..." He paused as a tear dragged itself from a pitiful eye finally realising that what little of his own future remained was not about to become a pleasant one. He went through the motions of attempting to swallow, there was nothing to swallow, he took a deep breath but even that seemed now pointless.

"...Be that as so, Æthelstan King, ye shall stand accountable for thy faults upon the final day of thy destiny."

"As shall we all" whispered Wulfric unafraid of being over-heard, "Some earlier than others."

The King was again calm. There was no point in continuing to echo his anger, the accused, his own Father's son, had all but conceded his guilt and nothing further could, or would be offered in mitigation. The now humble Bishop of Dorchester had previously attempted to interrupt, but even he thought more wisely and remained silent, even his God could not have reversed Edwin's self destruction.

Ælfric cleared his throat, assured himself that all were silent. "Edwin, thee by thine own admittance confess to the charges..." It wasn't a question.

The King's gesture was silent, a simple raising of an open palm and a shallow nod of the head made only for the attentions of Byrnstan who obediently stepped forward, Holy Book in one hand, seal of office in the shape of a cross in the other and a smug grin of self importance across his ashen face, it was to be he, and he alone who would benefit from this theatre.

Two lower clerics stood, one to either side of their Bishop, leaned slightly forward and between them opened a scroll that was rolled slowly from the top, then raised towards the light for Brynstan to read, poorly...

"Then Edwin of Wessex..." He spoke annoyingly in a melody, as if he were chanting vespers. It sounded very much out of place.

"...In the eyes of the Almighty, one true God, upon the divine Order of Æthelstan, Rex Saxonum et Anglorum...Thee hath been charged and upon thine own words found guilty of numerous acts of treason, revolt, and attempted murder..."

A slight pause as he dropped the melodic rhythm, swallowed, then wiped a bead of pious sweat from his greasy brow.

"...Therefore, as decreed by our Holy Laws, and the Common Laws of our Land, as punishment for the crimes of treason towards the personage of our King and the people of Winchester, for the crime of harrying revolt against the House of Wessex, thee be sentenced this day to banishment and exile from our lands for the remainder of thy life, and may the Lord, our only God grant mercy upon thy pitiful soul."

Sighs were expressed by the gathering which were only drowned by the sharp intakes of cool stale air as the 'blessing' was pondered and the sentencing continued. Some had thought the decision too severe, others, mostly all, had thought it to be insufficient.

Byrnstan continued. "Thine own estates, bequeathed to thee by thy late Father's death, shall be enclosed with those of the King, as compensation for such outrage…and a portion of thy lands, to be decided upon at a time hereafter, shall be granted to the family of the 'ealdwif' murdered by the blade of thine own assassin… So speaketh I, Byrnstan, Bishop of Winchester, by the will of our King so appointed by Almighty God…" and so on and so forth he blithered sanctimonious compliments towards the King's right to rule.

It had been arranged, prior to the trial, that Byrnstan should accord any sentence just in case Æthelstan should feel the right to mercifully intercede, but Edwin had asked for no mercy towards himself or his family…

But Æthelstan intervened nonetheless…

"If thee speaks any words that may be thought to be truth, as thee speaks of a God given right to the seat of Wessex, then such rights should come through divine order. So, if our Lord God had wished for it to be thee who should have been granted a right to rule, then it shall be upon him to ensure that thee lives long enough to complete such a Holy Order."

Now the silence could almost be heard as the court awaited their King's words…

For a split second Æthelstan held the urge to grab Edwin, shake him senseless until he realised his wrong, then hold his half-brother in forgiveness and tell him all would be right from then on, they would be brothers, cynn, friends, but such feelings soon left, and sense took back its hold. His glare towards the son of his Father would have cut through any man's resilience.

"Upon the morrow, ye shall be taken from this place and marched in bonds to the shores of our Kingdom, to a place named Bucgan Ora. There, thee shall be cast upon the waters of the 'fish road' within the oldest boat of the shire, without oar and without sail." He glanced about, there was not a single offer of argument "With nought but a single guard for thy attendances. There, thee shall be left to the mercy of the great waters, and God's will."

Before the echo of his final words had disappeared into the Minster's stone, the King had 'stormed' from the Hall leaving nothing more than a crash of oak in his wake and fifty or more pairs of eyes baring down upon the convicted person of a one-time Earl.

...And it happened. Just as the King had ordered. The fate of his half-brother had been sealed, and with it a lesson, sent out to all within his ever-growing Kingdom, of the punishments cast upon those who conspired to commit treason or revolt. If the instigator had been any other than his Father's son, Æthelstan knew that his retribution would have been more dreadful, but his own honesty would never pass his lips.

Within a matter of weeks after the sentence had been carried out, and the smallest of Noble gatherings bore witness as the oldest of rotten hulks had vanished into the growing swell of a raging sea, an 'Embassy' had been received at Winchester's 'still' Royal Court.

The foreign visitors had been dispatched by Æthelstan's distant, but loyal cousin, Aedolf, the Count of Boulogne. They informed the King that the body of his half-brother had been discovered, washed upon their shores. Aedolf had written, in a personal note, that he had escorted the body himself, to the Abbey of Saint Bertin in Saint Omer where it had been buried with the honour of a Noble, and the respectful love of a cousin.

Graciously Æthelstan had returned the embassy back, across the waters, and with a gracious donation of Alms for the Abbey, along with his unending gratitude for his cousin's kindness.

He was now relieved. The opposition from Winchester that had stood so stubbornly against his rule since the first days of his ascendance had finally ended, and with it the threats of any further uprisings from the nobles. Edwin's failed revolt had ironically cemented the union of the Anglo-Saxons into one land, and that land was finally, and officially named Engleland.

In the wake of Edwin's death, as if he had somehow regretted his decision, even if it had only been slight, Æthelstan paid penance. As if it had always been in his thoughts he set aside a suitable sum of money, a great sum of money, for the construction of a church at Milton in the Shire of Dorset, always to serve memory in Edwin's name. To ensure that the church would become efficient, therefore continuing long into the future, he granted the collegiate sixteen manors to provide the income that would be required.

Time passed, anger subdued and Æthelstan decided to leave Winchester, confident that news of the attempted revolt and its outcome would have spread through the shires like the northern winds, and that now the Wessex folk at the very least accepted him as their true King. He admitted in silent relief that the only memory he would savour was the meeting of a young boy with an innocent smile that beamed across a grubby face as he ruffled his unkempt hair. The simple and carefree attitude of one so young, who, despite the hunger and poverty, had brought back memories of himself at such an age. As he rode from the walls of the burg that same boy had raced alongside the column, straining his muscles to keep up, whilst smiling proudly as if he had waited forever for another sight of his King.

The lad had looked up through squinted eyes and passed a grin through still grubby cheeks, then raised a hand as he lost his ground, and a tear escaped as he waved 'God be with Ye' to a man he knew then to be his friend as well as his King.

Æthelstan had wanted to stop, gather up the boy, and place him in a court as another of those he had fostered, but that would have been incorrect. If he had done that for this child, then he would wish to do so for every child.

As the King had eased Abrecan's head towards the north he carefully dropped a sheathed seax into the grassy verge of the hollow way, modest and barely ornate, but to the youngster who had gathered it from the damp wayside it would be the greatest gift of all. He would treasure it for the remainder of his life, and the stories that he would tell his own son would ensure that the knife accompanied many more tales for the generations yet to follow.

Then the Dark Raven with horned beak

and the livid toad,

the eagles and kite,

the hound and wolf in mottled hue

were long refreshed with such delicacies.

In that Land,

no greater war was ever waged,

Nor did such slaughter

ever surpass that one...

[Æthelweard's chronicles]

CHAPTER 14

937 A.D. The Lands had emptied of all men. The armies of Olaf Guthfrithson, Constantine II of Scotland, Owen I of Strathclyde marched in their thousands to meet the armies of Æthelstan of England.

...Æthelstan shook his head before wiping the grimy sweat from a helmless brow. Staring across the plains of Brunanburh he enjoyed too much what little remained of the afternoon's sun and the peaceful silence of the pre-fight where all was now committed, and nothing could be changed. The 'game' had already commenced.

Then all would remain as it was, until Hel's own fury was sent to spoil the tranquillity of Nature's innocence.

Warm blood swept into numbed parts of his tired body as he slipped in one movement from Abrecan's saddle, landing with both feet upon the crispness of the northern sod. From neck to boot his painful cramps increased, then quickly eased as muscles stretched and joints flexed. A roll of the shoulders finally restored normality into his body. Eagerly snapping open the clasps on his side satchel he reached in, awkwardly withdrawing its contents, flat bread, ewes' cheese, and spring water would delay his hunger until the kitchen fires had been stoked within the thorny ringed burg that already neared completion, as expected, before the night could sweep out its cloud of shadow. The King began to eat ravenously before he had settled.

He sat alone, always preferring it that way, although the Huscarl were forever within eye's sight, and made himself reasonably comfortable, appropriately beneath the naked arms of a lonely oak. The cheese was good, the water too warm and his thoughts went deep into years gone by. The sad deaths of his guardians, how much he still missed their company as much almost as he had missed their advice...and the death of his Father, in yet another battle for his lands, and of the Dark Riders soon after, all before his ascendance to King.

It had been the longest of waits. An equally tortuous wait. A life time's wait. Yet as soon as he had found himself standing in front of that small, naïve alter in the grey weathered sandstone chapel of the All Saints, in Cynyngstan, the stress drove through his body. The time had finally arrived, warm, bright, and dry was that day for which he had been prepared since he could first speak the words of a man, yet his nerves caused him to almost wish otherwise, but only for the shortest of times...

Pausing from his thoughts of the past he recollected fondly the similarity of both days. The strength of the mid-day sun warmed through his body highlighting all that was good, even on such a day. The green plains of that unknown place named Brunanburh were strangely similar to that small yet adequate church where a King's stone lay.

927. The golden sun had then, on that most special of days, broken impressively through the half-shuttered windows on the western side of the aisles, casting its Holy rays upon the 'Sarsen' floor, enhancing the riven configuration of the natural stone. The modest structure was by no means equal to the grandeur of the western Minsters, some present had thought it far too modest to celebrate the ascendance of a King, but the flowered garlands and richly embossed tapestries that had been borrowed and donated were draped from the otherwise plain walls, achieving enough to impress the Regal importance of that day. There had been an abundance of blue colouring, brushed and washed upon every possible surface in a hurry to uplift the church's status, "Too much" he had thought but only to himself, that day was not one for criticism against those who had attempted to do only well...

The location for the day had been Æthelstan's choice, and his alone. Judging the mood of the folk in the southern shires, the uneasiness across Wessex and the uncertainty across his newly combined lands, he had thought Kingston the only place. Set almost upon the borders of Mercia and Wessex, Kingston boasted the only bridge across the Thames, other than London, making access easy and showing all that everyone may cross in peace from Wessex to Mercia and back, as one people, in one land, in Engleland.

The centre piece upon the alter boasted a golden cross that sat upon a heavily embroidered cloth of kingly purple, both gifts during Edward's reign, standing out proudly behind the robed body of the aged Archbishop. It stole the first glance of everyone as they entered.

Æthelstan also stood out. Proudly draped in the purple cloak long since a gift from his Grandfather, showing off the golden scabbard of the King's sword, also given by Alfred…

During that first year, since his Father's sudden death on the banks of the Dee River, many strange and unexplained happenings had filled his life. The Dark Riders who had 'flown' the length of the land to secure his rule had been his first inherent order. From the rugged plains of Chester's new Shire to Oxford in Wessex's south they had rode to 'spread' the news, telling all of Edward's death in battle, defending his people and their lands, and that now Æthelstan, eldest son and Ætheling had become 'in title' to the dead King's seat. Then came the rumours that had then followed the unexplained and premature death of his half-brother Ælfweard, just sixteen days after their Father's, rumours which had spread like a wild fire across the Saxon shires.

Edward's death had brought Æthelstan's own arguments against some sections of the Church, especially since Ælfweard's unexplainable death, but even they had finally conceded in recognising that He, who bore the name of Noble Stone had been the rightful heir to the Kingdoms occupied by the Engles and Saxons. Yet what it ever had to do with the church directly was anybody's guess, surely 'they' were only there to minster the 'Word' of their God over those whom he ruled, and not dictate where it was that he should do the ruling.

And naturally there were the Danes, and the Scots, and not forgetting the Welsh. There would always be the Welsh with one form of complaint or another.

Secretly though he was thankful of the Welsh. Were they not kin to the folk who had first walked those lands during the time of his own Mother's forefathers, at the very least he had always known where he stood with them. He used their 'favour' as much as they used his.

Where as far as the Dane and Scot were concerned, their day would soon arrive, and all would then be decided.

...The celebration of Æthelstan's ascendance to the ruling seat was always going to be unlike any that had come before him. From the instant Edward had passed from their world, the coming of the 'new' way had begun.

Overseen and greatly scripted by his half cousin, the Archbishop Æthelhelm had laboured tirelessly day and night for many a month ensuring the new way of appointing a King, their King, would be correct, and what's more, appropriate to the times that were fast approaching. Æthelhelm wanted that celebration to be remembered not just for his times, but for many years, or even centuries to follow.

...A line of clerics, eagerly in rhythm, recited a Latin script after the harmonious completion of a small choir's contribution to the ceremonial start, which heralded Æthelhelm's raising high the golden cross of office, whilst at the same time permitting himself a sly glance around the noble congregation. Many had gathered, yet not all those invited were in attendance, even his old eyes had not missed the absence of one highly important figure. There would now be a need to visit Winchester, where he would most certainly require of its Bishop, Frithestan, a solid explanation for his absence, and other Wessex nobles had copied, refusing even to send the smallest of blessings to 'their' new King. Nevertheless, the changes had been made with the inclusion for the first time, of a glorious crown created from the finest gold, it would stand as a definite change towards those new ways.

The crown had been just one of Æthelhelm's additions, unlike the usual 'helm' that had been traditional and symbolic as a remnant of their heritage from 'other' lands since before Offa's time. Carefully cast in the purest of gold with a silver Wyvern clutching a single red jewel, seated beneath a golden cross at its front, with four upturned points, one at each side signifying smaller crosses. The one jewel was significant in stating One Land, under One Rule, with the four smaller crosses depicting the lands of the north, south, west, and east, again under one rule.

Every door and window shutter had been opened to its fullest permitting the assembled crowds of common folk to get as close as possible, giving the impression that the proceedings took up the whole town, Æthelstan was eager that all should be part of the ceremony.

He took his last pace forward as Ætheling, stole the slightest glance before lowering his body into a kneeling position, nervously and proud alongside that sacred 'Stone of Kings'. A silent, but deep breath was gratefully taken before placing both hands carefully, one at each side of the sarsen block. Just as the ceremony now insisted, a silver penny had already been set in place next to one set previously by his own Father.

He lowered his head until his chin had settled upon his beating chest...

Æthelhelm lowered his also...

"In the name of Our Father, the Almighty one true God, I place this Crown, as s sign of thy rule, upon the head of our chosen King..."

He did, slowly, precisely and with dignity. Surprisingly it fit.

Then, just as a King should portray, he rose calmly to his feet, bowed a head respectfully towards the alter, then again towards the gathering, before taking one small step until he stood upon the surface of the ancient stone.

The Archbishop, observed closely by his young nephew and new apprentice, Dunstan, continued...

"Now, take ye the virga, to soothe the righteous and terrify the reprobate...Then on to teach right to those who may stray from the fold, always aiding the fallen..."

Æthelstan took the rod, plain and strait in gold with a silver twist, embellished with another, smaller cross at its head.

"...and accept the sword to impress thy word to mercifully grant aid to all widows and orphans, and restore desolate things."

Too heavy for fighting, the sword was placed, point downwards onto the stone's surface, hilt held tightly in the right hand, and on his left...

"The ring, that thee shall wear forever. The ring of our new Engle Land, marking the acceptance of thy responsibilities to support the faith." And the golden ring slipped easily onto the middle finger with an ingot separating the initials, A and R in its centre.

"...and now, through the powers of the Holy Father, I, Æthelhelm of Cantwaraburg, pronounce thee Guardian of the Faith, King of Wessex, Lord of Mercia and All the lands about. King Æthelstan, of these Isles...Thee shall establish and govern the apex of paternal glory over all folk, unitedly..." and a barrage of Latin scriptures in the forms of blessings and prayers from the mouths of the clerics echoed around the stonework, understood only by some, meaning almost nothing to the many, but the result would soon become the same in any language.

Æthelhelm continued for all to understand...

"Thee shall hold fast the state that thee now grasps as commanded by the Holy Father..."

More chants and religious sighs followed.

Æthelhelm leant forward taking the King's left hand in his right, then lifting it on to his own lips he kissed the golden ring to show all that he now bowed to Æthelstan, and with him the church would follow.

Then the Archbishop uttered the words that he had longed to speak for most of that year...

"Astanden Æthelstan, Cyning Seaxisc ac Engle…Rex Saxonum et Anglorum."

Now Æthelstan stood down from the stone alongside his Archbishop, glancing at his people as King of the Anglo-Saxons.

The gatherings inside and out remained in tentative silence, apart from the odd shuffle and cough and child cry, before Æthelhelm followed with another prayer. 'Omnipotens Sempiterne Deus' which he had 'stolen' from the earlier Carolingians. Another addition to the ceremony took place when Æthelstan's head was anointed with a mixture of perfumed oils as a sign of baptism into his sanctified position. The blend was made from a secret recipe of oils and herbs, blessed in private before the ceremony's commencement, and it would remain a secret for the next one thousand years, or more.

Æthelhelm's direct appeal to his God then commenced…

'To endow this new King with the qualities of Abraham's faithfulness, with the meekness of Moses, and the fortitude of Joshua, adding David's humility to accompany the greatest wisdom of Solomon.'

Further prayers still, telling of the good things from Alfred's reign and the continuing legacy of Edward's own rule, then, for the first time the term Engelcynn was used in a Holy context.

Æthelstan was now King in the eyes of his God, and with his God's blessing he would become ruler over those unconquered lands that had caused his Father, and those who had ruled before, so much discontent.

His mind drifted from the excitement within a southern church moving dreamlike onto the eyes of a girl child, with blonded locks and pretty cheeks, running and skipping and singing about a courtyard during one of Gloucester's finest mornings, before falling into the arms of a Mother whose eyes shone equally bright as she gathered up a daughter and swung her raggedly from left to right. How dizzy they had fallen together, as he permitted himself the rarest of smiles, landing in a crumpled pile both glanced into his eyes, how wonderful they were, a mother and her daughter, how painfully bitter the keeping of such a secret.

The day dreaming over, his stomach full and a thirst quenched, he found himself back in the saddle, over-looking the plains of Brunanburh, at the side of his only heir, rested, refreshed and ever vigilant.

To his left, the sun was threatening to escape for another day as the gloom of an impending eve rolled in from the east. The western breeze brought with its chill a hint of salt which settled upon his lips as if to prove their closeness to the great 'fish road'.

His eyes glanced across at the rider mounted to his left and remembering his own first battle, so long ago, he offered a comforting smile to ease the youngster's telling nerves.

"How proud would be our Father, to know that we be here, together, for the glory of our lands."

"I believe that he can see us bregu, here and now, he watches over us all."

"He does Edmund...As do they all who stand at his side..." Æthelstan smiled sympathetically "Then be thee ready my brother?"

"I be ready...A little afraid I confess, but only to thee, yet always ready."

He admired the honesty of his young sibling. "To be afraid Edmund is to be a man. Our Father taught that when thee stops being afraid, thee stops being a man, as to be afraid, is to be fearful of losing the great things about thee. Any thing be worth the fight only if thee be afraid of losing it."

Edward had not taught him any such thing, they had been Æthelred's words, whispered on his death bed. His own Father had never afforded the time to counsel such guidance, his harmless lie was spoken as an attempt to offer calm.

"...And what of the armies?" continued the King "Be they also eager to risk everything?"

"Yea, they be always ready to follow their King."

Those were the words every King had wished to hear on the brink of such a battle.

"Then on the morrow, we shall leave behind our one God, in His own peace with the pious ones upon the brow, where they shall all watch and whisper their 'pennig's' worth..." His head motioned to their rear as his excited voice grew a little louder "Then let us summon the sound of the Asgardian bells, so that we may stand as tall as Wyverns, and face together that which may be our final battle, and if that be so, then together we shall stand once more, alongside the spirits of our Ærfædas."

Even the smaller groups of Huscarl automatically summoned a riotous cheer as they nodded heads, shook spears, and thumped their shields noisily in agreement with their King. All had fire in their bellies for the coming fight, so long now overdue. At last the time had arrived. Even their horses were ready, stamping fetlock and shoe, snorting clouds of warm breath from bellowing lungs, shaking their manes in the western breeze, standing as tall as their riders.

The background support fell quiet as the King glanced down to his right where a standing man seemed to have appeared from nowhere, panting for his every breath after his sprint to the side of his Lord. Æthelstan saw him and asked...

"How far be their armies from this place?"

Gareth Greyhair looked up, squinting at the silhouette now masking the sun's last brightness, focussing upon his King, nodding a slight salute of the head. A hand poorly shaded his brow as the sweat poured through a belted jerkin ignoring the oncoming chill, mixing with the stains of mud that smeared his front, top to bottom betraying the many days he had spent in hiding, watching, waiting, until there was something worth reporting. Days and nights spying from the back of rotted tree stumps, through copse, under glade, seeing all from the silent shadows of nature's hides, nothing had moved so much as an inch across that part of the Isle without Gareth Greyhair, or another of his band knowing.

"We have followed them my Lord..." a pause for more breath and the clearing of a crusted throat, he would not spit in front of his King, so he swallowed the congealed phlegm noisily. Each of the eight men now arriving at his side heaved in unison for the luxury of air, all looking in need of a decent meal, appearing as if they had been running for weeks without rest, and they had.

"Since their feet crossed by the Latin wall we have followed them Lord. Constantine and his Scyttisc march clumsily, their bellies full of mead, beneath eight 'gupfanas', they shall be upon us as the next sun rises..."

Almost everything that he needed to know in one quick report, as it should have been. Constantine had broken the treaty months earlier and now marched four thousand well armed Scot out of Alba, into the middle lands, not the numbers he had been expecting.

"...On this night, they shall be forced to make their camp to our north, or march strait into Heorstan and his Wessex..." the Welshman spat his stomach refusing to accept more of that wretched filth...

Constantine mac Aed had returned from his exile on the Hibernian Isle many years earlier. On the death of his cousin Domnall mac Causantin he had claimed the rule over the Picts, but not before slaughtering many of the ancient clan. Constantine's grandfather Cinaed mac Ailpin had united the men north of the great wall years before Æthelstan's birth, settling the highlands for his own benefit, but Constantine had grown to be a man full of greed and assumed his forces had the strength to spread his rule the length and breadth of the Isle, all the way to the southern coasts of Wessex. He was the one to beat, as were the Danish forces from Dublin, who had started their march some weeks earlier. Yet on the other hand, Constantine's second ally the King of the Cumbric, whose banners had also been seen, would have probably agreed to any settlement to avoid a war with the English, if he had not been under strict command of the Scot.

...Lungs replenished, a little spring water from a side flask, and the report continued.

"The Dane comes from across the Gwyddeleg, beached his ships two days since and will find us mid morrow, and the armies of the Cumbric..." he spat again at the thought of his treasonous cousins, "they be..." he pointed towards the east, where small towers of fire smoke had started to rise from beyond a line of sweeping hyrsts.

Æthelstan's eyes followed the line of his scout's arm and calmly smiled...

"Ahhhhh, Ouuen be early." Another wry grin highlighted the King's face, the Cumbrian was always expected first as his lands were the closest.

"To the cook's tent Gareth, along with thy men. Fill thy bellies and rest thy bodies for it may be the final chance until we have this 'swinen' beat."

Gestures, murmurs of appreciation and relief were shown as the roughest looking group turned and hurried to be first in the line for hot food that would not remain so for long.

As the last Welshman disappeared, the King nodded a silent command to his half-brother, who in turn copied the Order in the direction of a shadowy figure who had barely been visible during the report. Masked against the backdrop of vegetation, with his strange array of clothing and dyed skin, he stood resilient and disciplined, awaiting a command.

The sinister figure was Wulfstrum, commander of a small band of anxious volunteers from the Shire of Kent, set on revenge with the Dane for the butchery of their cousins at Tettenhall.

The wordless command was nothing more than the wink of an eye, followed by a swift nod of a head which was readily accepted through a confident smile as the standing form of the leather clad Jute rolled a left arm high and wide, which caused a weapon man a short distance away to respond with a more vigorous wave of a coloured banner, first to his left, then to his right, rapidly repeating the actions, three, maybe four times, as if he had waited a lifetime to carry out the deed.

Wulfstrum moved into the shadow of his King watchful of the empty grounds around them, the wind caught his matted hair sweeping its Jutish redness free of his broadest shoulders. His mouth churned over the remnants of a 'tug' of dried deer meat as his eyes pierced through the evading light searching deep into the nothing for something he was certain to find, and eventually he did.

The silent signal, unseen by all except those who were meant to see, brought five hundred of his Cantwaran kinsmen to rise out of the dampened grasses, as if they had appeared magically out of the nothing, without noise nor fuss. They had been there, their dress camouflaging against the night, in hiding all along, covered in bracken and gorse, some beneath the hooves of the horses. None had seen them, not even the Ræcc hounds had taken their scent, and the smiles of achievement upon their faces bettered the look of shock upon the riders' expressions.

Each man shook himself down, evicting whatever livestock had thought to make a Jutish smock their home. They checked their weapons before stretching their frozen joints to face the noble pair horsed upon the hazy dune. Once satisfied that nothing further would be added, without a change of expression, they mechanically turned in unison to face North, walking forward as one, lightly, and in total silence as their brown stained bodies and auburn hair silhouetted against the impending sky until all had 'vanished' into the gloom as if they had never been, leaving in their wake a breeze that blew across their path carrying with it an odour which stank like nothing ever witnessed before.

"That be why the dogs did not find them" Edmund bellowed as his left hand failed to rid the stench.

Those quiet, modestly unassuming people were from the southernmost shire of Wessex, of whom Alfred's Mother had descended. Of pagan origin, as were they all, that unpretentious folk had long since derived from a peninsula far across the eastern waters. They were as proud and as valiant as they were trustworthy and loyal. Since the very beginnings of their time, when the word for 'war' had not yet been sought, the Jutes had perfected their 'hidden surprises'. For many days, even weeks their sagas had told, without exaggeration, they had been known to lie in wait with little to eat or drink save that which surrounded their hide, under cover of the natural vegetation, still and dangerous and secret, merging into its background until a deer or other beast had ventured upon their secluded place, then out of nowhere they would rise and kill a ghastly death of deadly shock. Naturally over the years, as man had found his greed and fighting became the way route to survival, their skills had been adapted into near perfection.

As he watched the misty band of warriors disappear Æthelstan leant across Abrecan's mane and called to his young heir, now mesmerised by the Jutes...

"It was said once, yet only in a spoken tale now almost forgotten to most, that the first Man to walk upon this Earth was a Jute who went by the name of Temes, many, many lifetimes passed. He, alone in that world of endless days, unguided and lost, had set out upon the barren lands of all he knew, wandering for many years. He passed through many mystical, empty places which hid all the torments until, eventually hungry and lost he ventured into a wonderful land of plenty where he came upon the Mother of All things. There, in that land, replenished and safe, he briefly fell in love with her for a single season of time, and that season, which seemed to last an eternity would become known as Spring. And from their love they begat a child, a single girl child with golden hair and the brightest eyes, who grew to be named Summer.

As she grew, Summer inherited all the talents and gifts that had been her Mothers, and the great strengths and bravery of her Father and used them to bring upon the world many great plants of all colours, with odours of the finest scents. Then she brought the wild things of all shapes and sizes, and good things to eat, but above all she brought peace and plenty to every land. Through the time that followed such things in those lands were virtuous and calm, safe and unending, until it all became spoiled with the coming of Winter, brought forth by the age of Man."

A pause, then, "And where, bregu, did man venture from?"

Æthelstan smiled unsurprised by the question he himself had asked when first told. He glared at his heir through squinting eyes "I told ye Edmund, it be just a tale."

Myths and legends long forgotten had told further of how the 'powers' and talents of the Jutish folk had been brought across many lands of that unsettled world, descending from the sand plains of the farthest eastern realms, by a persecuted people escaping the wrath of a fearsome and merciless enemy who ruled only in the name of greed and power. Long ago they had adapted their ways as a means of survival and had once been known to those who knew them as the 'Ungesewen folc'.

Edmund Ætheling, just fifteen years of age had always felt safe within his brother's shadow. Adjusting his windswept cloak to fit more comfortable upon his young shoulders he took in a breath of the chilled evening air and paced his mount closer to his brother's side, both now watching the disappearance of the irregular Jutish infantry in awe. Casually pulling his mount to a stand he rested his body further forward upon the cloth gullet of his fighting saddle, then let free a sigh before refilling his lungs...

"How magnificent be these Lands, and her people who hold in them so many talents and gifts, not just for warring. Surely there be right on our side, in this place where we shall be as one, as together our strengths will make us unbeatable. How great then will be these lands?"

The King smiled as if his own words had been echoed, "Edmund. Brother. In this short life that we be granted there walks only two kinds of men, the takers, and the makers, so it must be as thee says, for if victory be not ours then there shall remain nothing of any worth, for any man." In agreement, and in each other's silence, they continued their ride both secretly thinking of the catastrophe and mayhem that would engulf those lands should their quest fail.

Out of sight from their King, on the fringes of the darkest of nights, they had reached their positions deep enough into the place where the fighting was expected to be its fiercest. The Jutes, with their painted skins of browns and greens would conceal themselves behind or beneath the smallest piece of vegetation. A clump of fern, the thinnest of bog grasses, a winter green bush, or a rotting stump, they would lie through the night, as still and as silent as death itself, with meagre rations of food and water, for as long as they were required, just waiting, despite the cold, whatever the weather, whilst their darkened peat stained skins and concealed weapons remained beyond the eyes, and ears of any living creature.

More confirming reports had come to him by way of the Pecsæten, dispatched many days earlier, before the main armies had been readied to march. They had now informed their King of Olaf Guthfrithsson, the Danish King of Dublin who had crossed the Hibernian waters to the west. It had now been confirmed by all sources, the invasion had begun, his enemies were on their way in the greatest of numbers, all of them uniting as one single force as he had expected, now marching towards their assembly, just as he had expected.

Further news had been brought through the spies, there were always the spies available with their talents. Gatherers of information for all occasions, and loyal only to he who held the heaviest purse. Reports, gossips, snippets of information 'stolen' from within the ranks of their enemies, had told that the King of the Scot had intended to register his new found right to rule over all lands which would soon be 'once of the Saxon'.

The nearing Scot would soon be setting his camp, noisily and arrogant in the darkness. All would now be on their guard, many nervously on edge, until the rising of the winter sun when two days of preparation and information gathering would follow until the three invading armies were joined en mass, and the stragglers who lagged for one reason or another had caught up. Two further days of council would ensure that all who had sworn ally and honoured their word had marched their numbers of freemen and levied alike into their respective camps, and then the plans for victory would be agreed by the chieftains and jarls.

Under normal provision, in the 'build up' before any battle, during the planning stages, emissaries and embassies would be dispatched to the opposing camps, under the protection of 'griðlagu', to offer or ask for bounty, or levy, in the form of 'gafol' or hostage, to permit the other to vacate the field intact and return unharmed to whence they came. But not so on that occasion. There would be no bribes or bounties from that field. Æthelstan wanted a conflict, there would be no other way. He sought a war and had waited long for its coming as he was certain in both heart and mind that its result would bring about a true and lasting peace to all lands, a peace unlike any other before, but first he had to secure the victory.

There would have been no emotional welcomes from long lost friends or forgotten cousins as ally had met with ally when the armies from across the cold waters had merged with those from the even colder north. The Dane had sent the Scot fleeing from the lands of Niall Noigiallach and men who remembered the sagas still held a grudge, but not so much as the grudges that were held against the Anglo-Saxon. Yet reason for such a grudge had been long forgotten, if it were ever actually known.

As was their way, as each group had entered the swelling encampments, each would haggle, and demand by right, or name and title, for the best place to rest his army, and infighting could soon be heard scrapping over the hillock tops as Dane fought with Scot, and the first casualties were suffered without the new 'Englisc' having drawn a sword.

His enforced energy through that hurried march was the reason they had beat their enemies to the field, his Grandfather's legacy had ensured that his armies, and navy, were prepared to march or sail without notice, but it would have been solely down to Æthelstan's aggressive insistence to leave the burgs and homesteads with sufficient manpower to defend the thorp's and vils from any passing gangs of pirates or chancing marauders, or even a rebellion from an outraged Thegn, to ensure that the last of the crops were gathered before winter's rage fully stamped her claim upon the season and ensuring his armies had a place to return.

On that march. As he had passed through burgs and other strongholds he would increase the numbers of his fyrd from those who were able bodied and spare, replenishing his stocks from the homestead's supplies to keep the bellies of his warriors full, but not too full. All that energy and determination, forward planning and instant readiness would set the plan to start his enemy's demise.

He had dispatched the groups ahead to guarantee the fires were set correctly. Where cover would have suited the Dane and Scot they had burnt the vegetation and opened the ground to entice them into the damp and boggy areas where the ground was treacherous and unwelcoming, muddy and awkward. Downstream from the English camps fresh spring water had been ruined with the carcasses of rotting animals where the northern winds screamed through the crags and rocks and howled at their necks granting them little comfort to rest and sleep. All such things that would welcome an enemy to the lands of Middengærd.

...And of course, there were still the Pecsætan. The first of the hill folk tribes of the Engles who had stated their claim upon the heart of that Isle more than five hundred years passed. Having mixed their blood with the Brythonic Brigantes, and other local clans, they now lived, hunted, and farmed in the uplands of Mercia and had been ordered by their King's swift, single command... "Dispatch the Pecsætan!!!"

To forage their way north the instant he had decided to take his fight to the throats of his inherited enemies. Small bands of those peak landers had scampered about the north like insects until they had found the prime areas where their 'talents' would be best suited.

From the grassy carpets of the hillocks and hyrsts to the damper gullies and glades and hollow ways of the shire woods they would carry out small ambushes, using hit and run attacks upon the weakest flanks of the invading hoards, injuring rather than killing, maiming rather than slaughtering, for it was long proven since Ælfred's day, that an injured man took up more time and resources than the dead. When the main force had broken free from the assault and had left their injured behind with the sparsest of guards, the men of the Peak lands would return in silence to complete their task, viciously killing their prey, dead. Such talents were continued, slowing down the invaders until the time stood right to allow them to proceed, almost unhindered, to find their new fate.

Inevitably, such attacks did not always go the way they had been intended and many of the Pecsætan had been captured and most cruelly killed, their bodies mutilated and left upon the wayside, naked and open, often 'pinned' to a tree or its trunk, to bleed out, as a lesson to the local folk of what lay as fate for those who dared to stand against the Men from the North.

Final glimpses of the sun's light hesitated upon the western horizon and the darkening clouds threatened to steal away the last glimmers of precious light as Æthelstan glanced into the eyes of his brother…

"So, it shall soon be upon us Edmund. This coming time, when all men shall stake their claim to that which be not theirs. See how they all hasten to greet us…" a muffled laugh interrupted his speech, there was nobody to notice the nervous tremor that accompanied it. "…Here, in this finest of places shall it finally be settled. One last fight, a final slaughter, one final defeat, and so then to the victor shall go the Engle Lands."

As if she had been waiting for Man to complete his day, the sun finally conceded and dropped exhaustedly from view bidding all to hurry to the safety of the fires which had then began to glow and radiate across the scattered camps. In isolated pockets at first, but then, everywhere the beacons of all armies brought the orange light of man into the empty darkness of night, and Edmund, only then realising the magnitude of the gatherings uttered his nervous agreement, and both men turned their horses back towards their night tents.

Obediently on foot, Wulfstrum followed in the tracks of his men, chuckling to himself with a heightened excitement at the thought of the approaching battle. The Cantwarans were a people who had never grown used to failing, they had stood their ground across the ages, and the thoughts of war, and revenge delighted the Kentish Thegn, the last of his commanders reported that all their bands were 'settled'.

Edmund, although still young had become highly confident with his status as Ætheling, yet even so, he stuck close to the side of his brother, in the tightest of bonds. Through his young years he had watched as his own mother, Eadgifu, had ridiculed and conspired in her attempts to break Æthelstan's ties with their now dead Father. She had whispered and gossiped in the shadows of the courts to persuade others to counter his entitlement, turn the common folk against him and blacken his name as rightful heir, constantly harping that his birth had been produced out of wedlock and away from the praises of their God. However, she had not succeeded. Upon Edward's death, she had been banished to a small, barely known nunnery at Berclea, which was openly sponsored by the King. There she would remain, out of 'harms way' ending the consequences of her gossiping that had so often violated the peaceful corners of many a good Lady's court.

Eadgifu's spiteful ambitions were now done with, the pride and respect that he held for his older brother continued to grow as did his eternal loyalty. He had always, even in his first years, during those rare visits, tried to walk in Æthelstan's steps worshipping the ground they had left. Day by day, as he grew to a young adult and had been honoured as Ætheling in the Tamworth courts, he had shown keen eagerness to learn, for he knew, that should his God permit, one day he, and he alone would rule those lands in the stead of his brother King.

...Leading up to that day, where more men now stood upon the northern plains than did so anywhere else in the land, attentions, and concerns from those who had owned the smallest as well as the largest estates had always been paramount within that area and west along the Hibernian sea. Those sections of borderlands that were prone to attack held more burgs and beacons than any other that had been built by his Grandfather or added to by Æthelflæd, or his own Father. Now strengthened, every council within the land knew of the increasing threats from the Danes of Dublin, Limerick, Cork, and Waterford, and then talk of further invasion from across the Latin wall was the talk of the day. It would not have been a secret that such threats were soon to become harsh realities and reports of large scale invasion forces were always on the 'tongues' of travellers, messengers and of course, spies. The greed of the Northmen was unquenchable, the arrogance of the Scot unending, neither would ever be satisfied with that which they held, even if they held everything.

The spies had begun to report back almost weekly regarding the growing tensions and mass preparations for serious campaigns from the western island, with sightings of Anlaf's lieutenants massing their numbers in the Waterford strongholds a few weeks earlier affording the final clue that an invasion would soon become more than just a 'mead-hall' threat.

If such a report had not sent the hairs on the back of the English necks bristling with concern, then Guthfrithsson's own arrival ahead of a larger than normal escort, spotted beaching on the shores of Strathclyde that October, would certainly have their nerves tingling.

Before sailing from Hibernia Anlaf had left Loch Luimnigh in tatters. What few survivors remained alive were in complete devastation after the order for the merciless sacking of the complete province. Now he arrogantly marched his army across the Latin wall and into the lands north of the Humber River declaring that his only purpose left in life was to 'defeat and kill in the most terrible of ways that upstart Saxon, Æthelstan, who, thinks he holds the Right of His God to be granted total rule of that Isle.'

Around the same time as the Viking's arrival, the English King had coincidentally dispatched an 'ærende' of four Thegns to the lands between the Latin walls, to the main court of Constantine, which at that time was shared by Ouuain of the Welsh Cumbric. The message taken by the errand requested that 'As agreed in the treaty of Eadmont, Constantin mac Aeda King of Alba, a gracious and well thought of ally of Æthelstan, King of the Engle Lands, would assist in the speedy return of the Norse fugitives, namely Anlaf Guthfrithsson, and his Jarls."

Constantine poorly denied any knowledge of a Norse presence within his court, lying that he had not seen hide nor hair of a Viking for many a month, which itself bore insult against the treaty, as four of Anlaf's most trusted Jarls were seated at the Scot's own table as the message was being delivered, stuffing their faces with highland venison and spreading their greasy faces with the broadest of smirks as they were 'dully' entertained by the 'Saxon' Kings request.

There would be no compliance to Æthelstan's wishes, the treaty of Eadmont had been mere lip service paid by the Scot, to keep the 'Sasunnach' army away from his borders, allowing Constantine, and others, time to assemble forces suitable for invasion. The errand had been the final chance for compliance to the treaty, a last attempt for an unlikely resolution to what was then the coming of certain war.

No agreeable reply was returned, in fact, nothing more than the heads of three messengers and a fourth trussed and badly beaten, were sent back in answer to the English King. Wrapped haphazardly in the bloodied tatters of a Thegn's cloak and stuffed unceremoniously into a fraying fisher's basket, the remains of the three, and a fourth in accompaniment barely alive, had been 'dumped' outside Tamworth's gates on a misty wet morning, then horsed to Winchester to the King's assembly...

It had been some weeks before Anlaf had set his feet upon the shores of Alba that Æthelstan had summoned the 'Witan' to council, and after the speediest of agreements, had sent out the 'battle axes' for the fourth time in as many years. The handles were still warm since being dispatched to order the formation of another fyrd, but that time it had been more than just a fyrd of freemen that would be summoned to arms. Huscarl, Knights, Spearmen, all men at arms, butchers, bakers and cooks, anyone capable of carrying a weapon was summoned to Æthelstan's ranks, even women, and not just those fearful warriors who remained within Æthelflæd's ranks. The King had called for the assembly of every able-bodied man who had seen fourteen summers or more, and in many cases, the wifman also, from all corners of Engle Land.

Æthelstan's speech to the now loyal crowds of Winchester had been perfect. Rousing, patriotic, confident, and emotional, dictated by the scribes and carried by Huscarl and Knight, to every shire, burg, and homestead within his realm, and those of his allies also.

"...Ride them fast, ride them wide" came his command "So that my Earls, Thegns and Ealdormann, Freemen and Thræl know that again I ask of them, and all good folk of these Isles, that which no King should ever ask more than once. Tell them all the spirit of Engle land calls to them once more. But this time t'is certain to be the last, for if our lands be not our own after this final quest then they shall ne'er be and there shall be no further need for the axes, for there shall be no folk remaining to dispatch them...We start to gather on this day to march against the hoards from the western isle, and so to from the north, the Dane, the Norse, Viking, and Scot, the Pict and the

Cumbric and any other who so wishes to stand against us. We march for the future of the Engle and Jute, the Brython and Saxon, and for all who call this land their own. This day we march to protect the lives of us all, we march as one, we march as Engelcynn."

Now, far across the land they rode, leaving the echoes of cheering crowds in their wake. The smallest groups of 'ridend' with their black cloaks flapping in the winds of the west, carrying each an axe long ago bestowed upon the elders from the times forgotten even by their own forefathers, when they had once walked in far away lands, now carried by hand picked Knights to the farthest ends of the realm.

The first axe, from the days of Penda, long ago sent to hail the battle of Maserfield, now carried by 'dark riders' to the Halls of the East Saxons at Shoebury, where their eastern allies wasted little time in gathering their numbers to ride, run and march to the aide of the one who had been chosen to be King of All the Engle Lands.

How those axes had 'spoke'. Spreading the message and gathering the armies. Now had come the warriors of the old Saxons, mystical Jutes, proud Mercians, with the North and South Folk from the east...and from the valleys of the West came the Welsh, who had accepted the Saxon as best of the worst. Those too of smaller gangs, of Fleming and Lombard and Franc offering loyalties from their own Kings who had sworn over the years their own undying allegiances.

Almost unnoticed came the arrival of a small band of hefty well armed warriors, sent from the new province of the Northman across the 'suð sæ'. They had been sent, by the survivors of the recently deceased Rollo, at the command of their new leader William Longsword, to take Æthelstan's side, and to assist in his victory against Rollo's 'misguided' cousins. What would remain unknown was that a second group had been ordered to join the ranks of Constantine, swearing to him the same 'loyal' words. Normandy was still an unknown province, still lacking in substantial ally, and even less wealth, backing both sides was the surest way of supporting the victor, gaining at least one indebted ally, and a wealthy benefactor in the outcome.

...Two days and three evenings after the small group of Pecsætan had arrived in Winchester with the surviving messenger baring the Scyttisc King's reply, despite an extremely heavy snowfall across Alba's wastes, Constantine's garrisons were almost complete. By dispatching the heads of the English messengers back to where they had come, Constantine had shown his hand, and in turn, by breaking the 'griðlagu', had declared war on the English.

As they had prepared to march south the bulk of his northern forces had swept in behind the 'Scyttisc' King, crossing the stone border at the Old Roman garrison point at Vercovicium where they were inconvenienced with an enforced delay in the destruction of the small farmstead and its inhabitants, they had violently beset their purge upon foreign soil.

In their thousands, they flooded southwest leaving behind them the pitiful remnants of an aged farmer and his family leaving three generations of innocence bleeding into their own soil, dying over their winter crops. The family's roots had been firmly placed in that farmstead since the last of Rome's 'Augustas' had fled south, and now all traces of their line were extinguished forever.

The beacons had burned for longer than ten uncertain nights. Now they were all assembling, gathering from the shires on a ghostly morn of snowfall and grey, after the longest of marches, hurriedly setting their camps in an unknown field of white in the farthest of their northern lands, at last they had all joined together, united under one King.

Now they were the army of the Anglo-Saxon folk, now they were the army of Engle Land.

'Now was riot raised, the Ravens wheeled,

the eagle eager for carrion,

there was a cry on earth.

Then loosed they from the hand the file hard lance,

the sharp ground spears to fly.

Bows were busied, buckler met point

bitter was the battle rush, warriors fell,

on either hand the young men lay!...

...So, stood firm the stout hearted,

warriors in the war- they did keenly strive,

who with his point should be able from fey men to win life.

Warriors with weapons, rack fell on earth...'

The Battle of Maldon.

CHAPTER 15

On the third eve of the great army's gathering, of which no greater number had ever before assembled, at the time of the day when neither sun nor moon held dominance over the darkening skies, Æthelstan looked out towards the northern horizon.

Far out, in deep concentration, towards the camps of his enemies, where they would be stuffing their faces and filling their bellies on stolen meat, swigging the battlefield mead in their age-old preparations for war. They would soon be relishing in trancelike states brought on by herbs and pulses and witches brews, to give them strength and courage for the coming fight. The glowing shadows from their cooking fires illuminated the skyline from left to right without a pause, yet he resisted temptation to send out the archers and strike first blood, the time was not yet right. The lands glowed bright from the flickering torches of the Scyttisc, the large fires of the Cumbric Welsh and the spit roasts of the Irish Dane, and whoever else wished to enforce the enemy ranks that still poured in from coast and hill, without a stop...

When the threatening cries of battle broadcast their echoes across the hills of any land many assortments of people gather to answer its call. It is always the same, whenever, wherever. Fighters from everyone's gang, eager to take payment in whatever form it be offered, either through the weighted purse of an invading Jarl, or from the scraps and leavings and 'black mail' thieved at the battle's close, and of course, there were the whores, and tinkers and other wastefuls who always seemed to appear from nowhere in particular, selling their vast expanse of inflated wares and fares...there was no glory in war, there would never be glory in war...

He wore the great purple cloak that had been presented on passing his fifth year, by his grandfather...

Alfred's voice had spoken then in the rarest of gentle tones as he stood as a boy in miniature at his King's feet, staring up intently at the figure he had easily grown to love. The Royal entourage of white cloaked Huscarl and loyal Thegns filled the side chambers as the silence echoed its nothing into the wattle and stone panelled walls where a young Æthelstan had stared dumbstruck and mesmerised within the presence of such a great man whose tired eyes now betrayed the torment and stress of his earlier years, 'For use when thou shall become Thegn' he had told a doting boy as the heavy pile of neatly folded cloth was lowered onto his arms, then he ruffled the boy's hair affectionately with an agedly gnarled hand.

...And at his side hung the pure white 'heort' skin scabbard wrapped tightly with gilded wire, outlining the shape of long forgotten Brythonic words, that sheathed the immaculate blade, received also on the same day as his precious cloak. That second gift was even greater. Of true Saxon crafting, worthy enough to be Wayland's own, with a jewelled pommel that had been expertly fashioned into the shape of a double-headed wyvern with small red gemstones for eyes, it resembled closely the catch fitted to his cloak. Upon one face of the blade, scratched in the most fanciful of lettering sat the words...

'Ælfred gifsceatt me Æthelstan'

The opposite side of the blade had been left untouched for the addition of an inscription by the swords new owner.

The weapon had been forged by Cerdic, the finest blade-smyth in the land, maybe the finest in any land. He had been a man with a body size that you would expect of a large 'smithy', bearded, and full bellied with a reddened face from the long days bending over a burning forge, swilling weak mead to quench an unending thirst as he sang the words to the old songs in time with the smashing of heavy hammers onto the glowing steel of a forming blade.

Cerdic had inherited his craft, passed down to him through the line of many who had forged before him. From his ancestors, the Brythonic clan long since forgotten as the Brigantes, who had walked those lands hundreds of years earlier. Over many days, relentless against fatigue and urged on by the hollow chanting of ancient verses which seeped out from the shadows that surrounded his aged forge, the man had toiled and sweat every scrap of knowledge that had been ingrained into his spirit, battering the steel that had been gathered from five shires to complete the blades making. As each cloud of steam had screeched its quenching scald of the irons thirst an echo in the shadows beyond whispered a word of approval, as if the Gods themselves had agreed the making.

Asser wrote at the time...

'And the ancients sang their melodies across those lands as the blade's form had been fully complete...'

Alfred had said...

"...Æthelstan sunsunu. This fine blade be thine, for use when ye becomes a King..." Alfred had smiled his finish and turned to struggle his limped return to the padded settle. Those were the last words a young boy would hear from his Grandfather.

His guardian aunt had pitied him that same evening. As they had sat within the boy's bedchamber, both admiring the special gifts. Æthelflæd had watched her ward, as Alfred had staggered a painful return to his seat, and the frail look that had forced a smile from the dying King as the boy had been escorted from his Hall. The lad would surely miss the presence of such a man.

Whilst his mind had lain elsewhere she had whispered his name...

He looked up sheepishly, back in the land of now, and smiled innocently at the Lady with his blue eyes beaming at her gentle complexion...She was almost the prettiest woman he, and many others, had ever seen even though both her cheeks bore the scars of war, and her eyes suggested, no, confirmed, that she had witnessed things in her life that a Lady of such nobility should never see, which strangely added to her beauty.

"...Modrige?" a cheeky grin accompanied his response.

"It be custom among our folk, when a young warrior receives such a fine blade, for him to honour such a gift by granting the blade its own name…"

"For hwon?"

She smiled, there was always a why?

"Long ago…" her eyes beamed brightly like the war beacons as she recounted the tales told when a girl, "…long even, before our forefathers had heard of these lands, when Woden was known only as Þiðrir, and Oðinn Allr Faðir ruled the mighty worlds of Asgarðr, and our heaven was the glorious fields of Glassisvellir. In times when nought but peace had been bestowed upon us, a young warrior would name his 'langseax', and from that day onwards the weapon would be known in the Hall of the Slain, that 'langseax' belonged only to him, and would never be used by any other."

Again, the boy grinned, were her stories truth, or were they just like those told by the old Huscarl to keep him within his chambers at night, or persuade him to do as they wished?

"If all the ancients had been granted everlasting peace, then why would they need a langseax?"

She returned his smile, then sighed "Just in case, min deorlic…everything we do is always just in case. It be the way of men. It shall always be the way of men."

Æthelstan thought deep and long before answering. Such a good tale deserved a good response.

"Then Modrige, I shall name this blade in the words of the old folk who came from the lands of my Modor's folc…Caledfwlch, that shall be the name of my blade. It shall be 'Battle hard', for should it ever be drawn it shall be done so in 'true battle' for my lands, to bring close peace upon all men. Together in victory, Modrige, Caledfwlch. They be the ancient words from Ecwynn's Cynnfolc, and that be the name given to this finest of blades."

Through the night the smithy toiled upon that blade as the words 'Æthelstan namian me Caledfwlch' were etched deep onto its blank side.

In a peaceful copse to one side of Brunanburh's field Æthelstan slipped effortlessly from his mount onto the grassy pitch of a ruined hyrst and loosely tied Abrecan's restraints to the remnants of a lonely elm. It was nothing more than a token gesture, she would never have strayed. His right hand stroked her bright mane with gentle affection as his cheek rubbed against her own, he whispered softly 'Sundorwine' before turning from her stare.

As he walked his hesitant manner suggested he then bore every problem and concern of that world, and as he strode into the shadows of the Brunesweald glade, just as the sun had offered its ritual surrender to the night's glow, he let out a sigh of tired contemplation, almost as relief for the natural sanctuary that nature offered within her coppiced dominion. An owl called sharply in the distance disturbing the rarest of quiets as a breeze provided accompaniment as it rustled the points of a tree which were no longer visible in the dappled gloom of that woodland realm.

Alone at any time would always be a risk in those darkening days, it was a 'treat' rarely afforded. His death at that moment, without the turmoil and expense of a battle would see the most glorious of victories for any adversary, yet adamantly, he felt the draw of winter's night beckon him closer into its dimness, silently reassuring a safety within the chill of a whispered draft that slipped secretly between the leafy forms.

The privacy of a small, concealed clearing seemed to appear out of nothing, and once within, he settled gradually to his knees wrapping the thick cloak about his shoulders, then rested his weight against an aged trunk as a breeze became a wind and turned its path to bring a greater coldness from the north. He watched through the charcoal spindles as the final signs of any sun rested beneath the night of the west.

Oblivious to his surroundings his attentions remained fixed with growing concern for the huge numbers that were making up the magnificent force that would soon be unleashed against him, to his knowledge, never had such an army set foot within those shores to do battle, to his knowledge, never had such an army been defeated. Then his thoughts were cast towards those who had rallied to his call, answered the axes, followed their Jarl, or Thegn or Ealdormann, or just arrived to fight. Each pledged his, or her worth, to stand at his side on the morrow, when the sun would herald the new day and man would once again proceed to tear each other apart.

He allowed his eyes to ease shut for the meanest of seconds in a vain attempt to remove those rare thoughts of weakness and worry. For the first time in his noble career he felt afraid, uncertain to what the future may bring, his confidence threatened to fail him as he questioned his own actions.

'Had he wrongly taken up his Grandfather's quest, accepting it too easily, insisting on too much from others...Had he stood his ground once too often, taking it for granted that others would naturally follow his lead...Should he have granted more lee-way towards his neighbours...Should he have stood back from such aggression, granted more favour when confronting the Kings and Earls of the hordes who now flocked in their thousands readying their armies to destroy him and all that he held close?'

His thoughts raged, his body began to shake, sweat broke out despite the chill and confusion misted his mind as panic began to set in. Then...

"Naaa!!!" and a crack of thunder echoed its way far to the south.

Had he leapt to his feet as the unknown voice had startled his thoughts...

Or had he drifted into the deepest of sleeps?

"Naaa!!!" came the voice once again that time without the accompaniment of thunder.

...And Æthelstan opened his eyes...

Stunned. Silent. In total shock.

'Who had stolen his peace?'

The sun had risen, brought with it a new day, roused awake the wild things and beaten back the frigid darkness of night. It warmed his pallid cheeks bringing back the calm, easing the thoughts of frustration, and the chill slowly drifted from his body.

Adjusting his eyes to the changes within his 'new' surroundings he listened as the birds chirped and chippered on the thick leafy beams. The forest's inhabitants had awoken from a long winter's sleep, now exhaustively finding spring's sun to bask and warm their rested bodies, excited in the birth of a new season that already promised plenty.

Obviously, he had slept through the night, there in that glade with the warmth of a new morn to comfort his body as he stretched out his aches. The unknown voice that had awoken him had been temporarily dismissed from his thoughts as he stared about his surroundings, now clearly different. He may have been there before.

The trees seemed more golden and the grass bent tenderly under his leather soles as he warily paced forward, a step or two at a time, careful and suspicious as he remembered the voice that had disturbed his fretting. Whilst he searched the now brighter surrounds for traces of the speaker he could swear that Abrecan had earlier been tethered at the edge of that same clearing.

"Where are thee" calling finally "who be there and speaks to a King, alone here in this...this..."

The echoes of a gentle gust were followed by...

"T'is I Æthelstan Stormking, first Lord of the Engelcynn...Ruler of the wise...Ring giver to the brave...seeker of a true peace for the children of men."

He stopped, the right hand instinctively locating the blade's hilt, his left steadying for balance.

"Who be it that dares to hide himself?"

The slightest wisp of laughter was followed immediately by "I?... Why, son of Edward, t'is I...He who was once known by many names, to many folk. To thee I be no longer, to many I may still be forever more."

He looked up. High into the brightness that gave away nothing but its golden flare, those words rung through his mind over and over. There had been such riddles before, somewhere deep in his past, in his dreams, or...

"Ye hide within the brightness of suns, and speak to thy King in riddles...I do not understand thy words, and although I may recollect thy voice, I still do not know thee."

...And a face casually and cheekily emerged from the light, as if it peered through a golden curtain, not inches from his own face. It was a haggard face, a well-worn face bearded and set within a helm of gold and silver seated upon the blondest of locks, shining with more brightness, close enough to feel the warmth of the 'stranger's' breath upon his cheeks.

The English King stepped backwards, disturbed, in shock, ready to 'en guard', which also granted a more suitable vision of the stranger. He pulled at his blade, easing the scabbard across his waist into a drawing position should it be needed.

He stood tall, the 'stranger', but not as tall as the King. He was wide in his girth, but not so wide that there would not be room for more feastings. He appeared to be a noble man, dressed in well forged armour that bore markings from an unknown land, shining with other bright things, and a sword hung heavy at his side.

Æthelstan had seen that sword before, along with that brightness, or was it the chanting in the background of the shining clouds that recalled his memories? One thing that he almost knew, he had heard them all before.

Just at that time, when panic would normally have grappled for control, Æthelstan relaxed his shoulders releasing his grip around the sword's hilt...he sighed in relief as he relished the arrival of the familiar aroma of fresh honeysuckle and blackberry leaf. But that time there followed no female words.

"Maybe thee dream, Heahcyning Æthelstan, maybe thee only sees now that which thee hath forever been searching..." The voice eased as the figure completed a circle around the confused King.

"Oh, my son, my regal son, how proud I hear thy Forefathers sing of thy triumphs as they forever feast at my table. How they look down upon thee, thee, a Noble Stone in more than name. At the forefront of thy kingdom always ready and able to protect thy lands from those who shall only forever dream that it be theirs."

Æthelstan removed slowly his helm and shook free his matted hair trying to rid the confusion from his head. His eyes squinted, another deep breath was hastily sucked, then let out just as quick to drag in another to take its place.

Had he been drugged with a Wiccan's potion. Or was he injured, even dead, and now in heaven having lost the fight that he had thought had not yet begun?

"Nay. Thee be neither of those."

The warrior answered the King's thoughts, which threatened, just for a second, to bring more panic and he reached once again for his blade. Then again, the odour took his senses and he relaxed, the blade returned to its scabbard as the noble stranger slowly released a comforting grin, at the same time, his right hand rose in silent gesture for peace, there was to be no conflict within that place.

Another breath and a stern tone asked, "Then who be thee sir?"

"Thee knows of me, Lord of the Mercian, for I be the All Father, the Architect of everything. The maker of the kingdom of men...I be thy thoughts and thy wishes Æthelstan Old Blood, King of all."

A glance at the crystal grasses perfect at his feet he took a bold step forward then returned as he forced his mind to choose between reality and dream, back another step with another shake of his head "Nay, this cannot be. T'is no more than just a dream."

A chilling but innocent bout of laughter from the gleaming stranger holding tight his mid-drift as his belly vibrated in perfect time with his chuckles...

"Nay, son of Ælfred's elder, there be no tricks, nor potions, no spells, not in a place such as this, for this night, upon the eve of battle thee holds within all the doubts of every true man. Thine enemies have massed in the greatest of numbers, so vast an army, never seen before upon these Isles, not even in the dark times of thy own Mother's Forefathers."

"Then if thee be the All Father, Woden of sagas old, why hath thee brought me here, and not just smitten mine enemies from the northern plains?"

Again laughter, but much louder now, loud enough to echo through the wooded lands and up into the brightness until it threatened to disturb those who now slept in the Halls of the old Gods.

"Thee asks thy questions with a bluntness, just as thee did as a child." Inwardly he smiled remembering the boy who now stood as a man. "Thy enemies may not be my enemies, yet, even if they were it would be forbidden for one such as I to meddle in the fate of men. My own wars have either been fought, or be yet to follow."

"Then why am I here?"

Woden paced, and paced some more, willing this King to remember the visits of his younger years, it would have made things so much easier.

He began to explain...

"Such a war like that which shall soon follow may not be a war where I should do battle with blade aloft and Thunor at my side..." For a second he half-wished that it was. "...Yet there be other ways to assist the one who may bring forward the golden light into the future of these darkest of days. These be mine enemies, son of my brother, and enemies of any realm, yet it lies with thee, and thee alone, to halt their spread and hold fast thy rule upon these lands, as has been foretold. The Engelcynn land be that of our sons and not of those who simply wish it to be. This be the final chance for the Land of Men, the only chance remaining for the children of Saxnot, to live alongside those who still hold ties to those who once walked these lands. Thee be the last hope to the Council of Men, to lead them to live out their lives in one, eternal and everlasting peace."

Æthelstan's expression was humble. He gradually conceded that all he had been told not just the fantasies of dream, and slowly, as he remembered those strange encounters of his past he thought of his Mother, Ecgwynn, and the lessons she had taught in that strange world of a never-ending summer. The oaths and the pledges that had been made to him, and those he had made in return. The King's confidence had returned.

And just at that minute, as if further proof had been needed, he caught the odour of his own Father on the delicate breeze, and thought he had glanced his shadow in the corner of an eye, then that too of his Grandfather, and he would later swear, for he would now always remember those times, that he had heard their whispers in the secret of his mind...

"Æthelstan sunu, how proud we be of our Kingly son..."

Then a chorus of whispers, "Edward's son shall march forth his great armies of Men and unite his lands forever" and a clash of thunder rattled from above, yet the skies remained bright and clear.

A deep breath filled his greedy lungs as he straitened his body. He replaced the helm upon his head pushing under his over-long side locks as it sat snug, Æthelstan would be a different man from that moment on.

"Then Father" a sigh "what be it that I should do?"

The chanting echoes from the distance grew louder, but not too loud, and the welcome grew warmer, but not too warm and even though he could not see any others, Æthelstan knew that they were not alone, they had never been alone, the laughter and murmuring within the shadows became more obvious. He had the strangest feeling of being stared at by crowds of onlookers that he now knew could only be the spirits of the Einherjar, those who had fallen upon the countless fields of battles through ages passed, now graced to rest within the shores of Valhalla, his own Father amongst them.

As a mortal King he felt the privilege of being amongst such company, for filling their ranks would be Æthelberht and Oswald, Offa, and Penda and of course Ælfred, Æthelred and Æthelflæd. Then with increasing humility he lowered his eyes in modest recognition for those whom he knew were about him. He smelled again the odour of the woman he knew had granted his birth, the honeysuckle and blackberry leaf that remained fresh regardless of the season, he had eerily remembered it forever even though he had been too young at her passing. And the thoughts of a childish adventure filled his head. Of a day, long ago, when a child became a man, and he breathed again, deeply as if it were his last and closed his eyes as the rarest of tears drizzled its way down a cheek...

"La, Æthelstan, Cild fram se æfenleoht, beon thee stillan..."

...And the softness of a Mother's kiss stole away the tear as a keep-sake for eternity, and a second followed from a maternal eye dropping delicately onto a son's brow before running onto a ruffled beard, down his neck, beneath his jerkin, sinking into the flesh that guarded his heart...King Æthelstan of Engleland knew then for certain who he now was.

The unexplained lump in his throat vanished as he accepted that which he already knew, that which he had always known. Æthelstan now acknowledged without any doubt that part of him had truly originated from the old ways of that land. He was part born from the blood of the ones who had inhabited those isles since the first day of the long beginning. He was Mercian by birth, but Æthelstan of those lands was rightfully there as its ruler, for he was of the old times, Brythonic times. Those lands were once again ruled by those who belonged, and that is how it would remain, forever.

The All Father raised both hands to shoulder height. His left grasped Æthelstan tenderly, with certainty, just as a Father would a son. In Woden's right, brilliant, and white, he held a battle horn modestly gilded with traces of silver and a twisted braid that matched perfectly the colour of the King's cloak.

His eyes stared deep at the icon, curious to its meaning, in awe of its craftsmanship.

Woden's right pushed forward.

"Take ye this horn, Noble Maker of destinies...Such a horn, born out of a Siren's cry and forged by the ancient Smyths in the bowels of the fires cast down from Asgard through the Halls of the Val Hallan in readiness for Ragnarok's coming. T'is said by the ancients that it can call the Valkyres themselves...This very horn, inherent to Middengærd as the lands that have been gifted to the Children of Men, born now to those who shall soon come to be known forever as Engel Cynn..."

Stretching he nervously reached for Woden's hand and accepted the glorious bequest, with a tremble at the slightest touch of its coldness. Eventually he took a firm hold, his nervousness vanished and the coldness that had been within him turned to warmth, and comfortable ease. Gone now were the worries and doubts that had haunted him.

Before the All Father had totally relinquished his gift, just as the invisible sun had started to lower its brightness behind the still clouds which sheltered above, the chanting ceased in the distance. Gone also was the feeling of his Mother's presence, as had the laughter of those who had been his welcome.

Woden's tone changed, his words now spoken in serious warning...

"Know now my words spoken to thee as truth, as written in the Chronicles of Men, long, so very long ago..."

Æthelstan's expression held sincere.

"...Should thee lose this contest for thy lands, the final days of man shall come closer, closer than ever in the past. This war that ye makes be not just a war of two lands, it be a war of two beliefs, of two customs, of two worlds, of two destinies. For if a victory does not befall thee and there no longer be a land of men, then there shall be no further need for the lands of the Father's of men..."

A brief silence as the All Father refused to accept the images of that which he now spoke.

"Thee hath been told of Ragnarok?"

The King nodded remembering his previous visit as a young man. 'Ragnarok, the end of all things good, of all things Man.'

"Then now comes the time that shall determine its coming."

It was now clear to the English King. There would be no more riddles of confusion. The All Father was granting him a choice.

"Should the time come in battle, and it sorely may, when thy armies threaten to fall and all about thee begins to fail, and the future seems for thee no more…"

Not a murmur passed the King's lips.

"…Then before the darkness of defeat engulfs thee my son, sound thee this horn." Finally, the old God released the horn allowing Æthelstan to hold it fully. "Sound it with the tunes of thy heart, sound it hard and sound it long, to summon the aid of thy Forefathers, for in their mead halls they eagerly wait the coming of the time when they may march at thy side."

And in the mighty clouds that swept across Asgard's skies twenty thousand times ten reflections of the dying sun's rays mirrored upon the helms of those who were never to be forgotten, as if his Forefathers had waited for nothing more than the very sound of that horn.

Then Woden's tone changed once more. Now his tone lowered, its very depth hailed a warning…

"Heed ye my words…" and the shinings dimmed above. "Do not summon forth such aid if it not be needed, for the horn may only be used once in the life of a King."

Again, Æthelstan nodded an understanding. He did not quite believe all that he had been told, let alone all that he had seen, even that which he held tight in his grasp, but somewhere within his person he knew he must follow the All Father's words, besides, if the coming battle should turn for the worst any assistance would be accepted.

"Now, Æthelstan Trueheart, remember ye this." The giant took a step closer, and motioned towards the horn, "Should thee ever find the need to call upon this horn, thee must know that in return, thee shall sacrifice the grey years of thy life. Think hard on this King of Men, for it be thee, and thee alone who shall decide whether the future of thy lands be fairly exchanged for the winters of a King."

There was the hero,

with both his shoulders covered by a variegated shield,

possessing the swiftness of a war-like steed;

There was a noise in the mount of slaughter,

there was fire, impetuous were the lances,

there was a sunny gleam, there was food for ravens.

The raven there did triumph and before he would set them free

with the morning dew like the eagle in glad course,

he scattered them on either side,

and like a billow overwhelmed them in front.

The bards of the world judge those to be men of valour,

whose councils are not divulged to slaves.

The spears in the hands of warriors were causing devastation;

and ere was interred under the swan-like steed...

from Aneurin's Gododin

CHAPTER 16

It had been the stinging of the early morning's coldness that had woken the first King of all the Engle Lands from such an awkward sleep. The purple cloak had slipped from his shoulders and winter's bite had roused him uncomfortably as it bit uncaringly into his bones.

As he stood, King Æthelstan slowly eased the fatigue from his body shaking away the morning's tardiness before he began to walk from the Brunesweald glade leading the ever faithful Abrecan, who had remained in wait through the lonely chill.

He left forever the shadows of the trees.

His boots cracked the crusts of early frost as his thoughts cast back to the strangest of dreams. Æthelstan shook his head once more, almost embarrassed, positively ashamed that he had very nearly permitted himself to believe in the reality of his dreams, more so he was furious for stupidly falling asleep, alone in the woods without escort or guard...and the thirst in his throat, like the driest of bark from the oldest elm. Yet in his mind he was now in better spirits, more confident in his manner than previous days.

During those first few hours of daylight, as the English camps had set to stir from a night of nervously broken sleep, a lowly manservant entered the Royal tent with a ritualistic calic of almost warm goat's milk, still half asleep himself he had found the King's bed empty and untouched. The news that screeched its way into the half silence of an awakening war camp brought many from their shelters wielding sword and spear, falling about as they fumbled for clothing and weapons, and not all in that order.

Even the Scyttisc Constantine may have been awakened from his fur lined cot by the squeals and screams from the panicking erne...

"The King, the King, he hath gone..." as if he would be held to blame. "Our Lord King, he hath gone, taken by the Dane, or the Scot, or even the deofol, in the night...gone" and his cowering eyes had flickered left and right checking before a biting tongue greedily lapped at the milk that had clumsily spilled over grubby fingers.

As if the time and place for any such outburst had ever been so wrong to show such an overstated expression of panic, that morning was certain to be it, for at that very instant, as the serf's echoes still hung in the morning's mist, their 'lost' King had entered the camp's perimeter, alone yes, but well and in one piece, with his horse in file and almost a smile upon his chilled lips.

'Ætswige...Silence...'

'Fordettan, fordettan!!!...Shut up, shut up!!!'

'Dysig...'

'Nawiht' Were just some of the comments that had been verbally thrown at the foolish manservant by the closest of the angered knights, along with whatever suitable projectiles had been to hand.

The erne almost looked disappointed at the sight of his King.

The King's left hand outstretched fully as he tethered his horse to a convenient tent pole and the erne, known only as Wolstan, felt the calic confiscated rapidly from a trembling hand, he stared nervously at the sight of his master, too afraid to even lower his eyes in shame.

Æthelstan was not impressed.

"What ails ye man...what no good deeds hath thee been up to in my absence?"

"Nay bregu" and the weakly figure twisted the top half of his body into a half grovel as he cautiously paced a retreat until his pathetic form had disappeared behind the flapping side of the canopy. Feelings of disgrace and embarrassment had come often since he had been forced into his King's service, in lieu of a Fine brought against his true master, a penance for his failure to supply sufficient men for an earlier fyrd. If ever he could summon the courage to flee, then he most certainly would, if ever.

An uncertain smile spread across the King's lips, the oaf would never be worth the effort, and he was already out of range from a slap. How he wished that fool would make off in the night, fail to appear one morning, never to annoy him again, if only.

He lowered his head missing the trim of the cloth as he entered and acknowledged the half-dressed Viking still busy in his own rush from sleep. It was far from unusual, but few words ever passed between Æthelstan and Vidar, the Norseman. The fair Dane had found the mixture of Saxon and Mercian words difficult enough to understand, let alone the array of different dialects and slangs that had accompanied them. Usually the limited conversation had been down to Æthelstan's own knowledge of Norse, taught to him as a youngster. However, the relationship between the King and his aide was a healthy and especially trusting one despite their inherited differences, for it had been Æthelstan who had granted the Dane and his family their freedom after connived and treasonous charges brought against them by an unscrupulous Thegn had been instantly disproven. A small farm on the outskirts of Tamworth, paid for of course by the wrongful accuser, had been agreed as compensation for the slur, and for that, Vidar had sworn his undying allegiance to his new King, even if it meant that he would be set against his 'own' peoples, forever.

Refreshed, and as clean as could be expected from the facilities of a field camp at the start of winter, Æthelstan returned from his privacies accompanied by a fully dressed Vidar close behind, that would now be his position until the finish of the coming battle, whichever way the fates had deemed.

Together they entered the central clearing.

At first sight, any onlooker may have been forgiven in thinking that their campaign had been peaceful and for pleasure, maybe a courteous visit for an over exaggerated hunting expedition, or even a noble quest, not of a gathering for the greatest battle those lands would ever see.

Eventually the rousing of the camp would set right the onlooker's error as it became more apt for the situation with knights and huscarl beginning to muster at the ready, to be counted then reported by an Arthegn to an awaiting Ealdormann, Thegn or Earl, to take stock of their numbers, check for over-night desertions, deaths, illnesses or even the odd suicide.

The King had settled himself besides the open hearth of a morning fire soaking up its welcomed heat, allowing the flames to thaw through his battle-shirt as he listened intently to the on goings of the morn'. Then another calic of warmed milk and extra honey, that time served by one of sense, refreshed his senses and warmed his innards. He relaxed his mind away from thoughts of the passed night, almost closing his eyes in search for a little solitude, but as always, the metallic quiet of the morning was soon broken.

The heavy breathing and objective stamping from a group of stabled horses alerted the camp's attentions towards the ring wall and the western gate where a dishevelled Egill and his 'Here' burst their way unannounced into the camp's quiet, as if the end of days were about to descend.

Dripping with another's blood the northern Thegn lowered his head respectfully brief as he approached his King, clearly out of breath perspiration expired from every gland despite the chill.

Æthelstan almost laughed, "What be this at such an hour, so early on the morn', thee looks as if thee hath defeated the Scytisc single handed?" His grin was now more noticeable, if the newcomer's appearance had not been so alarming with the obvious smears of another's life glistening on every weapon, the knights who had gathered would have also found the humour of their King's greeting.

"Bregu, my King…" Egill's response was sharp, serious, and professional, the King's wit had been wasted. He panted like a hunting dog, desperate for the meanest breath as he sucked in between each sentence. "Bregu was wise to heed his Thegn's advice…For in the night, across the way…" he panted as he pointed to the slope of a small hillock, "…In the first camp, they came upon us, in the shadows of the half moon…"

Æthelstan offered the still panting Egill his calic. The gesture was instantly accepted with the remaining half of its contents greedily supped, choking, and spluttering into the precious liquid as he omitted to draw another breath, then he cordially passed the cup to his rear, to be refilled and shared amongst his thirsty spearmen.

"...We saw Anlaf, Bregu, agin with disguise, as we did see him as a spy in thy courts not a single year passed...Agin as a spy in the gloom of the night, searching for thy tent..."

"Well" asked Æthelstan angrily, "did he find it?"

"He did bregu" and he smiled triumphantly at the previous night's deceit. "He fled the Weardian when roused, for fear of capture..."

The camp's centre had now begun to fill as news of the night's disturbance had filtered through the waking tents, men nodded in agreement, hissed in approval, winced with caution as they listened to the report.

"I saw also his Jarls, Adils and Hryngr, with their own men approach from the dune's rise, through the moon's shadow..." he regained the calic as an eager Wulfhere refilled it urging the Mercian to continue his tale.

Men at arms and huscarl had started to take up their weapons around the thorny ring, but only as a gesture, just in case, but there was no threat.

"Adils entered the night-tent that had replaced thine own during the eve'..." Suspicious glares passed between King and Thegn.

"Then, how be Sherbourne's Bishop?" asked the King knowing it to have been the Bishop's tent that had replaced his, unknown of course to the Bishop.

"A slash to a forearm and a blackened eye bregu, and a set of badly stained hose."

Æthelstan lowered his head as an attempt to conceal the start of a grin. "Then t'is certain that he be able to use the other forearm to bless the folk, and pocket their pennig…after gaining a fresh set of hose" and a disrespectful laugh echoed through the gathering.

"Then what becomes of Ælfgar" asked the King "how did we fare?"

"Adil's folk attacked Ælfgar as my attack went to Hryngr and his islanders…" another pause "Sadly Ælfgar was not up to the fight" and another pause for the shame of a colleague's failure. "And when the Dane had near made short of him Ælfgar fled from our camp, heading off towards the coast with no more to him than which he wore." The embarrassment was shared by all before the King checked…

"Be thee certain?"

He was. And told his King once more.

"A coward, and in our ranks…" At that moment, Æthelstan's revulsion was more for the cowardice shown by his Thegn than for Scot or Dane. He kicked out at a fallen ember raising ash and smoke into the air. "Then let him so be exiled from our lands, never to return amongst us for fear of his own death."

Yea's and more yea's and more single worded agreements met with their King's command, there was no place in their camp for a coward, then all eyes returned to Egill Skallagrimsson.

"Adils then turned his 'here' upon me screaming for blood, and with short numbers I fought on 'til joined by mine own brother Thorolf, who hath but the fewest of folk, yet they be strong and proven warriors. I ordered the stand, we all stood firm, and those of Ælfgar's folk who were still able did join with us for our King and our Gods. As I fought my way to Hyrngr's side through what was then but a handful of Orc, I tore his banner from its shaft…"

He slipped a bloodied hand inside an equally bloodied 'serce' and pulled free a bloodied cloth, in the same movement he shook it free to reveal a black Raven amidst the stains of other men's life.

"...And on that sod, I called Hyrngr to meet his destiny's end and with the side of my blade and the point of his own banner's shaft I dispatched him from this world...and now he sleeps in Hel's own arms, and his body rests in the coldness of his own death, outside the thorn wall."

Æthelstan was as much relieved as he was grateful. He had not heard the attack, alone in the Brunesweald, silent in 'another' world, yet neither had others within the camp. The attack had been thwarted thanks, to the courage of 'most' of his Thegns, and more so, for once, he had listened to his Earls, allowing his tent to be moved to the west of the hill's side, out of sight, and out of sound.

"We have two dead of our own bregu, and four more with wounds that may never heal. Two more also have wounds that will not keep them from this day's fight...The Dane lost nine of his number in the struggle with four others finished as they fled. The rest who ran off with Adils are of no fit state for this coming fight, and shall not last too long if they are."

Æthelstan was again satisfied by the efforts of his Mercians, though they were lead by an Icelandic poet, even so, they could have turned tail and joined Ælfgar the deserter.

"Thy brother Thorolf?"

"He be at camp bregu, making safe...just in case."

"Let him know that he hath done a great service this day and that I be pleased with both the sons of Skalla Grimr. For thine efforts, should we live on from this place, Thorolf and thee shall divide Ælfgar's lands equally, and all his worth too, and from this day thee shall both be Thegn."

Egill accepted the rewards for himself and his brother, but had always intended returning to Iceland once his adventuring's were over, but who could know how that new day would fare?

Whilst the Icelander wittered out one of his famous poems Æthelstan found himself a seat away. Again, he settled with his thoughts on the coming day when another disturbance revoked his privacy.

"Thee hath found a great horn bregu?" from a half-dressed knight.

"A horn, what horn, of what doth ye speak?" and a second knight glanced down at his King's waist, to where the white horn hung from a chord.

Up until that moment he had given little or no thought to the previous night. With the news of the attack on the upper camp to distract his thoughts he had put the night's visit into the Brunesweald from his mind. But as he had followed the gaze of the passing knight, glancing down to his left, he was filled with shock as the memories of that previous evening flashed through his mind, registering once more in his thoughts, and then he knew…

'Those were no dreams.'

In his struggle to separate reality from fiction his right hand cautiously slipped across the width of his body grasping hold of the white horn, which, until that moment somehow had hung unnoticed, taken for granted, maybe as if it had hung there forever, part of his garb, part of himself. It brought another jolt of reality into his senses, kick starting his memory as his fingers delicately inspected the immaculate form, sliding along its shape, picking out the inlay.

He sat. Still as a post, holding the object in one hand, his eyes glued to its form, studying its every inch whilst he finished another mouthful of spiced milk. From his thoughts, the dreams of the passed night became an assured reality, the first King of All Engle land was renewed with confidence and zeal, and a new, more certain hope…

Which not for the first time that morning was threatening to become no more than a distant memory as an apprehensive outrider entered the camp at speed, interrupting more than just his King's thoughts as he clumsily dismounted from a lathered horse before the animal had come to a halt. The Wessex horseman slid the remaining distance almost collapsing into a kneeling position, stirring up clouds of brownish dust as he came to a stop at the foot of his now standing King.

He had travelled through the night.

Not across the longest of distances, but slowly and in quiet, through the lines of their enemies, hugging the outskirts of their camps, weaving in and out of their positions, hiding within weald and dale, in marsh and in heath, walking his horse silently within the shadows to bring his news to the camp of his King.

He choked on what little breath he could draw into his chest at the same time staring up into expectant eyes.

"Bregu, Cyning..." he desperately took another breath, but he sucked too greedily, and the embarrassed rider choked and spluttered phlegm and bile at the foot of his liege, finally "...There comes a fleet upon our shores, a fleet of the enemy's ships, beached at the place known to local folk as Roose."

None gathered had heard of such a place, it could have been anywhere, but already Æthelstan had formed a dislike for it. Seemingly he had begun to think that all he should do that morning was shake his head and bad news would be forthcoming, and a smash of pottery in the background as a platter fell from Wolstan's fingers gave him further proof... poor form from others.

He was certain, until then, that the numbers against him had gathered complete, surely there were no more owing levy to Constantine, unless...

"Whose ships, be they?"

His tone was strict, his question a formality, clarifying that which he already suspected. Æthelstan's stomach threatened to drop to his feet as the answer was given.

"They fly beneath the sign of the Black Raven my Lord. They be Danish mariners, but the weapon men they carry be painted with Pihtisc wode, there be hundreds of them, crawling now, across this land, screaming their unknown tongues as if the Deofol be their master."

"Oh, he be their master for certain" then returned his stares to the messenger who had started his second attempt of rising to his feet.

"Calm thyself man, Ye now be Englisc, and thee shall fear no man."

"My Lord…" and the rider was dismissed to the food tent.

The report had been correct.

There were hundreds of them, too many and too quick to count. As they had disembarked upon the shore, half crazed from potions and pulses, howling screams and whining curses hollered in their own strange tongues filled the winter's air with verbal poison that enhanced their pending threat. Those who had rights to that land, who had not fled as the invader's cries swept across the northern hills, were cut down in their fields, or in their cots whilst the oldest surviving clans of Alba approached Brunanburh's innocent plains.

They were Picts. They were the fiercest warriors north of the first Latin Wall. They were the oldest folk still to walk across the Caledonian hills, or at least that was how the stories had been told to scare the youngsters…

'Beasts from Hel's infernal pit, haunting the shadows of the night, whisking away any who dared to walk the darkness alone, never to be seen again…'

'Painted swine who wore little clothing, feasted on the young and defiled the innocent and Godly.'

'Hel's own forgotten folc.'

Long ago, at a time still remembered by the elders from tales told when young, the Picts were the strongest of all the northern armies, dedicated fighters who knew no limit and would have accepted no master. They believed that writings and records were unholy and blasphemous to their strangest beliefs which were held in total secrecy deep within their clans. They were the very reason that the Roman Hadrian had constructed the great wall, to hold back the menacing hoards who had already overcome the first wall of Antonine. Yet over the span of many tormented generations the countless feuding and warring had taken its toll and whole sections of the male population had been literally wiped from the face of their land. Æthelstan himself had sent many trusted messengers into their camps, on errands of peace, to discuss charters and trade, but none had returned to his courts. Many rumours were conjured regarding their fate, some said that they had been eaten alive, others had gossiped that great dragons had met them as they made their way north, carried them off into enchanted forests never to be heard of again. Whatever the truth, the Pict had wanted no charter, nor trade.

There and then.

In that desolate place known locally as Brunandune, across the plains of Othylynn, under the shadows of the Effien Hills gathered the last army of the mystical Pictish people. Once a mighty race, civilised in their own ways, masters of their own arts and crafts, now enveloped into the ranks of the Scot and governed by a false King named Constantin mac Aeda. Their loyalty to him came only through fear brought down by their 'new' neighbours. Their villages were left in ruins, their farms desolate and barren, their customs rarely observed, not even in secret, forgotten, along with the names of their forefathers. Young children were now being forced to speak in the foreign tongue of the Scot, and sit around the fires of foreign clans. Their unique belief and heritage would soon be eradicated from all memory, vanished forever, and weakening bloodlines already tainted with those of the Caleds and Scyttisc who freely forced themselves upon the women. Soon the word Pihtisc would be forgotten, even in the dreams of the old.

Fate had led them there, to that place, where those who remained able were left to swarm their hoards across the northern greenery, rampaging the last of their masses towards the Engelcynn with one single hope firmly in their thoughts...to die with glory and honour, in what would be their final battle, so that they may rightfully sit around the fires of their forefathers in whatever afterlife would been granted to them, soon there would be no place upon man's Earth for 'their' kind. A new dawn was approaching those lands, and their inclusion had been ignored.

Habitually, Æthelstan had again ignored the advice of his Earls and Thegns, taking to the saddle himself.

Loyally, Abrecan carried him across the vales and through the woodlands of the west where she waited reverently in the shadows as he took his guard behind rocks and ridges nearing the freezing shoreline, wrapped in the greyly tattered cloak of a serf, and protected by a modest gang of equally disguised knights.

He had watched them all from the shades of an old willow's canopy, the invaders as they noisily disembarked from their Danish carriers.

Close enough he had heard them gather along the water's edge then quick to disappear into the bog lands, fleeing east and south like the winds that had brought them, eager to reinforce their false King's army. With the Pictish additions to the invasion force they had combined to become dangerously greater than that of the English, by at least ten spears to each one of his own. The odds had now been heavily set against him, just as he had been told in the wooded glade the night before. Yet he remained confident. During his years as Ætheling, he had continuously warred against the northern clans who had often outnumbered his own army's strengths, nothing had changed, he would beat them once again.

'At least with them together and in the same place it would save him time' he had privately joked as he reached Abrecan's hide. Swiftly, and often too close to the raging invaders, he had returned to his armies as if he had never been away, informing his seconds of what he had learned, yet changing little of their previously agreed plans. There would be no place for hesitation, all knew now of their part, and that of the other, just in case. From the King himself, down to the spearmen and archers, even to the serfs and ernes whose purpose in battle was to replenish the fighters, carry away the wounded and hide in the woods keeping watch for a change to their enemy's tactics, everyone knew the duties of the other. No King could have done more to prepare his armies for that which approached.

Æthelstan stared out in cold defiance across the plains where he had chosen for battle. His glare penetrated harshly across the vast openness into the enemy formations whose numbers swelled with the passing hours, now too great to be counted by his spies. Abrecan paced on the spot, flexing her muscles, and declaring her stand, his right hand slipped into the velvet purse belted at his waist and withdrew a silver shilling. He smirked as he stared at the embossed head upon its surface, and at the words stamped inside the outer rim…'Rex Saxonum et Anglorum', his heart skipped as he realised all it had taken just to bring him to that point.

His chest rose as his lungs filled. "To be King of a land such as this land, a man must do much more than to leave his head upon a silver shilling…" And he spurred his horse into a light canter beginning the march into a battle where the outcome would set the future for time everlasting, possibly to every other land in that ever-changing world of men.

The morning was fresh, the air crisp and clean. A pleasant breeze skimmed against their backs as the waving banners of the Mercians' lead those from the House of Wessex and Kent towards the flatness of Brunanburh's frosted greenery, the turf glistened with a million crystals as if nature beckoned the coming of the end across those untouched plains, all accompanied by the naïve song of morning birds calling out their ageless fanfare for the coming of that new morn.

Was Nature adding her calls to fanfare the beginning of the fight or was she sounding her final songs before the coming slaughter would claim ten thousand lives, snatching all from her grasp forever.

To the rear of that newly formed army of Engle land the female entourage chanted through endless tears of mixed emotion calling loudly their ancient prayers spurring their menfolk onwards, towards a hopeful victory, begging to whoever may listen, for their safest return.

And the horns blew loudly as if a thousand thunders rattled the ranks and Nature's call was swept from the field.

At the edge of the gathering crowd of children, and maidens, and wishful dreamers, who had not the courage to march, an old man with one leg lacking below the knee pulled his frail and hurting body from its slouched position and looked on enviously as the colourful files marched passed. His many days of warring were long passed, only he could recall the warrior that he once was, and a tear of forgotten pride for his want to be among them ran from an eye as he remembered those who should have been at his side that day. As the front columns cantered by, their bridles chinking and their weapons thumping against wood and leather, the old man called out, loud and clear, too loud for one of such frailty, loud enough for those close to hear his words...

He'd spat the thickness from his throat...

"For that which hath been granted to us, through the blood of our Forefathers...Must be safeguarded, through the blood of our sons..."

And he pictured in an aged mind the holocaust that he knew would soon be inflicted upon the young men of his House, and the suggestion of a second tear crept onto his wrinkled cheek as he eased himself back into the slouch, gratefully closing his saddened eyes, nothing had changed since the terrors of his day. Now the old warrior was ready to walk the evergreen grasses of Neorxnawang.

As the old man's words had disappeared into the melee and his eyes had closed upon that mortal world for the final time, he had heard the young children in the distance, continuing to play their games at the rear of the columns with snapped off branches for spear or sword in the 'home ranks' as they imagined, in childish minds, that which their fathers and brothers were about to do for real.

Furthest back and the last to 'shuffle' in the safe lines of well-wishers were the Abbots and Priests and Clerics from the Minsters and Priories passed on route. Huddled in rugs and the thickest of furs Wulfhelm of Canterbury continuously signed the cross as he stumbled the Latin psalms, copied to his left by Brynstan who truly wanted to be elsewhere. On the right of Canterbury's Archbishop stood Ealhstan of London completing the Holy trio, chanting their blessings of good hope, promising God's forgiveness to those who offered themselves into the service of their King, and of course their Church. He too signed an invisible cross in the steam of his wine laced breath.

A thousand starlings glided their murmuration overhead as if they offered an escort and as they disappeared noisily to the south they left the field with an eerie silence, save for the thud of the horses' hooves and the clash, and crank of weapons. Not a word was spoken....

Not until both sides had arrived within hearing distance...

And then it all began...

The first signs of aggression simply brought both sides from their night's protection, forced marching their numbers over the 'duns', out of the bogs and crags, waving their spears and rattling their shields, finally coming to a strident halt a little more than an arrows flight apart. With their weapons smashing noisily against shield and thigh, intertwined with sparsely whispered mutterings to those behind the front line, relaying back details of the first sightings of an awaiting enemy in that first light of day.

Then the shouting increased becoming louder and less sporadic...

...It commenced with the Scytisc clans who taunted the Englisc ranks, and as each curse echoed in the distance it was immediately replaced with another obscener, and more vicious. That was soon accompanied by a Pictish chant emanating hatred and scorn towards their long-time enemy, and as if they were feeling outdone the Dane opened their voices with a barrage of obscenities and howls that would have embarrassed the devil himself.

In unison, the Mercians had been first to take up the verbal challenge, returning the insults of the Northman, as had always been the way, and it took little time for the Wessex and men of Cent to intervene with their renditions on how to insult one's enemy. Last, and the most discreet were the Cambric tongues who joined in only so as not to be left out. Their insults were secretly aimed at both sides, as they were truly unsure on whose side they were meant to be fighting, and whilst a dozen languages produced a thousand dialects the greying sky turned blue with shame and mortification as the crudest of phrases were conjoined by the rudest of hand gestures affronted by one group or another. Rapidly the din rose out of control growing into a deafening howl, louder and louder until it threatened to rip out the ear drums of everyone present...

'Ut...Ut...Ut...' from the Englisc armies.

'Alltud...Alltud...Alltud...' echoed the Welsh, on both sides.

'Englar saurr...Englar saurr...'spat the Dane, and everywhere pulsated with the sound of angry men.

Then suddenly, as if all were instantly struck dumb...Silence filled the morning air once more.

King looked sternly at King, dismissing any thoughts of a last-minute treaty.

Jarl glared at Thegn as each others worth was investigated.

And men at arms looked intently upon weapon men.

Æthelstan pondered in those final seconds of peace which almost seemed from another age. Out there, in his sight now was an alliance of pure hatred, vehement towards his kind, towards any kind not theirs.

To his centre was the Dublin Dane, standing with the Northumbrian Viking who stood to the left alongside their cousins from the western Isles, and a small group of Norse from Ellan Vannin filled the ground between them.

Then there were the Orcs. Vicious bastards from the Isles far to the north who gave no thought to another, not even their own. Though small in numbers, their reputation for ruthless barbarism was a growing legend in their own lifetime.

Added to all was the Cambric, and their closest neighbours the Scot, and again making up the space between them were the Picts who had nothing more to lose than a return to the lands that were no longer theirs, under the rule of a King who had turned against his own kind.

Not a voice dared to speak.

Not a single blade or shaft threatened to crash upon the limewood rounds, even the horses refused to break the wall of silence that had now started to send shivers along the backbones of every man and woman present, including Æthelstan.

Each warrior had gathered in those last few seconds, before Hel would erupt her evil doings upon the earth, staring across the brooding plain and into the supposed eyes of a not so distant foe, opposite were their beliefs, very similar was their intent. And as the sun woke fully from the east whispering its golden rays across the shoulders of the Engelcynn fyrds, terror rose from the bellies of the invaders as Englisc silhouettes swelled like giants, their blades and points glistening in the sun, their armours reflecting the brightness across the lowlands blinding the Dane and his engrossed allies. Some spewed out a hastily stuffed breakfast onto the sodden ground afoot, others emptied a nervous bladder where they stood, and a few began to shake from top to toe. But the majority, battle-hardened Dane, blooded Scot, war worthy Pict stood together in anticipation for the moment when they would bring down a final retribution upon their ancient enemy...

At the appropriate time, of which He alone had decided by the warmth of the morning sun caressing his cloaked back, the King who sought to rightfully rule in total the Lands of the Anglo-Saxon withdrew his regal sword from its gilded scabbard and raised it high towards the Halls of the Ancient Ones...High towards the morning sky into the arming rays of a winter's sun.

...And flaaaaaashhhhhh!!!!!! With a scream of perfect brilliance, the blade took hold of that day's light, transferring its brightness across a place that was then named Brunanburh...

Their King looked deep into the eyes of those closest and saw the faith within their hearts...

"Men of the West Shires…Thee be the very Heart of our Engle Lands!!!"

Then their backs straightened, their mouths moistened as every fear left the bellies of those Children of Men. And forward they went, on England's errand…

Now the horns had been sounded,

The beacons had been burned

And their warnings ignored;

Now all gathered within,

To do the slaughter for the future

Of the Children of Men...

Anon.

CHAPTER 17

For the first few paces they were cautious, no matter their Order, all moved with the greatest apprehension.

Watchful and sensitive, careful, and precise, treading their feet as if the very ground they stepped upon may open and swallow them whole, yet none seemed afraid, even though everyone would have had the right to be.

Both sides were on the move, and they did so in their thousands. So vigilant as they moved suspiciously onto the freshness of a winter's morn, many still not completely awake, until… just as the morning sun threatened to bare itself fully upon the world of men, they dismissed all other thoughts.

Nothing before that day now mattered. Nothing before that second as they gathered their speed together as one, despite another's heritage, despite their beliefs.

All moved faster.

As their horsemen raced into the gallop the weapon men to the rear hurled themselves into a frenzied sprint, closer to their enemy's front, the scurrying hoards had one common objective, to reach the front rank of the opposition and kill them as quickly and as painfully as possible.

To the rear of the dust cloud scarified by the knight's horses came the women, loud, rapid, and fierce just as if She, Æthelflæd, still held their Order. Their screams could be heard above everything, the ferocity sent a chill through the bodies of all who remembered their first encounter.

Edmund rode close. So close that he breathed Abrecan's dust and smelled the foamy sweat as it leached from the animal's hide mixing with that of his own mount. With shield and lance so tightly gripped, his gauntleted knuckles turned as blue as wode, he glanced about the plains to his front, then to the left and followed to his right as both armies neared, ready to smash into the mobile shield walls.

Edward's sons.

Æthelstan and Edmund. Their mill honed blades unsheathed, their English hearts unbared. Confidence beamed across their faces. Both knew that this was their time, the only time, to smite their oldest enemy, to destroy that northern threat forever. It was their time to bring peace upon the Lands of Men.

There was always that split second of silence…

In that final space of time. Before two armies would collide together on a field of war, there was always that eerie, haunting, frightening, almost enchanting breach in time, and that day would be no different.

There came, in that smallest space before the battle's clash, a single second of nothing, as if the Gods' were granting those who were about to die a second's thought, a chance, to change their minds, to talk, to agree, to live. A second of silence when everything around seemed to slow to an almost halt and the fear and pain that was about to be inflicted was momentarily held at bay while stomachs churned, and nerves rattled, hands quivered and bodies trembled…and as quick as it had come that second had vanished, man had lost his chance as the instant din of metal upon metal, followed by man upon man, horse upon horse, seemed to shake away all reason from the world. It was as frightening and as deadly as Hel's own roar bringing Dane and Scot and Jute and Saxon, and every other clan and house from that Isle together in the end's beginning.

Immediately before the first echoes of battle had disappeared, men had fallen. Dead and dying, dropping like frozen rain as the screams of pain and hatred and fear cascaded across the throws of death, and then…the Danish 'wedge' of leather and mail clad warriors brought themselves to a halt, as if time again had reached its end…

But of course, it had not. In the quickness of a spit most had turned to their left, with the remainder turning to their right, dividing their ranks at the centre as they dispersed from their 'swine-array' formation, into the outer flanks of the battle, perfectly to a plan.

The Dane's actions had hailed the archers bringing them quickly into place. Painted men from the ranks of the Picts who had swarmed from the woods to the north of the field, now raised a long bow, a short bow, or a crossbow, and eyed their range with the deepest of thought towards the stunned glares of the English lines, ordered by Constantine from his 'safe hide', somewhere away to the rear, it seemed the basic of all traps. Now they pulled back the strings, hugged their weapons tight to the shoulder, pointed their aim into England's Heart.

The expressions that flooded over the men from the shires told of their immediate fear as hundreds now faced slaughter, for there was nowhere for them to run, they were trapped on all flanks. To their front stood their enemy's archers whilst to their left and right came the Cumbric weapon men, and to their rear heaved the masses of their own reinforcements, they were trapped in the centre of certain death.

But Æthelstan was no fool, and neither were his commanders. They had anticipated such a ploy from an overconfident enemy who was too idle to ever change his tactics, believing that his way was the certain way.

As the Irish Danes had parted, Hywel Dda of the south Welsh had brought his horse to the side of his King. He had ridden hard and long, gathering his men en route, most of them only arriving as the early morning's ranks had begun to stir from the night. Tired, wet, and hungry they were, in desperate need of rest, but readily accepted the inevitable...

A fight was all that would greet them, and it would be the hardest fight of all.

Whilst the heathenish Picts had been taunting their prey, cursing, and promising to send their enemy viciously into their afterlife, in a language that would soon be unknown to any, the men of Hywel Dda had readied themselves in their secret positions, below, in the peat bogs of that unforgettable place.

Many had moved in the early morning mist whilst both camps still slept, but they, the men from the valleys of Brytenlande had dug themselves deep beneath the freezing grasses, only to be disturbed by the arrival of more of their kin.

As the leather strings of Pictish bows had been drawn, and hardwood quarrel's and slender arrows had been slipped into place, the Welshmen had steadied their nerve, took a grip of their weapons, and waited tensely for their master's signal...

Their wait was short.

"Ymosod Ar!!!...Ymosod Ar!!!..." The Welsh leaders scream erupted from the depths of his stomach, the horns blew out loudest as the banners of Brytenlande rattled against the wind. Hywel Dda urged his horse forward towards the fight as the bog lands had begun to explode as if they gave birth to the men of Deheubarth. Bursting free from their hides, sending tufts of peat and frosted grass in all directions, the Welshmen tore themselves free from England's skin, pouncing like demons possessed onto the stunned bowmen. The need for self preservation quickly replaced the sudden shock as the Picts desperately fought back against their ghostly attackers. The savagery that ensued was as shocking as it was quick and as sickening and devilish as it was real, but the bravery of both sides was indistinguishable, neither would succumb.

Remembered by time alone would be the screams of pain and dread, it would remain forever emblazoned in the memories of those who would be fortunate enough to survive such carnage. The intended shower of bolt and arrow that had been destined to take out the first waves of English was hoped by Constantine and his Danish allies to have been the first major blow against Æthelstan's forces, but it had been put down in an instant as the last volley of wooden projectiles fell aimlessly to the ground, along with the archers. No longer would they be a threat.

Had there been a double bluff?

Constantine had used the Pict as an expendable decoy, readily permitting their sacrifice to force the English King to show his hand and in turn expose his strengths too early in the battle. Almost forgotten until then Anlaf and his Irish Danes had emerged from the archers' rear commencing their claim on the battle with the heaviest of impacts upon the peat drenched Welsh, slaying without mercy as they began to carve their way through their masses leaving nothing alive in their wake.

Hywel Dda was enraged.

Hywel Dda was stunned. It must have been the spies, it always came down to the spies. His men were falling faster than leaves in a winter storm and there was nothing he could do about it...

In those distant flanks of growing horror, across to the south where the land dipped and the blood drained, Æthelflæd's legion of women had engaged Ouuen and his Cumbric warriors in brutal contest sending both lines of defence too'ing and fro'ing as each challenged the other for victory. The screams of the women highlighted the morning, but all that seemed certain was the blood pools would become deeper.

...Hywel's inherited instincts had urged him to unsheathe his lance, close his shield tight to his torso, ride into battle, and join with his warriors from Deheubarth accepting their fate as his own. It would be right that he should. It would have been that in which his forefathers would wish...but not in that battle. Æthelstan raised a hand reached out and grasped hold of the Welshman's 'byrnie', urging him to wait, motioning above the panic that all was not yet lost.

His wait would not be long.

As if they had heard the words of their King the ground erupted for a second time. Now around Anlaf's men, five hundred Cantwaran ghosts spewed their weapons into the onslaught halting the Danish advance.

Æthelstan had also played a 'double bluff'...

The Dane was stunned as much as he was angered. There had been no sign of an ambush when they reconnoitred that place under the earliest hours of the night's cloak. His advance scouts had reported nothing but the claggy morning mist.

...It seemed as if they had been hidden forever, deep in the bogs and tufts, always part of that land, unnoticed until then, and now unbeatable. They seemed to rise from everywhere. From the black pools of every sticky mess, from beneath every sod of plains grass, at every significant point, screeching and raging for a fight.

With the suggestion of a rescue the men from Deheubarth had found a second wind, pulled their depleted ranks together and reformed at the side of the Cantwaran Jutes where together, as one united force, those once enemies now fought as brothers, as equals, as countrymen, and pushed back the Norsemen...but not before Wulfstrum had shown Anlaf the final side of his blade.

The two men had come together purely by chance.

As the Jute erupted from his hide, with no immediate target in mind, he had startled the Dane's horse as he emerged from below, causing the animal to panic, throwing its rider awkwardly onto the bog land crust. Dripping wet, and as black as the peat that had concealed him, Wulfstrum had been equally surprised as both recognised each other from previous conflicts. Despite his frozen reflexes the Kentish man had been the quicker, more alert, and instinctively more reactive leaping towards the Dane's body, sweeping forward with his giant blade, slicing through the Danish stomach half killing the invading Jarl, in a single blow.

Now, as the groups of leaderless Danes staggered back in shocked retreat, Wulfstrum completed his act of savagery removing Anlaf's head cleanly from bloodied shoulders, and without ceremony glared across the field in satisfaction, proud and erect upon the hillock, holding high and obvious Anlaf's last expression for all to see, including his King, screaming his words of victory in an almost ancient tongue.

With a signalled acknowledgement from his King the Jute tossed away the severed head into a patch of bog grass, discarding it as if it were nothing, as then it was.

Anlaf's death should have summoned the beginning of a victorious slaughter against the invading masses, installed panic in the hearts of the Northmen, fear in the bowels of the Scot, and a deep sense of loss amongst all else, but that was not to be. It had the reverse effect.

It seemed that the Dane's death had called to arms every Viking, Scot and Pict that walked the earth. Even the small army from Ellen Vannin had found their muster, on the brink of the brow, overlooking Anlaf's brutalised body. A multitude of eyes, thousands of them, pierced through the English strengths as the battle motioned itself to an unscheduled standstill. The jumbled lines of the enemy forces pulled themselves free from the onslaught and retired to the perimeters of the fight, awaiting what they had hoped to be the greatest of surprises, and in turn, victory.

Æthelstan looked up from the carnage, "Surely it would not be that easy?".

Then...

Fear ran through his veins as he realised the fullness of their numbers. Their hoards had gathered as one, calling for the many in hiding, concealed, waiting for such a moment. Had he been out thought?

"Strælboran...Archers." He called.

"Garwigenda...Spearman." Called another.

"Ridend...Knights" and they flocked to his lines.

The English commanders copied the call and gathered their warriors, yet each man knew that despite his own strengths, and those too of his allies, they would be no match for the mass that now overlooked them from the hillock previously held by the English. The Scot and his allies encircled their flanks, chanting, insulting, laughing, and swelling.

They came out of nothing, without warning.

Swelling with hatred they were, noisily rampant, frighteningly threatening. Their strengths enforced as their numbers slowly began to descend from the rise, beating their shields with the shafts of their spears, hilts of their blades, and the heads of their hammers...

The army of the new English was about to become no more than a fireside tale.

That time there was no mystical second of silence before they hit, no chance for a treaty, no enchanting space where a choice to continue would be granted, they just hit, hard, mighty, and definite.

Positive was their counterattack, unexpected their brutality, valiant their push. Within the first few seconds of the contact more than five hundred English warriors had walked their final steps upon their Middengærd, Hel's hoards were melting their way through the outer ranks, closer to their centre by the second.

It may have been Ecgbehrt who had screamed "Ridend...swefaþ hæleþ... Knights and warriors sleep thy sleep of death" before the second impact had confirmed their dire predicament.

What could he do?

His shield wall would soon fall.

What should he do?

Every warrior and weapon had taken the line.

What was there left for him to do?

He thought as a man, for that was all he was, just a man, a King by station but nevertheless just a man, and the acceptance of defeat and certain death seemed to rise from his stomach.

A little further north than directly west stood Constantine's mercenaries, the shameful scourge of any battle. They had encircled their way from the east to find the most vulnerable flank of the enemy, and that is where they now stood, in groups of the vilest and cruellest of creatures ever to have assembled within those pitiful lands.

They had travelled from everywhere imaginable, and other places that were not. Multi coloured skins who between them spoke every language on earth had gathered to await the command of that day's employer. The merest sight of their presence radiated fear into the hearts of all who dreaded their coming.

Almost over weighted with their 'Black Market' weapons forged by foreign smyths into every shape and size, they stood eager and ready to earn their worth, they looked as Hel's own warriors.

Still out of sight their serfs and squires, a truly motley crew and as evil in looks as their masters, making themselves ready to fill their hand carts and satchels with battlefield booty, to sell or exchange at the nearest market town as soon as their victory had been declared. Of course, not all would survive but none would have ever agreed as they all believed themselves to be magnificent and unbeatable, and there for one single purpose.

Then Æthelstan picked out a single body from the growing massacre that littered between the places where men, and women, now almost stood their ground. A tarnished mail, a bloodied cloak, a severed arm and a dying face and a King wept a tear in the height of battle at the passing of his most trusted of all, at the death of his dearest of Thegns, the end of the man who had sworn as a child, to protect a boy who had become a King. He who had kept his secrets, followed him across the Isles through every day of his life, almost, now lay dying just feet away and there was nothing he could do to save the life of his loyal Ecgberht.

In his final throws, the Thegn smiled up at his King, cried a muffled word that went unheard as his heart missed its final beat, and his eyes closed forever from those lands allowing his spirit to enter the Halls of those who would truly never be forgotten.

Amidst his tears the King cried loud, "There lies Ecgberht, son of Ecgric, a much-loved friend to an unworthy King, may his blood bless these lands for ever more."

Then a King shed another tear as he turned his mount towards the fight.

"How many more would he lose that day?"

"How many settles would be empty around the tables of Engle land that eve?"

"How many wifmen would be screaming their last as an empty space stayed cold in their beds?"

A shattered King glanced across the small, lonesome space that separated him from his brother, his chosen heir, he felt sick to his stomach, almost vomiting, as he watched a handful of his precious knights fall from their mounts, struck down by spear and bolt and arrow to be finished off by the clubs and blades of brutish Picts. There in his very sight was the beginning of what now promised to be the end of his precious Engle Land, soon his heir would perish and so to their bloodline.

"Bloodline?"

And in his panic, as his heart tried its utmost to burst through his mail clad chest, and cold sweat ran furiously down his back, he took in the deepest of breaths and caught hold, with great relief, the odour of fresh honeysuckle and blackberry leaf... followed by a warmly comforting whisper at his side...

"La, Æthelstan...cild fram se æfenleoht...beon thee stillan."

His nerves were showing for fear of such an impending loss, but his courageous heart would never permit him to concede. He remembered those precious words spoken by his Mother, the promises of the All Father and the warmth of his Grandfather Ælfred.

Æthelstan looked once again at the turmoil around him, stretched long his neck skywards and screamed, loud, clear, and pertinent...

"Na Forlætan!!!"

He realised again his destiny.

He called again, "There would be no surrender." There would never be surrender, not on that day or on any other.

The words of the All Father echoed through his mind…. "Æthelstan Cyning…beorna beahgifa…" and the reassuring smiles of his Mother as he reached down to his left, easily finding the gifted horn.

There were no doubts in his intensions as he guided the horn to his mouth, no second thoughts of whether that which he was about to do was right, or ridiculous, as he spat free the battle's dust and readied the instrument. He spat again before it touched, ridding the nervous dryness from his mouth.

Now a horn that is carried into battle, when sounded to summon warriors of an impending attack, or a change in tactics, or call for aid in the heat of a fight, or just to instil courage when the enemy runs riot, that type of horn sends out a dull drone that slowly spreads through the air as it grows in pitch then peters away into nothing as it reaches the extent of its range.

But it wasn't so with that horn.

As Æthelstan blew, and blow he did until his lungs threatened to collapse, the sound which left that horn was fine, light, and melodic, as if it came from the lips of a thousand Sirens borne out of Asgard's tranquil lakes. From a mystical choir it came, spreading across the rampaging masses, lifting high towards the sky, seemingly increasing its tone as it rose, and as the King blew out a second and a third note the same tones emulated again skyward, through the clouds and on into the stars that surrounded the enchanted lands, awakening the spirits of those who had remained in the shadows through many centuries passed.

Loud enough the call, to wake the mighty Thunnor, and Loki, Saxnot and Fenrir, Baldæg, Ingui, Frea and Tiw, Wuldor and Woden. Calling them all and their brothers to arms, asking for aid, for now came the time that all had been waiting for, at the mead hall tables and around the hearth fires of every land.

Now came the time that ALL men were needed.

Now was the time when the Children of Men needed the aid of the Old Ones, and a tone called out a final hope.

And it would come.

At first there seemed no more than the smallest of rumbles, hill storms, threatening to disturb the day's end, hardly concerning the slaughter. From the west, came its rumbling, almost in silence as it rolled its way north, then turned towards the south, darkening more in colour as its breadth widened, cloaking the golden rays of an evening sun. As the slightest of tremors began to shake the green hillocks of the western rise, unnoticed still by those engrossed in the challenge of killing to survive, its noise grew louder, greying clouds became a battle's roof casting an ever-growing shadow beneath its eerie blanket.

Despite the chilling gusts that preceded the approaching gale the sweat poured relentlessly from beneath Æthelstan's helm. His eyes became glued to the coming squall, his lips fixed to the horn as he continued to blow, his free hand clenching nervously the blood drenched sword, he knew those clouds had come for him.

He blew again in desperation, staring in horror at the falling banners of his allies, crumpled and bloodied to the ground, as great swathes of corpses littered the field on every flank. Men screamed their agonies in ancient tongues, called out their final cries for mercy with modern words and gave their final plea to those holier than they, as a last breath accompanied that terrible hurt, once indomitable spirits left those lands forever.

The King of All Engle land blew a final time, one final call of desperation, one final plea before permitting the horn's tone to disappear amongst the cries of war as he released his grip, allowing it to nestle once again at his side.

At first, he felt ridiculous, stupid, even childish, for hoping the sound of a horn would change the outcome of a war, the few angelic notes doing no more than interrupt the screams of the approaching defeat…

Then, as a cloud of Scytisc arrows bit into another fruitless resistance something grabbed his attentions in the distance. He strained his senses in desperation to hear the noise that hovered above the battle's whine, heeding the first of the mystical replies, horned from beyond the greying clouds which now skirted above everything.

The feelings of self ridicule quickly vanished as he heard the answers to the Horn, an unknown calling from beyond that maybe offered hope. But would their coming be too late, defeat was approaching his armies by the second, his enemies from the north were gaining ground, his company began to diminish. Æthelstan himself seemed certain of one thing, if ever he had been unsure about anything else, if their destiny was to end in such a place then so too would his own, together, at the shoulders of his knights…

His left hand slipped to the rear of his fighting saddle grasping tightly a broken shaft, then pulled free a single, brightly magnificent, and very ancient spear from its sheath, a spear that had long since been named 'Rhongomyniad' beneath the eyes of one God.

He then nestled the pristine limewood shield against his forearm, wyverns up, and grasped Abrecan's reins, tightly with his fullest sword hand. As a smile beamed across his bearded set a tear spent onto a grimy cheek. If that was now his time, then he would face it head on and most definitely at the sides of those who had always offered their everything for him.

His knights were falling as the enemy's strength increased. His Earls were now battered and few, his Thegns in disarray, and panic threatened to rule his army. If that place named Brunanburh was to be the final throw of the English then it would also be his, in the vein of his forefathers, beneath the gaze of those who awaited his company.

King Æthelstan lifted his shoulders, pointed that mystical spear towards the enemy's middle and leant himself forward, against the horse's mane…

"Abrecan…min sundorwine. If our end be the wish of those much mightier, then be it so as we shall now pass into our afterlife as one."

The horse's noble head jerked high and proud more than once, agreeing with her master, a snort of heated breath left her nostrils in contempt for those who were about to feel her wrath, and a fetlock kicked out violently against the dying body of a Pictish warrior. Proudly she marched her King forward into their final battle.

And the distant horns grew louder.

As he neared the central onslaught of a battle he had sworn would be the fight to end all fights King Æthelstan glared across the field. He stared at the many who had fallen, and at the many who still managed to remain afoot and on horse, relentlessly hammering their enemy, certain to do so until they also fell alongside those of their brothers, and sisters. He caught the silhouette of his true brother Edmund, surrounded by many, still holding his part, so young. How proud he was of him that day, fearlessly laying all for his King, for his House and for his lands. At such a young age. What a knight he had made, what a King he would have made.

How proud would be their Father.

Again, glistening pride left the eye of Engle land's first King as he remembered the young girl he had named Æthgifu, in that courtyard of Saint Oswald's. A child whom he had been forced to ignore, a child whose innocence and humility had stunned him on every cherished encounter, so few they were, the child that he fought for that day, and all those others like her.

Edward's eldest son looked skywards as the clouds tumbled darker overhead. Lightning darted from east to west and the distant horns blew louder. He pushed Rhongomyniad upwards as a final salute to those who had permitted him to follow their path, and fire rose from the belly of the English King. Anger spun through his body, pride for his warriors shone through.

His eyes reddened, his cheeks puffed, and his heart pumped rapidly as the words came from his mouth, from his soul...

"Men of the West.... Men of the West." Louder. "For that which hath been granted to us, through the blood of our Forefathers, must be safeguarded through the blood of their sons...No surrender."

They heard his cry.

Above the chaos of the fight his warriors heard. No matter their House, no matter their tongue they heard the words of their King, and copied his screaming.

'Na Forlætan…Na Forlætan…" Their blood may also stain England's lands, there would be no surrender.

Was it all a dream?

Their words had echoed upwards, following the last note of the horn's tune. Had it disturbed the spirits of the fallen whose own horns had started to echo a response?

Now. There emerged something strange, something eerie, almost mystical from behind the Eyffien Hills.

Was it a dream? Rapidly and without warning a more intense, brighter, bolt of lightning flew across the darkened sky as the mischievous Loki, Father of Wolves and bringer of Hel angrily awoke from an ageless sleep, broke himself free from Woden's chains and sent forward his mischief from Asgard's depths, tumbling across the hills, descending horribly in an explosion of fire and torment upon the small armies of Ellen Vannin, shield rounds, weapons, and bodies alike were hurled into the bolt of fire that spread through their ranks leaving nothing more than the singed earth in its wake, no warriors would make their return to that most ancient of isles.

And Hel herself had followed her roguish mate to watch the slaughter from the seclusion of her underworld den, now awaiting with increased delight as she hovered to gather her due ration from that day's carnage and transport them back to her abyss, where an infinity of damnation loomed. Among them would be Anlaf, that wretched Dane whose cause had brought so much suffering to that 'gentle' world, how his voice would now squeal in perpetuity, unheard and forgotten.

Behind Loki had come his brother Thunnor, son of Woden and his Mother Earth. God of War, slayer of elves, basher of trolls, caretaker of the Saxon folk. He was not a God who took a challenge lightly, he would not tolerate the slightest threat against his folk from Middle Earth. A silent storm began to vibrate across the Danish lines brought about by Mjolnir's rage as she swore her magical allegiance to the army of her new people, Anlaf's remnants would soon be scattered without mercy, from the closest of victories. Those fortunate enough threw down their weapons as they fled, from that place of panic and fear, towards the coast whence they had first come.

And the horns still called as they neared the fight.

Æthelstan was aghast. At first, he had thought it a bolt of fire from Hel's own heart, raining down to destroy them all, until his nose caught yet again that enchanting odour of fresh honeysuckle and blackberry leaf.

He looked again high towards the grey and smiled "Modor" and another tear dribbled onto his gleaming mail.

"La Æthelstan beorn fram se æfenleohte, no more shall thee fear. Now comes the time, my only son…"

Her whispers paused as a tear fell free from an invisible eye disturbed only by the vibrations of the Scytisc hoards that heaved stronger in the growing winds.

"…Comes the time my son that hath been so long awaited by those who share thy blood. Such a time to take thy folk, all thy folk of every race, now for them to be of only one race, the race of Man…Time comes to take them forward into the new world and show all that thee now be their King granting unto everyone, all things that thee would wish to grant for thyself."

For a second it felt as if a kiss had been placed upon his cheek as a Mother's whispers echoed amongst the battle's din, for his ears only. Then the aroma of his sacred past drifted away for the final time…

His attentions were torn once more from the horrors that threatened to rip the very heart from his land. A sound had caught his ear, far away in the distance, high above the screaming scars of that worst of battles…

…It was the sound of linden shields that beat in the distance of the Eyffien Hills. Many shields.

The Mercians fought with continued rage, their numbers falling despite their intent, horse fell alongside rider as the ranks regrouped and charged once again, a hundred times again. Now their numbers would only grow in those golden fields of Glassisvellir…

There were ancient voices singing ancient songs now heard over the Eyffien rise, many voices...

Within the turmoil of the battle West Saxons, East Saxons, from the South too, men of Kent, of Anglia, of all, screamed their violent curses as a thousand more pitched into the battle's heart alongside the Jute, the Fleming, and the Welshman too.

The clouds were now parting over the Eyffien Hills and a golden sun was beginning to break its way through, quiet was the thunder, gone were the lightning bolts.

Æthelflæd's warrior women, so few now their numbers, amidst the chaos regrouped upon a solitary rise, weapons drawn, smiles of desperate reassurance about them, still ready to make a final stand.

There came many shadows, marching down the slopes of the Eyffien Hills.

Æthelstan clenched his knees gripped tightly Abrecan's girth and moved deeper into the butchery, cutting, and stabbing into the madness that would always be war.

There were many spears now glistening through the shadows of the Eyffien Hills, shields shining, mail gleaming, songs singing, out of the shadows of the Eyffien Hills.

Edmund found the side of his brother and grasped hold tightly the sword arm of his King, there was no time for words as both stared out to the golden sun now blazing down the rise of the Eyffien Hills.

There came many warriors, bearing many banners, eager for battle, marching towards them from the slopes which had brought them down from the Eyffien Hills.

Wulfric found the pair. He had fought his way slowly since the middle of the day to be at the side of his King. So many had fallen at his feet, good men all. Sweat and grime clung to his skin like an outer coat, blood dripped like water from his tired blade and his tarnished 'battle sark' gleamed no more, it would probably never do so again. He desperately sucked the foulness of the air as he tightened a cloth around an open wound that dribbled its redness from his left thigh, he paid it no further heed.

He panted tiredly. "Hwæt eart hie Bregu, they who march into our ranks with their much welcome army beneath unknown banners?"

Edmund also stared for an answer, he too had asked of the songs and of the tongues in which they were sung.

"Who be they?"

"Who be they?" as a sigh of relief and proud laughter erupted from their King's stomach.

Edmund and Wulfric both stared into the face of their King. Had he gone mad, on the verge of what now seemed their victory, had the stress and the strain of such a battle turned his head?

Æthelstan laughed loudly once more...then turned to them both...

"Why my friends...Alive hath come the sagas of the hearth fires, the tales of a child and the dreams of a coward...The sagas that told of the folk of these lands rising from the shadows, when all was but lost. They be the sons of those who first craved this land. They be those who have lived in the shadows of us all, who have strayed from our sight and lived their lives alone. They be the last of the Bryneich, the Corneu and the Cantiacci, they be the sons of the Cornovii, the Brigante and Icenae, Bernicians and Deirans and all other clans who begun this land. They be the ranks of those true to these lands, they be the ranks of our Engle land."

From every wood, crag, moor and down the ancient races had answered the call of their King who was said by many 'to be of their blood'. In the names of their forefathers the tribes and clans who still survived in the shadows of their tortured lands, who had lived in isolation and seclusion for countless years, now emerged with an air of magic about them as they made for the side of their King. Each man, and boy too, bare chested, in tattered old cloaks, clasping ancient weapons of every description, all supporting a small posy of fresh blackberry leaf and honeysuckle clipped to a jerkin. It was now the time for the Brython to once more march against another invader who threatened his lands.

Proudly and in amazement of what took place Æthelstan of England reached one final time for the horn and raised it slowly to his lips...

"Now, let us summon the heroes..." and the horn sounded its fanfare for the coming armies.

And before his two companions could confirm the truth of such actions a cloud of rage swept up from the approaching lines, flew towards the fight, screaming slaughter, violence, hurt and pain towards all who dared to draw arms against the Children of Men.

Death now flowed from the Eyffien Hills.

Anger, carnage, agony, and mayhem spread across the field of battle.

Revenge, glory, and victory now began to sweep from the shadows of Engle land's Eyffien Hills.

And Asser's Kin soon wrote...

937.

Here, Æthelstan King, of Earls the Lord, rewarder of heroes, and his brother also, Edmund Ætheling, elder of ancient race, slew in the fight, with the edge of their swords, the foe at Brunanburh!

The sons of Edward, their board-walls clove, and hewed their banners, with the wrecks of their hammers. So were they taught, by kindred zeal, that they at camp oft 'gainst any robber their land should defend, their hoards and homes.

Pursuing fell the Scytisc clans; the men of the fleet, in numbers fell; 'midst the din of the field the warrior swate. The field grew wet with the blood of men since the sun was up in the morning-tide, gigantic light! Glad over grounds. God's candle bright, eternal Lord- 'till the noble creature sat in the western main;

There lay many of the Northern heroes under a shower of arrows, shot over shields;

And Alba's boast, a Scythian race, the mighty seed of Mars!

With chosen troops, throughout the day, the West Saxons fierce press'd on the loathed bands; hew'd down the fugitives, and scattered the rear with strong, mill sharpened blades.

The Mercians too, their hard handplay spared not to any of those that with Anlaf over the briny deep, in the ship's bosom sought this land for the hardy fight.

Five Kings lay on the field of battle, in bloom of youth, pierced with swords. So too seven of the Earls of Anlaf; and of the ship's crew, outnumbered crowds.

There was dispersed, the little band of hardy Scot, the dread of northern hoards; urged to the noisy deep by unrelenting fate!

The King of the fleet with his slender craft escaped with his life the felon flood; and so too Constantine, the valiant chief, returned to the north in hasty flight. The hoary Hildrinc cared not to boast amongst his kindred.

Here was the remnant of kinfolk and friends slain with the sword in the crowded fight. His son too he left on the field, mangled with wounds, young at the fight. The fair-haired youth had no reason to boast of the slaughtering strife.

Nor Old Inwood and Anlaf the more with the wrecks of their army could laugh and say, that they on the field of stern command better workmen were, in the conflict of the banners, the clash of spears, the meeting of heroes, and the rustling of weapons, which they on the field of slaughter played with the sons of Edward.

The Northmen sailed in their nailed ships, a dreary remnant, on the roaring sea; over deep water, Dublin they sought, and Ireland's shores in great disgrace.

Such then the brothers both together, King and Ætheling sought their country, West-Saxon land, in right triumphant.

They left behind them, raw to devour, the sallow kite, the swarthy raven with horny nib, and the hoarse vulture, with the eagle swift to consume his prey; the greedy goshawk, and that grey beast, the wolf of the weald.

No slaughter yet was greater made e'er in this island, of people slain, before this same, with the edge of the sword; as the books inform us of the old historians; since hither came from the eastern shores the Engles and Saxons, over the broad sea, and Britain sought;

Fierce battle-smyths, o'ercame the Welsh, most valiant Earls, and gained a land.

Brunanburh 937. The greatest battle ever to be fought on English soil.

Eac Assers cynn hraðe writan...

937.

Here Æðelstan cyning, eorla dryhten, beorna beahgifa, ond his broþor eac, Eadmund Ætheling, ealdorlangne tir geslogen æt sæcce sweorda ecgum ymbe Brunanburh.

Bordweal clufan, heowan heaþolinde hamora lafan, afaran Eadwardes, swa him geæþele wæs from cneomægum, þæt hi æt campe oft wiþ laþra gehwæne land ealgodon, hord and hamas.

Hettend crungen, Sceotta leoda ond scipflotan fæge feollan, feld dæn ede secgas hwate, siðþan sunne up on morgentid, mære tungol, glad ofer grundas, Godes condel beorht, eces Drihtnes, oð sio æpele gesceaft sah to setle.

Þær læg secg mænig garum agetad, guma norþerna ofer scild scoten, swilce Scittisc eac, werig, wiges sæd.

Wesseaxe forð ondlonge dæg eorodcistum on last legdun laþum þeodum, heowan herefleman hindan þearle mecum mylenscearpan.

Myrce ne wyrndon heeardes hondplegan hæleþa nanum þæ mid Anlafe ofer æra gebland on lides bosme land gesohtun, fæge to gefeohte.

Fife lægun on þam campstede, cyninges giunge, sweordum aswefede, swilce seofene eac eorlas Anlafes, unrim heriges, flotan ond Sceotta.

Þær geflemed wearð Norðmanna bregu, need gebeded, to lides stefne little weorode; cread cnear on flot, cyning ut gewat on fealene flod, feorh generede.

Swilce þær eac se froda mid fleame com on his cyþþe norð, Costontinus, har hildering, hreman ne þorfte mæcan gemanan; he wæs his mæga sceard, freonda gefylled on folcstede, beslagen æt sæcce, and his sunu forlet on wælstowe wundun fergrunden, giungne æt guðe.

Gelpan ne þorfte beorn blanden feax bilgeslehtes, eald Inwidda, ne Anlaf þy ma; mid heora herelafum hlehan ne þorftun þæt heo beaduweorca beteran wurdun on campstede culbodgehnadtes garmittinge, gumena gemotes, wæpengewrixles, þæs hi on wælfelda wiþ Eadweardes afaran plegodan.

Gewitan him þa Norþmen nægledcnearrum, dreorig daraða laf, on Dinges mere ofer deop wæter Difelin secan, and eft Hiraland, æwiscmode.

Swilce þa gebroþor begen ætsamne, cyning and æþeling, cyþþe sohton, Wesswaxena land.

Wiges hrimge Letan him behindan hræ Bryttian saluwigpadan, þone sweartan hræfn, hyrnednebban, and þane hasewanpadan, earn æftan hwit, æses brucan, grædugne guðhafoc and þæt græge deor, wulf on wealde.

Ne wearð wæl mare on þis eiglende æfer gieta folces gefylled beforam þissum sweordes ecgum, þæs þe us secgað bec, ealde uðwtan, siþþan eastan hider Engle and Seaxe up becoman, ofer brad brimu Brytene sohtan.

Wlance wigsmiþas, Weelas ofercoman, eorlas arhwate eard begeaten.

Brunanburh 937 þa mæst beadu fohten on Brytene land.

Lo, there do I see my Father.

Lo, there do I see my Mother.

And my sister and my brother

Lo, there do I see the line of my people

Back to the beginning

Lo, they do call me.

They bid me to take my place among them,

In the Halls of Valhalla

Where the brave may live forever.

Prayer from the 13th Warrior.

Epilogue

Although he had not yet seen out his forty sixth winter completely Æthelstan was tired, more tired than one would normally be if he had seen twice the King's years, but then his life had been filled with twice as much as any man of his age.

Winterfilleth had arrived, in all its glory, some weeks earlier allowing the moon to take the longest part of the day as it beckoned the start of the dark months. Their world was getting colder, stock had been sold for the coming 'Bloodmonth' and the fields had been scythed of all that they had produced during the growing seasons. Now it was stored and jealously guarded, it would be all that would keep their bellies full during the grey months. The wall between their world and the afterlife was at its thinnest and appropriately only four days would pass before All Saint's Day.

A muscle ripped viciously through his shoulders causing Æthelstan's head to roll backwards too sharply sending a shock through his left side, agonisingly wrenching the muscles in his neck, bringing a painful jolt that trembled through his upper body, like most things now it was dismissed and blamed upon old age. Eventually the hurt faded into nothing.

It was the glow of the wall torches flickering their golden tongues, biting brightly into the haze around his crumbling vision that had been sufficient to convince him to ease shut the lids of his eyes and rest his enervated body gently against the cushioned back of his favourite settle. A chill flitted through the room bidding the flames to increase the tempo of dance as a shiver urged him to tug up the fur rug, but he was too tired.

For the first time, in many years maybe, he now felt content, fulfilled and at ease. Gone now were the aches of his battle wounds, the strains and tears of his muscles and the constant fatigue brought on from just being a King. He thought deeply of his part in those often-cruel winters that had brought him to that point. Of the arguing, the fighting and the dying as well as the laughing and the living. The smell of the feastings after each gathering still caught his senses as did the songs and the sagas that had echoed from the lips of the travelling bards. Then there were the tears and the cries of the wives and the mothers, the sons, and the daughters, as he had marched his armies home from their continuous warring's, the empty spaces of the fallen within the ranks, so many spaces.

He thought of his times as a boy, as a man, as Ætheling and as King, his public times, and his secret times. More apparent than anything else within his memory was that one night, such a stormy night so long ago, and his stay within Swine's Hill and a Thegn's daughter, Ymma, so long since passed. He remembered, no he had never forgotten, the young Æthgifu, born from that forbidden night, herself now a woman of intended purpose, who, despite the warnings of the All Father, would carry forth the blood of the Old Folk within her veins, into that new world, a closely guarded secret, a safeguard for the future that may one day far away save again the Children of Men. Had his ignorance of Woden's words meant that still no peace would come to those lands, or had he truly fulfilled his destiny?

In the ever-distant halls of his memory.

Through the mists of a tired mind Æthelstan pictured the hazy outline of a wattled old hus hidden deep in the shadows of his beloved Brunesweald, surrounded in nature's green, serenaded by the wild things at play. It became clearer as it neared. He knew well that he had been there before, long, so very long before as a boy, and instantly his thoughts jumped to the vision of his beloved mother Ecgwynn who had guided him in his dreams, so many worlds passed...

But not that time.

He remembered the old man, in even older clothes, who had dragged open the heavy oak door and scared a young lad half to death. But that time there would be no old man in even older clothes.

As the same old oak leaf squealed its way open, that King who had achieved all his life's wishes, and some also that had been wished for him, that King, that man, that boy, that lad, was no longer afraid.

At first, just as in those distant dreams, a darkly haunting space replaced the oak. Empty and eerie, and in his dreams Æthelstan willed desperately for the old man to appear just as he had so long ago, as if the presence of the All Father, in any form, would ease his pains and permit him to continue his glorious reign over that wonderful land of men.

...And he willed it, harder and more forceful, almost hard enough to snatch him from that deepest of sleeps, from that pleasant and most welcome of dreams.

...More so he willed for Woden's smile as the blackness slowly changed from dark to grey, and just as before, there emerged the stoutest of figures, but it was not that of the All Father before him, clad in shining mail, a golden helm and the tails of a fine cloak gathered to his left in one hand, whilst the strong hilt of a fine blade was gripped within the other.

An unchallenged echo bid silence to the wild things...And the words endorsed a peace within nature's quiet.

"Min sunu... Min deore sunu. How good my heart beats to stand with thee once again, after such a time...Now a man thee be, and the finest of all Kings, finer than I, more so maybe than even our Ælfred."

"Fæder?"

Edward answered with a Father's sadness...

"Æthelstan... Æthelcyning... Æthelmann... Æthelsunu. Ruler of our Engleland, how proud we all be of thee."

In his mind, just as the years before, he strained to understand such things within that woodland realm, yet he had also learned, long ago, that it was only normal in such a place, to allow such things to occur, just as they willed.

"How be thee here Father...be here also my Mother?" His whispers were struggled through the driest of throats, even such fewest of words were strained through his increasing fatigue.

A tired son glanced upwards, just a little, towards an unseen sky. He sniffed at the air and creaked back against his cushion in contentment as he breathed, after so long it was there once again, the odour of fresh honeysuckle and crushed blackberry leaf. Even though he could not see her he knew that Ecgwynn was close by.

"Modor."

A pleasing grin lit up Edward's face, "she be now where we all belong my son, where we are All destined to be together."

Slight disappointment entered his expression. "Then Father, if it be that I shall join with thee, when shall come my time?"

Sadness filled a Father's eyes briefly, but soon made way for happiness and delight.

"Why, Æthelstan sunu, King of all, thee be already here." And a Father's words surprised a son. "It now be time to join our Forefathers. Thy time in the world of man hath now come to its end..." and an arm pushed out from the opening as an invitation for the younger to follow, "...and thy time in the new world hath just begun."

An insignificant second that may have lasted an eternity passed as both men stared at each other in silence until a tear finally ran down Æthelstan's cheek as he realised his ealdorlegu, just as it had been foretold by the All Father years earlier in another world, and for the first time, in a lifetime, a son embraced his Father.

His stomach churned with the thought of a new adventure, and he felt again his youngness return. Just like his early years he had not been in a dream he had been standing at the gates of Neorxnawang, but unlike those earlier visits there would be no more returning to his beloved Engle Land, and without a further warning...

"Come, son of mine. It now be time to leave this Land of Men forever, and sit for eternity at the tables of thy Forefathers who so eagerly await thy presence...For no man shall ever say that thy place hath not been earned as much, if not more so than any other there."

A.D. 941.

This year King Æthelstan died in Gloucester,

On the sixth day before the calends of November,

About forty-one winters, bating one night,

from the time King Ælfred had died.

And Edmund Ætheling took to the kingdom.

He had eighteen winters.

King Æthelstan had reigned for fourteen years and ten weeks.

The Anglo-Saxon Chronicle.

King Æthelstan died on 27th October 939 a day before the anniversary of Ælfred's own death.

In 941 he was entombed at Maidulph Minster, now known as Malmesbury Abbey, along with his bravest of knights, and six of his cousins, all who had fallen at Brunanburh.

On his tomb was etched his epitaph, one of the lines proclaiming;

'Here lies one honoured by the world and grieved by his land.'

Æthelstan's story is the basis of the legends of King Arthur and has been lost in the fantasies and myths of those who need to invent their heroes.

He was undoubtedly the last King to rule with the ancient blood of the 'Brythonic people' in his veins, the Anglo-Saxon Chronicles tell us ...'Elder of ancient race...'

He was the first King to be invested with a crown.

He was first to unite the English and Scottish in the first treaty between both kingdoms. He was first to support the Guilds and the Masons, some claim the modern-day Freemasons stem from his rule.

He was first to openly trade with other countries, starting a European trade union.

He was first to support the European heads of state.

He was first to have the Holy Bible translated into Anglo-Saxon, for his people to read the Holy words for themselves.

He was first King of All the English. He was the first King.

.... Then why is he the LAST King we are taught about?

On life ge on legere

Ure ancenned cyning.

ungecnawen.

In life and death

Our only begotten King.

Anon.

Historical Key/ Glossary of terms.

Abrecan	a violent storm from the north.
acbeam	Oak tree.
adleg	Flames of a funeral pyre.
Æcermann	Farmer, field worker, land man.
æfenleoht	Evening light.
Ælfen/ælf	Of elves.
Ælfred	Alfred. Elf counsel, advisor.
Ælfscreon	Elf's cry.
Ælfwyn	Elf's friend.
Ælmes/ælmesse	Alms/aid given to the poor by a King or Noble.
Ærende	Message. Embassy, visiting diplomatic body.
Ærfæda [s]	Forefather [s].
Æthelflæd	Noble beauty.
Ætheling.	Son of a King, heir to a ruling house.
Æthgifu	Æthelstan's illegitimate daughter. Noble gift.
Aglæca	Male name, fighter, warrior.
Alltud.	Old Welsh: Outcast/ Cast Out.

Angelcyning/Engelcynn	King of the Engles,
Angon	Long weighted barbed spear.
Arthegn	High positioned servant.
arwe	Arrow.
bære	Barley.
Baldæg	God of light.
bar [a]	Boar [s]
Battle sark	Body armour [kenning].
beacen	Beacon/banner/warning flag
beadu serce	battle-shirt/war tunic
Beaggiefa	Ring-giver. Lord King
Beamfleot	Benfleet in Essex
Bedas ford	Bedford, [Bedas crossing]
Beormingas	Birmingham
beorn	Man
Bernicia	6th century Anglian realm Northumberland etc.
bidsteall	To halt and stand
blodfolc	Relative. One of the same blood
bord	Board/table/shield
bordweall	shield-wall

Bregu	Old Mercian; Lord
bremelberie	bramble/blackberry
breostnett	coat of mail
brimrad	Sea road, large watery channel between two lands
brimwudu	Sea wood, ship
brodor	brother
brodorsunu	nephew
Brytenlande	Wales. The land of the Britons
Brython	One of many names for England
Bucca's meadow	Buckingham
Bucgan Ora	Bucga's landing. Bognor Regis
Burgtun	City. Capital city
burg/burh/bur	A fortified place. Modern day borough
byrnie	Padded leather or cloth jerkin
Caledfwlch	Old Welsh; battle hard. Welsh name for Excalibur
calic	Chalice, goblet
Cantwara	Modern day Kent. Of the Brythonic Cantii people
Cantwaraburg	Canterbury, old shire town of Kent
Ceapmann	Market trader, stall holder, salesman
Ceapstow	Market. Modern day Chepstow

ceorl	Lowest of free men. Small land owner
Ciannachta	Ancient Irish people of county Louth
Cirice [an]	Church [s]
Cniht	Boy soldier, armed youth. Knight.
coc [as]	Cook [s]
Corneu/Kernou	Cornovii. Ancient people of Cornwall
cot/cote	Hut/sleeping place, bed chamber
cycene [n]	Kitchen
cild/cyldru	child/children
Cyning	King
dægcandel	Day candle. Sun
Dearaldia	Mystical forest surrounding Asgard
Deira	5th century Northern Brythonic realm
Deorby	Old Norse; village on the Derwent, Now Derby
Deorlic/Deorling	Deer like, brave one, bold one. Darling
dohtir	daughter
Eadmund	Edmund. Blessed protector
Eadweard	Edward. Blessed guardian
ealdorlegu	destiny/fate or future
ealdspell	old saying, story, tale

ealdwif	old woman
Ealdefæder	Grandfather
Eallfæder	All Father/Woden
eardling/earðlinga	Farmer/land worker
Eborac	Lost Brythonic realm of the north
efeste	to hurry
Einherjar	Dead warriors carried to Valhalla by Valkyries
Ellan Vannin	Old name for Isle of Man
Elmet	5th century realm, now part of the West Riding
Englar	Old Norse; Angle, Engle English
Engle Land [e]	England up until 15th century
Eoforwic	York
eorðcynn	One of the earth, earth child
Eorlwerod	A band of noble warriors
Eostre	A/S Goddess
Eastermonaþ	Easter month/April
erne	lowest of male servants
Eyland	Old Norse; Island
Fædra	Mercian dialect for Fæder...Father
Feldhus	field house/tent

Fenrir	Norse/Saxon wolf God
ferend	traveller
Foederati	Engle/Saxon/Jute Roman mercenary
ford	a river crossing, bridgeless crossing
foregeleoran	go/pass to your death
Framganga saman	Old Norse; to go forward as one
Frige	A/S Goddess of physical love
frith	peace
fyrd	Anglo-Saxon army of free men
fyrdrinc	Soldier/warrior
Gafol	Tax/bounty paid to stop an attack or invasion
Gaini	Saxon tribe settling in Lincolnshire
Gainiburg	Fortified town of the Gaini, Gainsborough
ganggteld	large tent
Geat [as]	Jute
gebedstow	A place for prayers
geleoran	to depart a life
gelt/geld	Ransom, bribe
gemot	Anglo-Saxon council. See Witan
Gerefa	Reeve, Shire Reeve, later sheriff. Slang; gaffa

Gese [Yehseh]	Yeah/Yes
Griðlagu	Law of temporary peace
Gododdin	Brythonic inhabitants of Hen Ogledd [Old North]
godwine	good friend. Modern surname Goodwin
guþfana [n]	battle flag, banner. Standard [s]
Gwyddeleg	Old Welsh; Irish/Ireland
halda	Old Norse; to hold, stand fast, wait
hælwyrt	the herb, pennyroyal, fleabane, fleawort
Hæsere	Lord, Master
ham	home
Hamm	part of a pasture or field
Heahcyning	High King
healsbeorg	Mail 'coif' for neck and shoulder protection
Hel	A/S Goddess of the underworld
helm	Helmet, head covering, high fortification
hemejje	undergarment with short sleeves, a shirt
Hen Ogledd	Brythonic; Old North
heort	Hart, male deer over 5 years. Original; Horn head
here	Band, group of armed free men
herklæði	Old Norse; Armour

Herla	Herla cyning. A/S mythical leader of the hunt [Hern]
Herlið	Old Norse; Army
Hleothop	Saxon oracle, companion of Mimir the remembered
Hrot	Scum, filth
Hurst/hyrst	Hillock upon where a copse or small wood grows
Huscarl	House guard. Military escort, armed servant
Hvitakristr	Old Norse; The White Christ
Inthinen	Female servant
Irskr	Old Norse; Irish
Karve	Shallow bottomed long ship used for war
Kenning	compound expression, metaphorical meaning
Konungr	Old Norse; Chieftain/King
Læcehus	hostelry of pilgrimage, hospital
Læce [as]	Doctor/physician
Langlocc	Long hair
Legacæstir	City of the Legions. Modern day Chester
Lin	flax linen cloth, napkin, towel
Litha	The summer solstice
Longphort	Term used in Ireland for a ship enclosure/fortress

lytling	small child, little one
Maidulph	Old name for Malmesbury, Æthelstan's burial place
Mancynn	Mankind
Middangeard	Middle Earth, Earth, the world of Men
Modor	Mother
Modrige	Aunt
Myrce/Mercia	A/S for 'Land of the border folk'
Nawiht	Worthless, useless person
Neorxnawang	A/S paradise/ heaven. Heavenly field
Nese	Nay. No
Nihtgeng	Night goer, goblin
Nihtweard	night watch, guard, watchman, guardian
Nihtwic	Night camp
Pecsætan	Peak dweller. Early Engle tribe
Ræcc	Setter dog that hunts only by scent, war dog
Ridend	rider, horseman, knight
Rond	Old Norse' Shield
Samhain	Halloween. Celtic feast, Brythonic; Calan Gæaf
Saurr	Old Norse; filth, scum
Saxon/Seaxisc	Men of the knife

Sceot/Scyttisc	Scot, Irish clan ejected from Ireland by the Dane
Scield/scild	shield
Scitte	shit, excrement
scylen	female servant, slave, concubine
seax	small knife, short sword
See	a Bishop's official seat
Scir	shire, Cheshire, Lancashire
scop	travelling story teller
scramseax	sheathed blade
sculan	shall
Sigethuf/sigeþuf	victory banner
sipwif	noble lady
skrud	Old Norse Mail coat, padded cloth, armour
snekkja	Old Norse; Thin, sleek ship used up until 1066
Spæwif	a female seer, one who prophesises, or spies.
Spanghelm	preferred helmet of the Anglo-Saxon
stræl	wooden shaft, arrow
strælbora [n]	archer [s]
sundorwine	special, best friend
sunsunnu	son of a son, grandson

Suð sæ	South sea, English Channel
Suþseaxe	South Saxons/Sussex
Swatlin	Handkerchief/personal cloth
Sycan	nurse
Temes	River Thames
Tid/tyd	or tide, meaning time. Winter tide etc
Tig/Tir/Tiw	Norse/Anglo-Saxon God of war and battles
Thræll/Þræll	Servant/slave/serf
Thunor	Anglo-Saxon God of thunder, as Norse Thor
Toft	Old Norse; Homestead, site of a house
Undernmete	breakfast, first daily meal
Ungesewen	invisible, unseen
Ut	out
Utlaga	Outlaw, criminal
Virga	Latin for Rod or noble office
Wælcyrie	Valkyrie, chooser of the slain
wælfyr	Funeral pyre
Ward	room within the walls of a fort or burg
Wealas	Anglo-Saxon for the Welsh, meaning foreigner or slave

Westseaxe	West Saxon, Wessex
Wicca	wiccan, witch [s]
Wicing	Viking, pirate, sea borne raider
Wiltunscir	Wiltshire
Winterfylleth	October. Winter full moon
Witan/gemot	assembly of King's council, government
Woad	Yellow flowering plant grown for its blue dye.

Printed in Great Britain
by Amazon